Never Greener

www.**penguin**.co.uk

Never Greener

Ruth Jones

BANTAM PRESS

LONDON · TORONTO · SYDNEY · AUCKLAND · JOHANNESBURG

TRANSWORLD PUBLISHERS
61–63 Uxbridge Road, London W5 5SA
www.penguin.co.uk

Transworld is part of the Penguin Random House group of companies
whose addresses can be found at global.penguinrandomhouse.com

First published in Great Britain in 2018 by Bantam Press
an imprint of Transworld Publishers

A CIP catalogue record for this book
is available from the British Library.

ISBNs 9780593078068 (hb)
9780593078075 (tpb)

Typeset in 11¼/15¼pt Sabon by Falcon Oast Graphic Art Ltd.
Printed and bound by Clays Ltd, Bungay, Suffolk.

Penguin Random House is committed to a sustainable
future for our business, our readers and our planet. This book
is made from Forest Stewardship Council® certified paper.

MIX
Paper from
responsible sources
FSC
www.fsc.org   FSC® C018179

1 3 5 7 9 10 8 6 4 2

This book is dedicated to Lucy Matthews –
a passionate reader and wonderful friend.

Truly, though our element is time,
We are not suited to the long perspectives
Open at each instant of our lives.
They link us to our losses: worse,
They show us what we have as it once was,
Blindingly undiminished, just as though
By acting differently, we could have kept it so.

Philip Larkin

1985

Fergus was getting tetchy. The new girl should've been there at six. And now it was twenty past. A Saturday night at the height of the summer season was *not* a time to be short-staffed. He'd already roped poor Callum in to help. And obviously *he*'d rather be elsewhere. He looked over at him serving behind the bar and thought, as he often did, how good he looked for his age, definitely younger than his thirty-eight years. Fergus's kid brother, Callum. Funny he still thought of him as the baby. Even though he was a towering six foot four. He watched him now, chatting easily to a couple of the locals. That was the thing about Callum. He was *easy*. With absolutely everyone. Whoever he was talking to – no matter who they were, their background, their age – he had this way of sounding interested. It's what made him such a good teacher. And such a good dad. Fergus envied his brother's enduring patience.

Callum was listening to old Stuey Jameson berating the latest goings-on in the news, putting the world to rights – Ach, how things'd be if *he* ran the show. It was part of the job, listening to the regulars – the old boys who staked their territory at the bar and refused to move, no matter how busy it got in the pub. Always sitting in the same place, on the same bar stools, drinking the same brand of bitter. Even in winter, when the place was sunk into sad hibernation and waves from the North Sea smashed relentlessly against the sand, hurling their beige foam high over the roofs of the seafront hotels; when the promenade was no longer peopled with ice-cream-holding holidaymakers – even then, in those dark, tradeless months, regulars like Stuey religiously came and sat at the bar, downing their pints in perfectly timed rhythm, to the tune of sparse, empty chat. Yes, Stuey and his like were the pub's bread and butter out of season, and could never be taken for granted.

Fergus nodded at Callum and headed out to the beer garden. Where the hell was this barmaid? He knew it was a mistake taking her on. The girl – Kate something-or-other – had come to him last week when he was particularly busy. The daughter of a mate of a mate, looking for a holiday job and apparently a bit lively, but weren't they all these days? Fancied herself as a bit of an actress. But didn't they all these days? Fergus reckoned actresses were probably good with people, good at chatting to the likes of Wheezy Ron and Jackie Legg. And she'd had this smile. And before he knew it, there he was saying, 'OK, come in on Saturday at six, let's see how it goes.' And looking at his watch, it was now six thirty-five. So it wasn't going well at all.

He started clearing crisp-packet debris from one of the tables. A group of kids who'd made the mess whooped and cheered as Fergus deftly collected five pint glasses in each practised hand. One of the crowd, enthusiastic with drink, drained his whisky chaser and brought the tumbler down too hard, smashing it to pieces and eliciting more cheers and whoops.

'Hey! You can cut that out RIGHT now, d'ye hear!'

Fergus took the glasses back to the bar. 'Have a word with that lot, will you, Cal? They're doin' my nut in and it's only half six.' He handed him a dustpan and brush. 'And where the hell is this girl?'

Heading outside to the rowdy crowd, Callum wondered again why Fergus had ever wanted a pub. He hated the hours, hated the customers and didn't even like a drink! He started clearing up the broken glass. 'Take it easy now, lads. My brother's in a strop tonight and it's me that'll get it in the neck.'

4

'Aye. Cheers, Cal.'

Callum's gentle-giant demeanour was always a calming force. Friends joked he should have worked for the UN. His quiet confidence and lovely-ugly-rugby-player soul made those around him feel safe. He never lost his temper and yet no one would ever want to get on the wrong side of him. His rugby days long gone, Callum's body still bore the war wounds from years of playing on weather-beaten pitches, taking hit after hit in the scrum, battered by thousands of tackles, bashed, cut, bruised and scarred. He'd never been an oil painting in the traditional sense, but what made him so attractive was the fact that he didn't know he *was*, his features now more rugged than the Scottish coastline he'd grown up on. And as Denise at the club often liked to say, no matter how old he got, Callum MacGregor would never lose his sexy-as-fuck factor.

'Look boys – it's magic!' A voice came from behind them. An alien Welsh accent amidst the cacophony of Scottish. 'Daddy's got a pan and brush in his hands and he's actually USING it!'

Callum beamed as he turned to see Belinda, his heavily pregnant, tenaciously blooming thirty-six-year-old wife, holding the hands of his two little sons, Ben and Cory. 'Ey, watch it, you!'

'Daddy, we're goin' the beach!'

Callum leant down and tickled Ben, making him squeal with delight. 'Wish *I* was!' He kissed Belinda softly on the cheek. 'You OK?'

'Oh y'know, so-so. Car's out the front.' She handed him the keys. 'You sure you're alright walking back?'

Belinda rubbed her tummy. 'Yeah – the exercise'll do me good. Might jog this one into getting a move on. Don't reckon I can take another four weeks of this.'

'Good curry – that's what you need.'

'No more kids! That's what I need, Callum MacGregor. I'm never letting you near me ever again!'

Callum nuzzled discreetly into her neck, whispering, 'And we all know *that*'s not gonna happen.'

Belinda caught her breath. He could still make her tingle even now, ten years down the road and on baby number three. 'Behave,' she whispered back, blushing. And scooping up Cory, who clutched his bucket and spade, she headed out, calling over her shoulder, 'What time you back? Twelveish?'

'Yeah, won't be any later.'

He watched her go. Ten years older now than when they'd first met. Ten years wiser – if Belinda could actually *be* any wiser – and ten years more gorgeous, a child in each hand and another about to arrive. Yes, he looked at his wife and thought how very, very lucky he was.

If he could have replayed his life like a VHS tape, he'd have made it freeze-frame, put it on pause, and asked to pick up again from there. From that life-changing moment when he watched his beloved Belinda walk away and the whirlwind that was Kate Andrews come hurtling into his safe little world.

She was eating candy-floss.
She was twenty-two.
She was breathtakingly beautiful.

'Alright, boys?'

The lads round the table were delighted. 'Oi! Give us a bite!'

'Sorry – I never share anything. Don't know what I might catch!' She winked at them, then headed indoors, not even noticing Callum, who still stood, pan and brush in hand.

Inside, the bar was getting busier. 'Sorry I'm late. I went to the fair!' Kate looked around for a bin and threw away her candyfloss stick. The annoyance on Fergus's face was masked by the steam that poured out of the glass-washer. He'd like to sack her before she'd even started, but he desperately needed a barmaid. He knew Kate knew this.

'Right. I'm not impressed. And if you're this late again, you can forget the job. Now get these glasses stacked and start serving. It'll be eight deep in here in an hour.'

Callum went behind the bar and grabbed one of the many pint glasses being thrust his way from the other side.

'The Seventy Shilling needs changing . . .'

'I'll do it,' Callum offered.

'No, you're alright, just do me a pint for Alec, will you?' And Fergus was off to the cellar.

'OK, who's next?' Kate beamed at the sea of customers, seemingly unbothered by Fergus's ticking-off. A chorus of thirsty voices each claiming their turn.

'Is he always that miserable?' she asked Callum as she began serving. It was the first time she'd spoken to him and all Callum could think about was the fact that her bare arm was touching his as they pulled their pints of lager in unison.

In defence of his brother, he tried to sound pissed off.

'You *were* forty minutes late.'

'Ha! You sound like a teacher!' Kate laughed.

'That's because I *am* one.'

'You're kidding!' Kate stopped, pint in hand.

'No. This is just . . . well, I help Fergus out when it's busy.'

She turned, noticing him for the first time. 'Where d'you teach?'

'St Mary's down the road – top juniors.'

'Ah, we used to play them in netball.'

'Which school did *you* go to then?'

'Other side of town. North Park on the Queensferry Road.' Her smile was mesmerizing. 'I'm Kate, by the way.'

'I know.'

She held his gaze.

Five hours later, she was astride him, her lacy knickers discarded on the sandy ground beneath their feet and her little denim skirt confidently pulled up. The wooden slats of the shelter's bench groaned along with every thrust, joining in. She sat facing him, taking all of him in, relentlessly delighted to feel him inside her, as if discovering sex for the first time. But she was too well versed in what she was doing for this to be the first time. She stopped for a moment to catch her breath and held his face, disbelievingly – 'Jesus!' His smile spread slowly, then, without warning, he picked her up in one deft movement and pushed her against the wall. She whispered 'Yes' and he carried on fucking her. 'God, you're good.'

What are you doing? The question flashed through his mind but he swiftly ignored it.

They came together. Stood there indecorously, his jeans around his ankles, her legs around his waist and the North Sea pounding. Suddenly, over the yelling of the waves, they heard singing: a drunken voice, getting closer. *'I'm ne'er ginna dance agin, Guilty feelin' got nae rhythm.'*

'Shit!' Kate giggled. Callum covered her mouth with his hand. Which turned her on even more.

'Don't move!'

She didn't. Nor did Callum. She buried her head in his neck as the well-oiled George Michael tribute act turned the corner at the other end of the shelter, leant up against the wall, unleashed his tackle and had an almighty pish. It seemed to go on forever, accompanied by bursts of *'Shoulda known better than to cheat a friend . . .'*

Kate, still amused, started biting Callum's palm. Every second that passed, they waited for the man to look up and see them, but he was oblivious. When he eventually finished, he shook himself down, tucked himself in and stumbled away.

Kate whispered, 'D'you think he—'

'Not a thing.'

But from a little way off came a shout. 'G'nigh, pal. Nice arse, by the way.' And Kate collapsed in giggles.

It was nearly one a.m. when he drove her into the city centre, tatty bits of Body Shop make-up messy in her lap. The vanity mirror was down and she was scooping her hair up into a scrunchy. She had big rich glossy brown curls, masses of them. He wanted to put his hands through them again, bury his face in them and inhale.

She saw him looking. 'Oi, keep your eyes on the road.'

He smiled and did what he was told.

Shaking a blue mascara wand into action, she began topping up her lashes, mouth open in concentration.

'How old are your kids?'

'Who says I got kids?'

'You gonna tell me you haven't?'

He smiled. 'Three and five. And there's another one on the way.'

'Christ, you been busy. No wonder you need the extra cash.' She was onto lipliner now. Callum stole a glance as she meticulously lined her fleshy lips with confident expertise. She knew he was watching again. 'I can do this with my eyes closed, y'know. It's my party trick.'

'Bet you couldn't do someone else's.'

She smiled. 'Just here's fine. I'll walk the rest.' And she swept up her make-up and shoved it into her little beaded bag as Callum stopped the car.

'You sure you don't want me to take you home?'

'It's a Saturday night in Edinburgh, man! Remember those? Nightclubs? Curry houses? Hangovers the next day? You're not *that* old.'

'Thirty-nine next month!'

She smirked at him and got out of the car. 'Thanks for the lift!'

He watched as she walked away. And then, as if remembering something, she turned on her heel and came back to his side of the car. He wound down the window and she leant inside to kiss him.

Jesus, those lips, he thought.

She looked him straight in the eye. 'You. Are going. To break my heart, Callum MacGregor.' And she was off again, banging the roof of the car as she left. 'Toodle-pip!' This time she didn't turn around.

He tried to take in what had just happened. Was it some kind of set-up, an elaborate joke played by one of the boys at the club? No. This was no joke.

And then it came.

The guilt.

Belinda.

He took a deep breath. Where would he say he'd been tonight? For the briefest of moments, he thought about telling her. *What?* Fuck, no. How could he even think that was a good idea?

Went up the club, had a bit of a lock-in.

Gary would cover for him. He owed him more than one favour on that front – Callum was always covering for Gary. Christ, is that what he'd become now? A rugby-club-shagger bore?

In the distance he saw Kate join a group of friends, laughing. One of them picked her up and swung her round. Callum turned the key in the ignition and his car pulled away. He was headed home. Ready to start lying.

2002

1

'I fell for him so hard. It was like riding a bicycle really fast down a very steep hill and realizing my brakes weren't working.' Kate Andrews – now thirty-nine, tearful, smartly dressed and more stunning with age – was talking to a therapist, hands crossed neatly in her lap.

'And what about him? What d'you think *he* was feeling at the time?' The therapist was softly spoken, kind.

Kate took a deep breath. 'Well, to be honest, most of the time I think he was feeling . . .' she hesitated and the therapist nodded, willing her to speak, '. . . my arse.' And she burst out laughing, covering her face in her hands.

The director and the TV crew were used to this from Kate. The actor playing the therapist looked bemused. The camera guys shared a smile.

'Sorry, I'm so sorry, I just couldn't resist. It's this script! The lines are just so – y'know, crap sometimes . . .'

'Yes, thanks, really helpful that.' The director wasn't impressed. They were already running over time.

Kate rolled her eyes. Christ, what was wrong with people? It was only a bit of a laugh. 'For God's sake, I said I was sorry!'

'OK everyone, we'll pick this up again on Friday. Hopefully by then Ms Andrews will have pulled herself together. That's a wrap.'

Like a scolded child, Kate headed off to her trailer, shouting goodnight to various crew members. Betsy, her make-up artist, called out to her, 'You wanna get your slap off, sweetheart?'

'No, I'll do it at home.'

'Your loss,' Betsy joked. 'I'd've done you a lovely head massage!'

'Next time, babe! Love you!'

And she climbed up the metal steps of the Winnebago, her smile dropping as she shut the door behind her. She started changing out of her character's clothes into her Armani jeans.

The wall lights were on and the electric fire. Something she held dear about being in her trailer when it was dark and cold outside. Her own little sanctuary. She loved night shoots when there were hours of hanging around. She'd climb into her little trailer bed and pretend she was eight again, all cosied up and safe. She pulled on her cashmere V-neck and caught her reflection staring back from the mirror on the laminated wall. She looked her age today. The dark circles were pushing their way through the matt concealer under her eyes. She needed another vitamin B shot from that doctor in Harley Street. Couldn't afford to get run down with another eight weeks' filming to do. And she really must give up smoking. She picked up her packet of Marlboro Lights, lit one and inhaled defiantly at the sign by the fridge – *Strictly no smoking inside this trailer*. They all knew she smoked in there, but no one dared say a word.

A timid knock on the trailer door.

'Don't come in!'

'Sorry, Kate, just to say your car's ready when you are.' It was Becky, one of the runners, a sweet and lovely girl whose kindness never ceased to amaze.

'OK, thanks, Becs. Be there now.'

Kate took four more rapid puffs on her cigarette, squeezing out every last drop of nicotine, before running the stub under the tap and throwing it in the bin.

She shut her eyes for a few seconds and sighed. The blackness was heading her way. That godawful, disempowering gloom that crept up from time to time and engulfed her. She could feel it, deep in the pit of her stomach – an anxiety, a fear of the unknown, an irrational sense of impending sorrow. She had to banish it before it sank its claws into her again.

She looked at her reflection, determined, gritted her teeth and said, 'Come on. Get. A. Grip.' Then she painted on the well-known Kate Andrews smile and opened the trailer door.

Dougie, her driver, was waiting by his black Mercedes, drinking coffee from his ubiquitous Thermos mug. He shouted across to her, 'Got anything you want carrying, sweetcheeks?'

'Only my sorry ass!'

'Can be arranged.'

'Oh you old smoothie, Doug.'

And Dougie laughed, slightly too loudly. Sometimes the film-set banter was exhausting. Always having to keep up this pretence of 'all mates together', having to be constantly upbeat, constantly cracking jokes, constantly being a 'really good sport'. She imagined Dougie telling his wife, or the other drivers, *She's a little diamond, that Kate Andrews. Won't hear a word said against her. Down-to-earth, heart of gold, wicked sense of humour* . . . Kate knew how important it was to stay in Dougie's good books. She never knew when she'd need to call in a favour.

Kate dug deep and went into overtly jolly mode. 'Come along then, Douglas! Take me home and don't spare the horses!'

Forty minutes later, Kate was fast asleep in the back of the car. She always slept on her way home. Dougie knew the routine: ten minutes before arriving at her house, he would wake her so she could have a sneaky ciggie out the window.

'Kate . . .' he whispered. He didn't want to alarm her. 'Not far now.'

'Hmmmnn.'

She stretched and yawned, waiting for Dougie to say the inevitable, 'Careful – you'll start catching flies you stay like that too long!'

'What time is it?'

'Quarter past, treacle.'

She reached into her bag for her fags, took one out and lit it, rapidly winding down the window to blow out the smoke and relishing the comforting blast of cool air on her face. The Chiswick traffic was slow. She adored this time of evening, passing houses when it was dark: people with their curtains open and their lights on unwittingly presenting private shows for passers-by who peeked anonymously into their lives.

'I'm sorry for smoking in your car, Doug, it's really selfish of me.'

He was thrown by her uncharacteristic humility. 'That's alright, darlin'. What the eye don't see, eh?'

The traffic drew to a halt again. Kate looked inside the front room of a ground-floor flat. A woman sat on her own, an empty dinner plate in front of her, flicking channels on her remote. She gave up, threw the remote across the room and buried her head in her hands. In the house next door a couple were rowing – the woman raised her arms, gesturing in defiance, the man just kept shaking his head. He appeared to be trying to speak, but she was talking over him. The car moved slowly on. Three houses down, two women were laughing at something one of them was reading from a letter, wiping their eyes with joy. The joy turned to a hug. The hug turned to a kiss.

'Are you happy, Doug?'

'Oh y'know me, Miss! Can't complain!'

Can't complain, mustn't grumble, could be worse – all the trite expressions people relentlessly churn out, making light of all that pain, giving away not the slightest hint that they're feeling demolished inside. Unless of course they weren't. Maybe she was alone in knowing this hollowness of spirit, this bankruptcy of the soul that caught her out when she least expected it.

What must it be like to be normal, she wondered? The world's idea of normal anyway. She thought about Dougie's wife. Dougie's wife would be normal. Hairdresser's on a Tuesday, Aerobics on a Wednesday, girls' night on a Thursday (Dougie's wife would call them 'girls', even though their average age was sixty-two), curry night with Doug on a Friday, *Unless he's workin' – these television shows, he's out all hours ferryin' the stars back an' forth, bless him.* Then Dougie's wife'd have the grandchildren on a Saturday or go shopping with her daughter-in-law, and do a nice roast on the Sunday. Every Sunday. Dougie's wife probably had a little part-time job in a gift shop or a cafe and did her Christmas shopping by October the first every year. Kate longed to be normal. To never have to overthink or listen to the running commentary whirring in her head, telling her she was never good enough or real enough, calling her useless and ugly and fat.

'What plans you got for your day off then?' Dougie interrupted her thoughts.

'Sod all, thank God.' She reached into her bag for her diary. 'Long lie-in, nice brunch at Carlo's, maybe a little massage in the . . . Oh fuck.' She'd found tomorrow's date and there it was, staring back at her. She grabbed her mobile from her bag, scrolling through her contacts for her agent's number.

'You been booked?' said Doug.

'Looks like it.' The call had connected. 'Cynthia, it's me. Sorry to ring out of hours but I've got no details for this thing tomorrow – it just says "school visit".'

'Yes, love, *your* old school.'

'You're kidding me?'

''Fraid not. You're on the seven ten from Euston. They booked you a good six months ago and they're very excited about it.'

'How come I don't remember agreeing to this? Edinburgh!! For fuck's sake, Cynth!'

Cynthia Kane had been Kate's agent for over fifteen years. She was used to Kate's volatile temperament and her habit of not listening to information then claiming later not to have been told. Cynthia never took offence. 'You want me to cancel?'

Kate sighed. Yes, she did. But in all conscience she knew it'd be too harsh. 'No, it's fine. Sorry. Could've just done with a day off, that's all.'

Cynthia hung up, promising to have a word with the producer

to see if they could find a few days' grace in the filming schedule so that Kate could get some R & R.

'Thanks, Cynthia.' Kate sighed and looked out of the window. She knew what Dougie would say next and predictably he did. 'No peace for the wicked, eh?'

'Oh, can't complain, mustn't grumble, could be worse . . .' Dougie was oblivious to her sarcasm and she took a deep draw on her fag before throwing it out the window, just as they pulled into her road.

2

Inside Number 29, Matt Fenton was adding red wine to a big pan of chilli. Despite the frilly pinny he was wearing, he still looked remarkably masculine, his white-blond hair and Scandinavian features adding to the image of a thirty-seven-year-old dad in touch with his feminine side. His daughter Tallulah watched him as she drank her bedtime milk, her stuffed panda, known as Panda, on her lap.

'Why doesn't Mummy ever make the supper?'

Tallulah was five. Tallulah was a Daddy's girl.

'Because Mummy is too busy earning money to keep you in Coco Pops and ice-cream.' He leant down and picked her up. 'Now young lady, time for your bed! And you, Panda.'

'Panda didn't like what you gave him for tea.'

'Complaints in writing to the management, please.'

They'd just got to the top of the stairs when the front door opened.

'Hello?'

'Mummy!'

Kate threw down her bag and her coat.

'Hey, gorgeous!' called Matt.

'My favourite two people in the whole wide world! Let me just get a drink.'

And as she went off to the kitchen, Matt tried to ignore the slight irritation he felt. Kate had a habit of putting her glass of red before anything else, even kissing her five-year-old daughter goodnight.

'I want to see Mummy!'

'Tell you what, let's tuck you in first, then I'll get her to come and read you a story.'

'OK.' Tallulah preferred Mummy's stories because she always put on silly voices.

In the kitchen, Kate drained her glass of Rioja in one before pouring another, which she would pretend to Matt was her first. When he came in, she was tasting the chilli. 'Mm, this is *good*.'

'She wants you to read her a story.'

'Yeah, I will in a sec.'

They kissed. And Kate snuggled into his neck and shut her eyes for a moment. He put his arm around her and inhaled the smell of her hair, the familiar mix of hairspray, cigarette smoke and very expensive perfume. He could tell her mind was elsewhere.

'We sold the Berlotti prints today. Restaurant in Hackney.'

'Nice.' She drank more of her wine, her eyes still shut.

'And then I spent a good two hours designing your cake with Lula. But sssshh. It's a secret.'

Kate smiled and pulled away from him. 'She loves other people's birthdays more than her own, I think.'

'I know, and she's particularly excited about yours, even though I've told her ladies of a certain age prefer to forget!'

'Christ, is that what I am now – a "lady of a certain age"?'

'You're still a top bit of totty in my book.' And he kissed her left ear. 'You OK?'

'Yep.'

She wasn't. He knew the signs.

'I'll go see Lula.'

He followed her as she made her way upstairs, glass of wine in hand.

Tallulah was already out for the count, her tiny arms holding on tight to Panda as she dreamt. Kate stood in the doorway watching her little girl sleep as Matt came up quietly behind her.

'She's such a precious baby.' Kate was barely audible.

Matt held her hand and they stood there in silence. Watching. Loving. 'What d'you want to do for your birthday?' he whispered. 'She keeps asking.'

'Oh, I dunno. I'll be filming, won't I?' She thought for a moment. 'Wish we could run away. Just the three of us.'

Matt looked at her. 'Not getting sad again, are you, babe?'

She didn't return his gaze. 'No, course not.'

'You would tell me, wouldn't you?'

'I'm fine, honestly. Just hate the idea of being another year older, that's all. It's alright for you. You're still technically mid thirties.' And before Matt could pursue it, Kate changed the subject. 'I've got that school thing tomorrow.'

'I know. It was on the calendar. I'll take you to the station if you like.'

Kate hesitated. 'Come with me.' It was more of a plea than a request.

'It's Lula's little concert, remember? One of us has to be there.'

'You having a dig?'

'What? No, don't be daft! Look, you'll be in Edinburgh by twelve, back home by eight. I'll book us a table at Porto's tomorrow night, shall I?'

'Fucking school. They've only asked me back 'cos I'm famous.'

'Er, well yes, I think that's the whole point. They want to show you off. *Look how successful the pupils of North Park Primary have turned out to be.*'

'Don't tell my mother I'm going. She'll be furious at me for not visiting.'

'You can't do everything, sweetheart.' Matt stroked her cheek. 'Come on. Bit of my lovely chilli and an early night. That's what you need.'

It wasn't. But then Kate didn't really *know* what she needed. She let Matt take her hand and lead her downstairs, pushing away the suffocating gloom that was doing press-ups in the corner, biding its time, getting ready to pounce . . .

In bed that night Matt dreamt he was trying to fix a leaking roof. He was standing next to a cement mixer – churn, swish, churn, swish – but every time he reached in for more cement to fill a hole, another one would open up. And all the time the cement mixer kept turning – churn, swish, churn, swish.

He woke up, breathless and shaking, desperately trying to make sense of where he was. The bedroom. Good. That's good. But he could still hear the noise – churn, swish, churn, swish. He looked at Kate's side of the bed. She wasn't there. And then he realized where the sound was coming from . . .

They'd lived in their home for six years. Moved in when Kate was pregnant with Tallulah. It should have been way beyond their budget, but Kate had just finished working on a lucrative drama series in the States so money was far from tight. A gorgeous Georgian detached house in Chiswick: they'd fallen deeply in love at first viewing.

There was nothing to do to it. Even the nursery was ready and waiting. Just one thing was missing: Kate wanted a gym. It was non-negotiable. And the room that Matt had hoped would be his study was clearly the only candidate for conversion. 'It's essential to my well-being and how I look for work.' He'd been thrown by her unfamiliar tone – so much so that he didn't argue back. 'My looks are my assets, Matt.' Then she'd laughed and kissed him and the subject was closed. This was the first time he'd had any insight into Kate's determination to get what she wanted. But the more he got to know her, the more he saw this side of Kate's personality – and he grew to understand that despite her vulnerability, her insecurities and this craving to be loved, she also had a ruthless ambition and an inner drive that could obliterate any obstacle in her way. He found himself respecting his wife for this.

And there he stood now, in the doorway of Kate's gym, watching as she pounded away at the treadmill – churn, swish, churn, swish – sweat flying off her, headphones on, the muscles in her perfectly toned arms and legs rippling with every gruelling step. She was oblivious, muttering to herself through gritted teeth, 'Come on, come ON!' He felt that to disturb her would be akin to waking a sleepwalker, but what he was watching was insane. It was three thirty in the morning, for God's sake. She had her back to him, the music in her headphones so loud he could hear the lyrics to the high-energy dance track even over the noise of the treadmill.

Then, out of nowhere, Kate slammed her hand down on the stop button and stood there panting. She ripped off her headphones and put her head onto the console. The tinny music carried on as the treadmill shut down. Matt didn't want to frighten her but he knew whatever sound he made would make her jump. 'Kate?' he whispered.

'Jesus! How long've you been there for?'

'Few minutes.'

She grabbed her gym towel and wiped the sweat from her forehead as she sat at the end of the machine.

'Couldn't sleep. I was trying to wear myself out.'

'Kill yourself, more like.' He was sat now on the weights bench by the treadmill. She was within arm's reach of him, and he could see how drawn she looked despite the flush of her cheeks and the perspiration glistening on her skin. He held out his hand to her.

'Don't. I'm all sweaty and disgusting.'

He hid his rejection as she got up and headed to the door. 'Gonna jump in the shower. Won't be long. Go back to bed.' And she left him there.

The tinny dance track came to an end and in the silence Matt felt very alone.

3

Eight hours later, sitting in a first-class seat on the InterCity 125, Kate stared out of the window at the drenched and muddy fields, bordered with bracken and withering autumn trees. Electricity pylons stood proud like miniature Eiffel Towers, and empty training pitches cried out for players to come stamping across their sodden turf. Occasionally there'd be a group of sheep all facing the same way, munching grass like it was going out of fashion and showing no signs of feeling the cold, nestled inside their thick woolly fleeces.

Kate sipped her stewed and tasteless coffee and wondered when British train companies would catch up with the rest of the country and start serving a decent brew. Her stomach rumbled and, embarrassed, she looked round to check no one else had heard it. God, she was starving. She'd hardly touched the chilli the night before, nor the porridge Matt had made her before she left.

Not that Matt was aware. Over the years, she'd devised a handful of food-concealing techniques – chucking stuff down the loo, mixing it into plant-pot soil, hiding it in the dog bowl, or even – and this was the most extreme – when Tallulah was a baby, secreting unwanted food inside dirty nappies in the nappy bag. Sometimes she felt guilty for not telling Matt. But she knew he wouldn't understand and he'd start lecturing her about nutrition and how unhealthy it was to be underweight. Easy for him to say – TV was ruthless. It wasn't true what people said about the camera adding ten pounds: it added twenty. And Kate knew how important it was to look good – especially as she got older. She just needed to lose five pounds, and then she'd feel settled.

Across the carriage from her, an overweight businesswoman in an ill-fitting suit was talking on her mobile whilst intermittently sinking her teeth into a breakfast baguette. Kate couldn't help but surreptitiously watch. It comforted her, seeing fat people eat – made her feel secure in her hunger and the knowledge that she herself was nowhere near that size, or that out of control. The woman was discussing quarterly figures. She appeared to work for some kind of national retailer.

'Well, Paul will have to take that up with you, Dave,' she was saying, 'because the report I'm reading tells a very different story.'

As Dave presumably justified his actions on the other end of the phone, the woman took the opportunity to take another mouthful of her baguette. But she was too enthusiastic and her bite burst the yolk of the fried egg, splattering yellow goo all over her chin and right down the front of her shirt.

She didn't know she was being watched, silently swearing and looking around for a tissue to mop up the mess. Not wanting to waste anything, she scooped up the spillage with her forefinger before licking it clean.

'Yeah, yeah . . . no, go on, I'm listening.' She clearly wasn't. She reached into the vast handbag stuffed under her feet and began scrabbling around inside, still feigning interest in the phone call. Eventually she pulled out a packet of wet wipes, struggling to free one single-handedly. She ended up extracting two, and vigorously wiped her chin with them before attempting to clean up her shirt. In the process, she dropped her phone.

'Bollocks!' It went right underneath the woman's seat. Kate could see 'Dave – Bolton Branch' flashing merrily away on the screen whilst his little voice cried out for help. 'Hello? Hello? You still there?'

Kate looked away as the businesswoman's hand flailed around

under her seat, fruitlessly searching for the handset like one of those grabber machines in a seedy seaside arcade.

Suddenly there was a kerfuffle and Kate looked back again to see the woman now on her hands and knees, her broad backside majestically swaying between the two seats as she stretched for the phone. Her calves were thick and dimpled and the cracked skin on the heels of her feet peeped through the twenty-denier tights she was wearing. Kate offered up a silent prayer of gratitude that *she* didn't look like that.

Phone retrieved, the woman clambered back into her seat, sweat now running down the sides of her neck. 'Sorry about that, Dave. Where were we?'

Kate and the woman caught each other's eye momentarily before looking away, mutually embarrassed, until the embarrassment on the businesswoman's face turned to delighted recognition when she realized that she was staring at *the* Kate Andrews! Unable to withstand the awkwardness, Kate picked up her bag and headed towards the smoking carriage.

She stood in the vestibule at the far end of the train and lit up, the window open slightly for her to blow out the smoke. She thought about earlier that morning at home, waking up late to find Tallulah at the end of the bed, clutching Panda.

'Hello, gorgeous. You gonna have a cuddle with Mummy before school?'

Tallulah snuggled up. 'Daddy said *you're* going to school today.'

'That's right, pumpkin. Mummy's old school back in Scotland.'

'Was Mrs Pickering your teacher?'

'No darling – I doubt Mrs Pickering was even born when I was in school!'

Matt came in with Kate's porridge and handed her a coffee.

'Thanks.' She took a big slurp. 'Oh *why* do I have to go, Matt?'

'Babe, you just have to show your face, that's all. Let them take a photo, say a few words about how humbling it is to be there. They'll be *so* disappointed if you cancel. It's their centenary!'

26

'Yeah, but it's not like I *went* there a hundred years ago, is it?'

'State of you, this morning, you look like you might have done!'

'Cheers, mate!'

Matt laughed. 'Honestly, what was all that about? Bloody marathon in the middle of the night.'

Kate sighed and looked away.

'Daddy, you said a bad word! – Panda says you're very naughty.'

'Yes I am. Sorry, Panda. Now let's leave Mummy to get dressed – she's got a train to catch.'

Tallulah jumped off the bed and ran out onto the landing. Alone with Kate for a moment, Matt leant over and smoothed her cheek. 'I'll see you tonight, bub. I'm going to ask Hetty to come. You don't mind, do you?'

'Course not.'

'I mean, if you'd rather it was just us two . . .'

'Hetty is *always* welcome, you know that. She's one of the few people in my life who never irritates me.' She took his hand, kissed it and whispered, 'I love you so much, Matt. I'm sorry I'm such a monumental pain in the arse.'

Kate knew how much it meant to him when she was kind, how it pulled the rug from under him when she showed him any rare sweetness. Berating herself for not treating Matt better, she vowed to try harder. Whatever demons took up occasional residence in her head were certainly not put there by Matt.

'Eat your porridge, Goldilocks,' he'd said and she watched him chase after Tallulah, sighing at the prospect of the day ahead. What had she been thinking, saying yes to this school visit? She must've been drunk at the time. Or distracted. Because going home to Edinburgh was not something Kate did unless absolutely necessary, like when she'd returned for her grandmother's funeral, or for Christmas five years ago when her mother refused to take no for an answer. There were too many ghosts in the Scottish capital and she already felt haunted enough.

*

She lit up a second cigarette. Chain-smoking helped alleviate the anxiety gnawing away inside her like a rat on a bone, but only briefly. She closed her eyes and let the brutal force of the air outside blast her face as it rushed in through the window.

It had been seventeen years.

In the early days, she'd patiently waited for the healing power of Time to work its legendary magic, to mend her and make her feel better again, just like the aphorism always promised it would. And yes, the pain had diminished considerably since then. But she'd eventually come to realize it would never leave her completely, and hardly a day went by without her thinking about what had happened or wondering how her life might have turned out had a different choice been made.

Time had given her something else, though: an expert ability to steel herself in the face of any unwelcome emotion, to never allow in anything which she couldn't control. It wasn't much of a consolation prize, but it was better than being at the mercy of her enemies: Weakness and Vulnerability. When it came to self-admonishment, Kate was a boot-camp bully. 'Pull yourself together, for fuck's sake,' she whispered, drowned out by the invading wind.

'We will shortly be arriving in Berwick-upon-Tweed,' the distorted tannoy voice of the train manager announced. Kate took her final puff and threw her stub out of the window before cramming two sugar-free mints into her mouth.

As the sliding door of the carriage opened to let her back in, she noticed the businesswoman now tucking into a large croissant and jam. Kate's stomach rumbled again and she inwardly purred with self-righteousness. The woman called over to her, flakes of pastry framing her mouth, 'Can I just say, I'm a *big* fan of your work, Miss Andrews!' and she smiled as she carried on munching.

4

The taxi driver was also a fan. Not only that, he was a fan with career advice and not afraid to dish it out. 'Aye, see when y'did that show on the BBC? About the nurse?'

'Ah, you mean *Sisters*?'

'Nooo, they were nurses, nae sisters!'

Kate bit her tongue. *Keep smiling.* 'Yes, it was called *Sisters* – did you like it?'

'What a load of bollockin' baloney!'

'Thanks,' she muttered.

'Ey, don't get me wrong, ye were terrific in it! Full o' sass an' spark, eh? But your wee fella, the guy with the eyes . . .'

'Jimmy McColl.'

'That's him. I canna stand the man. With his wee gurnin' face all twisted up like a neep.'

'A lot of women find him very attractive.'

'Pfff, the man's a prize jessie, no mistake. Calls himself a detective? They say he shaves his chest! I mean, have ye ever heard anythin' so—'

'You can pull up just here actually, I'll walk the rest.' Kate had had enough of his blethering.

'You sure, hen? It's nae bother for me to—'

'No, it's fine. Honestly. I fancy walking.' She took out a twenty from her purse. 'Keep the change.'

'You little angel. Tell you what, it's nice to have you back in your home town, Miss Andrews. A lot of folk they leave an' come back all pumped up with their English airs and graces, but you—'

'Hey, I'm married to an Englishman, y'know!' She chided him with a smile.

'Well, we can't all be perfect.' And he laughed. 'Ye take care now – here's my card in case you need fetching back.'

She took it and got out of the car, absorbing the sight before her. Just a hundred or so yards away stood the school gates of North Park Primary, now painted green instead of the shabby white they'd once been. Behind her the taxi pulled away with a cheeky hoot of his horn.

Walking through the gates felt strangely comforting. On the rare occasions she came back – a handful in the last seventeen years – she'd pretty much stayed at her parents' house for the duration of her short visits. She'd certainly never ventured up the Queensferry Road to the site of her old school. But returning here now, to a place where she'd only spent six years of her life, really did feel like coming home.

She made her way to the main reception. The large oak and glass door with its brass fittings had been there in Kate's day. She turned the handle just like she would've done thirty-odd years ago – but nothing happened. It was locked. A face appeared on the other side.

'You have to buzz the buzzer.' This was Mrs Crocombe, the school secretary.

'Can't you just let me in?'

'No, you have to buzz the buzzer.' Mrs Crocombe was a stickler for school rules, even when they didn't make sense.

Kate, on best behaviour, smiled politely and buzzed the buzzer. 'Hi, I'm Kate Andrews and I'm—'

Mrs Crocombe cut her short. 'I know who you are, my dear. In you come.' And she opened the door to let her in. Kate resisted commenting as she stepped into the foyer. 'Headmaster will be with you shortly.'

'Right. OK, thanks.'

Something about Mrs Crocombe's reverence for the term 'headmaster' and the fact that she missed out the word 'the' when referring to him made Kate want to rebel and unforgivably misbehave.

Mrs Crocombe left Kate standing alone, serenaded by the sound of small children singing a hymn in the hall nearby.

'*Dance, dance, wherever you may be* . . .'

She looked up at a huge mosaic-effect banner, made no doubt by hundreds of small hands holding Pritt Sticks and bits of coloured paper. It declared 'North Park Primary 100 years! Welcome'. And scattered beneath it on several noticeboards were dozens of photographs of the school since its opening in 1902. She peered closely at the smiling, fading faces.

'Recognize anyone?' The Headmaster was looking over her shoulder.

'Oh, hello. I was just—'

'Brian Boyd. It's an enormous pleasure.' He held out his firm hand for an even firmer handshake. 'Of course, I never taught you, but I was trying to work out when you left.'

'Nineteen seventy-four!'

The Headmaster whistled his incredulity. 'So Colin Marshall was in charge then, I believe. I wasn't sure if . . .'

But Kate wasn't really listening. She was still trying to take it all in. 'It's almost exactly the same . . . the kingfisher statue, and . . . and the floor . . . the woodblock floor . . . and the door handles, and even the smell . . . What *is* that smell?'

'I like to think it's a mixture of hard work and happy times!' This was Brian Boyd's mantra. He was so proud of its invention that he used it whenever the opportunity arose.

Kate edged towards the main hall, drawn by the sound of the singing. '*Dance, dance, wherever you may be* . . .'

'Can I have a little peek?'

'Be my guest. Infants' assembly.'

'*I am the Lord of the Dance, said he* . . .'

Tiptoeing up to the window in the door at the back of the hall, she looked inside and saw a hundred kids, the oldest no more than seven years of age, sat cross-legged, dutifully singing words they didn't really understand. 'I remember this one!' She blinked back sudden tears as she sang along in a whisper.

'And I'll lead you all, wherever you may be . . .'

She hadn't expected this. To be taken hostage by emotion and led down Memory Lane, transported back to a simpler, painless time in life, unfettered by the complications and inexplicable fears of a grown-up world.

'And I'll lead you all in the dance, said he!'

'I thought you could meet the Year Sixes first.' The Headmaster was always on the go and oblivious to Kate's nostalgia. 'Year Six translates as top juniors in old money!'

'Yes, I know.' She snapped out of her reverie. 'I've got a five-year-old myself, so . . .'

'Right. Well, it's in the same place that it always was – up the stairs, end of the corridor. Shall we?'

As they mounted the steps, she remembered instantly the feel of the handrail and the sensation of running her little fingers up and down its polished mahogany. She carried on down the corridor, the Headmaster by her side wittering something about class sizes and downturns in economy. Kate could hear children laughing, reciting, shouting in the classrooms as she passed, their voices blending with those of the ghosts of pupils past.

Blissfully ignorant of what she was thinking, the Headmaster trampled all over her private thoughts and announced, 'Course, we've had eighteen fire doors put in since you left. And a computer suite. Right, here we are.'

They'd stopped outside the final classroom. This used to be Mrs Jackson's room when Kate was there nearly thirty years ago. But now the plate on the door bore the name of a different teacher.

Mr MacGregor

Kate felt simultaneously sick and exhilarated. It couldn't be, could it? A loud rushing in her ears and she subtly steadied herself with her hand on the door frame. Fortunately, Mr Boyd didn't notice. Kate gathered herself.

'Not . . . *Callum* MacGregor?'

The Headmaster knocked enthusiastically on the door. 'That's right. Joined us last year from St Mary's in Portobello. Deputy head. Quite a coup!'

A voice came from inside the room.

'Come in.'

Kate couldn't focus, could barely hear. Her mouth felt like it was filled with sand. The Headmaster, still wittering, opened the door and made way for her to go in. But her feet wouldn't move. She stood rooted to the herringbone tiles of the junior-school corridor floor.

Sitting at his desk, in front of a classful of excitable eleven-year-olds, was the man she had fallen in love with seventeen years ago. Her voice wouldn't work. Nothing would work.

Callum looked at her. Gentle. Unsurprised.

'Hello, Kate.'

5

Matt stood up from his desk in the little office at the back of the shop, drained the dregs of his espresso and stretched. He hated doing paperwork – the downside of having his own business. But the upside was being able to work around Tallulah and her school hours. With Kate working such long days, she couldn't be relied upon for childcare. Not that this was something Kate had ever negotiated – she simply expected Matt to accept that her career came first. It was a practicality and he justified it by telling himself his job meant he could have the best of both worlds: running a small and flexible business whilst being a stay-at-home dad. Well, not quite stay-at-home – more stay-at-shop. Or stay-at-gallery, to be more precise.

At Warwick he'd studied History of Art. He was passionate about other people's work. Probably because he himself couldn't paint, or draw. Not so much as a wonky stickman or potato print. Yet he could talk in detail about portraits and landscapes and abstract pieces till the cows in a Julien Dupré painting came home. And when his grandmother died, she left him a tidy enough sum to set up his own small art gallery in Brackenbury Village. He'd agreed with his mum after she'd gladly signed over the money that 'those who can, paint – and those who can't, open a gallery'. It did surprisingly well. Well enough to pay for Peter, his part-time assistant and old school friend of his mum's, who could mind the shop when Matt needed to be a dad – like now, when he was about to head off to watch Lula in her school play. Of course, he'd prefer it if Kate could be there next to him, but he'd long since learned not to point this out: he knew she felt guilty at being such an absent mother and reminding her of the fact would only lead to a storming row that could last for two or three days. Life was easier when Matt just accepted Kate's rules. And although at times he felt like a single dad, spending more time with Tallulah could hardly be called a challenge.

Above the gallery was a fabulous studio space, big and light and airy, which Matt rented out to local artists for a nominal fee. Its current inhabitant was Chloe, an intense-looking Brummie with candy-pink hair who wouldn't say boo to a goose but did amazing things with pastels. Matt had sold one of her creations only last week – a riot of greens and blues depicting the mossy, dank underside of Hammersmith Bridge. There was something darkly Dickensian about it, and it had fetched £1,500 along with a nice seller's commission for Matt.

He checked the time – probably a good moment to catch Hetty on her lunch break. Matt and Hetty had been best friends since uni and she was his first port of call when he needed to talk. And today he wanted to talk about Kate. Something was bugging him about her – she was probably just working too hard, but that gym routine in the middle of the night was just one of many symptoms – symptoms of a deep-down sorrow that reared its head from time to time. A chat with Hetty would sort him out. And probably some TLC time with Kate – she always responded well to being spoilt, loved up and boosted with confidence. He picked up his mobile, pressed 'call Hetty' and waited.

Hetty had worked for a small magazine in Hampstead called *Vegetarian Living* for the past ten years, and Matt knew what a stickler her boss Glen was when it came to taking private phone calls during office hours.

'Hello?'

'Why do you always answer your mobile like you don't know who it is?'

'Do I?'

'Yes! Why don't you just say "Hi Matt"? 'Cos you *know* it's me.'

Hetty thought about this for a second. 'Well, I suppose it feels like I'm sort of spoiling your surprise!'

Matt laughed. Kate was right about Hetty – she was one of life's sweetest and funniest people.

'Hey, guess what?' she said, full of excitement and not waiting for the answer. 'I've done it! Announced the reunion thingy.'

The bloody university reunion! Hetty had been planning it for at least the past two years. Matt felt relieved it was finally happening, because that meant it would soon be over and he would stop having to listen to her going on.

'But what if no one comes?' She was off at a hundred miles an hour, worrying, wondering, projecting, forgetting there was someone else on the other end of the phone. 'You'll come, won't you? I mean, even if it's just you and me, that's still technically a reunion . . .'

'Hetty, slow down! I need to pick your brains about Kate. I think she's getting . . . y'know . . . unsettled again.'

But Hetty wasn't listening. She was distracted by Ivor the magazine's accountant signalling to her that their boss was back. 'Sweetheart, I have to go . . .' she flapped. 'Glen's about to walk in!'

'OK, well can you babysit tonight?' Matt blurted. 'I thought I'd take her out for dinner – we need a bit of grown-up time—'

'Yes, yes!'

Ivor was now waving at her manically.

'Great. See you at seven.'

'Yes OK, now go!' She was panicking.

'Oh, one last thing – shall I get you something special to eat? Pizza?'

Hetty could see Glen's silhouette moving along the corridor to the office door and just managed to frantically screech-whisper, 'Brown-rice-and-broccoli-I'm-CLEANSING!' before hurling her mobile into a wastepaper bin and plonking herself down so hard on her ergonomic office kneeling chair that she slipped and landed on the floor. A second before Glen walked in, she clambered back up and tried to look engrossed in her computer whilst surreptitiously rubbing her left knee.

At the gallery, Matt smiled and pulled on his jacket. 'I'm off then, Pete. You're OK to close up?'

'Of course. We're running low on the Ketterlock postcards, by the way.'

'OK, I'll call them tomorrow.' And he stepped out into the brisk October lunchtime.

Porto's restaurant was a five-minute walk away, en route to the school. He'd taken Kate there on their first date, and since then it had become their most regular haunt. They loved its unpretentiousness and authentic Portuguese décor and, more than that, its delicious fresh fish and seafood. Porto's was owned by Ralph, who prided himself on creating a little Mediterranean bolthole in the middle of West London. Ralph's brother did the cooking, using their mother's recipes, and Ralph himself was a kind of maître d' slash head waiter.

He was outside now, talking to some customers. When he saw Matt he beamed. 'Hey my friend, when are you bringing your beautiful wife to see me?'

'Can you fit us in tonight, around half eight?'

'Of course. Usual table?'

Matt laughed. 'Ralph, how come you can *always* fit us in? What if someone else wants that table?'

'Then I throw them out my restaurant. Out on the street. On their backsides. See you tonight, Mattango.'

Matt shook his head, smiling at Ralph's sense of melodrama. He headed towards Tallulah's school, bracing himself for a performance of 'What the Octopus Did On His Holiday'.

He called Kate. Straight to voicemail. 'Hey gorgeous, just checking in. How's it going up there? You finding it all a bit weird? Call me when you're done. I've booked Porto's and Hetty's babysitting. I love you.'

As he hung up, on cue a text came through from Hetty. 'OH MY GOD! ALREADY THREE REPLIES TO THE REUNION! XX' She always texted in capitals.

Matt answered, 'Awesome! X'

A few seconds later, another text: 'PS, ONE OF THEM IS FROM ADAM LATIMER!!'

Matt's smile dropped. That *wasn't* so awesome. He stopped for a moment, then texted back, 'GR8 – gotta go. School play. C U 2nite. X'

Christ, Adam Latimer. Thinking of him left Matt cold. The guy was an idiot, only Hetty refused to accept it. Despite how much he'd hurt her, Matt's lovely friend, over and over again. He could handle Hetty's incessant talk of Adam, but the thought of actually seeing him after all that had happened was . . . well, anyway, she hadn't said Adam was actually *coming* to the reunion, just that he'd replied.

So we live in hope, thought Matt as he arrived at Tallulah's school, a tiny Adam Latimer-shaped cloud threatening to darken his otherwise sunny day.

6

Kate sat on the child-sized toilet seat of a child-sized toilet in the girls' lavs and willed herself not to cry. She shut her eyes and squeezed back the tears, forcing lungfuls of air in through her nose and out through her mouth like she was in some advanced meditation class for superheroes. In. And out. And in. And out.

She had thought she was going to faint. God, she was a good actress. No one would've suspected the torment she was going through, stood there in front of Callum MacGregor's Year Six pupils, with the Headmaster watching proudly from the sidelines, as she answered question after question, her wit, warmth and charm winning over the kids. She'd signed over thirty autographs, including one for Alice MacDonald's gran. 'Miss! Miss!' Amidst a sea of raised hands, Callum – also appearing to be calmer than a duck pond – had taken on the unofficial role of MC and had selected the questioners from the class.

'OK, Gregory Lang. And don't even think about saying anything rude, pal.'

Kate had smiled, but hadn't dare look in Callum's direction, keeping her focus firmly on little Gregory.

'Miss, see when you was in Australia doing that film . . .'

'Yes?'

'Why d'ye not go on *Home and Away*?'

'Hm, well, I don't think they'd have me, to be honest.'

'She couldn't do the accent, stupid!'

'Yes she could, she's an actress, stupid!'

'Miss! Are you a millionaire?'

'Er . . .'

'Have you got a mansion and a car made of gold?'

'Right, that's enough questions, I think it's time we said goodbye to our guest now, don't you?' Callum MacGregor's 'teacher' voice was well practised and unfailingly effective. He'd always managed to garner respect even from his most wayward of pupils.

'Thank-you-very-MUCH-Mrs-Andrews,' the kids had chanted in the listless sing-song way that only schoolchildren know how to do.

'It's *Miss* Andrews, actually.'

'You never married, then?' Callum had asked.

And this time she couldn't help but look at him. Well, a vague approximation of him anyway. She couldn't actually meet his eye, acknowledge his physical presence, say 'hi' to the elephant in the room, so huge it was straining against the walls and the ceiling, threatening to bring the whole place down around them in pieces.

'Oh, y'know,' she muttered, trying with all her might to sound casual. 'Equity name an' all that. My married name is Fenton.'

There was a butterfly-flutter-sized hiatus that nobody else could've detected. The kids had already started talking about lunch and the Headmaster was chomping at the bit, ready for the next part of his tour. 'OK then, Kate – are we ready to meet Mrs Baldwin?'

'Mrs Baldwin! God, is she still teaching?' Kate's enthusiasm was a little too hearty.

'Only just! She retires in June. She's been really looking forward to your visit.'

'Excellent!' And as she followed Mr Boyd towards the door, Kate gathered all her strength, turned to Callum and gave the performance of her lifetime. Ultra cool, unflustered, in control. 'Nice to see you again, Callum.'

In return he simply touched his temple with his forefinger in a tiny mock salute.

Outside in the corridor the Headmaster was off like a rocket, striding towards Mrs Baldwin's room with Kate following behind in a daze.

'She's where she always was – same classroom since she started in 1960!' And then he added, 'I didn't realize you and Callum already knew each other.'

'Oh.' Kate was caught off guard. 'We don't really – we had a mutual acquaintance . . .' She tried concentrating on not being sick. 'Actually, I think I drank too much coffee on the train. Can I just pop to the loo?'

The Headmaster wasn't impressed. He had an itinerary. He *knew* she'd start messing it up – she was an actress, after all. Very needy they could be. And disruptive. Or so his wife had warned him. He glanced at his watch and mustered a smile.

'Well, we *are* up against it, schedule-wise. Probably best if you use the junior girls' lavatory rather than popping back to the staffroom. I'll wait up ahead with Mrs B – you can find your own way, can't you?'

Kate had stumbled into the girls' toilets. Empty and silent apart from the hiss of the leaky water fountain, which somewhere in her subconscious she noted had still not been fixed since even when she was a pupil. She headed into a cubicle, locked the door and sat down. How she longed for a cigarette.

Their affair had been earth-shatteringly erotic.

Snatched moments in the pub's beer cellar when they'd both offered to change a barrel, the lifts home afterwards, the joyous and dangerous risk-taking sex on the beach, in his car, in her bedroom when her parents were out – even *his* house on occasion.

But it had always been more than just a fling. She'd known as soon as she'd looked at him that first night behind the bar how frighteningly powerful this thing between them actually was. She'd known. Something inside her had simultaneously died and sprung to life. Totally without control of where it could lead, totally without care

41

for whom it would hurt, including herself. She'd been continuously both thrilled and filled with terror every second she was with him, every minute she was not.

And there it was. Alive in her again. Electricity restored in the wake of a power cut. Lights back on. Business as usual. Exactly how it felt seventeen years ago.

Before it all came crashing down around them . . .

Don't cry.
Do. Not. Cry.
She reached for her cigarettes. She knew the Headmaster would be tapping his foot by now, but he would just have to wait. She held the lighter up, her hand shaking, let the flame ignite the tobacco and inhaled. Three deep draws on her Marlboro Light before tossing it half finished into the bowl. She flushed, grabbed her Chanel from her bag and smothered the smoke in a blanket of scent.

When she came out of the cubicle, she was startled to see a little girl stood staring, as if she'd been waiting for her.

'Oh! You made me jump!' Kate attempted a smile, but the little girl just frowned.

'The Headmaster says Mrs Baldwin is waiting,' she announced, and ran off. Kate wished she could run off too.

'On my way!' she shouted, faking brightness brilliantly.

7

The school bell rang announcing home time and his twenty-seven pupils scraped their chairs, grabbed their bags and were gone, Callum pointlessly shouting after them, 'No running!' He began clearing the desks and sighed.

He'd known for several weeks that she was coming. Brian Boyd had smugly announced it on the staff noticeboard at the beginning of term: *Centenary Celebration – VIP visit by former pupil and TV star Kate Andrews*. Most of his colleagues were excited at the prospect, especially the female staff who 'loved everything she was in, especially that thing about the nurses' – Callum kept schtum, feigning disinterest whenever the subject came up.

Seeing Kate's name up there in black and white had left him inwardly reeling, taking in the enormity of what it would feel like to see her again. But at least he'd had a few weeks to get used to the idea, and being forewarned would make him forearmed. He'd be prepared for the challenging hour or so she'd be standing in his classroom; she'd be gone as quickly as she'd arrived, leaving him to carry on with his day. She wouldn't have been expecting to see *him* though, would she? She'd have presumed he still taught in Portobello – not that he'd become deputy head of her old school in Queensferry. He could've taken a sickie, he supposed, and avoided the whole thing. But he'd not been teaching there that long, it wouldn't look good taking a day off so soon in the job. Plus, if he was honest, once he'd grown accustomed to the idea of seeing Kate again, he'd been curious to know what she looked like these days. In the flesh.

Seventeen years.

It came rushing back to him like it had happened only weeks ago. The chaos that had ensued, the disintegration of his until then very solid life. The whole experience, laid to rest in recent years, now hauled glaringly back into the spotlight.

He thought of the guilt he'd felt after that first night on the beach.

The only way to handle it – more importantly, the only way to prevent any danger of giving himself away – had been to act with total confidence, as if it had never happened. So there he was, up by eight the following morning, seeing to the boys' breakfast and making Belinda a cup of tea. He buttered three rounds of toast and cut them into soldiers. Then lifted two soft-boiled eggs from the pan, neatly placing them inside two ceramic Thomas the Tank Engine eggcups before handing them to his sons. 'There you go.'

'Yummeeeee!' Ben started smashing the top of his egg straight away with a spoon.

'Hey, careful, let Daddy do it.'

Cory just stared at *his* egg, unsure what to do next, and waited to copy his older brother like he did with everything else in his little life. Soon they were both dipping their soldiers into the rich, amber yolks, and Callum returned to making the tea. Three bags in the pot, he waited for the kettle to boil.

But forgetting the night before had been easier thought than done. Kate Bush was playing on the radio and he was back in the beach shelter, the waves applauding them, his eyes closed, Kate kneeling on the sandy ground, watching his face with delight as she loosened his belt, his jeans . . . she'd known exactly what she was doing, what she wanted . . . and when she got it she began devouring him with erotic expertise. Christ. *And if I only could, I'd make a deal with God, And I'd get him to swap our places . . .*

The kettle had clicked to announce the boiling of the water.

'I am gaspin' for a cuppa.'

It was Belinda. Callum's earlier determination to banish his guilt had gone out the window the instant he saw his wife walk cumbersomely into the kitchen, heavy with sleep and a month away from childbirth. He dug deep and with desperate and forced casualness managed, 'I was hoping you'd have a lie-in.'

'Try telling this one that.' Belinda smoothed her hand over her baby bump. 'We been practising a few drop goals in my tummy this morning, haven't we?'

'Start 'em young, eh?' Callum kissed the top of her head and put his arms around her. They both stood in silence for a moment, comfortable in the embrace, watching their boys demolish their eggshells. 'Funny to think of there being three when it's just been those two for so long.'

'I know. Things change though, don't they, Callumagico?'

She looked up and smiled at him and he willed himself to stay calm, even though his heart was thumping and remorse was coursing through his veins at a rate of knots.

Belinda's antennae started to twitch. 'You OK, babes?'

Inwardly Callum started making a rapid deal with a God he didn't believe in – *Let this go, make this OK, and I will never go near that woman again.*

'Yeah, why?' He tried and failed to sound nonchalant, and if the phone hadn't rung at that precise moment, the game might have been well and truly up.

'Daddy, it's Uncle Fergus,' said Ben, his mouth full of toast.

Callum took the receiver, his hand slightly shaking. 'Bit early for you, Ferg?' As he spoke he watched Belinda pour herself some tea and kiss the boys. Distraction successful.

'I know. Look, I hate to do this to you, but I've got two coachloads arriving today and Chris has just rung in sick. I've tried Polly and Liam, but it's no go. Is there any chance . . . ?'

'What time?'

'Evening shift – sixish? You'll be done by ten, most probs.'

'I'll have to check with Belinda.'

Belinda was ahead of him. 'If he wants you to work, then go for it. I ain't goin' nowhere in this state.'

Callum turned back to the phone. 'Guess that's a yes then.'

'She's a bloody saint, your wife, d'you know that?'

Callum laughed. 'Yeah, she is.'

He'd been about to hang up when Fergus had added, 'Oh, and don't worry, you won't be completely on your own. I'm getting that girl back in. She wasn't totally useless.'

And there it was.

The shortest-lived resolution ever made, dissolving into weak-willed air. He knew he'd be with Kate again that night, and probably the next and the next . . .

Locking up the store-room, Callum pocketed the key and headed out relieved that the day he'd been dreading for so long was now done with and he'd come out of it unscathed, with no complications or repercussions. He'd decided against telling Belinda about the 'celebrity visit' to the school. What would be the point? Best to just keep things simple.

And anyway she was gone now.

Panic over.

8

Kids were milling around her, the Headmaster was flapping them away and an ancient reporter was trying to get a few shots for the local press. They were stood in the school foyer and, all the while, Kate's professional painted-on smile belied the simultaneous agony and thrill she still felt from seeing Callum three hours earlier.

'Your taxi should be here any minute,' the Headmaster was saying. 'Can I reiterate what an honour it's been to welcome you back to North Park Primary.'

He was talking unnaturally loudly, looking around to make sure the reporter was in earshot. He wanted to be quoted word for word, he'd had it all planned. But Kate was distracted and not really playing ball.

'Er, yeah, sure,' she mumbled.

The usual home-time chaos was exacerbated by her being there. Parents collecting their kids wanted a sneak peek of the actress they'd seen so many times on their TVs that they felt she was an old friend. People were calling her name, some had cameras with them, others were clamouring for autographs, and all the while Kate was searching the crowd for Callum, desperate for one last look at the man who'd broken her heart all those years ago.

And then she saw him.

*

Unnoticed by anyone but her, he was making his way to the oak and glass door, car keys and a pile of books in his hands. She watched him stand aside to allow in another couple of parents keen to see the VIP. As he waited to let them through, he glanced back and Kate caught his eye. He managed the briefest of smiles and her heart lurched so violently she thought it would cease beating.

A schoolchild eager for her attention ran straight at her, knocking her momentarily off balance.

'Richard Blair! If I've told you once I've told you a thousand times, we do NOT run on school premises!' Mrs Crocombe the school secretary was yelling at the running child.

When Kate looked up, Callum had gone.

'I said your taxi's here, Miss Andrews!' The Headmaster was finding her a tad annoying now. That was the third time he'd said it. She was a pretty vacant sort, didn't answer his questions a lot of the time – probably on drugs. Most of them were, weren't they? Or so his wife had told him.

'Oh. Right. OK, thanks.' Kate felt overwhelmed by the crowd and needed to get out of there pronto. 'Thanks for . . . I dunno, thanks for having me,' she blurted out and made her way to the exit.

Outside, the taxi was waiting. It was the same driver who'd dropped her off earlier.

'Ha! You're stuck wi' me again, hen!'

She got into the back of the cab without speaking. Behind her, kids and parents had followed her out, still calling after her in the hope of an autograph or a smile.

'So is it Waverley or Haymarket you'll be wanting?' said the driver.

Kate didn't really know. She didn't really know anything at that moment, just wanted to be away from there, just wanted some air. 'Er, Haymarket, I think.' And she opened the window as he pulled away from the school. Her head was thumping. She needed a fag. 'Can I smoke out of the window?'

The driver laughed. 'As long as you don't mind if I join you!' And he lit up a Benson, glad of the excuse for a sneaky puff.

Kate put her head back and inhaled, consoling herself with the acrid burn of tobacco, before daring herself to think about him. She'd kept it together all afternoon, holding in the pain so tight every muscle in her body had ached with longing, but none as deeply as her heart. She wanted to scream, to weep, to cry out in agony.

'Y'alright in the back there, hen?' The taxi driver had caught sight of Kate in his rear-view mirror as she looked out of the window, taking in the passing houses and streets, a tear trickling down her cheek. He mistook her melancholy for homesickness. 'Aye, it's not a bad place to be brought up. I'll bet y'sometimes wish y'd never gone away!'

She managed a dry smile, embarrassedly wiping away the stray tear and cursing herself for not being more discreet. They were approaching a set of lights. As the driver blathered on about the evils of the English, Kate continued looking out of her window. A car in the next lane pulled up and stopped at the lights alongside them.

At first it didn't register. But then, like something out of a cartoon, Kate did a double take and her stomach somersaulted.

It was Callum.

He hadn't seen her.

She grabbed a twenty-pound note from her bag, hurled it at the driver and said, 'Sorry, babe, gotta get out – just seen someone I know.'

And she clambered out of the car and slammed the door shut on the driver's protestations – 'You're mad, hen! Yer off yer heed!' – and his delight at the twenty: 'Still, thanks very much – very kind.'

She opened the passenger door of Callum's car and climbed inside.

He was too stunned to react.

'Any chance of a lift?' She smiled, doing up her seatbelt. 'Didn't like the look of my driver. Shifty eyes.'

The lights turned green and Callum pulled away.

9

'This really isn't helping, you know.'

Matt was still laughing as he poured her a glass of tap water. They were in Kate and Matt's big open-plan kitchen. Tallulah was with them, eating her pasta, Panda sitting loyally next to her, trying to share the joke, although she couldn't really understand what had been making her daddy laugh quite so much.

'Oh Het, I'm sorry, it's just – only *you* could do something like that.'

'Thanks a lot.'

Hetty had turned up to babysit, still blushing and wracked with embarrassment as she told him about the email she'd received from Adam Latimer earlier that afternoon. 'Of course, you can imagine, when I saw his name I nearly had a cardiac arrest!' It had said, '*Well, well, well . . . little Hetty Strong! How's life? Would love to come to the bash. Call me. Adam xx*'. 'Two kisses, Matt. Two kisses!'

'Right.' Matt had wondered where this was leading.

'So then I thought, *OK Het, keep it casual. Keep it light . . .* and I wrote back, "*Wey hey!*" But that made me sound like . . .'

'A children's TV presenter?' Matt offered.

'Exactly.' Sometimes Matt and Hetty thought uncannily along the same lines, often finishing each other's sentences. 'I finally decided on *"Hey stranger. Glad you can make the reunion. Will call you tomorrow for poss catch-up?"'*

'So far, so good . . .' Matt always enjoyed Hetty's tales of social disaster.

'Then, of course, I was in a kerfuffle about the kiss. Should I put one or two or none? Because, to me, ONE kiss looks too intimate . . .'

'You overthink things, Het.'

'. . . but then, if I didn't put any, would that look too frosty?'

'So, in the end . . . ?'

'So, in the end, I thought, *Sod it, I'll put two, just like he did,* pressed send and shut down the computer before I had time to change my mind.'

'Great. Job done.'

'Oh my goodness! But then, Matty, I was just putting my cardigan back on when terror struck!'

Matt adored Hetty's natural bent towards melodrama and was already starting to chuckle.

'So I turned the computer back on and went into my sent box and there it was! Mortification clouding the blood in my veins like iodine in water.' Sometimes Hetty sounded quite Shakespearean.

'Why? What? Tell me!'

'Well, when I re-read my email, I realized instead of writing *Will call tomorrow for poss catch-up* I'd written *piss* instead of *poss*.'

Matt was in his element. 'Oh joy!'

'So now he'll think I'm some kind of wee-wee fetishist!'

Tears were seeping out of Matt's eyes. 'But why didn't you check?'

'Because I was too excited! It's been fourteen years, Matty, since I've had any contact whatsoever!'

Matt's laughter subsided when he thought about Adam and the effect he still had on his best friend, even after all this time.

'Oh mate, what is it about that guy? He treated you like a moron.'

Matt began slicing an apple and put the pieces on a little plate with some jumbo sultanas, shaping them into a smiling face. He handed it to Tallulah and kissed the top of her head.

'He wasn't *all* bad.' Hetty looked sad now and Matt, as ever, regretted criticizing the love of her life.

'Sorry. Listen, I'm just gonna jump in the shower. Lules, why don't you tell Hetty about the octopus song you had to sing in the concert today?'

Upstairs, Matt turned on the taps in their en-suite shower and undressed, waiting for the water to get warmer. He looked at himself in the mirrored wall – still tanned from their holiday in Morocco less than a month ago – and smiled.

That was a *good* holiday. Matt's mum Sylvia had come with them to help with Tallulah, which meant they had more time to themselves, which meant more time for sex. As he stepped under the power blast of hot water he indulged in a rock-hard horny image of himself and Kate in their hotel shower – a vast and expensively tiled wet-room with five different water jets and granite ridge shelving at just the right height – water pounding at them relentlessly from all directions as they fucked against the wall. It was fantastic, the power of the shower and the steam drowning out their unstoppable moans. What was it about sex in a hot climate, he thought? Warm-weather sex was always so much more of a turn-on. He was desperate now to see Kate. He looked down at his clean, wet body: yes, *every* part of him was desperate to see her.

He stepped out of the shower, grabbed a big fluffy towel and wrapped himself in it. Still dripping, he sat on the bed and called Kate's number. This time it rang. And rang. And *then* it went to voicemail. He lay back on the bed and waited for the familiar sound of her voice inviting him to *leave a message and I'll call you back.* After the beep he dived in: 'Where are you, Mrs Fenton, because I need to see you. I was just thinking about Morocco. God, it was good, wasn't it? Mmmm. I think you and I could do with a dirty weekend somewhere, what d'you reckon?'

He laughed at himself then and said, 'Right. I'm in danger of turning this into a sex-pest call, so ring me back. I'm presuming you must be on the train by now. Probably best if we meet at the restaurant? We can skip starters, go straight to main, then come back here and shag each other senseless. Call me.'

He pressed 'end call' and then went to the wardrobe to pick out a soft blue linen shirt which, he remembered, he'd worn a lot in Morocco, and which he also remembered Kate had really liked.

10

In the end he'd driven her to Edinburgh airport – or at least the car park of a Travelodge nearby, where she'd figured it would be more private. It was pointless going to the station – Kate knew she'd missed her train and at the back of her mind she thought she could maybe get a flight instead. But she wasn't thinking properly; all she really wanted to do was sit with Callum and look at him, talk to him – actually she didn't really know *what* she wanted. For a woman so outwardly in total control she'd become a sea of confusion, a weak and helpless mess.

They sat in the car park of the Travelodge, the rumble of jet engines coming in and out of the nearby airport ripping up the silence between them. They hadn't said much on the way there. Her phone had rung at one point – Matt. She'd let it ring.

'Aren't you gonna answer that?' Callum had asked.

'No.'

He stayed eyes fixed forward the whole time, watching the goings-on outside, people exiting and entering the hotel. He knew Kate was staring at him, but he daren't return the look. He didn't trust himself to.

What was he doing here? This was insane. What if someone saw them together?

Kate gazed at him. He must be fifty-six by now. She longed to reach out and touch the rough features of his coarsely attractive face. They were drawing her in again, still as engaging as they'd always been, even with seventeen years' worth of living added to the lines around his eyes and on his forehead, and the salt and peppering of his thick-as-ever hair. *Age has made him more beautiful*, she thought. His skin glowed with a familiar ruddiness, from time spent outdoors – holidays with *her*, of course, with Belinda, time spent gardening in *their* garden, hours standing on the sidelines watching *their* kids playing cricket and rugby and netball. And she felt dizzy with envy imagining his happily married life.

Callum unscrewed the cap on a bottle of water and took a huge glug before offering it to Kate, wiping his mouth with the back of his hand. She took it from him and drank, not because she was thirsty but because she wanted to put her lips where his had been.

'So how old are your kids now?' she asked, with fake lightheartedness. She could have been catching up with a distant cousin.

'Ailsa's sixteen, just started sixth form. Ben is twenty-one – on a gap year in Borneo.'

'Blimey!' This small talk was ludicrous, she thought.

'And Cory is nearly twenty. Second year at St Andrews.'

'What's he reading?' Not that she cared.

'History.' Not that he cared to tell her.

'Good choice.' What a pointless thing to say, she thought. And the silence that followed continued in its awkwardness.

A taxi pulled up outside the main doors of the hotel and two businessmen got out, both with overnight cases, one laughing at something the other had said, unaware of the weird and unlikely reunion that was taking place just metres away from them.

Kate was still thinking about Callum's kids.

'They were just babies . . .' she said.

'I know.'

And then they both started talking simultaneously, the sham of polite conversation no longer sustainable.

'I probably shouldn't have come in today,' he blurted.

'You must have *known* I was – Oh, sorry,' she backed down.

'No, go on.'

'Well, I saw a notice in the staffroom, saying I was visiting the school – so you must have *known* I was coming.'

'Of course I did! But what was I supposed to do? Tell the Head it wasn't a good idea because seventeen years ago I got you pregnant? Christ!'

There was something about the way he said it, his blatant acknowledgement of this primal connection that existed between them. And before she knew it she'd reached out and turned his face towards her, clumsily attempting to kiss him.

He pulled back, shocked. 'What the hell are you doing?!'

'Sorry, I don't know . . .'

He turned away from her, looking out of the window and focusing on a travel-weary businessman pulling an overnight bag from his travel-wearier car. Matt shut his eyes in the hope of calming down, but unable to avoid the anger surging up inside him as he remembered what she'd done. He couldn't look at her when he said it. 'You should have discussed it with me, Kate. Not just gone ahead and—'

'Oh, like you'd have stood by me, would you, Callum? I don't think so!' Kate was tearful now.

'I just . . .' He faltered, because he knew she was right. He *wouldn't* have been there for her but his resentment was still raw. 'I dunno . . . Phoning me like that. Announcing it like a done deal.'

'I need to explain something,' she sobbed. 'About what happened – it wasn't . . . straightforward . . .' But before she could finish, her mobile phone interrupted her train of thought, ringing obliviously in her bag. She didn't move.

'Well, answer it then.' He was on edge. But then felt guilty for snapping. 'It might be important.' Callum hadn't had a mobile himself that long; he still thought they were only really used for emergencies.

She did as she was told and he watched as she searched in her bag. When she eventually found the phone, he noticed that her hands were shaking. He felt a sudden pang of pity and found himself wanting to comfort her. As she talked she looked away, and this time he allowed himself to take in the sheer loveliness of her that, if

56

he was honest, he'd never forgotten. The inviting fullness of those gorgeous lips, the grey-green eyes that could knock you over with a single glance, and the creamy flawlessness of her complexion. When she'd been talking to the kids in the classroom earlier that day, he hadn't dared look at her, not properly. Because he knew how it would make him feel, and he was right. Oh fuck.

'Hi.' Her voice was emotionless and flat.

'Finally!' Matt on the other end was buoyant. 'Did you get my voicemails?'

'Um, no, not yet.'

'Well, I thought we should meet at Porto's – you won't have time to come home first. Whereabouts are you now? Peterborough?'

'Babe, I'm so sorry . . .'

Silence on the other end. Matt knew what was coming. He was well used to the tone that prefixed Kate's letting him down gently.

'I bumped into an old friend. We went for a drink.' She took a deep breath. 'So I missed the train.' She shut her eyes tight as she lied to him, forcing her voice to stay level and calm.

There was another pause as Matt took in what he was hearing. 'You're still in Edinburgh,' he sighed.

'Yeah, look, it was just . . . we haven't seen each other for so long! For . . . well, for years!'

'What friend?'

She hesitated. 'Sorry?'

Then she turned to look at Callum, realizing he'd been watching her the whole time, his expression different now, softer than it had been earlier, his defences down. She ventured to look him straight in the eye and this time he didn't look away.

'Paula. Paula McGee – you wouldn't know her.'

Then Callum, without dropping his gaze, slowly reached out and put his right hand under the hemline of her skirt, touching the soft bare flesh of her inner thigh and confidently parting her legs. She gasped, shut her eyes again and tried steadying her voice, but when she spoke her words came rushing out. 'Matt, this line's a bit crap. I'm gonna get a flight, OK? I'll ring you soon as I've got the details.'

Callum's hand went slowly higher. The anticipation alone of his fingers inside her was too much to bear . . .

'Dinner's off then, I take it?' The resignation in Matt's voice was palpable.

'Let's go tomorrow instead, yeah? I'll call you in a bit.'

She didn't wait to hear his response.

Within fifteen minutes of ending the call, Kate and Callum had shut the door to room 210 of the Travelodge and were making up for the seventeen years they'd spent apart. Half a mile away, the planes continued to land and take off.

11

Becky was trying her best to balance a plastic tray that held a fizzing Berocca, a full-to-the-brim cafetière and a polystyrene bowl of sliced melon covered in tin foil, all whilst battling the gusting October winds. Head down, her wet-weather gear impeding fast movements, she headed to the make-up truck. As she reached the steps, Benno, the assistant director, was already there.

'That lot for Kate?' he asked.

'Yeah. It's all she wanted.'

'OK, I'll deal with it.'

He took the tray in one hand and deftly nipped up the steps of the truck, opening the door with his elbow. It was six fifteen a.m. and still dark.

Inside the make-up truck, Radio 2 was playing quietly in the background, and a combination of warm air and hairspray danced up Benno's nostrils.

'One ridiculously low-calorie, highly caffeinated breakfast for Miss Kate Andrews!' he called out, all smiles.

Kate was sitting in the make-up chair down the far end of the truck, head back, an eye mask over her eyes. She didn't move and looked for all the world like she had died. Betsy the make-up artist raised an eyebrow at Benno as she carried on painting Kate's nails.

'Just stick it anywhere,' Kate mumbled.

'Don't tempt me.' The film-set double entendres were prone to strike at any moment of the day, no matter how unsociable the hour.

Benno put the tray down next to Betsy's make-up station. 'Give us a minute, would you, Bets?'

'Sure.' And she replaced the nail-varnish brush and screwed on the lid, pointlessly attempting to blow Kate's nails dry before she got up and left.

Benno grabbed a mug from above the sink and poured Kate's coffee. On the mug it said, *Yes, you do have to be mad to work here!*

'So . . . Doug tells me you called him last night and asked him to pick you up . . .'

'Dobber.' Kate could barely speak.

'. . . from Sheffield!'

Kate sighed and slowly removed her eye mask.

'You look like shit.' Being direct was often part of Benno's job.

'Cheers, Brad Pitt.' Kate reached out and grabbed her coffee, her hand shaking slightly. She downed a big mouthful and Benno took the foil off the melon slices.

'What's goin' on, Kate?'

'Late night, that's all. With an old school friend.'

'Yeah well great, you've got four major scenes today, including that pick-up from Wednesday, fourteen pages of dialogue, and you can barely keep your eyes open.' He forked a piece of melon and stuck it in front of her mouth, feeding her like a toddler.

'Few Red Bulls, I'll be right as rain. You know me, Benno, show must go on and all that!' She nibbled at the melon, then pushed it away, searching in her bag for some Panadol.

'Don't make me have to say it.'

She burst the pills out of their foil film and swallowed them with more coffee.

'It won't happen again.' She was barely audible, like a sulking teenager, the chalkiness of the painkillers bitter in her mouth.

'Good.' He headed towards the door. 'Oh and by the way,' he smiled, 'happy birthday, mate!'

*

When she and Callum had shut the door of the hotel room they didn't speak for an hour, barely looked at each other, in fact. It was almost as though the sex was a necessity, a formality to be gone through before their lives could carry on. It had all been surprisingly easy, no awkward moments, no shyness – everything as it used to be, as it always was. And of course unspeakably, intensely good.

Afterwards they lay there in the gloaming, the fading Scottish light dancing through the characterless and tiny hotel window. Her head on his chest, him looking up at the Artexed ceiling. He spoke first.

'So . . .' he whispered, smiling. 'You never *write*, you never *call* . . . !'

She laughed without looking up at him, just kept stroking his arm, the feel of his skin so surprisingly familiar, as if she'd touched it only yesterday, not seventeen years ago.

'What were you going to tell me? Earlier. In the car,' he asked.

'Nothing. It wasn't important.'

They'd stayed like that till eight o'clock, the by now black sky illuminated by unforgiving car-park lights, which cast an eerie orange glow over their bodies. Both their mobiles had rung several times and neither of them had answered. They knew that with each avoided call the demand for an explanation was building, and yet they couldn't bring themselves to move.

Eventually it was Kate who did. There were no words, nothing either of them could say to soften the inevitability of separation. So she just stood up, dressed in silence and left. He stared at the door for minutes after she'd gone, reading the fire-drill sign above the handle over and over again: *In case of fire* . . .

When she arrived at the airport, the information board showed there were no more flights to London that evening. Bollocks. But there *was* one to Birmingham, leaving in an hour. *Oh well, better than nothing*, she thought. She headed to the desk to buy a ticket. It would cost her a fortune, no doubt, but needs must.

'Sorry Madam, but the flight is completely full.'

Kate laughed. Was this a wind-up? 'Don't be ridiculous! Are you telling me you haven't got one single seat?'

'I'm afraid not. Due to the cancellation of the earlier Manchester flight.'

Kate put her head on the desk before her, the sound of metaphorical chickens coming home to roost, ringing in her ears. And people were staring at her. She forgot sometimes that her face was famous.

Panicking, she walked to the ATM a few yards away, taking out a stack of cash before heading over to the taxi rank. The driver's expression was a picture when she told him to head south and just keep driving. Then she took a deep breath, looked at her mobile and rang Doug. She was dreading the melodrama, the indebtedness she'd be made to feel for weeks to come, but she had no option. He answered the call. She tried to sound light and ditzy.

'Hey Doug, guess what silly mare has gone and missed her flight?'

A beat and then Doug launched automatically into crisis mode. 'Where are you, sweetheart?' His voice was low and gravelly; his London accent wouldn't be out of place in an episode of *EastEnders*.

'Oh Doug, you don't wanna know . . .' She was dreading telling him.

'If there's a road that leads there, I'm on it.'

She could almost hear the look he was giving his wife as she stared over the rim of her cocoa mug and Kate knew he was actually enjoying the heroism of all this. So, probably, was Mrs Doug. 'I'm in a cab, and I'm currently two miles south of Edinburgh airport.'

Doug gave a long whistle down the phone and Kate rolled her eyes. 'OK. No problem! Give me ten minutes to fix myself a flask and I'll be on that M1 before you know it. Tell the cabby to head for Sheffield.'

'Sheffield! Good Lord!' Mrs Doug in the background was probably now choking on her cocoa, Kate thought.

'Yeah, there's a service station just after Junction 30, I think it is. We time it right, you shouldn't have to wait too long. Hang tight, angel. Your Uncle Doug is on his way!'

'Thanks, Doug. Drive safe.' And she hung up.

'Y'know this is gonna cost ye hen, don' ye?' the taxi driver had said unhelpfully.

'Yeah, don't worry. I got the cash.'

'Could be two, three hundred quid!'

'Like I said, I've got the cash.' And his face lit up. 'Now if you don't mind, I'm gonna get some kip.' She shut her eyes and thought about her friend Lynette, a recovering alcoholic. Lynette had told her once about the first step of recovery – what was it? Something about being powerless over alcohol, and that 'our lives had become unmanageable'. There wasn't a glass of wine in sight, but Kate's life had never felt more unmanageable.

And yet. And yet . . . there was also this warmth, this smile that stretched from her head to her toes, her whole being bathed in bliss. She felt like she'd found the missing piece, the piece she'd always known but never dared admit was missing. Until today.

The taxi turned onto the A1 and headed for Sheffield as Kate dozed off in the back seat, smiling in her sleep.

She crept into bed at three a.m. Matt was out for the count, his back turned away from her. He hadn't been angry when she'd rung him about the flight, just resigned. And silent. She hated those silences. She knew them well. But she also knew she only hated them because they were justified. She was married to the kindest, sweetest, loveliest man on the planet, and yet she let him down again and again and again.

Surpassed yourself this time though! She'd curled up behind him, spooning him and inexplicably needing to feel the comfort of his body next to hers. As if she was telepathically willing him to forgive her for what she'd done. In his sleep, his hand reached up and held hers. *It's OK, baby, it's OK.*

Her eyes were closed for what seemed like only ten seconds before the timid alarm tone on her phone was urging her to wake up again. She'd had two and a half hours' sleep and now it was time for work. When she left the bedroom she looked back at Matt. He was still sleeping, on his side in the same position as when she'd come home.

12

'Take heed, Ailsa Cerys Louise! Before you stands the shadow of your father's former self, victim of a mid-week drinking sesh and a man steeped in shame!'

Fifty-four-year-old Belinda MacGregor was clearing the breakfast things when her dishevelled husband came in, doing up his tie.

'Aw Dad, you look minging!' Ailsa was munching on a bowl of Shreddies and reading *King Lear.*

'Yeah, alright.'

'You didn' even seem that pissed!'

'Oi, language, missy.' Belinda had always been strict about swearing. When it came to her kids, at least.

'Aye, well I can handle my drink, can't I? Because *I* am a grown-up, and *you* are still underage. Don't forget it.' Callum was glad of the subject change. It was a long, long time since he'd had to tell lies, and he was on very shaky ground now.

'Who was he again? This old mate?' Belinda pulled open the dishwasher door and started loading the plates.

Callum took a swig of tea, buying himself a nanosecond of thinking time. 'Paul McGee. I told you! Emigrated to Oz thirty-odd years ago, back visiting his mother.'

'I swear I'm losing my marbles. I can't for the life of me remember him!'

He kissed her forehead. 'Why should you remember every single person I was ever in college with?' He threw away the rest of his tea and stuck his mug in the rack. 'I'd give you a lift,' he said to Ailsa, 'but I've got to pick up the car from town.'

'Oh it's shamin'!' Belinda winked at him, her greying hair swept back into a tight pony, a stone heavier now than in her thirties, but her eyes still bright and her smile still sexy.

'Not going in till after break,' Ailsa said through her munching. 'Study period.'

'Which is meant for studying!'

'Er, what d'you think this is?' And she held up her *King Lear*.

Callum rolled his eyes and made for the door.

'See you tonight, you dirty stop-out!' Belinda watched him go, calling after him, 'And do your own tea, 'member. I've got Legs, Bums and Tums.' She smiled, waiting for him to shout back at her, as he did every Friday morning, *'And yours are the best in the world!'* But for some reason, today he didn't say it. She frowned for a second, and put it down to his hangover.

'*I'*ll take you, Ails. My shift's not till ten.' And she switched the dishwasher to rinse, extinguishing the flicker of doubt from her mind.

The night before, Callum had left the car outside a pub called the Griffin. It wasn't a regular haunt of his and he reckoned he could get away without seeing anyone he knew. Three hours earlier, he'd left the room that Kate had paid for and made his way to the hotel bar. The two businessmen he'd seen that afternoon were sharing a couple of beers, and a woman in a corner was staring despairingly at her laptop. Apart from them, the bar was deserted. He was about to order a drink when he was overcome by the urge to get away from there – not home, not yet. Just away from that place. Where it'd happened. As if putting distance between himself and the hotel would erase the memory. Erase the event. He needed booze. Something to help make it all OK. Something to help him come up with a story, to help him think.

The Griffin was busy, thank God. Plenty of Thursday-night

drinkers to hide amongst and keep him anonymous as he downed five pints and worked out a strategy. OK, so he'd met up with this old college friend, and one pint had led to another. *Who was he?* Oh, you wouldn't know him. *Do you want to invite him over? Will you be seeing him again?*

No. Definitely not. It was a one-off.

The pub was closed up now, save for the drayman unloading his early-morning barrels. Callum got into his car, parked a little way off, and sat staring ahead of him. It was eight thirty a.m. He should've been in school by this time. He felt numb, not even daring to think about the night before. Every time Kate came prowling into his mind, he banished her from it. Desperate for some kind of sanity, he turned on the radio, yearning for the normal and the humdrum to bring him back to his normal and humdrum but lovely, loved life. Liberty X were singing, '*Boy if you could read my mind, I'm sure that you could find, what you've been searching for.*'

But he couldn't stop Kate from prowling. And he couldn't stop remembering: those lips, her legs wrapped tightly around him and how it felt to be inside her again.

He turned the dial quickly to a local station, where the presenter was discussing yesterday's visit to North Park Primary by the famous actress Kate Andrews. 'By all accounts, she was lovely!'

Callum turned the dial again and finally found solace in Radio 4. He took a deep breath and headed towards school.

13

'It's magnificent, don't you think?' Peter at the gallery was holding up a large canvas, received that morning and still half-wrapped in brown paper. Called 'Sunrise at Coggleshell', it had captured all the potency and optimism of a new day with confident sweeping colours that dared the observer to question them, and, despite his grey mood, Matt couldn't help but be transported by it. The artist, Mark Lavender, had a quirk of style that neither Matt nor Peter could articulate. But his work always made them smile. They'd sold three of his paintings in the past, all for a good price.

'He's looking for two grand,' Peter said.

'Then put it on for three.'

'Are you sure?'

'Not really. But then I'm not very sure of *anything* today.'

Peter frowned and was about to ask more, but Matt got in first, 'Oh, just ignore me. I've got to go anyway. Picking Tallulah up so we can deliver Kate's birthday cake.'

'Send her my regards.'

It was the best Peter could manage. He always tried to hide his real feelings about Kate, but never managed to succeed, because he'd simply never been very keen on her. He always felt she gave Matthew the runaround. And he wasn't just intimidated by her because she was a flighty actress – no, the TV world didn't impress or faze Peter, having himself been in a relationship with a reasonably successful actor – Julius – for over ten years. There was just something untrustworthy about her.

In fact, Julius had worked with Kate a number of years ago on an episode of *Midsomer Murders*. She'd been playing the red herring, the young wife of a local dignitary who everyone suspected had a motive for killing her husband. Turned out it wasn't her whodunnit but the lollipop lady. Julius had played the murdered dignitary, and so he and Kate had shared a few scenes. He said she was charming and witty and highly professional, but there was something not quite hinged about her. 'Her cannon is most definitely loose!' he'd confided in Peter one evening after filming. 'A bit too fond of her friend Charlie.' He tapped his nose conspiratorially. Peter had never tried cocaine, unlike Julius. 'And there's something else. Can't quite put my finger on it, but believe you me, she'll come to no good.'

So when Sylvia – Matt's mother and Peter's lifelong friend – had told him that her 'darling Matthew' was going out with a famous actress – 'y'know, the one who was in the Scottish thing about the thing. On a Sunday night!' – Peter's alarm bells gave a faint tinkle. When Sylvia said they were getting *married*, the bells rang loud and long. But what could he say?

'She's ever so beautiful, Pete!' Sylvia had said to him, all excited, as if stunning beauty would make up for any shortcomings.

And then when baby Tallulah arrived, Sylvia had been beside herself with joy. For a while, daughter-in-law Saint Kate could do no wrong. She'd given Sylvia a granddaughter, after all!

But in the past two years, Sylvia had started confiding in Peter that she didn't think all was well with her son's marriage.

'I know Kate's under an enormous amount of pressure,' she said to justify it. 'But she gets these . . . *episodes* . . . where there's no stopping her. She goes on a self-destruct mission. Gets drunk, then goes crazy with exercise for days. Or worse, Matt says, she'll buy a stack of food – sausages and cheesecake and the like – and eat it secretly in the middle of the night. One time he came downstairs and found her almost head first in a bowl of trifle.'

Peter never forgave himself for his involuntary guffaw when

Sylvia told him this. But as he repeatedly said to her afterwards, 'It was just the way you said it, dear. Of course it's disturbing. It's just Kate doesn't strike me as someone who'd even be in the same *room* as a trifle, let alone *gorge* on one.'

'She . . . y'know, makes herself *sick* afterwards, Matthew says. It's really upsetting.'

Peter did feel sorry for her when he heard this. Kate Andrews was the last person on earth he'd have down as someone with an eating disorder. Somehow booze and drugs, even gambling, there was something 'cool' about being addicted to those, something worthy of a trip to the Priory, he thought, but *food*! How embarrassing. How humiliating for her.

He watched Matt, preoccupied now, pick up his keys and his phone and make for the gallery door, turning before he left. 'Hey Pete, well done again with the Lavender painting.' And he was gone.

Troubled soul, thought Peter, and the old-fashioned bell above the door pinged obliviously as the door shut behind him.

14

At *Vegetarian Living*, Ivor from Accounts was hovering by Hetty's desk. He was holding half a dozen eggs. Hetty was ignoring him, engrossed in her computer, trying to work out if Adam was flirting with her or laughing at her in his most recent email when he'd said, 'Piss catch-up? Didn't realize you were into "water sports", Betty Strong?'

She clicked on reply but couldn't concentrate, too aware now of Ivor's presence.

'They're totally free-range,' he was saying, 'and organic. Happy hens, y'see. My cousin's. He's got four.'

He put the eggs down on her desk and she suddenly felt awful for ignoring him, especially in the light of Adam's crude email. 'Oh Ivor, that's so kind of you. I'll have one for my breakfast.' She looked at him, smiling, silently communicating that this was the end of the conversation.

But he just stood there and smiled back, noticing Hetty's left eyebrow was bushier than her right, but loving her even more for it. He found the courage and said, 'How was babysitting?'

'Didn't do it in the end.' And still they stared. Hetty's computer pinged; she glanced sideways at it: Adam! She inwardly gasped when she saw his name.

'Who's that, your boyfriend?' Ivor asked jokingly.

But Hetty was distracted by the email and unthinkingly said, 'Er . . . yes . . .'

And just like that, Ivor's fears that Hetty might be seeing someone were callously confirmed. He scuttled off like a scolded puppy, mumbling, 'Oh, OK,' and leaving his eggs behind him.

Hetty opened the email: 'Sorry, am worried I might have offended you. Let me take you out for lunch to make up for it. How about Sunday?' For a moment, she wondered if this was the same person as the Adam she knew. He sounded so earnest, so kind . . . and then it hit her. He was actually asking her out! She was going on a date! With Adam Latimer!! She must get her eyebrows waxed, she thought.

At lunchtime, she headed out alone. Usually Ivor tagged along but this time she managed to dodge him, leaving the office without his noticing. She just needed space to think.

She made for the small park area a stone's throw from the magazine building. It was usually packed at lunchtime with desk-bound workers desperate for a bit of greenery and slightly fresher air than the conditioned stuff that was pumped through their offices. But today the weather had turned, and most workers had opted to eat indoors.

Hetty took out her little sandwich box, filled with a wholesome salad of brown rice, pumpkin seeds, avocado, tomato and spring onion. She started munching, then thought better of the spring onions, fishing them out and throwing them to the birds. She ought to be careful what she ate between now and the Big Day. She didn't want to put Adam off with overpowering breath – God forbid! A pigeon pecked at the discarded spring onion but wasn't impressed and moved on to an unwanted burger bap on top of a bin.

Lunch! Adam Latimer was taking her out to lunch!

She had to stay calm. She mustn't read anything into it. He was just being friendly, that was all, catching up with an old friend.

Yes, but what if . . . what if it was *more* than that? Time does funny things to people. He may have been a bit immature back then, a bit thoughtless maybe. But now they weren't far off forty. Maybe he'd been in an unhappy relationship? Maybe he was reassessing his life? Maybe she, Hetty, was just what he was looking for now. Maybe . . .

She took out her notebook and pen and started amending her never-ending list. She'd booked a venue for the reunion – the Marmant Hotel in Holborn on December 20th. She'd had to pay a huge deposit but it was worth it. It was classy and bijou, could cater for a hundred people, and the price per head was reasonable. Especially by London standards. She knew she was taking on a lot organizing this on her own, but she was actually really enjoying it. So far she'd had sixty-seven replies.

Ooh, disco! They needed a DJ to play some of the old eighties hits. And name badges – otherwise how would anyone recognize anyone else? Some people would look exactly the same, of course. She wondered how Adam looked now and her stomach flipped in anticipation of seeing him again.

When she got back to the office, she would send her reply. Keep it brief and to the point. She'd already more or less planned the wording: *Lunch on Sunday would be wonderful. How about Le Corale on Marylebone High St, 1 o'clock?* That's all she was going to say. Firm. Confident. No kisses. And no reference to the 'piss catch-up' disaster. That was best forgotten.

She finished the remnants of her salad and realized she still felt hungry. But she wouldn't eat anything else. Even if Ivor offered her some of that delicious organic chocolate, she'd say no. She had to look her best for Adam.

Ooh – eyebrows. She put it on the list. She'd wait till the day before to get those done because they were like bindweed, her brows: the minute she waxed them, the minute they'd start sprouting again.

She put the lid back on her sandwich box and was about to set off for the office when a voice came from behind her, 'Buy some flowers for some luck, luvvy! Buy some flowers for some luck!' A Romany woman with two front teeth missing and clutching a few pieces of heather wrapped badly in silver foil was standing far too close, invading Hetty's personal space.

'Oh! Right! Erm . . .'

'Don't turn me away, luvvy, don't turn your luck away!'

'No, of course, it's just . . .'

Hetty reached into her pocket and pulled out a ten-pound note. She couldn't possibly give her that. 'Hang on . . .' She tried the other pocket. Twenty pence. 'I don't suppose you've got any change, have you?'

Unimpressed, the Romany woman ignored her and carried on, 'There's an old flame been burning a long time. A man. He'll bring you love, luvvy.'

Hetty looked at the tenner and thought, *Sod it*. The woman had her hooked. She pressed the note into the Romany's hand.

'Time to bring him out now, luvvy. He's been at the back of your mind a long time – time to bring him out.'

Hetty was transfixed. 'Is his name Adam?' she whispered, like a child who thought she'd seen Santa Claus.

The woman looked slightly annoyed by the question and ignored it, finishing with a flourish, 'And there'll be a child – just the one. And not straight away.'

'Oh my goodness!' There was so much more that Hetty wanted to ask, but the woman was backing off now, her easily earned tenner clasped tight in her hand, and she was gone.

Hetty beamed. Today was a *good day*!

15

The only thing Kate needed at lunchtime was sleep. She wanted to not eat but Benno wouldn't hear of it and told her he wasn't leaving the trailer till she'd had some mashed potato and a bit of cauliflower cheese.

She did as she was told. She couldn't be bothered to argue, and could probably afford a few calories – being so tired had depleted her energy. She'd do whatever it took to get her to the end of the day. She momentarily thought about taking a line. She was sure the actor playing Ramesh had a stash. But she hadn't touched the stuff since she'd got pregnant with Tallulah. And let's face it, her life was enough of a mess without adding to her problems.

Once Benno was satisfied she'd eaten 'at least enough to keep a mouse going for the day', he promised she'd be left in peace. She climbed onto her bed in the tiny little trailer bedroom, crept under the covers and closed her eyes.

In the distance she could hear Benno barking instructions at his team: 'Do not let ANYONE near Kate's trailer without my say-so. She's getting some shut-eye.' He ran a tight ship, did Benno – she'd give him that.

Her eyelids felt gritty and sore. She felt too tired to sleep and there was a very loud hissing in her ears. If she could just have twenty minutes, that would be *something* . . .

She dozed off straight away. A deep, healthy sleep engulfed

her, and she dreamt, of course, about Callum. Nothing she could remember later, no tangible narrative, just the sensation of having been with him, of knowing he'd been there inside her head. And it felt so good. When she woke up she found her right hand hot between her legs and she knew she'd made herself come in her sleep, just as he'd made her come the night before. Christ, it wasn't even twenty-four hours yet.

She stretched her arms above her head and yawned for Britain. Then she climbed out of bed and pulled herself into the tiny shower in the trailer bathroom. The water was slow, but at least it was warm. She longed to put her face underneath its refreshing flow – anything to help wake up again – but she knew Betsy would kill her if she messed up her make-up any more than she already had. The shower did the best it could and she stepped out onto the mat, drying herself with the big purple towel from the rack. She felt marginally better. Wrapping the towel around her, she headed into the living area, grabbed a cigarette and lit up before pulling out another Red Bull from the fridge. She sat down and picked up her mobile.

'Directory Enquiries. How may I help?'

'Yes, it's an Edinburgh number. A school on the Queensferry Road – North Park Primary.'

'Would you like us to text you the number?'

'Yes please.'

She hung up and waited for the text to come through. Her heart was racing as she keyed in the number and pressed call.

In the staffroom at North Park Primary, the Headmaster was making himself a coffee. They'd all been discussing the article in the *Edinburgh Gazette*. Brian Boyd was particularly proud of himself – they'd quoted him virtually word for word, in all fairness. And the photograph of him with Kate Andrews was a cracker. He'd already asked Mrs Crocombe to contact the *Gazette* and ask for a copy. He'd have it framed and put up above his desk. Alongside the one of him with Sean Connery. 'I thought she was a wee bit batty, if I'm honest,' he announced. 'Probably a cocaine freak. I mean they all are these days, aren't they, these actresses?'

Callum didn't look up from his marking. The Head could be such a prat sometimes, he'd rather not get involved.

'I take it you didn't warm to her then, Bri?' asked Cathy McBride from Year Four, who had a bit of a crush on the Headmaster.

'Ach, not really, no. Just can't be doin' with ditzy airheads, that's all.'

Mrs Crocombe came bustling in. 'There's a call for you, Callum.'

He looked up from his marking, red pen in hand, and Mrs Crocombe looked quickly around the room, checking her audience before she announced, 'It's Kate Andrews!'

Brian Boyd glanced sideways at Cathy McBride, who raised her eyebrows.

Cool as a can of chilled cola, Callum barely blinked and said, 'Yeah. She said she was going to organize a trip for the kids to her film set – let them go behind the scenes an' all that.'

He got up from his chair and made for the office, leaning in to the Headmaster en route. 'So she can't be all bad, can she, Brian?'

In the school office, Mrs Crocombe was holding the receiver. She put on her best telephone voice, a touch of Morningside creeping in. 'I'll pass you onto Mr MacGregor just now.' And she held the phone out to him.

He took it and stared at Mrs Crocombe, unnerving her enough to finally leave the room as he said, 'Kate! Thanks for coming back to me so quickly!' In her trailer four hundred miles away, Kate inhaled so rapidly on her Marlboro Light it made her a little light-headed. Or was that just because she was hearing his voice again?

Safe in the knowledge that the door was now tightly shut, Callum carried on, not waiting for an answer, 'What the fuck are you doing, calling me here?'

'I've got to see you.'

'You're insane!'

'I've got to see you, Callum. I'm coming up tomorrow night.'

'No.'

'There's a hotel in Leith – the Barrington. I'll be there, in the Lomond Suite. From seven o'clock.'

Callum couldn't believe what he was hearing. He took a deep breath – OK, time to calm things down. 'Listen,' he said gently. 'Last night was incredible, but it was a mistake. I'm married, for God's sake.'

'So am I.'

'And I'm not unhappy!'

'Nor am I.'

There was a knock on Kate's door and Becky shouted from outside, 'Kate?'

'Yeah, give me a minute, Becky.'

Callum had had enough. 'I've got to go. Don't call me here again, OK?'

Kate shut her eyes, her voice level and calm. 'Callum, I'm coming up tomorrow night. I have to see you. If you don't come to the hotel I will come to your house. I mean it.'

'Jesus, you're nuts.'

'I'm not.' Her voice cracked a little. 'I know you want to see me too.'

The awful truth was that he did.

Mrs Crocombe came back in at that moment, mouthing her apologies and looking for a file with her 'don't-mind-me' demeanour.

Callum's voice changed immediately. 'Right, great! Well, thanks for that. The kids'll be really excited.' He was about to hang up when he heard Kate add, 'The Barrington Hotel in Leith. I'll see you there.' But all Callum could manage in return was, 'Bye now! Thanks for calling.'

He hung up and Mrs Crocombe turned to him, all smiles. 'Oh she's a wee sweetheart, isn't she? I've always said that about her. A genuine, warm lassie.'

Callum tried to hide the fact he was shaking as he headed back to the staffroom.

16

'That's it, sweetheart, make sure it clicks in properly!' Matt was helping Tallulah secure the large Tupperware box containing Kate's birthday cake. They'd placed it carefully on the back seat of his car and were fastening the seatbelt around it.

'OK, now let's put you in next to it, shall we?'

'Mummy's going to have a SURPRISE!'

'She certainly is, my darling!'

Tallulah was so excited. She loved birthdays, she loved birthday cakes, and she loved going to visit Mummy at work. She held Panda tightly on her lap as Matt fastened her in, towering over the Tupperware box on her My Little Pony booster seat. Matt kissed the top of her head and shut the car door.

They'd finished making the cake that morning before school. It was huge. Three tiers of sponge sandwiched with two different flavours of jam, apricot and raspberry, and layers of whipped cream. Next, they'd covered it in ready-made icing, which they'd rolled out together – shocking pink, just as Tallulah had directed. The lettering was to be in lime green.

Matt had carefully squeezed the icing bag and piped the words 'Happy Birthday', before letting Tallulah loose on 'Mummy' below. It had taken her ages, her little tongue sticking out the side of her mouth as she put all her efforts into getting it right. He watched as she struggled with the second 'm', concentrating as if her life depended on it.

He had wanted to cry. Not just because Tallulah looked so earnest and sweet. But because he knew Kate wouldn't touch a single piece of that cake.

When she had finished, Tallulah turned to Matt, beaming. 'I've done it, Daddy!'

'Yes, you have! Well done, Lules.'

'This is the best cake Mummy's ever had.'

He had smiled at her and ruffled her hair. 'Come on, let's get it in the box.'

And now they were taking it to the film set. Matt had rung Becky the runner to warn her they were coming but to keep it a surprise. The idea was that they would get there in time for the afternoon tea break at four, sing 'Happy Birthday' and share the cake with the cast and crew.

'Did you bring the candles, Daddy?'

'Yes I did, don't worry.'

It was easy for him to say 'don't worry' – not so easy for him to follow his own advice.

Kate hadn't been right for some time now. Very slowly she'd started to withdraw, shutting him out of what she was thinking, shutting him down with a look or a snapped response. She'd been getting really weird about food again – he knew she wasn't eating. She tried to hide it, thinking he wouldn't notice, but he knew all her tricks and techniques: telling him in detail what she'd had to eat for lunch that day – as if by telling him it would make it true. Or making out she'd seen some amazing dessert on a menu or in a bakery and 'just couldn't resist it'.

But he knew even if she *had* bought the dessert, and even if she *had* eaten it, it wouldn't have been long before she was sticking her fingers down her throat in a private bathroom purge, ridding herself of the evil calories she'd been 'weak' enough to consume.

He'd once gone on the computer after she'd been using it. She'd accidentally left the page open – a horrific website featuring scores of anorexic women, celebrating their obscenely skeletal and flesh-deficient bodies. He'd panicked then and confronted her about it. Big mistake. She didn't get angry, just told him calmly it was research for a script she'd been sent. To play the part of a thera-pist who worked with self-harmers. She managed to make Matt feel stupid for even asking. 'You don't think *I'm* anorexic, do you, Matt?'

'What? No, it's not that. I just . . . well, I don't know what to think. Sometimes I don't think you look after yourself properly, that's all. I worry about you.'

'I'm perfectly fine.' She'd smiled. 'Please don't spy on me.' Her tone had turned cold, unfamiliar, estranged, and it alarmed him. He knew never to mention her eating habits again.

She must've always had this side to her, he thought now as he slowed down for a red light. It had just taken a while for him to discover it. After all, Kate was an incredibly talented actress and knew how to hide her feelings well.

In the back, Tallulah was singing – 'Happy Birthday, de-ar Mumm-ee, happy birthday to you!' He looked at her in the rear-view mirror and sighed.

They'd first met at the gallery, he and Kate. Almost seven years ago.

It was pouring with rain outside, torrential, healthy, chunky rain that saturated clothes in seconds and made its victims laugh with disbelief. Matt was working on his own that day, Peter was away in France on a wine tour with Julius. It was a Wednesday morning and the downpour was out of the blue, considering the gorgeous Indian summer they'd been experiencing for ten days.

Matt stood looking out of the gallery window, coffee mug in hand, feeling safe and warm and dry. The perfect people-watching post. Outside, intrepid pedestrians either huddled in doorways or dashed from pillar to post, feebly shielding themselves with news-papers and carrier bags, very few holding umbrellas, very few having been prepared for rain.

Further down the road, three big vehicles were parked outside one of the houses: a camera van, a lighting truck and a minibus. They were part of the film crew that had been filming at Number 23, the front windows of the house covered with big swathes of blackout drapes. Passers-by had stopped to look, often standing there for an hour at a time. But there really wasn't anything to see. An occasional electrician would wander out to the truck to fetch a lamp and have a sneaky fag while they were at it. Or a runner would come to the makeshift tea table to make a cuppa for one of the cast.

Three of the crew were erecting an emergency canopy over the table to protect the plastic cups and sachets of sugar from getting wet through. Matt watched them trying their best, failing, laughing – the rain was ridiculously heavy and had defeated them all.

He didn't see her approach. Must've been looking the other way. He heard the confident ping of the door and in she flew, laughing, breathless, soaked to the skin and shockingly gorgeous.

'Oh my God!' She was bordering hysterical. 'My make-up artist is gonna kill me!' She stood there, thirty-two years old, hair dripping, face drenched, a puddle forming around her feet. Matt recognized her straight away but was oddly unintimidated by her fame.

'D'you want a coffee?'

'Of course I do.' It turned out she'd been told she wasn't needed for an hour but not to wander too far.

'I've got a towel somewhere, hang on.'

Everything between them felt unexpectedly comfortable – as if he'd met her before. He couldn't have, of course. It was just the peculiar familiarity that comes with seeing a famous face – a highly recognizable stranger. At least, he presumed that's what it was.

Five minutes later, the rain had eased off and Kate was looking at the vast canvas on the back wall of the gallery, the towel round her shoulders, occasionally rubbing her hair with it. Matt handed her the coffee. She took it without looking at him, mesmerized by the artwork before her. A woman's face filled the frame, eyes closed and head tossed back. She was laughing, joy unrestrained.

'I wish I could paint,' she said.

'Me too.'

She turned to him, surprised. 'I thought that was a prerequisite for the job. Didn't your boss insist?'

'Er, no, well because . . . well, I *am* the boss. It's my gallery.' He felt himself uncharacteristically blush. As if he was showing off.

'Good for you!' She turned back to the canvas. 'How much for this? It's spectacular.'

'Yes, it is. But it's already been sold. Four grand.'

'Ah, shame. I'd have given you five.' She winked at him then, and when she did, something unexpected stirred inside him. Just momentarily. She looked at her watch. 'Oh bollocks, I better get going. Thanks for the coffee.' She drained the mug and handed it back to him. 'You've got a lovely place here. Little oasis.'

'Yeah, I suppose it is.'

She was gone as suddenly as she'd arrived. Matt stood there lemon-like, holding two mugs, a damp towel over his arm and a feeling inside that he'd just been taken captive by some inexplicable and deeply pleasant force.

He spent the next two days surreptitiously glancing out of the window towards the film-set house, hoping he might catch a glimpse of Kate. He went online and googled her – he was amazed at how many TV dramas she'd been in. He'd seen a few of them, of course, but it looked like she'd been acting pretty much continuously from day one of her career. He clicked on 'images'. A variety of photos came up, some of them of Kate in character, others taken at red-carpet events, awards ceremonies and the like. He noticed she was with a different guy in practically every shot and when he looked up her relationship status it starkly shouted out at him 'single!' He slammed his laptop shut. Oh God, what was he becoming? Was he *stalking* her?

When he told Hetty, she calmed him down. 'Of course you're not a stalker, you silly sausage. You're just a bit fascinated by fame – we all are. And you had a famous person in your shop and she's pretty and you fancied her . . .'

'Hey come on, I wouldn't say I *fancied* her.'

'Of course you did, Matt! Half the population does. She's stunning! And *because* she's famous you can look her up on the internet. Unlike ordinary stunning women like me! Who remain sadly undiscovered.' And she laughed and threw a ball of wool at him – Hetty was knitting a scarf. She'd been at it for eighteen months and it was only thirty centimetres long.

'She's older than me, y'know. By three years,' Matt said.

'Well then, you don't wanna be getting involved with an older woman, now do you?'

Matt had laughed. He was glad he'd told Hetty – it somehow dispelled the myth and stopped him obsessing about Kate Andrews.

He ought to go out more. Literally. He'd been seeing a girl called Gillian up until a couple of months ago. She was nice enough, and the sex was rather good. But they'd both agreed it wasn't going anywhere fast.

'The trouble with you, Matthew,' his mother had said to him once, 'is you like your own company more than other people's.' This wasn't strictly true. He just couldn't be bothered to spend time with people who didn't interest him. And for a few flashing moments when Kate had come into the gallery, he thought he'd found someone he *did* want to spend time with. Still, it wasn't to be. *Pull yourself together, lad, and find yourself a new girlfriend.*

The next day he took a phone call from Fiona Barker, the buyer of the *Laughing Woman* canvas. She was ringing to say she'd changed her mind and was terribly sorry but she hoped he'd understand. Under normal circumstances Matt would've been cross, a deal's a deal and all that.

But the moment she told him, he found himself saying, 'No problem at all, Mrs Barker. These things happen.'

As soon as he put down the phone, he scribbled a note on a piece of gallery paper – *'Laughing Woman' back on sale if you're interested, Matt* – shoved it in an envelope with his business card and headed outside, locking the shop door and leaving a *Back in five minutes* sign stuck to the glass.

Outside the film-set house, people were milling back and forth. A couple of the cast were by the tea table smoking and laughing, and a costume assistant was giving one of the props guys a shoulder massage in a camping chair. Electricians and camera crew were going back and forth from the house carrying big bulky equipment, and someone who looked like he might be the producer was talking animatedly on his mobile. 'Get it here as SOON as you can, Barry. This isn't on, mate, it just isn't on.'

Matt waited for a while, conscious that he looked like all the other rubber-neckers having a nosy. There was no sign of Kate. He thought about giving the envelope to one of the runners – but wouldn't they just think he was some weirdo groupie, a deranged fan seeking Kate's attention just like a million others? And then he saw a familiar face – Les the Sound guy. Les had come into the gallery the day before – a dour and unsmiling chap in a baseball cap and wet-weather gear. He'd talked for half an hour about why he adored Gauguin so much, before going on to spend ninety quid on a print for his wife. 'Wedding anniversary,' he'd muttered, still unsmiling. 'Twenty-seven years and I still love the very bones of that woman.' Matt had taken a shine to Les, but it might have been because he recognized his native South Yorkshire brogue. Yorkshiremen could do no wrong in Matt's book.

'Les!' he called out, a little desperately. At first, Les looked daggers, annoyed that someone should intrude upon him like that.

But then he recognized Matt and a sea of warmth swept over his face. He almost smiled. 'Ey up, Matt lad!'

'Do me a favour, mate, give this to Kate Andrews. She was in the shop the other day – it's about a painting she were after.' Matt was conscious he'd launched into a broad Yorkshire accent in his bid to win Les over.

'Aye, no worries. She's not in today.' Momentarily Matt's heart sank. 'But I'll see she gets it next week.'

The following Friday evening, Matt found himself helping two removal men unload the giant canvas, now wrapped in protective fabric, from the back of their large van. He oversaw them carry it into Kate's three-bed Pimlico apartment and affix it to the wall of her spacious living area. It looked spectacular. She knew what she was doing when she chose it. Matt refused to accept the five grand she'd originally offered, taking only a cheque for four. She told him he must be a very honest person but was probably a rubbish businessman.

He laughed and their eyes locked. That stirring again. When the removal men had finished, they all stood back and admired their handiwork. Matt paid the men and they left. As soon as they were alone, Matt turned to Kate and, pointing at her new acquisition, said, 'I hope you'll both be very happy together.'

That was his cue to go, but he stood still; that was her cue to say goodbye, but she remained silent. After a few seconds, she simply held out her hand and he took it. He didn't leave the flat again until five o'clock the following afternoon.

'Are we nearly there yet?' asked Tallulah – the prerequisite question for any car journey.

The guy behind him was banging on his horn. The lights had been green so long they were about to turn amber again. Matt snapped out of his sad reverie, held up his hand in a pointless apology and moved off. 'Not far now, petal.'

17

That afternoon, Kate could barely concentrate, her head in turmoil after hearing Callum's voice. She didn't really know her lines and, unluckily for her, the scene was an intense two-hander demanding total commitment and her wits about her. She had no idea where her wits had gone and she longed for the day to end.

It didn't help that the other actor in the scene, Ellis Marks, was one of those annoying worthy types who was word perfect and clearly judged her for not being as up to speed as he was.

Ellis had this annoying habit of interrupting the take if Kate got a phrase wrong or missed out a line, looking at Benno with a supercilious, pained expression and whining, 'I'm *so* sorry to stop, it's just Kate should have said *I won't be going there any more* rather than *I doubt I'll go there again.*'

Benno was good at hiding his frustration. It wasn't Ellis's place to point out anyone else's mistakes. Benno had worked with plenty of actors like him: those who rarely did TV work and, when they did, insisted on showing the world they knew all about the mechanics of filming.

The third time Ellis stopped, Kate just sighed a 'Fuck this!', got up and left the set, mumbling 'I need five minutes' as she went.

Benno, conscious that they were all walking an emotional tightrope today given Kate's fragile physical state, was only too keen to go along with her.

'No worries, babe. You want a coffee? Jase! Get Kate a coffee, will you?' he shouted, before Kate had even answered him.

The on-set crew, aware of an atmosphere brewing, busied themselves with jobs that didn't need doing, staying well out of the firing line. Ellis looked round for an ally, caught the eye of the young camera assistant and whispered with camp innocence, 'Was it something I said?' The camera assistant just blushed, not daring to conspire. He'd had it drilled into him by the director of photography never to engage with cast members on set unless it was life or death.

Outside, the October sun was still shining. Just. Kate sank down into the discomfort of a camping chair and shut her eyes, drinking in the afternoon's lukewarm rays. Tears threatened to sneak down her cheeks but she forced them away. She was just tired, she convinced herself. She wanted to blame it on Ellis Marks, but in all fairness to him, he had a point. She didn't know her lines, didn't even care about work today, and that was irresponsible of her.

She'd always managed in the past to put her work first. No matter what else was going on in her life, she never let it affect her work. But now everything was unravelling. She thought how much simpler things would have been if she'd never made that trip to the school. How much easier it would have been to carry on with life, using her well-worn coping techniques, her mechanisms for expelling the demons. But the truth was, seeing Callum again had shown her how dead she'd been. All these years. Christ only knew how this was going to play out. The only thing she could focus on was seeing him one more time. It was a need, not a desire.

Jason the runner came striding up, breathless, holding a cup of black coffee. Kate smiled at him. Jason, like Becky, lived in fear of Kate and she knew it.

'Thanks darling, you're a saint,' she said, momentarily fazing him. And she took a big gulp of the warm, tasteless liquid.

'Benno said you're to take your time, but when you come back there's a little surprise for you.'

Kate knew straight away what this meant. Nobody ever escaped having a birthday without some kind of fuss being made. Almost on a daily basis, greetings cards were passed around set and signatures surreptitiously collected. Everyone knew it was her birthday today. They'd make no exception.

'How intriguing!' Kate managed to look excited and handed Jason the half-finished drink before making her way back on set. She was prepared for a cake, she was prepared to see the entire crew gathered smiling and singing the inevitable 'Happy Birthday'.

What she *wasn't* prepared for was seeing Matt and Tallulah stood there with them – Tallulah proudly standing behind the cake she'd so lovingly helped to make.

'Oh my goodness! What are *you* doing here?' Kate knew what was expected of her and Tallulah wasn't disappointed by her mother's 'surprised' reaction, giggling delightedly.

'Mummy, look what me and Daddy made you!'

There were lots of oohs and aahs and *Doesn't she look like Kate?* from the costume and make-up girls.

'Wow! That is spectacular!' And she gave Tallulah a huge, slightly-too-hard hug.

Matt leant over and touched her arm, kissing her cheek politely. 'Sorry, she insisted on coming to see you.'

Before Kate had a chance to convey some kind of apology for the way she'd behaved, Tallulah was shouting, 'Blow out the candles quick and make a wish!'

Matt pulled back, letting Tallulah have her moment as Kate dutifully did what she was told.

Everyone watched and smiled. Kate couldn't be more in the spotlight if she tried. She looked at Matt, and the look he returned spoke volumes, silently willing her to keep up the front for Tallulah's sake, to play the game. This was the first time they'd spoken that day, so they'd had no chance to discuss what had happened to her last night and why she'd so monumentally let him down. Matt's look caught her off guard and she felt her throat tighten. Jesus, she was going to cry.

No. Stop it. Keep. It. Together. She blew out the candles and everyone clapped. She wanted to speak, to say, 'OK, can we all get back to work now, because I know where I am if I'm working,' but she knew the instant her voice came out it would crack with sorrow. So she kept smiling. The rictus grin of a woman battling her tears.

'Make a wish, Mummy. You haven't made a wish!'

Kate shut her eyes and made a wish. Thank God she'd never have to tell anyone what it was.

'Speech! Speech!' shouted Benno, keen to get back to filming but careful not to offend his leading lady. And once again all eyes were on Kate.

'Oh God, no!' She tried really hard to look faux annoyed and everyone laughed. Finding her voice from somewhere, she started to say a few words and it seemed for all the world that she'd got away with it. 'Well, thank you everyone for that *incredible* singing. Especially you, Rocky,' she looked directly at the boom operator, 'those dulcet tones were a bit of a shocker!'

And dutifully everyone laughed again. 'Um . . . it's great working with you guys, you make coming to work every day such a joy.' Kate was so good at lying. She caught Benno's eye and he winked at her. He knew she was talking bullshit.

'So thank you for that. But thank you most of all for my wonderful cake made by my . . .'

And that's when it went wrong.

'Made by my . . .' She tried to say 'my fantastic husband and my beautiful little girl', but the words just wouldn't come out. They got jammed in her throat like paper in an unruly photocopier, and a dry, incoherent rasping emerged from her mouth instead.

No one was embarrassed at first – aw, it was *sweet*! But then Kate's exhaustion finally got the better of her; the emotional backlog of the past twenty-four hours could no longer be contained – the guilt at what she'd done, the lack of food, the lack of sleep, the torment of seeing Callum again and knowing that it wouldn't be the last time . . . all of it, like a tsunami of surrender, swept over her, threatening to force her to her knees.

The tears were unstoppable now, her apologies incoherent. The smiles on the faces of the crew turned first to confusion then to concern, and then to fear. She steadied herself on the edge of the tea table and Tallulah, upset at seeing her mother like this, also began to cry. The hiss in Kate's ears became louder and louder, her mind turned to slush, her surroundings to slo-mo – Benno reaching out to help, Matt picking up Tallulah and making her feel safe. Everything was strangely outside of her and she didn't know where she was. And then – nothing.

Silence.

Kate had passed out.

18

The window panes of St Andrew's church hall were damp and clouded with condensation. Inside, twenty-two women of various shapes and ages were finishing their class. At the front, Rowena, their toned and lithe instructor, was urging them all to feel the stretch and breathe it out, for one final time. And then up she leapt, eager and brimming with fitness. 'Thank you, ladies! I think tonight you've surpassed yourselves.' She said that every week. The women applauded her and began rolling up their exercise mats, feeling the benefit of their workout in their legs and bums and tums.

Belinda turned to her friend Sue. 'It's bloody torture, isn't it? Why do we do it?'

'Because,' Sue replied quietly, 'we may be in our fifties, but we're still foxy fuckers who know how to get the old man turned on. Got to keep the machinery workin', haven't we?'

'You're appalling, Sue Crosby,' Belinda laughed.

Sue worked with Belinda at the hospital; they'd been friends ever since Sue moved to Edinburgh from London twenty years ago. One of their classmates, Sheilagh, came puffing over, pink in the face and a light sheen of sweat on her forehead. 'Who's coming to the pub to cash in all the calories we've just burnt?'

'Ah not me, love, I'm knackered,' Belinda said. And she was.

'I expect you'll be wanting to get back to your famous husband?'

'Sorry?' Belinda was confused.

'Don't tell me you didn't see him? In the *Gazette*?' Sheilagh started rustling around in her bag. 'I've got it here somewhere.'

'What you witterin' on about now, Sheil?' Sue found Sheilagh annoying at the best of times. She watched her as she dug deep and pulled out a tatty copy of the Edinburgh weekly paper.

'Look at him – all mysterious and enigmatic!'

On the front page, beneath a story about a local bird sanctuary, was the headline 'FAMOUS ACTRESS RETURNS TO QUEENS-FERRY SCHOOL' with a big photo of Kate Andrews and Brian Boyd at North Park Primary. Behind them, trying to avoid the camera and failing, was Callum.

'That Kate Andrews came back to talk to the kids yesterday. So glamorous. And look at your Callum, sneaking off in the background! You can keep it if you like.'

Belinda held the paper and focused on the photo, willing her hands to stop shaking.

'D'you see?'

But Belinda couldn't speak, her throat tight with tears. With superhero speed Sue came to her rescue. 'Bollocks, I left the sodding iron on! Get me home will you, Lind, before the bloody house burns down!' And she snatched the paper out of Belinda's hand, mumbling, 'Sorry, Sheil, gotta scoot!' before manhandling Belinda out of the muggy church hall and into the cool air outside.

Once she was through the door, Belinda steadied herself against the wall and whispered, 'Give me a fag.'

'Don't be an idiot, you haven't smoked for over thirty years.'

'So it's time I started again.'

'Right, well let's at least get in the car.'

A minute later they were sat in the church car park, the windows of Belinda's Fiesta wound down as they both puffed away on Sue's menthol cigarettes. Belinda only took a couple of drags before throwing hers onto the gravel outside. 'Christ, that's disgusting!'

'I know.'

Sue examined the front of the paper. 'It doesn't mean anything,' she ventured gently.

Belinda didn't answer.

'She was only visiting the school. Knowing Callum, he won't have even spoken to her, he'll have stayed out of her way.'

Belinda took an extra-strong mint out of her pocket and crunched on it hard. 'I think about her most days, y'know. What she did . . . what *they* did.'

'Yeah, I'll bet.'

They sat in silence. Sue had been there all those years ago to pick up the pieces when Callum's affair had been found out. She still bore a grudge against him for hurting her best mate, but she'd never tell Belinda that.

'When she's in something on the telly, Callum always grabs the remote and switches over.' She paused. 'And we never, ever mention her.'

'You'll mention her tonight though, won't you?'

'I don't know.' She crunched the remainder of the mint until it disintegrated in her mouth, started the car and drove off.

They didn't speak again until they pulled up outside Sue's house. As she got out of the car, Sue turned to her. 'Just stay calm, love. I mean it's not like he's done anything wrong, is it? It's not *his* fault she hurled her marriage-wrecking body up north for a school visit.'

Belinda ignored her. 'I'll call you tomorrow.'

'You can *call* me *any time*, you silly cow. Promise me you will.'

'Of course.'

But as she watched her drive away, Sue knew Belinda wouldn't.

When the truth had finally been revealed, Belinda thought she would dissolve into nothingness. The pain was suffocating, debilitating. And she'd have put money on their marriage not surviving the onslaught. Because how could she ever forgive him or like him or love him or even be in the same room as him again, after that?

They *had* survived, of course. And she thought they were stronger now than ever. But here she was, facing those same doubts and armies of distrust that had invaded their happy marriage seventeen years ago. She took a deep breath and went inside the house, clutching the *Edinburgh Gazette*.

Callum was in the kitchen making a stir-fry. Wafts of steaming chilli and garlic rose up noisily from the wok. He didn't hear her come in.

'Callum.'

He turned round, smiling. 'I've done enough for two if you fancy it?'

She took a deep breath and then launched in, her voice cold and hard.

'Tell me you really were out with someone called Paul McGee last night and not with Kate Andrews.' She slammed the *Gazette* hard onto the kitchen table.

His eyes flickered down at the black and white photo of the smiling woman he'd had sex with the night before. Neither he nor Belinda moved for five seconds. It felt to both of them like five hours. Eventually Callum spoke, finding within him the ability to sound completely affronted.

'Of course I was with Paul! Jesus, Belinda, what d'you take me for?'

And because she wanted to, she chose to believe him, and felt ashamed for ever doubting him and relieved to the core of her soul. 'I'm sorry. I'm so sorry.' She was tearful now and sat down on the hard wood of the kitchen bench. 'It's just seeing her there in that photo, with you . . .'

Callum sat down next to her, wrapped her in his arms and cursed himself for being such an appalling example of humankind as he comforted her. 'I didn't mention the school visit because I knew it would upset you . . .'

'Did you speak to her?'

'Well yeah, I said hello, but in front of the class and Brian Boyd. I was never on my own with her – I couldn't wait for the day to end, to be honest.'

For a moment they sat like that, Belinda cuddled up, made safe in his embrace. And then she asked him, 'What did it feel like? Seeing her again.'

He was grateful his chin was resting a-top Belinda's head, preventing her from seeing the deceit in his eyes. 'I didn't feel anything. She was just . . . nobody.'

'I'm so sorry, Callum.' Belinda cried anew. 'I hate myself for not trusting you.'

'Sssh, sweetheart. It's done. Gone. It was nothing.'

In the wok, the abandoned, blackening vegetables began filling the kitchen with the unmistakable smell of burnt food and the smoke detector screeched out its warning high and loud around the house.

19

'And you paid a fiver to be told that?'

'Well no, ten actually.'

'You idiot.'

Hetty had been regaling Matt with her Romany experience from lunchtime, which *she* thought was *extraordinary*.

They were sitting in the living room, sharing a bottle of vegan wine that Hetty had brought over to try. Tallulah and Panda were cuddled up next to Hetty on the vast leather sofa, reading – or at least pretending to read – *The Cat in the Hat*, whilst Hetty absent-mindedly smoothed her goddaughter's hair. Tallulah preferred to recite her own version of the story to herself – in an American accent – because it involved a three-legged dog and was much more interesting.

Bathed and pyjama'd, and comfortably full of warm milk, she was savouring the naughtiness of staying up late to wait for Mummy to come home. Matt had told her it was a treat for being such a good girl, but really he wanted to ensure Tallulah could see Kate was well again after her dramatic collapse that afternoon. He didn't want her having nightmares, and although Tallulah now believed Mummy had just 'fallen down' at work, Matt wanted to be doubly certain.

When Kate had passed out, the on-set nurse had rushed to her aid within seconds, and after taking her blood pressure and administering a hot, sweet tea, he pronounced her fit and well, just a little 'over-tired' – the standard industry euphemism for 'hungover'.

Kate had been mortified at her very public loss of control and, ever the professional, threatened to kick up a fuss with the executive producers if they didn't allow filming to continue. Everyone knew better than to argue with Kate when she was in one of her deter-mined moods, so they did exactly what they were told.

Matt and Tallulah had headed home, and by the time the film crew wrapped that evening Benno was delighted to discover they'd filmed everything they needed, despite the day's major hiccups.

'But don't you think it's amazing? That I should hear from Adam just two days ago, and then today this lady tells me there's some-one from my past who's come back into my life! *And* that there's going to be a baby!' Hetty was still dumbfounded by the Romany's predictions.

'No, I don't think it's remotely amazing. It's generic bullshit.' Hetty pointlessly covered the innocent ears of Tallulah, who wasn't listening anyway, lost in her nonsensical chatter, her eyelids fighting sleep. 'You could apply that "prediction" to anything. One size fits all. Honestly, Het, I'm surprised at you for being so gullible!'

'What's the matter with you, Mr Mardy Pants?'

Matt couldn't help but smile. 'Sorry. Been a bit of a day.'

'I know, sweetheart, but she's OK now. Isn't she, Lules? Your Mummy's better now.'

But as if put under by a stage hypnotist, Tallulah had fallen asleep clutching Panda and tucked in tight to her Aunty Het, *The Cat in the Hat* still open on her lap.

'It wasn't just what happened today, though,' he whispered. 'Things have been building for a while. Last night she didn't come home till three a.m.'

'But I thought she was with an old friend? Paula someone?'

'Oh Het, get with it, there *is* no Paula McGee. She was lying.'

'Really?'

Matt sighed and took a slug of wine before admitting, 'I think she might be . . .' Matt lowered his voice even more, in case Tallulah woke up and heard. 'I think she might be *using* again.'

'Oh dear. Oh no, that's not good . . .'

Hetty didn't know much about drugs. She'd smoked a joint at uni once, with dire consequences that involved vomiting over her bed after eating a dozen French Fancies. But she'd known Kate had a bit of a problem with cocaine after Matt turned up on Hetty's doorstep one night six years ago. He and Kate had only known each other a year and had had a massive row at a friend's party – Matt had had a bit too much wine, granted, but Kate was off her head on coke as well. It wasn't a revelation to him that she took it – he'd known since he met her that she did, in fact they'd even done it together once or twice in the early days. But although its appeal to Matt had long since waned, Kate's indulgence had carried on and gone way beyond recreational. At the party she just wouldn't shut up. Gurning in people's faces, shiny-eyed and, according to Matt, 'just talking and talking and talking shit. Thinking she was SO interesting – when really, Het, she was boring the arse off everyone. Everyone who wasn't high themselves, that is. And then she stood on a table and stripped off! Like a proper strip act.'

Hetty had put him up for the night, but when he'd returned home the next morning, expecting to find a repentant girlfriend in his bed, Kate wasn't there. Nor the next day, nor the next. She stayed at the party house for three days, and when she eventually came home she was on such a downer she trailed a nihilistic cloud of gloom everywhere she went. He thought this would put paid to their relationship. But a week later, Kate announced she'd signed up to a therapist and was going to 'get rid of this crap from my life – you're too precious to me, darling Matthew.' It wasn't long after that that Kate had got pregnant with Tallulah and, with the confidence of a new convert to sobriety, had sworn off drugs for ever.

And she'd apparently kept her promise. But Kate's recent strange behaviour could only be attributed to one of two things, probably both: that her depression was returning, and with it the accompanying need to take mood-altering substances.

And he didn't just mean wine. 'Her food's gone mental again too. She's doing the starving-herself thing, and the purging.'

'Oh I'm sorry, Matt.' Hetty looked at her dear friend, aching to make him feel better. 'Look, you need to talk to her. You need to be honest, to tell her your fears.'

'She's not . . . *easy*, though. To talk to, I mean.'

'Why don't you take her away for a few days? Go to Prague or Brussels or somewhere. Just the two of you. I can look after this one.'

They both looked at the sleeping Tallulah, contentedly snuffling like a newborn lamb, her dreams most likely filled with three-legged dogs and a cat in a strange stripy hat.

'Yeah, I know. I'll have a word with Benno, find out what her schedule is and see what I can organize.'

They both sat with their own thoughts for a moment.

'This wine is dire, isn't it?'

'Yeah, it's pretty weird.' And they laughed.

Matt wanted to change the subject, to lighten the mood. He hated unloading all his woes onto Hetty like this. He knew what a worrier she was.

'Right. So, this reunion. How many replies to date?'

'Oh, it's marvellous! Seventy-two!'

'Surely we won't know them all though?'

'Oh no, there are people coming from all sorts of backgrounds – mathematicians, computer scientists . . .'

'Remember Richard Whatsisname, with the beard? *He* did computers, and he stole one, d'you remember, and hid it in your wardrobe when you went home for reading week?'

'Oh my God, yes! And when I came back he just walked into my room, all cocky as a crab, picked up the computer and said, "I'll just relieve you of this!"'

'"I'll just relieve you of this!"' Matt laughed as he headed over to the wine rack to get a more palatable alternative to Hetty's vegan offering. He uncorked it with a practised hand and pulled out two fresh glasses from the cupboard. 'I wonder if there'll be any Manscis there.' Mansci was the nickname for Management Science, a term that had always bewildered Matt – was it the management of science, or the science of management?

'Yes, there's definitely one. Greta from the floor below us in first year.'

'Wasn't she Finnish slash Brummie?'

'Yes, and I used to love it when she swore – "fwckin sheet!" she'd say! Oh God, this tastes *so* much better.' And the warmth of the wine gliding down their throats made them feel buoyant and optimistic.

Matt held out his glass to clink with Hetty's. 'Here's to Greta and Richard and all those lovely people coming to your lovely reunion!'

'Including Adam.'

Begrudgingly, Matt said, 'Yeah, alright, and to him. Though I still think he's a dick!'

They were laughing so much when Kate arrived that they didn't see her come in. She watched them for a second from the doorway, two old mates, happy in each other's company, sharing a trusted, reliable and utterly solid friendship, and was filled momentarily with envy. 'Is it party time?'

'Kate!'

Hearing her mother's name woke Tallulah out of her slumber. 'Mummy!!!' Despite her sleepiness, the excitement at seeing her mother energized her enough to run towards Kate and throw herself into her arms.

'Hello, my gorgeous girl!' And she showered her with kisses.

'Daddy said I could stay up to see you!'

'So I see!' Over Tallulah's shoulder Kate winked at Matt, once again flooring him with an unexpected show of affection. 'Hello, Hetty, what a joy to see you!'

Hetty got up and gave Kate a hug. 'Aw, happy birthday. I bought you a cactus.'

'Blimey – are you trying to tell me something?'

'What? No. It's quite unusual, I just thought you'd . . .'

'Relax, Het, I'm joking.'

'Hetty's also brought us some vegan wine.'

'Which is really rather shocking,' Hetty said, slightly shame-faced.

Kate laughed and passed Tallulah over to their friend. 'Well, I've got something slightly better than that . . .' She went back into the hall and returned with two bottles of Cristal champagne. 'And there's another four where they came from!'

'Kate, that's too much!' Matt protested.

'Yes, I've got work in the morning and I don't think I should have any more!' Hetty was panicking.

'We don't have to drink *all* of it, silly. Production gave it to me as a present. Thought we could have a little party – this *is* the last year of my thirties, after all!' She went to the cabinet and took out three elegant champagne flutes.

Matt raised his eyebrows at Hetty in a look that was an obvious comment on the unpredictability of his wife. 'Oh well, Het – in for a penny!'

'That's the spirit!' And Kate popped the champagne cork, which blasted up to the ceiling with firework speed, eliciting a little yelp from Hetty and Tallulah, followed by a peal of giggles.

'Mummy, can I have some?'

'Daddy will give you a special glass, won't you, Daddy?'

And on cue, Matt got up and made for the Tupperware cupboard, pulling out a glamorous pink plastic cocktail glass and duly filling it with lemonade whilst Kate charged the champagne flutes. 'I'm sorry about today. I was just so exhausted.'

'Are you feeling better now, Kate?' asked Hetty nervously.

'I will when I've had this. Bottoms up!' And she downed her champagne in one before proceeding to refill her glass.

Hetty glanced unnoticed at Matt, and detected a hint of sadness flash across his face before it transformed into a big smile and he announced, 'Happy birthday, darling!'

'Ha! Yes, happy birthday to me!' They all took a sip, followed by a moment's awkward silence, broken by Kate. 'Ooh, and we're celebrating something else tonight.'

'Are we?'

Kate took another drink, inwardly finding strength to break the news. 'Yes, it looks like I've found the funds to pay for our new shower room – well, to part-pay for it anyway.'

'Overtime?' Matt asked. Tallulah was now ensconced on his lap, her short-lived excitement fading and sleep once again defeating her.

'Not quite. I've got a PA.'

'She means a personal appearance,' Matt explained to Hetty.

'Yes. Not a terribly glamorous one. I've been asked to open a casino.'

'Sounds glamorous to me,' said Hetty, the champagne bubbles rushing up her nose and making her light-headed.

'Well, the fee is *certainly* glamorous – they're going to pay me ten grand!'

'Blimey!' Matt reached for the bottle and topped up his glass.

'The downside is, they want me tomorrow night.'

Matt absorbed the information, annoyed that once again their weekend would be disrupted by Kate's work schedule. 'Bit last-minute, isn't it?'

'Ha! You don't think I was first choice, do you? They wanted Sarah Lancashire, but she dropped out, and apparently I was their second choice.'

'Well, more fool her!' offered Hetty, raising her glass in a solitary toast.

'Exactly. Matt, d'you think you should take her up?' Kate indicated the now sleeping Tallulah, her head resting on Matt's shoulder, her mouth half open.

'Yeah, I will in a minute.' He had the distinct impression that Kate was holding something back. 'So where is it? This unglamorous casino.'

Kate took another over-zealous drink, swallowing down her nerves with a big dose of Cristal before finding the courage to say, 'Edinburgh. I'm going back to Edinburgh.'

1985

20

'You're off yer head, man!' Callum said, emptying the contents of an ashtray into a bucket and dusting it clean with the paintbrush reserved especially for the gruesome task.

It was a Saturday night in mid September and although Callum had started back at school, he still helped out in the pub at weekends. They'd closed up for the night, and it was just him and Fergus. Who was airing his suspicions.

'But I've seen the way she looks at you, Cal. Sly little glances, always laughing at your jokes.'

'Can't help it if I'm hysterically funny,' he tried to appease him.

But Fergus was having none of it. 'I'm not stupid. And Belinda most *certainly* isn't.'

Callum put down the ashtray and looked at him. 'For Christ's sake, I thought you were kidding! She's in her twenties!'

'So?'

'Read my lips: there is nothing going on between me and Kate . . . Whatever-Her-Name-Is . . . Andrews.' He looked hard at his older brother, defying him to doubt further.

Eventually Fergus looked away and carried on totalling up the till, whilst Callum took the bucket of fags and ash out to the bin behind the back door. As they passed each other, Callum said, 'Listen, I get on with the girl, she's bright, she's a laugh. But that's all, I promise.'

Fergus nodded and smiled weakly. 'OK, I believe you.' He waited a moment. 'So I'll see you tomorrow night?'

Callum nodded and headed out, turning at the door. 'Oh, it's me and her down on the rota – I can swap if it'll make you feel better?'

'I said I believed you, didn't I? Now fuck off.' He threw a damp cloth at Callum, who laughed and ducked. But after he'd gone, Fergus was left with a gnawing feeling in the pit of his stomach.

Twenty minutes later, when Callum met with Kate in the little side street off the marketplace as arranged, he was distracted.

'I can't stay,' he told her. 'Get in, I'll drop you back home.'

They were meant to go to their secret place, a dead-end lane they'd discovered only five minutes out of town. But Callum didn't want sex; his conversation with Fergus had unnerved him.

'He doesn't miss a thing,' he complained. 'I dunno, maybe we should cool things for a few days, just let the dust settle.'

The thought of not seeing him knocked Kate off balance for a moment. 'We don't need to do that,' she said calmly.

'Kate, for God's sake, you've got nothing to lose here. I've got everything.'

'So let me solve it then.' And she smiled her wicked smile, and his bad mood instantly evaporated.

True to her word, the next night at the pub Kate caused a stir that convinced Fergus that Callum *had* been telling the truth, after all. Shortly after they opened at six, in walked a group of lads, all suntanned and sandy, with shaggy hair and toned biceps. They sat at a corner table whilst one of their crowd headed for the bar to order the drinks.

When Kate saw him, she squealed with delight – 'Oh my God! Oh my GOD!' – lifted the bar hatch and ran towards him.

He picked her up, swung her round and then kissed her full on the lips. There weren't many customers in the pub at that point, just Jackie Legg and Stuey Jameson, and one or two tourists – but those who were there stared open-mouthed at the spectacle.

When they finally stopped kissing, Kate said, 'When did you get back?'

'Couple of hours ago. Thought I'd surprise you.'

Kate looked at him for a few seconds longer, then turned, holding his hand, and led him up to the bar.

'Fergus, Callum, this is Jake. My boyfriend.'

'Hello!' Fergus said, bemused.

Callum didn't know where to put himself and managed to mutter a 'Pleased to meet you,' holding out his hand to shake. Jake, a bit thrown by this, turned it into a high five and the moment became very awkward.

'He's been travelling. Just got back!' Kate said, before turning to Jake. 'You're so wicked. Why didn't you tell me!' And she kissed him, whispering loudly enough for the others to hear, 'God, I've missed you!'

Fergus, feeling a little swept along with the whole thing, suddenly announced, 'Look, I don't think we're gonna be busy tonight, and me and Callum can cope, can't we, Cal?'

'Er . . . yeah.' Callum seemed preoccupied with the glass-washer, stacking glasses as if there was a mad rush of customers desperate to be served.

'Why don't you take the night off?'

Kate's eyes lit up. 'Really?'

'Yeah, go on, looks like you two have got some catching up to do!'

Callum couldn't look at Kate, who now had her head tucked into Jake's shoulder.

'Thing is, Fergie, that's very kind of you, but I really need the dosh . . . Tell you what, how about me and Jake go off for a couple of hours and I'll come back around eight?'

'Aye, go on then, seems like a good compromise.'

They watched Kate leave the pub, arm in arm with Jake. Fergus shook his head and chuckled. 'Well, that was a turn-up for the books! I take back everything I said!'

Callum managed to smile, but inside he found himself ludicrously and uncharacteristically eaten up with jealousy.

When Kate *did* come back as promised, just after eight, Callum couldn't bring himself to speak to her. She found it all highly amusing, and when she finally cornered him alone in the beer cellar – free now to come and go as they pleased, free from all suspicion in Fergus's doubting eyes – Callum's passion was fired up.

'So, d'you fuck him?'

'Babe . . . ?' His anger didn't scare her. Far from it. In fact, it turned her on – this new possessive side of Callum.

'Of course not! We sat on the beach, that's all. And talked for an hour.'

'But I watched you kiss him!'

'Er, duh! We were *acting*? That was the point, stupid!'

'Was it as good as this?'

And he pressed his mouth against hers, enveloping her in an angry, consuming kiss, stamping his territory and leaving her in no doubt about how he felt. She responded, her hand searching to feel how hard she'd made him, before breaking away to leave him wanting more. She loved how desperate he was for her. The power she held over him.

'Jake's a friend of mine from drama college,' she whispered. 'I dared him to do it . . .' And she flicked her tongue along the curve of his ear, sucking gently on the lobe, her hot breath making him want her even more. 'I'm a good actress, don't you think?'

He conceded with a nod. But inside he didn't like how he'd behaved, or what he was becoming. This just wasn't him.

'Look, I'm sorry. It freaked me out, that's all, seeing you with someone else. Even if it was a set-up.'

'Hey,' she said, lightening the mood, 'at least you'll get no more accusations from your brother – he was well and truly convinced.' And she walked back to the bar, smiling as she savoured her little victory.

21

Nineteen-year-old Matthew Fenton let himself into room 125 of Benfield Hall and tried to hide his dismay. 'As you can see, you've basically got everything you need in one small space,' said the steward (whose name, weirdly, *was* Stewart). 'You've got your desk overlooking the grounds, you've got your cupboard for your clothes, you've got your bed – obviously.' Stewart laughed at this, it was part of the patter that he gave to all Freshers who moved into Benfield. 'And the *pièce de résistance*, your very own sink. With mirror! At no extra cost!'

Matt was now regretting having left it so late in the day to choose his accommodation. The university was a campus one, so most students would be living in halls like these – but surely he could have done better than this?

'Its design is based on a Swedish women's prison! Ha! Weren't expecting that, now were you?'

Actually, Matt thought to himself as he surveyed the sparse room with its insultingly narrow bed, *I can well believe it is.*

He put his suitcase on the bed and his guitar next to the sink. Stewart nodded towards it. 'D'you play?' he asked, affecting the persona of someone in the music industry.

Matt was sorely tempted to say, *No, I just carry one round with me so I can look like a wanker*, but managed to resist and said, 'Just a bit.'

'Well, check out the Guitar Society at Freshers' Fair. You'll meet a few like-minded people, no doubt – maybe set yourselves up for a bit of a jam.'

'Right.' Matt tried to sound keen. But the thought of joining any society or even speaking to another human being for the three years he was here filled him with utter dread. He was going to hate them all, he knew it.

Stewart was about to leave when he remembered something. 'Oh, by the way, History of Art, right?'

'Er, yeah.'

'Girl down the corridor in 135, same course as you. You might want to hook up. See ya!'

The last thing Matt wanted to do was 'hook up' with anyone. He just wanted to be left to his own devices and was starting to think university was a big mistake. He'd spent a year touring Europe – bought the predictable Inter-rail ticket, but had set off on his own, not with a gang of mates. Not for him the booze-soaked, sun-drenched Greek islands or Spanish coastline: Matt sought out the galleries of Rome and Paris, the art trails of Holland and Germany. His passion for art was like an addiction: he needed it, thrived on it. And the only reasons he'd signed up for a History of Art degree were a) to please his parents, and b) because he wasn't so arrogant that he didn't think there was much more to learn. But it was this socializing bit that bugged him. Mixing with strangers, all that bonhomie and ra-ra-ra. He was a regular comprehensive kid from Rotherham. His family were no great shakes, *he* was no great shakes – he just had this thirst for learning, which he needed to quench. Freshers' Fair and fake friendships were not part of the plan.

He lay back on his bed. His mother would be *so* disappointed if he pulled out now. 'Just give it two weeks,' she'd said to him before he left – he'd refused to let her come with him. Didn't want to be like all those other kids, caught in that awful place between trying to be an independent adult and terrified of cutting the apron strings by actually saying goodbye to their mums and dads. Having had that year out made it easier to do this on his own. He sighed, then gave himself an imaginary kick up the arse, stood up and opened his wardrobe. Seven sad hangers jangled a feeble hello. He unlocked his case and tried to muster the enthusiasm to unpack.

A knock. Was it Stewart returning with more advice? Matt thought about not answering, but realized he'd never get away with it. He was, after all, living in a female open prison of sorts . . .

He opened the door. There in the corridor, brandishing an open tin of misshapen cakes, was a girl dressed in a white cheesecloth shirt, 1940s waistcoat, dirndl skirt, and leg-warmers over cowboy boots. An odd combination. Her hair was badly permed and she'd drawn shiny green eyeliner under her eyelashes. 'Rock cake?' She thrust the tin at him.

'Er . . .'

But before he could answer, she was talking again. Really fast.

'The Steward chappy, Stewart, suggested I said hello. We're on the same course. Not me and Stewart – he's doing a PhD – in Physics, I think – no, you and me. So here I am. Saying hello. I brought rock cakes with me – my mother thought they'd be a good ice-breaker. More of a good tooth-breaker, to be honest. I'm not the best of bakers.'

He looked at her. Silence.

'Oh, and I'm Hetty,' she blurted out. 'I'm middle-class, live in Hampstead, and I don't really understand the Miners' Strike. And I'm a vegetarian.'

Matt smiled at her, bewildered. 'I've never met one of those before,' he said. And an instant friendship was formed.

Later that night they walked back together from the Milking Parlour, the bar nearest to Benfield Hall. They'd already discussed the obligatory A-level results, pets and parents, and now Hetty wanted to talk about weight. But Matt said he'd never stood on weighing scales in his life and wouldn't have the first idea how much he weighed.

'I'm ten stone two,' Hetty announced.

'You're mistaking me for someone who cares?' he laughed.

'OK, tell me something about yourself that nobody else would know,' Hetty said suddenly.

Matt was caught off guard. 'Oh, right, OK. Well, I don't really want to be here, and I doubt I'll last the week.'

Hetty didn't answer straight away. 'That's a shame,' she said. 'But you've got to do what you've got to do.'

He felt an unexpected respect for her when she said this. Hetty was . . . well, she was OK. Maybe. 'Right, your turn,' he announced. 'Tell me something surprising about yourself, Hetty Strong.'

She was quiet for a while as they stomped through the wet September grass back towards their would-be Swedish women's prison. 'OK . . . I only came to Warwick because there's a guy who's come here, who I was at sixth-form college with, and with whom I'm in love – Gosh, I sounded quite Shakespearean then – and if he hadn't come here, then I wouldn't have either. Oh, and he doesn't know I love him. In fact, he doesn't even know I exist.'

Matt didn't know what to say, then managed, 'Far out,' in a homage to some unknown hippy student from the seventies.

'And what's his name, this guy?'

'Adam,' she said. 'Adam Latimer.'

22

When the phone rang they were lying on her bedroom floor, dozing, the late-September sun peeping politely through the blinds, not wishing to interrupt them. Outside, nothing much was happening except the Sunday thrum of a strimmer and the indecipherable chat of two car-washers.

Kate and Callum had been there since ten a.m. They'd had almost three hours of delicious, undisturbed sex: focused, determined and exhausting. Her parents were away on holiday and this room had become their haven.

He'd taken the kids to his mother's that morning, left Belinda lying in bed. Sleep eluded her these days and she had to grab it when she could. He'd kissed her forehead and asked her if she needed anything before he left.

She'd half opened her eyes and smiled at him. 'I suppose a shag's out of the question?' And then she'd gone back to sleep, entertaining herself with the ridiculousness of such an idea. It'd be a long time before she was up to any shenanigans. She'd frequently joke she was the size of a cross-Channel ferry right now. Not remotely feminine, her ankles swollen beyond recognition – 'They could literally be someone else's, Callum, probably my Aunt Betty's' – and her breasts were so heavy they hurt every time she yawned.

Callum had watched her gently snoring, her mouth slightly open, and felt relieved that she was finally getting some rest.

He wasn't consumed with remorse any more. *Because what you're doing is so abhorrent*, he thought, *it's beyond repentance and certainly beyond forgiveness*. And the devil inside his head said, *So you may as well enjoy it while it lasts, Cally boy, 'cos believe me, when she finds out, which she WILL, the whole shooting match is gonna come crashing down around you.* He knew all this, and still he couldn't give it up.

It's just sex though, isn't it? Isn't it? That's what he kept telling himself, but he didn't know any more. He was lost, defeated. He only knew he was addicted to her, to the smell of her, the taste of her – oh God, the taste of her! – the feel of her skin next to his, and Jesus, what it was to be inside her. If he thought about it too much, he knew he'd go insane.

When he'd arrived at Kate's house that morning, she'd opened the front door wearing nothing but a pair of knee-high boots made of tan suede and a black silk shirt that was too big for her. She looked amazing and she pulled him inside without saying a word. First she'd kissed him, then cupped his face in her hands, looking him straight in the eye before a broad smile spread across her face. 'You are SO gonna get it, MacGregor,' she promised. Then, holding his gaze, she undid his belt and dropped slowly to her knees. There she began consuming him, delighting in his every surrendering groan as he stared at her parents' cuckoo clock on the opposite wall.

Now, three hours later, they lay in a post-sex tangle of tired limbs and sated smiles, halfway between sleep and wakefulness, the phone ringing some distance away in the hall.

They would have just ignored it, of course. Even when the answer machine clicked into play and the voice of Kate's mother could be vaguely heard, politely inviting the caller to please speak clearly after the beep.

And they would've ignored it *still*, even when they heard Fergus begin his message. 'Hello, it's Fergus here from the pub.'

'He'll be wanting to change my shifts . . .' Kate sleepily mumbled and kissed Callum's chest, inhaling the familiar smell of his skin, her eyes still shut.

'Kate, can you give me a call when you get this?'

He ran his fingers along the small of her back.

'The thing is, I'm trying to get hold of Callum.'

And that's when they both stopped. *What?*

'I just wondered if you'd seen him, by any chance?'

They sat up.

'Y'see, it's his wife, she's gone into labour . . .'

And they didn't hear the rest of the message as Fergus carried on in the background, fruitlessly explaining how everyone had been looking for Callum everywhere and now they were running out of ideas, otherwise he wouldn't have rung.

Kate sat on the edge of her bed, still naked, calmly watching as Callum frantically picked up his scattered clothes from the floor.

'Fuck! *Fuck!*' The panic was making him shake and he stumbled as he tried to climb into his jeans. 'I've got to get to the hospital.'

'No.'

This didn't register, his mind on other things. Other pretty fucking life-changing things.

'Callum, listen to me.' She made him look at her. 'You mustn't go straight to the hospital.'

'What you on about? Of course I'm going straight there!'

'If you do, the game's up. Fergus will know you found out from me because you were *with* me.'

'And you think I care?'

'CALLUM!' There was a cold edge to her voice he'd not heard before and it caught his attention. 'It may feel like that now – like you don't give a shit about people finding out – but later on you'll regret it, I promise you. Now do what I tell you and it'll all be OK.'

The blood drained from his head and he had to sit down, the reality of the situation kicking in, the awful enormity of what he'd done finally overwhelming him: his wife was giving birth less than two miles away, and here he was in a strange house with a woman he barely knew, seventeen years younger than him, fulfilling some middle-aged man's fantasy, flying high on a selfish, destructive ego trip that could make him lose everything he had.

He looked up at Kate, and felt useless. 'What have I done?'

She looked back, determination on her face, totally in control.

'OK, what you need to do is go back to the house. To *your* house. Just like you would've done if you hadn't been here.' She spoke clearly, authoritatively. 'Where did you say you were going today?'

'I don't know . . .'

She could barely hear him.

'Callum! Pull yourself together, this is really important!'

He thought for a moment. 'DIY place over at Craigleith. The kids are with my mum.'

'Right. The only way you're gonna get through this is by lying, and I mean *big* lying.'

She went across the room to her stylishly messy dressing table, a jumble of scarves and little painted boxes, lipsticks and nail polish vying for space with half-burnt candles and incense sticks. Sitting on one of the shelves was a scuffed leather jewellery case, its contents lazily spilling out of the sides, silver chains and pearls tangled together with little Spanish beads and cheap bangles. She opened a tiny drawer at the base and took out a small antique box. She opened it to check inside, snapped it shut and then handed it to Callum. He stared at it, confused.

'Now listen to everything I say and you'll be alright,' she said. 'This is your story, OK?'

23

Although she wouldn't admit it to Matt, Hetty had spent most of her first week hunting for Adam Latimer. Under the pretext of 'exploring my environs', she'd scoured the campus for him – pretty much all the halls of residence, the Union, the Arts Centre – desperate for just a glimpse. On the eighth day, when she still hadn't seen him, she started to think she might have made a terrible mistake and that Adam hadn't come to Warwick after all!

It was in the launderette she'd finally stumbled upon him. Quite literally. He'd emptied his clean wet clothes into a white plastic basket and gone to get change for the tumble dryer. Hetty, carrying her own load of dirty laundry towards a washer, didn't see Adam's basket, tripped and went flying. A collection of her underwear and bedding, as well as an embarrassing orthopaedic sock, shot out before her and landed in an undignified heap on the floor. Hetty followed.

'Hey, watch where you're going!' Adam said as he came back in, jangling a handful of twenty-pence pieces. He looked annoyed.

Hetty hadn't turned round; she was on her knees, her back to the door, scrabbling around for any stray items and shoving them into the basket before someone saw. 'Sorry!' She laughed nervously. 'Don't know why I'm apologizing!'

And it was then that she looked up and discovered it was Adam standing there. She was holding a pair of tired panties in her right hand and a seen-better-days bra in her left. Mortified to see the boy she loved in front of her, she managed a stifled, 'Adam!'

He picked up his basket and took it over to the dryer. 'How d'you know my name?' He opened the vast circular door and started piling his wet clothes into the drum.

Hetty clambered to her feet and followed him. 'I'm Hetty. Strong. We were in sixth-form college together?'

He stopped to look at her now, half smiling and inquisitive. 'Were we? Hated that place, didn't you?' And he slammed the door and put five twenty pences into the slot. The machine rumbled slowly into tumbling action. 'Fancy a pint while this lot is drying?' He was already halfway to the door.

'Er, yes, I've just got to . . .' and she indicated her laundry.

'I'll see you in there,' he called over his shoulder. 'Mandela Bar. What you drinking?'

Hetty thought she would explode with excitement and couldn't think straight. She tried to sound cool and failed miserably. 'Oh anything, I'll have whatever you have.'

And he was gone.

She found him ten minutes later in the Union, laughing by the bar with a couple of drama students. A Eurythmics song was playing in the background. At first she was too shy to join them and stood watching from a distance, catching her breath as she took in the glorious sight of Adam Latimer in his donkey jacket and turned-up jeans and Doc Martens. '*No one on earth could feel like this . . .*' He was undeniably handsome, his ear pierced twice and his hair shaved at the sides, long and spiky at the top and bleached à la Depeche Mode. '*I'm thrown and overblown with bliss . . .*' Taking a large gulp of his purple pint, he turned and caught Hetty looking at him. 'There you are! Come on, your pint's getting warm.'

She walked over to the bar and Adam lazily introduced them all. 'Kev, Rick – Betty.'

'It's Hetty actually,' she timidly corrected him.

'Hetty, Betty – same thing. Here y'go.' And he handed her a pint the same colour as his. 'Snakebite and black.' It smelt revolting. But Adam had bought it for her, so she had to drink it. She took a mouthful and tried to hide her disgust. 'It was 68p, by the way.'

'Oh.' Embarrassed at the misunderstanding, she reached into her pocket and counted out some change.

Adam seemed to know Kev and Rick really well. They were talking about the forthcoming Drama Society auditions for *Twelfth Night*. He handed her a flyer. 'Come along if you like. We're casting the bit parts. I'm playing Orlando. And directing.' Then he turned back to Kev and Rick and carried on a conversation Hetty couldn't follow. But she didn't care . . .

She clutched the flyer for the audition, stood silently sipping her horrible purple pint and thinking how desperately she wanted to be in this play with him. Inside she felt warm and fuzzy – she didn't know whether it was the effect of the snakebite or the fact that she was standing just inches away from the Most Beautiful Boy on Earth. Adam, unaware of the silent adulation pouring forth from her, continued talking and joking with his friends, and for all the world, Hetty may as well have not been there. But for all the world, she was over the moon that she was.

24

'Absolutely stunnin'.'

Belinda was cradling her nine-pound-five-ounce newborn and the latest addition to the MacGregor clan, Ailsa Cerys Louise: Ailsa after Callum's godmother, Cerys after Belinda's best friend in school, and Louise because – well, because she and Callum both just liked the name. A shock of matted raven hair atop her shiny warm head, her face alternating between a pout and a gurn. Ailsa Cerys Louise was still affronted at being out and about in this clanky, bright world, when all she'd known hitherto had been warmth, peace, and the comforting continuity of her mother's loving heartbeat.

'I don't know what to say.'

Belinda was tearful. But she wasn't referring to the baby: she was looking at the antique emerald-studded eternity ring on her left hand, nestling in nicely next to her modest gold wedding band. 'I still can't believe you went and bought it.'

'Aw, stop goin' on, will you?' Callum smiled at her as he confidently extricated his daughter from her mother's embrace and settled her into a cuddle of his own, his arms, vast and protective, enveloping their tiny, delicate cargo.

'But it's so unlike you, Callum. You hardly remembered to get me a sodding engagement ring!' She beamed at him, relaxed now, despite the battle cries of childbirth still echoing round her exhausted body.

'Yeah well, I'm just glad it fits. Now stop embarrassin' me.' He was desperate to change the subject and he kissed baby Ailsa gently on her confused and crumpled forehead. 'Colostrum OK now, is it?' They'd been through the routine before.

'Yep, all good. She's gonna have an appetite on her, I reckon.' At which point Ailsa opened her perfect little mouth and started yelling, screeching, protesting, as if it had finally dawned on her that she was now actually BORN! And expected to get on with the indecorous job of being a baby.

'And a healthy pair of lungs!' Callum laughed. And he marvelled at how instantaneous and all-consuming was the love for a child; how it simply manifested itself in a parent's life, gate-crashing it without warning.

When Ben was born, he'd thought his heart would burst its walls with love. The advent of this alien force had completely hijacked him – he was busted. Lambasted. Transformed into a shaking, gibbering wreck. He'd heard boys at the rugby club go on about being a dad and he thought they were being big jessies who'd read too many 'New Man' articles in their girlfriends' magazines, that this fatherhood lark couldn't possibly be as debilitating as they were making it out to be. But then he held his firstborn in his arms, felt all the helplessness and dependency of that miniature mass of limbs and lungs and those grasping wee fingers, all that unconditional affiliation, an overwhelming sense of 'I've-got-your-back-son-and-that-will-never-change', and he wept like a fool. Couldn't stop.

So the thought of having a *second* child was unbearable. How could he ever love another child the same? In fact, when Belinda was pregnant with Cory, he had to sit her down and tell her in no uncertain terms, 'I'm sorry, Lindy, I just don't think I've got any love left over for another one.'

And she'd smiled at him – slightly patronizingly, he'd subsequently pointed out – and said there would *always* be enough love. More than enough, in fact.

And now here he was, holding his baby girl, inhaling the sweet, moist fragrance of her brand-new skin. She was yelling: obstinate, determined and utterly furious with him. He rocked her gently, and wiped away an escaping and unexpected tear. He wished he was only crying out of fatherly love. But he knew, deep down, he was crying with shame. With the behemoth-sized guilt that over-shadowed him. With the awful truth of what he was, and how he'd behaved, and the lies he'd told and would have to keep on telling. And he looked down at this tiny, angry face and he thought, *No. No, this is going to stop. I'm not going to be that person any more.* Simple as that. Holding a nine-pound-five-ounce bundle of love in his arms, he made the decision. Him and Kate. It was over.

That lunchtime, he'd gone back to the house, just as Kate had advised. He was in too much of a mess to think for himself and just went along with her instructions, unable to question, to change course. All he could do was stick to the plan. Inside, his guts were churning, his heart heaving, his brain and his synapses fizzing with overload, losing the ability to function. What the fuck had he become?

He parked the car and took out two tins of unopened paint that Kate had thankfully found in her father's shed. They looked brand new. Not forgetting the ring – small enough to keep safe in his pocket – he made his way to the front door. Shaking, he tried to put his key in the lock, but his mother was there in seconds. 'Callum! Oh, Callum!'

'What you doing here? Where are the boys?' It wasn't difficult for him to look shocked and railroaded, this was exactly how he was feeling.

'It's Belinda! She's in labour, son!'

And there it was. The licence he'd been waiting for since leaving Kate's house twenty minutes earlier. Now he could legitimately react.

'Right.' He put down the paint and turned on his heel, heading back to the car, his mother calling behind him, 'We've been looking all over for you!'

'I was at the DIY place in Craigleith.' He was into his automatic script now, rehearsed over and over out loud as he'd driven home from Kate's house. He felt like a murderer covering his tracks.

'But we tried there! We called them!'

He was ready for this. 'Yeah, well then I went over to Glasgow . . .'

'Glasgow!'

'Yeah, to this antique place . . . I've got to go, I'll call you when I get there.'

And he slammed his car door and started the engine. By now, Ben and Cory had come out of the house and were waving their daddy goodbye, confusion reigned, and he waved back. Challenge number one overcome.

He could hear Belinda's screams a hundred yards down the corridor. Even amidst the cacophony of other women's child-birthing cries, he'd recognize hers anywhere. Other-worldly, primitive and, dare he say it, bovine. Octaves lower and utterly terrifying. She was seconds away from delivery.

He walked through the door and there she was, his beautiful wife, on all fours, his brother stood next to her at a complete loss, surplus to requirements but feeling it would be too rude to leave.

When Fergus saw Callum he yelped, 'Jesus! Where the fuck have you been?'

'Calluuuuum!' Belinda didn't turn around. She had other things on her mind.

'It's OK, sweetheart, I'm here now. I'm so sorry . . .'

'Calluuuuum!' And she launched into an impressive tranche of deep and even outward breaths.

The midwife managed a smile at Callum as she prepared to grab the emerging baby. 'OK, here we go – one more push, Belinda, and we're there.'

Belinda dug deep, focused every sinew and fibre of her being, and PUSHED!

Fergus had stood aside to let Callum take his place. He bent down, his face parallel with Belinda's, and whispered, 'I love you so much, Lindy. I am so, so sorry . . .'

But Belinda wasn't listening. 'Gaaaaaaaaaaagggghhhhh!!!!'

And there it was. Birth number three for Belinda MacGregor, née Lewis. A gorgeous wee girl, instantly loved and welcomed into the world. The midwife handed Callum his daughter and helped Belinda slowly turn so she could finally rest on the bed. He placed their baby on her mother's chest and the midwife helped him cut the cord.

All the while, Fergus stood aside and watched, weeping like a fool.

'Typical of you, Callum MacGregor,' Belinda joked wearily. 'Wait till all the hard work's done, then turn up for the crowning glory. Literally.'

A few minutes passed with nobody saying anything, just the back-and-forth of the post-birth routine, the comforting sound-scape of the maternity ward going about its business, nurses and doctors coming and going, notes taken, blood pressure checked.

Belinda reached out and held her husband's hand, and innocently enquired, 'So, where were you?'

Stay calm, steady voice, you know the drill.

'Don't ask. What an idiot. Just rest now.'

She smiled at him and he kissed her hand. 'We've got a daughter, babes.'

'I know.'

Breathe. Breathe, for fuck's sake.

Later that evening, after the family had all been to visit and said hello to Ailsa Cerys Louise and when everyone had gone home and it was just Belinda and Callum and their sleepy, grouchy new bairn, in the tired dim lighting and dry heat of the maternity ward, Callum handed the little box to Belinda. Swallowing down the urge to be sick, guilt oozing from every pore, he did what he knew he *had* to do and lied to save his marriage, to save his life.

'This is the reason I was late.' The line was well practised, written by Kate. 'It's an eternity ring.'

She took the box and opened it, shocked and delighted, lifted the ring from its setting and put it on the third finger of her left hand. She completely believed his story – of the trip to Bradshaw's in Glasgow, of the purchase of this antique emerald ring, of the love he felt for her, of the fidelity that coursed through his veins.

And now, after one of the most tiring days of her life, Belinda MacGregor fell asleep, smiling, the emeralds on her left hand glinting in the harsh neon light of the hospital ward. And Callum felt lost, and sad, and bereft.

25

The gears on the Student Union minibus crunched reluctantly into reverse as Matt pulled into the loading bay. He was usually quite a good driver, but this ancient vehicle was getting the better of him. 'Bloody thing,' he muttered as he parked as near as dammit to the foreboding doors of the scenery dock. He was collecting props and staging for *Twelfth Night*, not a task he'd wanted but one which he'd offered to do for Hetty. As payback. For nearly coming to blows with Adam Latimer.

Two weeks earlier, Matt had gone with her to the auditions for *Twelfth Night*, solely for moral support. And, admittedly, Hetty's audition had been embarrassing. For some unknown reason, she'd chosen to do a speech as Maria ('the cute funny one' as Hetty described her), but with a Newcastle accent.

'Swayt Sir Tooby, be pare-shunt for t'neet; since tha youth of tha coont was today with tha' laydee, she is much outta quiet.'

She sounded Jamaican, but Matt hadn't the heart to tell her.

Adam Latimer was running the auditions as well as playing the lead and directing the play. He had been less kind. 'Hetty, that was shite! What's with the accent, man?'

'Well, I wanted to try something different,' Hetty offered, surprisingly unaffected by Adam's response.

'Yeah well, you shouldn't have bothered. Waste of time. Now do it again and drop the silly voice.'

'I don't think I can, though, it's how I learnt it.'

'Don't be such a tit, of course you can drop it.'

Suddenly Matt, who hadn't been paying much attention, desperate only to get out of the room without being noticed, felt his hackles rising. He'd only known Hetty a week or so, but he found himself feeling enormously protective of her, especially when this dickhead started throwing his weight around. He stood up.

'Hang on, mate, this is fuckin' am-dram. Who d'you think you are, Derek fucking Jacobi?'

'It's alright, Matt, really.' Hetty was blushing and an awkward silence filled the room. Adam was both shocked and delighted, noticing Matthew for the first time. 'Well, well, the Quiet Man speaks! You sure we can't tempt you to audition?'

Matt stared back at him. 'So you gonna give her a part or what? 'Cos I didn't see them queuing round the block just now to be in your little play.'

They both stared each other out, eventually interrupted by Moj the stage manager, authoritative in her dungarees and baseball hat and carrying an oversized ringbinder. 'OK, well, thanks for coming in, Hetty. We'll post the cast list up on the Dram Soc noticeboard tomorrow, OK?'

Adam laughed and broke away, leaving Matt looking slightly foolish.

In the end, Hetty had been cast as Officer Number Two. She had two lines: *'Come sir away!'* and *'Come sir, I pray you go!'* She was delighted with them both.

Matt felt bad for losing his temper and was now making up for it by helping transport a few large items borrowed from the Belgrade Theatre for the production, which was due to open in three weeks. His opinion of Adam hadn't wavered – the guy was a complete idiot. But Hetty was his friend – and he was doing it for her.

A stagehand from the theatre, who'd been sent out to show him the way, banged on the back of the minibus to stop him reversing further and crashing into the gates. 'Whoah! OK, Trigger, that's enough!'

Matt got out from behind the wheel, annoyed at the guy's patronizing tone.

'You'll have to come in and wait for five minutes. The stuff needs to be signed off before you can take it.'

Matt could think of twenty other things he'd rather be doing this Friday afternoon, but he dutifully followed the stagehand through the vast scenery dock and was shown to a seating area. 'Help yourself to coffee if you like. It tastes awful, but it's free.' Matt decided against it, grabbed an old copy of *Plays and Players* and sat in one of the Green Room's well-worn chairs.

He was halfway through reading a review of *Titus Andronicus* at Stratford when the door was opened by a kindly-looking woman who reminded him of his gran. 'If you could just wait here,' she was saying to a younger woman following behind, 'Oliver won't be long. Have you got your audition piece?'

'Yes. All sorted, thanks.'

The kindly-looking woman checked her clipboard before looking at Matt, confused. 'Oh, have I ticked you off the list?'

'What?'

'What's your name, dear?'

'Er . . . Matt.'

The woman looked at her list again. 'No . . . I don't seem to have a Matt. Are you Grumpy? Or Sleepy? Or Dopey, perhaps?'

'Well, at this moment in time I'm all three.'

'Sorry?'

The joke was lost on her, though not on the younger woman.

'I'm here to pick up a large table and a clothes chest. Oh, and some yellow stockings and cross garters, whatever they are.'

The younger woman was now sitting across the room from him, her legs crossed and a script in her lap, marked up with green highlighter pen. She smiled at the misunderstanding as the kindly woman continued, 'Ah, right. Thought as much. You don't really look like an actor.' And with that she disappeared out of the Green Room.

Matt looked at the younger woman and grinned. 'My feelings have never been so hurt.'

She grinned back. 'Don't suppose you'd test me, would you? On my lines?'

'Er, yeah, OK.'

She handed him the script. 'You say everything that's not in green and I—'

Matt interrupted her. 'Oh, I'm an old hand at this. My friend's an actress. Well, sort of . . .'

'This is my first audition out of drama school.'

As she spoke, Matt noticed the soft lilt of her Scottish accent and how captivating her eyes were. Not wanting to look like a staring weirdo, he turned his attentions to the script. 'Right. Here we go. This is the wicked stepmother . . .' He cleared his throat and suddenly became very self-conscious. He tried to counter this with forced confidence, but his voice came out a tad loud. '*Hark, who's that beneath the tree? She's sleeping fast and doesn't see. SNOW WHITE WAKES UP* . . . Oh sorry, d'you want me to read the stage directions?'

'No, it's OK. *Kind lady, glad I am to find you here, For I am lost and full of fear . . .*'

The door opened again and an energetic man in red Spandex appeared. 'OK, sweetheart, d'you want to come with me?' And he swept out as flamboyantly as he'd swept in.

'Wish me luck,' she whispered to Matt as she gathered her things.

'I can't,' he whispered. 'I don't know your name.'

She smiled at him. 'It's Kate.'

'Good luck, Kate,' Matt said. 'You'll storm it.'

An hour later, Matt was unloading his cargo into the storage area of Warwick Arts Centre, helped by Hetty. Where she got her strength from Matt really didn't know.

'I met Snow White today,' he told her. 'Well, a potential Snow White anyway.'

'Ah yes, the Belgrade panto. Adam was hoping he might get seen for that.'

'Why should he? He's not a professional actor.'

'Matt, will you please give the guy a break? He's immensely talented, y'know.'

'So he keeps telling you.'

And then on cue, with burning ears, Adam came up behind them, lighting a cigarette and blowing smoke into Hetty's face. She gave a slight cough, but didn't complain.

'God, what a fucking 'mare of a day. Matt, you're a star for getting this lot. Let me know if I can ever repay the favour.'

Matt couldn't be sure but he wondered if Adam had winked at him when he said it. Adam always made him uneasy. He wished to God Hetty would fall in love with someone else, but it didn't look like that was going to happen any time soon. 'And *you*, my dear, are a fucking angel. I swear to God, Matt, she keeps me sane, this woman does.' And the next thing, Adam was looking into Hetty's eyes before kissing her full on the lips. Matt looked away. Not because he was embarrassed by the kiss, but because he couldn't bear to see Hetty so vulnerable and gullible.

'Right, you can manage the rest, can't you?' he said. 'I better get this bus back to the Union.'

'Cheers, mate,' Adam called out to him as Matt headed for the driver's door. Adam and Hetty were standing together now, his arm louchely draped over her shoulder. 'By the way, you're invited to the after-show party on the last night. It's in Dom's house in Earlsdon. Gonna be major.'

'Maybe.' Matt started the engine, crunching the gears inelegantly into place and giving the appearance of being flustered. Which he wasn't. Just overly keen to get away from this creep.

The minibus kangaroo-jumped away and Matt swore Adam was laughing at him as he watched his reflection in the rear-view mirror.

26

The lunchtime rush was over. Just a table of five finishing off their coffees, Jackie Legg nursing a pint at the bar and an American couple studying a map of the Central Highlands, making notes on a pad. Kate looked at her watch. An hour to go before the end of her shift.

'See you tomorrow!' Izzie the cook shouted as she headed out the door.

Kate waved back and started collecting the empties left by a group of businessmen. The afternoon lull had descended on the pub, shaded and cool now, a sly film of tobacco smoke snaking its way through the shafts of sunshine that crept in through the windows.

Kate sighed as she loaded the glasses into the washer. It was nearly three weeks since she'd seen Callum, sent him packing from her parents' house armed with two tins of unused paint that he could claim he'd bought from the DIY store and an antique ring left her by her grandmother.

That Callum would give to his wife.

There'd been no kiss when he left – he was in such a state. The only thing she could do was to coach him, make sure he had his story straight, that he wouldn't get caught out. 'I'm saving your sorry ass,' she'd joked. But Callum was in no mood to joke.

She hadn't expected to hear from him straight away – of course she hadn't. She knew she'd have to be patient. She'd tried filling her days as best she could, taking on extra shifts at the pub, reading *The Stage* from front to back, applying for auditions. She'd even *had* an audition, which in fact had gone quite well – a pantomime in Coventry. But if truth be told, her initial enthusiasm for being an actress had left her. And the thought of living and working in a different city from Callum was anathema to her. She had to be where he was.

The evening after it'd all happened, she'd gone into work as planned. And when Fergus asked her if she'd got the phone message, she feigned ignorance – said she'd been out with her boyfriend Jake all day, they'd had a picnic up Arthur's Seat. 'Why? What's up?'

Fergus relished the invitation to launch into the drama of the day and re-tell the tale: how Callum's wife had gone into labour, how they couldn't find him, how they'd looked everywhere! How Fergus had nearly been the birthing partner, but then Callum had turned up right at the last moment.

'Oh my God! That's such a cool story. And what did she have in the end?' Kate had been rehearsing her 'excited' look, her 'I'm-so-pleased-for-Callum' look.

'A little girl. Ailsa.'

'Sweet!'

'Ailsa Cerys Louise. Nine pounds five. Between you and me, I thought they might have named her after our mother, but hey ho, it's their baby!' Fergus was clearly a bit put out that they hadn't.

'And so where was he? Callum?' She kept her voice steady, her eyes unblinking.

'Aw, well, it was really romantic. Turns out he'd gone to Glasgow to buy an eternity ring for Belinda. As a surprise!'

'Who'd have thought!'

'I've got a photo here, have a look at the wee thing!'

Fergus produced from his back pocket a Polaroid taken just hours before by a nurse at the hospital. A little crumpled now, it'd been passed round all the regulars and anyone who showed an interest in Fergus's news. Kate was thrown. She wasn't ready for this and she focused hard on the slightly blurred image before her, blurred even more by the unwelcome tears that were welling up in her eyes. Callum's dazed face stared back at her, his arm around Belinda, baby Ailsa between them.

'Aww. Gorgeous!' was the best she could manage. And she had to keep staring, had to keep her eyes looking down as she willed the tears to stop. Thankfully, Fergus was distracted by old Stuey, who'd just walked in and wanted to hear the news. 'What's all this 'bout Cal's bairn?'

Fergus wandered over to pull him a pint, repeating his story once more and leaving Kate holding the photo, giving her time to pull herself together.

It was seeing Callum there, in that three-inch vinyl square of hazy technicolour, looking so blown apart, so shattered, that she had known for certain she was in love with him. He was hers. Without a trace of bitterness or envy, she simply understood in that moment that Callum didn't belong inside the photograph's little unit. He belonged with her. She felt remarkably calm about it. Like everything had fallen into place. She just needed to be patient.

And she was. Patient.

Every day she came to work. And every day she limited the number of times she would ask Fergus about the new baby, throwing in the odd 'How's Callum finding fatherhood again? Can he still change a nappy?' It was the only connection – despite it being a tenuous one – that she had with the man she loved. She knew she couldn't ask too many questions, that she had to ask about Belinda and Ailsa, even the boys, not just Callum. She couldn't risk raising any suspicions from Fergus.

And still she remained patient.

But still she heard nothing.

And only once did she ask when Callum might be coming back to work, straining to sound casual, as if it didn't matter to her if she never saw him behind that bar again. For more credibility she added, 'If he's not coming back, Jake's looking for bar work – just let me know.'

Fergus said he would, that he had no idea what Callum's plans were. That when him and the missus had called round to see them the day before, Callum was so besotted with the baby and Belinda, waiting on her hand and foot, he didn't dare bring up the subject of work.

Oof! It was like Kate had been punched in the stomach: *besotted with the baby and Belinda* . . . She showed nothing, just smiled and turned to serve a customer.

But when she'd woken up the next morning, and counted the days without hearing his voice, without touching him, kissing him, fucking him . . . something inside her snapped. And she knew what she had to do.

27

'Hi! I'm Kate.'

She was standing on the doorstep of 24 Sutherland Avenue, partially hidden behind a huge bouquet, defended by her captivating smile.

Belinda had opened the door with Ailsa in her arms. She'd been expecting Sue to call round and was thrown by the sight of this bright and beautiful young woman beaming at her and proffering flowers. 'Sorry, do I know—?'

'I work with Callum at the pub,' Kate interrupted. 'You must be Belinda!' Her enthusiasm was bordering on maniacal and she made a mental note to calm down. 'And *this* must be the beautiful Ailsa we've all heard so much about!'

Caught off guard by the praise for her newborn, Belinda smiled back, flattered but confused. 'Yes! She's only just woken up.'

'Awww, she's gorgeous! I'm sorry to call unannounced, it's just a couple of us clubbed together to get you these and I promised I'd drop them off on my way over to my boyfriend's.'

Belinda found her social bearings along with her manners. 'Oh, there's lovely! Look, why don't you come in? I was just about to make coffee.'

'Sounds fantastic.' Kate didn't need asking twice and was soon following Belinda into the kitchen.

Don't. Ask. About. Callum.

'I can only offer you black, I'm afraid,' Belinda said, adroitly filling the kettle with one hand.

'Just how I like it.'

'We're out of milk till Callum gets back with the shopping. He'll be sorry to have missed you.'

Kate shivered at the sound of his name. 'How's he handling fatherhood this time round? I hope he's helping with the night-time feeds!'

The boldness of the question threw Belinda slightly. 'Er . . . yes. He's doing his bit, y'know.'

A small hiatus, interrupted by Belinda: 'Those flowers are stunning, by the way!'

Kate held them out. 'Look at me hanging onto them like a fool. Do you want me to put them in water for you?'

'Tell you what, let's do a swap and I'll get a vase from upstairs.'

Kate was wrong-footed by this, and surprise registered on her face.

'Don't worry, she won't bite!' Belinda laughed as she exchanged bouquet for baby, handing Ailsa over with the ease and self-assurance afforded to a mother of three. As she did so, Kate noticed her grandmother's eternity ring adorning the third finger on Belinda's left hand.

Kate, for once, was lost for words, unable to get her head round the fact that here she was, sitting in Callum's kitchen, holding Callum's baby, whilst Callum's wife fetched a vase and left her like that alone. A lovely calm enveloped her. She could hear birds in the garden, and the distant bark of a dog. Time paused. Life was momentarily perfect.

She looked down at the velvety head and soft, plump skin of Ailsa's milky little face, her eyes bright and inquisitive, not quite focusing but staring in Kate's direction, full of trust and contentment.

'Don't you look like your daddy?' she whispered, and Ailsa gurgled back at her.

She'd never really paid much attention to babies to date. Found them a bit annoying and needy. But *this* baby, this little bundle of mini-Callum, was the most beautiful baby she'd ever seen.

The timing couldn't have been more uncanny. Or more unfortunate – depending on the perspective – because just then the back door opened and Callum stumbled in, laden with bulging carrier bags full of groceries and disposable nappies. He was watching his step and looking down.

'Sorry I took so long. Bumped into Arthur Noctor.'

'Hello,' Kate said timidly.

He couldn't process it at first. The sight before him.

Kate.

Holding his three-week-old daughter.

He stood as still as a stag in a glen, searching for words or reason, his breathing rapid and short. 'What the fuck?'

Then Belinda called from the hallway, 'Callum? Is that you?' He may as well have been tasered. But before he could answer she was with them in the kitchen, a vase in one hand, flowers in the other, unwittingly saving him from himself. 'Kate's brought us these – from all the gang at the Lamb and Flag. Aren't they gorgeous?'

From somewhere he managed to find his voice. 'Yeah. Nice.'

'He's a man of few words, is Callum.' Belinda smiled at Kate, in the way wives do to excuse their husbands' awkward social behaviour.

Kate smiled back, finding her ground now and safe in the knowledge that they were getting away with it, secretly enjoying the thrill.

'I'm makin' us a cuppa – you fancy one, love?' said Belinda. And she turned on the tap, waiting for the water to run cold before filling the blue ceramic vase.

'No, I'm goin' out again. They'd run out of wet wipes and nappy bags in Tesco.'

'This is the sort of glamorous life we lead, Kate – bet you're jealous!' Belinda laughed, unaware of the truth in her joke.

Whilst Belinda was turned away from them at the sink, Kate ventured a glance at Callum.

He didn't return it. 'Thanks for the flowers – send my best to everyone,' he said, lifting the shopping bags onto the kitchen table. 'Lind, I'll pop down to Dawsons and put this lot away when I come back.' And he made to leave.

Panicking, Kate exclaimed, 'God, is that the time? Jake's expecting me – my boyfriend,' she explained to Belinda, simultaneously conveying to Callum that she had her story straight. 'Actually, Jake's not far from Dawsons – you couldn't drop me off, could you, Callum?' She didn't wait for an answer. 'We're meant to be seeing a film at half past.'

There was no way out. Especially as Belinda simply assumed he'd do the favour. 'Come on then, Madam, let's have you back,' she said, as she lifted Ailsa out of Kate's arms.

'Yeah, OK. Car's out the back.'

'Nice to meet you, Kate, albeit briefly! And thanks again.'

'My pleasure.'

Kate buckled up the seatbelt in Callum's car, her hand shaking. They sat in silence, as *he* concentrated on reversing out of the garage and *she* concentrated on stopping herself from reaching out to touch him. As soon as they'd turned onto the road, Callum spoke.

'You're sick, d'you know that?'

'Probably.' Kate was barely audible.

'Coming to my house! Drinking coffee with my fucking wife! Jesus!' Callum was consumed with contempt.

'I'm not asking you to leave her, Callum.'

He was so taken aback by this he laughed.

They sat in silence again as he drove past Dawsons and up to the end of the high street, turning into a small car park at the edge of some common land where people walked their dogs. He pulled into a parking space and switched off the engine, shutting his eyes, exhausted.

Kate reached out and took his hand, terrified he'd reject her, but happily surprised when he simply let her hold it.

'Ailsa's beautiful.'

138

'Please don't talk about the baby.'

'Sorry.'

A few yards away from them, a man in mud-soaked trainers returned to his van with a soggy black Labrador and opened the back door. The dog refused to jump in, despite entreaties with biscuits and bits of cheese, and instead sat staring at his owner, demanding a longer walk. The man was patient, but in the end resorted to hoisting the dog up into the back of the van. He petted him before shutting the door, and the dog's sad face stared back at Callum and Kate as he was driven away.

Still Callum looked ahead of him. 'This whole thing between you and me, it's been . . . I dunno . . .'

'A complete mind-fuck?'

'Yes.'

He found the courage and turned to her. 'I wish I'd never met you.'

Defiantly, she held his gaze. 'I know.'

He should've looked away, told her to get out of the car, to never contact him again, to leave him and his family the fuck alone. But it was too late. Those hypnotic, desperate eyes were drawing him in.

She leant in to him, reaching her hand up to his face, his skin hot with nerves and desire. And then her lips were on his, shy at first, but when he inevitably responded she needed no more encouragement, kissing him ferociously, her tongue finding his and sealing their mutual passion.

A woman in well-worn wellies and a coat covered in dog hair walked past them with two eager spaniels. She let them off the lead and they bounded away in search of adventure. All three were oblivious to the desperation steaming up the windows of Callum MacGregor's car.

'My parents are away at a wedding tomorrow,' Kate whispered.

'No.'

'Just for a night. Say it's work, a conference . . . anything.'

'Kate, you know I can't.'

Her voice broke as she pleaded with him. 'Please, Callum.' And without looking at him again, she got out of the car, shut the door and disappeared.

And Callum knew that within twenty-four hours he'd be lying in bed with Kate and wondering how this whole sorry, glorious mess would end.

It wouldn't be long before he found out.

28

The Smiths blared out of the terraced house in Earlsdon where the after-show party was in full swing. Student houses were easily identifiable by the collection of bulging black bin bags outside the front door, cracked window panes, half-hung curtains and the distinct whiff of hash wafting onto the pavement, mixed with patchouli oil and economy burgers.

When Matt arrived, a couple of Goths were sitting on the small broken wall that bordered the weed-strewn garden – though it hardly did justice to the word 'garden'. A shopping trolley with three wheels still lay where it had been abandoned in Freshers' Week. What was this obsession students had with shopping trolleys, Matt wondered as he made his way through the already open door.

Inside, the airless house was throbbing with party sweat and sex potential. Dom, who'd played Cesario, was stood at the bottom of the stairs kissing a third-year English student with a shaved head.

'Alright, Dom?' Matt shouted over the music. 'You seen Hetty?'

Without breaking out of the snog, Dom pointed vaguely in the direction of the kitchen and Matt headed through, picking up an abandoned can of Woodpecker in the hall. He took a swig and immediately spat it out, realizing too late that it had been used as an ashtray.

'MATTHEW!!' Hetty screeched when she saw him. He knew

straight away she was pissed – it was the only time she didn't call him Matt.

'Got any mints?' he asked. 'Just had a mouthful of ash.'

But she ignored him, thrust a bottle of cheap wine into his hand and pulled him into the front room. 'Let's dance.'

'Whoah, no thanks, I'm sober.'

'Oh don't be such a bore.' Hetty wasn't taking no for an answer and threw herself into her own particular style of dancing. Matt tried to blot out his embarrassment by downing the wine as fast as possible, soon realizing that nobody was watching him anyway – they were all engrossed in their own party head space.

'So what did you think?' Hetty shouted.

'You were amazing!' he laughed. 'Really . . . interesting.'

'Oh, thanks Matty. I LO-O-O-VED doing it.' She'd been really quite terrible in the play, not that he'd ever tell her. 'And what about Adam? Wasn't he captivating?' she yelled, dewy-eyed.

'Yep. Captivating.' And he finished off the wine, welcoming the hit he needed to get through this party he hadn't wanted to come to, full of people he didn't know.

He started doing a few dance moves of his own, going with the flow and singing along to Dexys Midnight Runners. '*Come on Eileen, oh I swear, at this moment you mean everything!*'

Half an hour later, he was sitting on an upturned bin in the tiny backyard, catching his breath and cooling down. A few feet away, Hetty was sharing a spliff with a couple of trendy girls, Mel and Zukie, from the cast.

'I know you won't believe it,' Hetty slurred, 'but I've never ever never even tried any drugs. The hardest thing I've ever taken is Benylin.'

Zukie, already pretty mashed, found this hysterical, whilst Mel just stared, concentrating hard.

'Though to be fair to me, it *wasn't* the one that makes you drowsy, so . . .'

Zukie laughed all the harder and Matt joined in. 'You're priceless,

Het!' He watched his friend drag on the joint like a teenager trying a cigarette for the first time.

The smoke tripped itself up in her throat and she spluttered, 'That is *sooooo* good.'

'Liar!' Matt laughed and held his hand out for a toke.

The effect on Hetty was instantaneous. 'You know what's funny about your name, Matt, is that it's "Mat". Like a bathroom mat. Or a place mat.'

'I'm gonna wet myself!' Zukie squealed, and it really looked like she meant it.

Matt was no stranger to smoking dope. He loved it occasionally, loved its instant chilling-out and perspective-changing properties. He inhaled the coarse burnt weed mixed with cheap loose tobacco, held his breath and waited for the hit. As he breathed out, he closed his eyes and enjoyed that feeling of transcendence, the assurance that everything was just as it should be and more.

But his little zone of calm was soon disrupted by the sound of shouting coming from inside the house. 'No, come on, SAY IT!' Adam was in the middle of a row with Dom over what appeared to be 'artistic differences'. A few party-goers had squeezed into the tiny kitchen to watch and a couple of earnest-looking girls were trying to calm things down. 'Say it to my fucking face, don't hide behind Liesl.'

'OK, you're a fraud, alright? A fucked-up little fake who thinks he's God's gift to theatre, lording it round the place like you're Kenneth fuckin' Branagh. Well you're not, OK?'

A few muffled gasps filled the room, a mixture of relish and shock that someone was daring to stand up to the great Adam Latimer.

'You're a poxy drama student with an ego the size of Manchester. My grandmother can act better than you. And she's been dead five years.'

People were sniggering now, because the whole thing was ludicrous. And for a moment, Adam seemed to think so too, looking round at his audience and allowing himself a small chuckle. He began turning away, and the fight seemed to be over more quickly than it'd started, until SMASH! Adam's punch came from nowhere, catching Dom firmly on the left side of his jaw and sending him crashing into the sink. The over-stacked draining board shuddered under his weight, sending mismatched crockery crashing to the floor. The girls screamed and the boys squared up like bouncers in a nightclub, placing themselves between Dom and Adam in case more was to follow. It wasn't.

'You're a prick.' Adam delivered his parting shot with utter contempt, before pushing past a huddle of onlookers in the kitchen doorway and making his dramatic exit.

Matt, now stoned, found the whole thing hysterical. But Hetty was beside herself, calling after Adam, desperate to follow him, struggling to get through the sea of people blocking her way.

Siobhan, the English student with the shaved head, was checking Dom was OK. As Hetty pushed past her, Siobhan turned on her. 'Call yourself a pacifist, and you're letting that little Hitler sleep in your bed every night? You should be ashamed.'

Hetty ignored her, partly because she didn't understand what she meant and partly because she was determined to get out of that house and find Adam. Matt, who was close behind, still clutching the spliff, was suddenly mesmerized by Siobhan's shaved head. So much so, he had to stop and stare at it.

Siobhan was thrown. 'What?'

Matt reached up and touched the warm, stubbled skin of her scalp.

'Get off, you weirdo!' Siobhan pushed his hand away.

Matt drew on the spliff and said, 'You feel like a baked potato.' It sounded insulting, but it wasn't meant to be.

'Come on! We'll lose him!' Hetty was pulling Matt's arm, unwittingly rescuing him from Siobhan, who called him a tosser as he left the party, throwing an empty beer can in his wake.

They found Adam at the bus stop, waiting for the Number 12. He barely spoke all the way back to campus. Hetty, on the other hand, was starving and all she could talk about was food. When they arrived at Benfield Hall, she headed straight for the kitchen, the munchies chasing manners out the window as she scoured cupboards and tins for something to sate her hunger, without a care for whose supply she was plundering, and making off with two boxes of French Fancies secretly stashed away by Sarah the Goth.

Matt, meanwhile, had let himself into his room without switching on the light and lain on the bed. His head was spinning – not unpleasantly – and the moonlight crept through his window, casting vast and Gothic shadows on the walls.

He must have fallen asleep for a couple of hours, although it felt like a few minutes, because when he woke up, the moon was no longer spying on him and the room was dark.

It took a good five seconds for him to register that Adam was sitting on the end of his bed. Still a bit stoned, he didn't feel shocked to see him. 'Where's Het?' he mumbled.

Adam stared at the floor. 'I think she ate eleven French Fancies. She puked them all over the bed.'

'Oh fuck.' Matt laughed and Adam looked up.

'Can I sleep here? Her room stinks.'

'Er, no.' Matt was clear-headed enough to know that Adam Latimer wasn't someone he'd ever want as a room-mate – even for one night.

'Oh come on, Matt, I've had a crap evening, I just need some shut-eye.'

And for reasons he'd later search for and never discover, Matt found himself saying, 'OK. But if you start snoring, you can piss off.'

Matt turned to face the wall and go back to sleep, feeling slightly guilty that he wasn't checking on Hetty after her French Fancy binge and deciding she was probably alright.

He heard the swish of denim and cotton as Adam pulled off his jeans and T-shirt and dropped them to the floor. And he felt the unfamiliar warmth of a male body next to his as Adam climbed into the bed. His head still murky from the weed, he convinced himself that everything was fine, that Adam just needed somewhere to sleep and Matt's bed was the only place on offer. They lay like that for several minutes, Matt pretending to sleep, Adam seemingly trying to.

And then, in the middle-of-the-night silence, Adam whispered, 'You really don't like me, do you, Matt?'

At first Matt ignored him – *Best policy*, he thought, *don't need to get into some heavy discussion – not at this hour.* But there was something uncomfortably vulnerable about the way Adam had said it, something uncharacteristically gentle from this tough man in Hetty's life. Matt should've followed his instincts and kept quiet, but his instincts were warped from too much spliff and, without moving, he said, 'No. No, I don't like you.'

The moments that followed were charged with uncertainty, unreadable and packed with risk. 'But do you like me doing *this*?' Adam said as he reached his hand around and inside Matt's boxers. Adam's delight matched Matt's horror on discovering he was rock hard to his touch.

Matt remained silent, his breathing accelerated as repulsion and desire simultaneously surged through his body.

'I think you do.'

Matt knew without even looking round that Adam was smiling his sardonic, triumphant smile, and he wanted to punch him. But not as much as he wanted him to carry on doing what he was doing . . .

Matt had never kissed a man before; never experienced the sensation of hot male skin, male lips pressed against his own, more confident and determined than any girl he'd ever kissed, harsher, muscular, powerful. And he couldn't believe this was happening; couldn't believe he wasn't stopping it in its tracks. It was as if he stood a short distance away watching it happen to someone else, voyeuristically observing one man seduce another: the seduced yielding, uncomplaining and wanting more. He knew how ridiculous it would sound, but he felt he had to say it: 'I'm not gay.'

Adam was kneeling astride him now and grinning, breathless. 'Nor am I.'

When Matt woke up the next morning, Adam had gone. The relief was overwhelming; he didn't know what he'd have done if he'd had to face him in daylight. He lay still, eyes open, not daring to move for fear of starting the day: the first day after his first-ever sexual encounter with a guy. He couldn't allow himself to articulate the events that had taken place in this tiny rectangle of a bedroom. He wanted to erase it all – not because he was disgusted at having had sex with a man – though admittedly he was surprised – just disgusted that that man was Adam – someone for whom he felt no respect or affection or warmth.

He steeled himself and got out of bed, turning on the taps of his utilitarian sink so hard the water bounced out and crashed onto the thin orange carpet tiles. He scooped some from the basin into his hands and soaked his face, over and over, cold, clean freshness erasing the memory, washing away the guilt. He stared back at his reflection in the mirror and was certain of two things: one, what happened last night would never happen again, and two, the sex with Adam was the most erotic he would ever have in his life.

Both of these convictions would turn out to be untrue.

29

'I've been on a bloody train before, Callum. I know what I'm doing!'

Belinda laughed and carried on packing three lots of kids' clothes into a holdall. She was leaving for Wales that afternoon with Ben, Cory and the baby.

'Yeah, but you've never done the journey on your own. With three of them, for God's sake! Look, maybe I should come.' It was a sly bit of reverse psychology on his part, because *he* knew *Belinda* knew how important the upcoming inspection was. Not just for the sake of the school, but for Callum's career. He was in line for promotion and a trip to Belinda's parents' wasn't about to scupper his chances. At least, that's what she'd told him, and he had no reason not to believe that's what she thought.

'Callum, how many times . . . ?'

'OK, so wait till the inspection is over. And then we'll *all* go.' He knew this would fall on deaf ears too.

She stopped packing and looked at him incredulously. 'You seriously think I'd do that to my dad? Come on now.'

Belinda's father had suffered a stroke a month before Ailsa was born. He was doing OK, but was desperate to meet his new and only granddaughter. There was an unspoken fear within the family that Gareth Lewis wasn't long for this world, and whether it was an overreaction or not, Belinda had sworn she'd be on that train heading south as soon as she was back on her post-birth feet.

But this wasn't the only reason she was going to Wales. Despite her outward smile, inside she felt sick with dread. Because she couldn't put it off any longer. She had to find out. And this was the only way . . .

It was Callum's younger cousin, Angela, who'd slipped up. Inadvertently, of course. The whole family had gathered to celebrate Grannie MacGregor's ninetieth birthday. Fergus had cordoned off the restaurant in the pub and the place was buzzing with long-time-no-sees and don't-you-look-wells. They were a close-knit family, the MacGregors, and genuinely enjoyed each other's company.

Having had a few glasses of bubbly, Angela was particularly demonstrative with her familial affection that afternoon. She loved Belinda's Welsh accent, but more than that, she loved Belinda and saw her as something of a role model. 'The thing about you, hen,' she was saying, 'is how you still keep things, y'know, *alive*. In the old marriage department. You're so damn sexy, for one thing!'

Belinda, who was breastfeeding Ailsa, was feeling far from sexy at the time, Ailsa's little gums sucking so hard it made Belinda's nipples scream out at her in agony.

'And like, even after three babies, you've still got it goin' on, haven't you?' Angela's breath, metallic from champagne, was too close for comfort as she leant into Belinda and whispered, 'But I know your little secret. To a healthy marriage.'

'That'll be my roast dinners?'

'Ha ha, if that's what you want to call it . . . No, you were *seen*.'

'What?'

'Yesterday at the cinema out at Fellgate. My friend Gilly was there and she saw you two kissing in the back row. She knows Callum from the gym – said even at a distance she'd recognize him. She was going to shout hello but he looked otherwise . . . well . . . occupied. Honestly, you two, ten years married and still as in love as ever, what are you like!'

Belinda calmly stopped feeding Ailsa, pulled down her top and turned to Angela, smiling. 'We didn't go the cinema yesterday.'

Angela blustered. 'Oh! Oh, right.' She struggled for words as she watched Belinda deftly put Ailsa over her shoulder, patting her back to alleviate her post-feed hiccups. 'Well, it can't have been Callum then!'

'No. It can't have been Callum,' Belinda repeated, still smiling.

'I mean she's a dizzy mare, is Gilly, and her eyesight is awful. And it was dark.'

'Could you pass me the Moses basket?' Belinda asked, her voice revealing nothing of the desolation building up inside her. 'I need to get this one home.'

And she put the baby in her crib, got up and left the party. It was twenty minutes before Callum realized she'd gone.

Belinda wouldn't have thought twice about Angela's case of mistaken identity, were it not for the fact that her suspicions had already been raised: there'd been a couple of boys' nights out recently when Callum hadn't quite accounted for his whereabouts. And then there'd been the regular late-night returns after working his shifts at the pub, where he'd said there'd been a lock-in. But when on one of these occasions Belinda had found the courage to check with Fergus whether this was true – 'Bit of a late one last night, was it, Ferg?' – her stomach had churned when her brother-in-law had answered, 'No, not particularly – pretty quiet, in fact.' Where she found the ability to shrug it off and smile, she never knew.

When Callum had returned from the party, she didn't mention her conversation with Angela. She wasn't strong enough to find out the truth just yet. She wanted to bide her time, to give him even more benefit of the doubt, until she found concrete evidence one way or another. So much for the woman who claimed zero toler-ance when it came to infidelity. The truth was, she'd rather remain in denial than deal with the crippling thought of Callum having an affair.

He took her to Edinburgh Waverley station, seeing her onto the train and settling his brood in safely for their trip. They'd booked table seats so that Cory and Ben could do their colouring-in and

Belinda would have enough space to spread out her collection of treat-filled Tupperware boxes, cold drinks and games to entertain them all for the eight-hour journey ahead.

Callum stood in the carriage and despaired. 'How you gonna manage if you need the loo?'

'I'll ask the train manager to mind them.'

'And what about when Ailsa needs changing?'

'Callum, will you stop fussing? It's all sorted. Honestly, you're worse than my mother!'

'Yeah, well I should be coming with you. I should be driving you there.'

'But you're not. So.'

A flicker of sorrow made her catch her breath before she smiled at him and wrapped her arms around him, ignoring the passengers pushing past to their seats and the boys making faces at the guard on the platform.

'Please take care of yourself, Bel,' Callum whispered, unashamedly displaying public affection.

'You sure I shouldn't be saying that to you?'

And he looked at her, confused. 'What?'

But before he had time to wonder further why she'd said it, she pulled herself out of the hug and laughed. 'You've gotta do your own cooking for five days, for God's sake. That lasagne you made last week should've carried a government health warning! Now bugger off before the train starts moving.'

And on cue, the train manager announced in very bored tones that the 14.30 Edinburgh to Bristol was about to depart, and would anyone not intending to travel please leave the train immediately.

Callum stood on the platform and watched the InterCity 125 snake its way out of the station. He didn't stop waving, even though he could no longer see his boys or his baby or his wife, until the train had rounded the bend and gone.

Inside the carriage, Belinda watched as the familiar figure of her husband grew smaller and smaller and finally disappeared from view. She thought back to their courting days – only ten years ago, but it felt so much longer – when she'd make the long journey up to Edinburgh on a Friday night, only to leave again on the Sunday. Shockingly in love, every second they could spend together they would grab and relish. Oh, those precious, beautiful weekends. She nervously turned the eternity ring around on her finger, reassuring herself it was still there, subconsciously questioning the existence of the love it represented.

Don't break it, Callum.

'Mummy, are you crying?' Ben asked her, rousing her from her reverie.

'No, babes.' She smiled, discreetly wiping away an escaping tear. 'Now, who's for a game of Connect Four?'

30

Their time together was intricately planned. Callum had gone to school after dropping Belinda and the kids off at the station, before launching himself into final preparations for the inspection the following week.

Nobody could have faulted him on the work he'd done. His own classroom was immaculate, even his store-room had been spring-cleaned and sorted, shelves labelled and dusted, junk thrown out – the fruits of a few late nights' cleaning, long after the end-of-day bell had rung. He had all his termly figures and pupil assessment reports up to date, and his extra-curricular activities were a shining example of how after-school clubs should be run.

He'd like to put his zeal down to enthusiasm for his job, but he knew deep down he was paving the way, getting the work done so that he could maximize his spare time with Kate. They'd arranged that she would come to his house after dark, and stay holed up there for the weekend. He knew that what he was doing was reprehensible, but he also knew he was too far in to turn back.

Three whole days together. The sex was relentless. Something had shifted within them both. Maybe it was because their time together wasn't so limited – not just a stolen hour after work or a rare weekend morning. Now they could fall asleep, wake up, have breakfast and lunch together, and to all intents and purposes pretend they were a real couple. For three days, at least. This wasn't just a game or a summer fling any more; they both knew they were in trouble and this was getting out of control.

It was the Sunday evening. Callum had school in the morning, so they'd planned that Kate would leave around two a.m., when neighbours' curtains were unlikely to twitch. Kate had cooked them a meal: mussels in white-wine sauce with freshly baked bread, followed by risotto. She'd wanted to impress – stupid really, but she wanted him to know she was so much more than just good in bed, that she was proper girlfriend material. No – who was she trying to kid? – that she was proper *wife* material, and, more than that, proper *mother-to-his-children* material.

They were sitting at the heavy pine dining table Callum and Belinda had bought just after they'd moved in five years previously. Belinda had been heavily pregnant with Ben, so Callum wouldn't let her so much as push it an inch. Instead, she was in charge of telling him where the table should go. It had taken four attempts, and by the time they'd finally decided on the right place, they were both in stitches. Callum laughingly accused Belinda of being a control freak, winding him up by continually changing her mind. After years of use, the table bore hallmarks of an established family life: faded felt-tip from the children's colourings-in, stubborn red-wine stains from numerous Sunday lunches, occasional ink blots from the evenings Callum had sat marking homework. And now he was eating dinner at it. With his lover.

'That was outstanding.' Callum pushed his plate away, grinning, and held his hand out for Kate to come sit on his lap. She did so, giggling at the thought of herself as some medieval serving wench. 'Why, thank you, kind sir!' she drawled, in a bad West Country accent. 'See! I told you I'm so much more than a good shag.'

'You're so common,' he joked and she laughed.

But her smile faded and she looked at him, brushing aside the hair that had fallen forward over his eyes. 'I got offered that pantomime, by the way,' she said unenthusiastically.

'Sweetheart, that's brilliant! Why didn't you say?'

''Cos I'm gonna turn it down. I can't move away from here, Callum. Away from you.'

'Kate . . .'

'I hate how much I love you. I feel like I'm in a permanent state of car crash. If someone offered me a single wish, I wouldn't give a toss about world peace – it would be to never have met you.'

She put her head against his and neither of them spoke, listening to the November rain lashing angrily against the window, both lost in painful thought. He put his hand up to her face and ran his fingers along the line of her cheek and her jaw. How she adored his hands. The reassurance of them, the weight of them, so much bigger than hers, so confident, so capable those fingers . . . inside her . . . touching her in ways no one else had ever done . . . oh God.

'What are we going to do?' he said, more to himself than her.

'I know what we *should* do . . .'

'Kate, don't.'

'We should end it, right now, and I *should* move away, go abroad even, meet someone, marry them, have their babies and ERASE you from my head!' She got up from his lap, angry at their hopeless situation, unable to contain her frustration. 'Nobody – *nobody!* – will ever come close to what you are to me. You know that, don't you? Meeting you has fucked up the rest of my life.' The tears came and she tried to swallow them down with more wine, drinking straight from the bottle on the table. 'I haven't told *anyone*, Callum. D'you realize what that's like?'

'Well, of course I do – I'm in the same boat, aren't I?' He was growing uneasy, sensing her rising anger.

'Living with this secret. Lying to my friends, to my parents – never being able to tell them I'm in love. I think my mother thinks I'm gay! And no. No, you are not in the same fucking boat as me, because *you*'ve got it all. You've got your perfect wife and your perfect children – and you've still got *me*, hanging on like the pathetic little bitch that I am, because *you* know and *I* know that I can never give you up. What's it like, Callum?! Having it ALL!?'

'Alright, keep your voice down, will you? These walls are paper thin.'

'I don't give a fuck.' She was weeping now. It had come from nowhere, this rage, this fury at their situation, as if only tonight she'd been made aware of the prison in which she was held – a prison of her own making, true, but a prison nonetheless. She was trapped.

'You're right, we're not in the same boat, because I've got so much more to lose than you. What d'you think it's like, Kate? Knowing what I'm doing, the guilt that's with me every waking minute. *You* don't have that guilt, because *you* don't have a family, so shut the fuck up with your sob stories and how badly off you are – you can walk away any time you like . . .'

This was a pattern between him and Kate – he'd seen it before. He put it down to the passion they shared, the way they could be idyllic and bright one minute and within thirty seconds at each other's throats. He despised himself for making comparisons, but this never happened with Belinda.

Overcome by the realization that this might be their last night together for a while, he swallowed his pride, got up and went to her, encircling her with his rugby player's arms, kissing the top of her head and soothing her. 'Hey, come on, ssshhh . . . let's not fight.'

They stood like that for a while, in the kitchen that belonged to a different world, a different family, Kate gently sobbing, Callum inhaling the scent of her hair. Until she found the courage to break away and, without looking up at him, said calmly, 'I promised myself I'd never ask you this . . .'

'Kate . . .' He knew exactly what was coming.

'. . . but I have to, Callum, because I swear, I cannot go on like this. It's destroying me.' And then she looked up at him, daring him to look away as she made the ultimate request. Barely whispering, her voice shook with tears.

'Will you leave her for me?'

31

She had no luggage, just her purse and a thin mac, defenceless against the torrents of Scottish rain as she stood waiting in the queue for a taxi. She hadn't been thinking when she left Wales, hadn't planned ahead. Hadn't even brought an umbrella. But getting wet was the least of her worries right now.

After waiting fifteen minutes, it was eventually her turn. She climbed into the back of the cab. 'Twenty-four Sutherland Avenue, please. In Portobello.' It was a horrible night and neither she nor the driver were in the mood for chat. Accompanied by the frantic squeaks of the windscreen wipers as they fought a losing battle, Belinda sat back and looked out at the black, wet night, thinking about when they'd first met.

It hadn't been love at first sight. That was the one thing Belinda and Callum had always agreed on. A rugby international – St David's Day 1975, Scotland versus Wales. And the most chaotic match in Murrayfield's history. The ground was saturated with supporters, bulging at the fences. Both sides had the Triple Crown in their sights so the atmosphere was more than just a bit tense. Belinda had come up from Wales on a coach with her local club, her dad by her side. She'd lost count of how many rugby games she'd been to with him. And unlike a lot of women who went to internationals, she was a genuine fan of the game. Not just there to get boozed up and cop off with a local. She knew her stuff. Learnt it all from her old man, who'd been quite a star in his time – a couple of seasons for Llanelli and a cap for Wales Under 21s. Belinda was the daughter of rugby royalty.

And there she stood, in her angry red Welsh jersey, no make-up and clutching her can of cider, screeching at the referee, at the teams, at anyone who'd listen. The injustice! The blatantly wrong decisions! The cheating Scots! 'Knock on, knock on!' Callum hadn't noticed her, nor she him. They were too busy supporting their teams. He was in the row behind, kilted and bevvied up, surrounded by his kilted and bevvied-up mates. It was a ten-all draw and they were well into injury time. But when Ian McGeechan finally scored the defining drop goal, Scotland exploded in glory and the souls of the entire Welsh nation – or at least the thirty thousand of them at Murrayfield that day – simply gave up the ghost and died. The Scots went crazy. Spontaneous bursts of 'Flower of Scotland' starting up all round, whilst the defeated Welsh woefully wept. Belinda was silent, turned to her heartbroken dad and shook her head. You'd swear they'd just lost a relative.

Callum, on the other hand, was buoyed up by the Scottish win and a few pints inside him. He noticed her despair and said, 'Hey, come on, Taffy, it's only a game!'

She stared at him for a moment. Opened her mouth to speak, then thought better of it. Then opened her mouth to speak again. Then thought better of it. Callum was thrown by her speechlessness, and not knowing what to say, blurted out, 'You look like a goldfish when you do that.'

He was trying to defuse the situation, not entertain his mates, but they made things worse by laughing and cheering him on as Belinda continued to stare. And then out it came, the fiery Welsh spirit he'd long since grown to adore.

'And *you*, good boy, look like a *wanker* when I do *this*!' And with that, she lifted up his kilt and flashed his boxers to the world. Which, as Belinda had since pointed out many, many times, he shouldn't strictly have been wearing if he was a true Scotsman.

'Hey! What you doin'!' he yelled, as she started pouring cider into his sporran. 'Fuck's sake!' It was one of the very few times in his life that Callum actually went red, and with his mates laughing at him as he fumbled with his soggy kilt and fading dignity, he couldn't have been gladder to see the back of Belinda Lewis weaving her way through the stand. So no, it wasn't love at first sight.

But later that night, Belinda was sat in a pub in Rose Street, putting the world, or at least the world of rugby, to rights. Her dad long gone to the B&B, Belinda was left with a few die-hards from the club – mainly men old enough to be her granddad – and a couple of Scots who'd latched on for the craic. 'He shouldn't have allowed that second penalty.' Her voice was croaky now. She was repeating what she'd been saying all day. But no one had the energy to join in any more. The sorrow of Wales's loss and the hours of drinking were taking their toll.

'Yeah alright, I agree with you!' came a Scottish voice from the bar. It was Callum, not long stumbled into the pub with fewer of his bevvied-up friends in tow.

'Ah look, it's the wee goldfish Taffy lass!'

'Ignore 'em,' Callum said. 'They're sore winners.'

Belinda was too sad and tired to fight back. 'Sorry about earlier, with your kilt an' that. It was just bad timing . . . We should've won, y'know.'

He actually found himself feeling sorry for her. And also found himself staring at her extraordinarily long eyelashes.

'Let me buy you a drink to commiserate.'

'Nah. Sick of drinking, I am.' And she picked up her denim jacket from the back of her chair and put it on, ready to leave.

'Oh! Right.' He felt strangely disappointed – he wasn't used to getting the brush-off. With the arrogance of youth on his side, at twenty-eight he thought of himself as pretty good with women.

'I could murder some chips, mind.'

Something about the way she said it made him see she wasn't like any other girl he'd ever met, especially on an international day . . . No agenda, she just wanted some chips.

'But just to be clear, you're not gonna shag me. Chips is chips, that's all, good boy.'

Callum opened the door for her and wondered how she'd managed to read his mind.

True to her word, she didn't let him shag her. Or even kiss her. Not that night anyhow. Though she did let him have her address and phone number, telling him that if he really was that keen he'd have to prove it. Which he did. Because twenty-seven phone calls, fourteen letters, two postcards and three months later, she agreed to visit him in Edinburgh.

Belinda blamed it on the Scottish air and the walk up Arthur's Seat; *Callum* blamed it on his irresistible seduction technique – either way, she finally gave in and had sex with him, announcing at the end, 'Well, that was certainly worth the wait!'

'Yep!'

She'd turned to him in all seriousness, unexpectedly welling up. 'No really, Cal, it was. You've got me now, babes.'

And he kissed her extraordinarily long and tear-laden lashes, and said, 'About fucking time.'

When Belinda fell in love with Callum, she fell in love with Scotland too. And a year later she was moving into his flat in Portobello, twenty minutes' drive from Edinburgh city centre, the new Mrs Callum MacGregor.

She watched the taxi pull away, its tyres sending rain hurtling in a perfect arc, from the gutter onto the pavement. She turned to face the house, but despite the rain, she couldn't bring herself to walk up to the door. Because she couldn't bring herself to discover what was on the other side of it.

She thought about what she'd do if she was wrong. If she put her key in the lock and went in to discover him with a Chinese take-away on his lap, watching re-runs of the Grand Prix, or trying to iron his own shirt for school tomorrow. She laughed at the image and then fought back tears as she prayed that that's what she *would* see. She knew what she'd say to him if she found him there alone – 'Surprise! My parents have got the kids for a couple of days, thought I'd come back so we could spend some time together . . . How long is it since it was just you and me, Callum?' And maybe she *was* wrong. Maybe this was all part of some post-natal paranoia.

The lights were on in the front room. She could turn around now and go back, never find out. But she was wet through and cold and exhausted and shaking. And she just needed to know.

She let herself in quietly. There was music coming from the kitchen: Sade was singing 'Smooth Operator' and the comforting smell of baked bread filled the hallway, welcoming her back into her own home.

Except Callum had never baked bread in his life.

Her feet left sodden footprints on the carpet as she made her way to the kitchen, her heart pounding louder than the music. The door was slightly ajar and she could see him sitting with his back to her, lost in thought. He was alone.

He was alone!

She felt dizzy with relief. And she wanted to sob with joy and go to him, smother him in kisses, tell him she'd been a stupid arse but everything was fine now and couldn't they have an early night seeing as the kids were safe at her mum's—

And just as she was about to call out his name, he turned and smiled.

But it wasn't Belinda he was smiling at.

32

At first, Kate didn't recognize her. She'd lost weight since the only time they'd met, just three weeks after Ailsa was born. And the rain-soaked mac she was wearing clung mercilessly to her shivering limbs, making her all the more unrecognizable, wet hair framing her horrified face. Nobody spoke. Sade still sang in the background.

'This is no sad and sorry dream . . .

Your love is real.'

Calmly, and with perfect aim, Belinda picked up the near-empty bottle of wine within arm's reach and hurled it at the music centre, silencing the cruel lyrics that seeped out of the speakers. She stared at Kate, defying her to look away. Kate struggled, but held her gaze.

The silence was painful. Only the rain outside smashing against the windows filled the excruciating void.

'How long?'

'Bel—'

'Since before Ailsa or after?'

'Sit down. You're soaking. Let's just . . . stay calm.'

But Belinda was beyond calm. She'd found an indescribable strength inside her that, had she been required to, would have made lifting a small car very easy.

Callum stepped towards her, and only then did she turn to look at him.

'DON'T . . .' She hissed like an angry cat, spitting the words out. 'Even. Think. About touching me.'

Kate knew that she should go, but she also knew this was crunch time. This was when it would all get real. No more hiding, no more meeting in secret, this was when Callum and she would finally get to be the couple she always knew in her heart they should be. This was the start of it. And no matter how awful this next bit felt, it *was* going to happen.

'Since the summer. When Kate started working at the pub.' There was no point in lying, Callum thought.

Belinda nodded at this, as if it was part of the jigsaw in her head that she was frantically piecing together. *You start with the corners*, she thought. *And then the edges.* She fought back the urge to be sick.

'Jesus, you came here before! When Ailsa was born. You brought me flowers! I made you coffee!' And as the jigsaw began revealing its picture, Belinda gained more clarity. Looking out of the window at the black and rain-sodden night, she said quietly, 'Get out of my house.'

Kate didn't move. Surprised, and thrown, Belinda turned and said it again. 'I said, *get out of my house.*'

Kate looked Belinda straight in the eye, her turn to be strong now. 'No.'

'Kate . . .' Callum could see where this was going, but it was too late – the furnace flared, and with a bestial roar from within her, Belinda launched at the woman threatening to steal her husband and shatter her life, and pushed her to the floor, hitting her wildly, screaming, weeping, raging.

Callum pulled her away and forced his arms around her, partly to protect Kate and partly to comfort Belinda. Helpless within the circle of his familiar embrace, Belinda's fight drained away from her and she stood there sobbing, letting him rock her gently in his arms.

'Tell her, Callum.'

'Shut up, Kate.'

'Tell her what you just told me. He's leaving you, Belinda. I'm sorry, but you were going to—'

But Callum didn't let her finish. 'I said shut up. And go.'

33

New Year's Eve, and the cast of *Snow White* had piled into the Dog and Duck, long-time haunt of anyone working at the Belgrade Theatre. Barney Bennett, aka Dame Lose-it-All, was ordering a round of drinks at the busy bar. The atmosphere was buoyant and festive: they'd had a full house that night and, despite there being a matinee the following afternoon, the cast were all set to get hammered. Except Kate. Who stood a little way off from the rest of them, preferring instead the company of old Mick the stage hand, who was only staying for one because he wanted to get back home to watch Big Ben and the fireworks on the telly with his wife.

'I don't blame you,' said Kate. 'It's always been overrated, New Year's Eve.'

'Well, I'm surprised to hear you say that, being Scottish. You near as dammit invented Hogmanay, bab!'

Barney Bennett handed Kate her orange juice. 'You sure you don't want a little vodka in there, you boring old moo?' he said, smiling.

'No, thanks. Don't think I could handle the matinee with a hangover. Cheers!'

'Ah, see! You can tell it's her first job – but she'll learn, she'll learn!' Barney joked with the rest of the cast.

Kate smiled. She'd known them all for just two weeks and they were a nice bunch. But all she really wanted to do was sleep. She planned on staying for one drink like Mick, then heading back to her digs – a lovely attic room at the top of a family home in Canley. They were away skiing at the moment, so Kate had the house to herself. She smiled at the irony of this – how the old Kate would have seen this as a brilliant excuse for a party, would've invited the whole cast back for an all-nighter and worried about the carnage the next morning. But things were different now. Things were sadder. Kate was a different person from the party girl she'd been just a few months earlier.

A week after the night at his house when it all came crashing down, she'd called him at work.

To tell him the news.

At first he wouldn't take the call – the school secretary kept palming her off with flimsy excuses. But Kate persisted every day for five days, until eventually he came to the phone during his lunch hour. The call lasted just over a minute. She knew there'd be people around him, that he wouldn't be able to talk freely, but she had no choice.

'I'm pregnant.'

Silence.

'Callum, did you hear me?'

'Yes.' And then she heard him address the secretary, 'Irene, can you give me a moment, please? It's a personal matter.' In the background she heard the door shut and Callum gave a deep sigh.

'I'm having an abortion. Tomorrow,' Kate said, willing her voice not to crack. 'There's a place in London. It's all arranged.'

'Whoah, hang on a minute . . . you can't just throw this at me!' His distress was palpable and she wished more than anything that she could hold him now, inhale the smell of him, kiss his hair.

'I'm sorry, Callum. I know this is difficult for you, but there's nothing more to discuss. I'm not really sure why I'm even telling you . . .'

'Nor am I. You've obviously made the decision.'

This made her angry. 'You got a better solution then?'

He sighed again. 'No. No, of course . . . I just . . . wish things were different, that's all.' And hearing this sliver of tenderness in his voice made her inwardly collapse. 'Yes. So do I.' She steadied her voice before finally saying, 'Goodbye, Callum. I won't contact you again.' And as she began replacing the receiver she heard his voice again, weak and muted. 'Kate?'

'Yes?' She didn't know what she was hoping he would say, but she would cling onto any scrap of hope he might chuck at her right now.

'Look after yourself, won't you?'

She paused, incapable of finding any more words, and then hung up, resting her forehead on the coin box before weeping herself hoarse. Her prediction had come true. Her heart had broken.

She brushed aside a tear that had annoyingly escaped as she remembered the conversation from over a month ago. And she wondered what he was doing tonight. If he was with *her*. Whether Belinda had forgiven him and taken him back. Or whether their marriage was irreversibly destroyed. She surprised herself by wanting it *not* to be. Seemed a waste to have all three of them suffer. She also figured if Callum and Belinda *had* split up, then surely he'd have come looking for her? He knew where she was. If he'd wanted to, he could've tracked her down and they could've got together after all. OK, so it'd be difficult at first – dealing with custody and living arrangements – but they'd have worked something out eventually. She didn't dare to hope. She hated it when she hoped. Hope was the worst and most debilitating emotion to come out of this mess. She didn't want to hope. She wanted to accept and move on. She wanted to stop wondering, she wanted to forget about the man who'd enslaved her heart and smashed it to pieces. What was the saying? – 'Pain is inevitable, suffering is optional' – OK, well she wanted to stop suffering now. New Year. New life. And the steely determination she'd begun cultivating these past few weeks was upon her again, slamming the door shut on any hint of tenderness or vulnerability.

She'd surprised herself with her own efficiency in terms of *what to do next.* The most important thing was not to tell anyone what had happened. To keep everything on a need-to-know basis. She'd been offered a three-month contract with the BBC radio drama company, starting a week after the panto finished. It couldn't have been more ideal, given the circumstances. She loved radio. She could lose herself in it all and still maintain a level of order in her life. Routine and security – that's what she needed right now. She'd stay with her friend Josie at a knock-down rent in her Brixton flat, then take herself off to Cornwall for six months in April, where her mate Sam had offered her a job in his gift shop for the summer season and the tiny flat upstairs. Yes. It was all mapped out. Routine and security. Routine and security. Until she was through the pain and Callum became nothing more than a big mistake in her sad and sorry past.

'Blimey, you look like you're ready to kill!' Nicci the stage manager was offering Kate some prawn cocktail crisps, snapping her out of her reverie.

'Do I? No thanks. Ha! I think I've got a bit of indigestion, that's all.'

'You sure you won't have a drink? A brandy or something?'

'Nah, I'm gonna head off soon. Need my beauty sleep!' And she smiled as she watched the merry cast get merrier, hurtling headlong into a mammoth hangover which Kate was glad she wouldn't have to share.

She caught a bus halfway back to Canley and walked the rest, passing happy drunks, angry drunks, silly drunks and weeping drunks as she headed for the tranquillity of her attic bedroom and warm, welcoming duvet. It was good to walk. Good for her head, as clear as the December night sky. She let herself in to the quiet house and made her way up to her room.

On a whim, she picked up the phone and dialled the speaking clock, listening to it as she lay on her bed in the semi-darkness, a mixture of street lighting and moonshine streaming in through the dormer windows, illuminating the room. The automated voice of the clock lady, squeezed through the phone's receiver, dutifully and

167

politely measured out the time. 'At the first stroke it will be twelve midnight precisely.'

And bang on cue, the city soundscape erupted into muffled cheers, bursts of fireworks, both distant and nearby, and tuneless renditions of 'Auld Lang Syne'. She replaced the receiver.

The celebrations beyond the silent house carried on without her.

'No looking back now,' she whispered, caressing her warm tummy, kept cosy under brushed-cotton pyjamas.

There'd been no choice in the end: she simply couldn't do it. She couldn't get rid of Callum's baby, now kicking delightedly inside her.

'Happy New Year, sweetheart,' she said. And she closed her eyes.

34

Three hundred miles north-west of Coventry, Belinda had just settled Ailsa back to sleep. Ben and Cory had been in bed for hours, out for the count, despite the partying in the streets and houses around them.

Portobello was no exception to the unique madness of Hogmanay and Belinda had long since learnt you couldn't beat it, you just had to join it. As best you could with three children under the age of six and no other adult to help you celebrate. She didn't really feel she was missing out – she'd never been a fan of New Year's Eve. When she was eleven her grandmother had died on 31 December and she'd always associated it with sad times. Of course, things had been different when she got together with Callum – and she learnt to enjoy the two-day celebration as consummately as any self-respecting Scot. But tonight she longed for sleep, and the chance to put this particular year behind her.

1985.

The year of Live Aid, third-time motherhood, the discovery of her husband's infidelity and the start of divorce proceedings. Fucking hell, who'd have thought? Watching Ailsa gently snuffling into much-needed sleep, Belinda felt safe, and loved – by her children, at least – but also very, very alone. And surprisingly homesick. She'd been thinking for some time about moving back to Wales, the comfort of being near her mum and her sister, her friends from school . . . but it wasn't fair to uproot the children, and despite what she thought of Callum, she couldn't separate him from his kids like that.

She headed downstairs and poured herself a glass of champagne. Seemed a bit frivolous really, she'd probably only manage the one and chuck away the remainder. Sue and Jeff had given it to her after they'd tried persuading her to join them for New Year's Eve – 'Bring the kids, they can sleep over, it'll be fun! We're gonna play Twister!' – but Belinda knew it would just remind her of the previous New Year's Eve, when she and Callum had got drunk and stayed there into the wee small hours.

It'd been a brilliant party, one of the best they'd ever known. And at a quarter to midnight, they'd sneaked into Sue and Jeff's en-suite bathroom for a private celebration of their own – exceptionally passionate and unplanned sex on the double-sink unit, knocking night cream and toothpaste onto the black tiled floor and bringing the whole thing to a perfectly timed climax as the party-goers in the street counted down to midnight. *'Five, four, three, two, one . . .'*

'Jesus! God!' Callum seemed to come for ages.

'Fuck, I love you, Callum!' Belinda held onto him hard and they kissed each other with such loving ferocity they could barely breathe. Outside, the revellers were singing 'Auld Lang Syne' as Belinda and Callum untangled themselves from their clinch to survey the debris of bottles on the floor. Belinda started picking them up. Thankfully none had smashed.

'Hey, leave that a minute. Come here.' Callum pulled her into him again. 'Happy New Year, Mrs MacGregor.'

'1985. Ten years, Callum. Not bad going, eh?' She rested her head on his shoulder and he quietly and uncharacteristically began serenading his wife, joining in with the singing outside.

'And there's a hand, my trusty friend,
And gie's a hand o' thine . . .'

Belinda found herself overcome with emotion, happy tears lolloping down her cheeks as she joined in with the song:

'We'll tak' a cup o' kindness yet,

For the sake of auld lang syne.'
That was the night Belinda fell pregnant with Ailsa.

How could so much happen in a year, she wondered? How could their lives have changed so drastically, beyond all recognition? Belinda sipped her champagne and looked out of her living-room window.

In any other circumstance, the coloured lights in the houses and gardens, the collection of illuminated Santas and reindeer and stars, transformed by a light dusting of snow, would have made the perfect Christmas-card scene. There was just one thing missing, she thought.

The gentle tapping on the front door was a welcome distraction from her maudlin and melancholy mood. She didn't really know who it might be – a merry neighbour, perhaps?

She certainly wasn't expecting to see *him*.

Callum.

Her heart lurched. It always did – it always would. And they stared at each other in silence.

'I can't do this, Bel.'

He didn't want champagne. He had nothing to celebrate. So she made him a cup of tea instead. The midnight countdown had passed unnoticed by both of them, the New Year being far from welcomed in. The scene couldn't have been more different from the same time last year.

Since Belinda had thrown him out, Callum had been living at Gary's, who, in all fairness, had turned out to be a really good friend. He hadn't judged, and he hadn't taken sides – unlike Sue and Jeff, who didn't hold back from telling Callum what a wanker he'd been.

'That woman is worth a hundred of you!' Sue had spat the words at him when she'd seen him one afternoon at the garage. And all Callum could do was agree.

He'd lost weight, and lost his spark. Because he'd lost his wife.

'She's not dead, pal,' Gary had tried to console him.

'She may as well be.'

He'd tried going back to work when it first happened. Attempting to normalize everything. But he was in denial. And the phone call from Kate that lunchtime had sent him spiralling downwards. It was the final straw. The ultimate manifestation of the wreckage he'd caused. Not one usually given to self-loathing, Callum plumbed depths of despair he hadn't known existed as he sank lower and lower.

School knew there'd been trouble at home, but, despite the conjecture flying around, none of Callum's colleagues really knew what had gone on.

'They'll not get any details from me,' Gary had told him. ''Cos it's none of their fuckin' business!'

When Callum had moved his stuff into Gary's, he'd been numb to his surroundings and could just as easily have moved into a dustbin. But gradually, as the weeks passed, he began to notice that Gary was quite domesticated. He was actually very tidy, in fact bordering on neurotic when it came to housework. The kids never came there to visit – both Belinda and Callum thought this would be disorientating for them. So they told Cory and Ben that Daddy was going to stay with his friend Gary for a while, but that he'd come to visit them every weekend.

Callum lived for those weekends, though the first time he visited was a disaster: he was unshaven and shaking, wearing tracksuit bottoms and an old rugby shirt he'd not been out of for days, smelling of beer and takeaways and virtually unrecognizable. Belinda sent him packing after half an hour, telling him to sort himself out and come back when he was more together – 'Don't be turning up like a down-and-out and frightening the living daylights out of your kids. They don't deserve that.' As soon as she'd shut the door behind him, she broke down in silent tears and sank to the floor, horrified at what he'd become and desperate to make him better.

After two weeks of Callum hardly speaking and seldom leaving his room, Gary decided it was time to intervene. He sat Callum down and asked him if he wanted his family back. Of course he did, what sort of question was that meant to be? In which case, Gary said in tough-love tones, it was time for Callum to get his arse in gear, get back to work, get back to life, get back to Belinda and the kids.

And, miraculously, Callum listened. Listened to this hardened bachelor, who had no kids of his own and had never known the love of a good woman like Belinda, but who could still see the excruciating pain in which his friend was drowning.

Callum returned to school, and started training again, eating properly and calling the children every day. The weekends were meticulously planned with a sensible balance of fun activities and quiet time, and whenever Belinda levelled any accusations at him or got irritated by him or let her justifiable anger get the better of her, he took it on the chin and continued to apologize.

He offered to babysit whenever she wanted a night out – not that she felt much like socializing these days – and he did the shopping, even the housework during his weekend visits. He treated it all like an exam he had to pass – and not just scrape through, but pass with distinction. He would pay whatever price he had to pay to get his family back.

And whenever Kate entered his head, he quickly deleted the image, banished and replaced her with images of Belinda in happier times.

Christmas had been really hard. Belinda said he should come to the house mid morning to open presents – but he wouldn't get to be Santa on Christmas Eve, she'd manage that by herself. When she told him this, it was like a punch to the stomach, but he took his punishment without complaint. 'You can stay for lunch,' she said, 'and watch a film with the kids. But I'm having my friends round in the afternoon and I don't want you here the same time.'

Callum noticed *their* friends had now become *Belinda*'s friends. In only a matter of weeks. There were always going to be casualties when a couple split up, but Callum would have far more of them than Belinda – in fact, Belinda would have no casualties at all.

So he'd done as he was told on Christmas Day and the kids were none the wiser, it seemed. Ben was maybe a little more confused than usual, but Belinda and Callum kept the mood so buoyant and friendly that the little soul was reassured all was well. He slept soundly that night.

Unlike Callum, who returned to Gary's empty house in the darkness of a Scottish Christmas afternoon. Gary had gone to his mother's in Morningside and was not planning to return till Boxing Day. Callum cut a lonely and forlorn figure as he let himself in, sitting in the big chair in the living room and watching in silence as the Christmas tree lights flashed on. And off. And on. And off. He sat like that for hours, wondering whether his efforts were doing any good. He soon found out that they weren't.

On 29 December, Belinda told Callum she was planning to see a solicitor in the New Year, in order to start divorce proceedings. Her voice had broken when she said she'd be citing his infidelity as reason for the divorce, and that yes, she would be naming that disgusting little whore he'd had an affair with – she couldn't bring herself to say Kate's actual name.

Callum tried to stay calm, but failed. He knew he didn't deserve any sympathy, but *divorce*? What happened to second chances? Belinda just laughed in his face. And for the first time since that fateful night in November when both their worlds had fallen apart, Callum and Belinda had an argument. A full-blown, crockery-smashing, accusation-hurling row, with Callum once again pointing out that he'd chosen *her*, hadn't he? He'd chosen Belinda – not Kate! To which Belinda once again expressed amazement that Callum should think she ought to be *grateful* for this!

'Say thank you, Belinda! The nice husband has chosen the sad old wifey over the twenty-two-year-old sex-mad beauty. Aren't you the lucky one!'

Callum had, of course, told her she'd got it all wrong, that that's not what he meant, but Belinda ignored him and the row ended with her screaming that she wished she'd never met him and couldn't wait to be divorced so she could start her life all over again.

She hadn't meant a word of it, but it was too late, she'd said it now. The only thing she could be grateful for was the fact that the kids were over at Callum's mother's at the time, and oblivious to their parents' massive fight.

So now, forty-eight hours later, with 1986 only a few minutes old, Belinda and Callum sat in their kitchen, drinking tea in silence, sadly and pensively surveying the room where their marriage had been destroyed, with their three bonny bairns asleep upstairs.

Belinda was the first to speak. 'I'm so tired.'

'Me too.'

And they both tentatively dared to look up. Callum wished he knew how to play it, but he didn't. 'I swear to you, Bel, it was a stupid ego trip and nothing more.'

Belinda remained impassive as he clumsily ploughed on, clutching at anything, any feeble straw of hope.

'You are the only woman I ever, ever want to be with . . .'

Belinda interrupted him. 'And don't tell me, *It will never happen again* – you've turned yourself into a cliché, Callum MacGregor.'

'Belinda, I'm desperate. And I will do anything. Whatever it takes. You can hire a private detective to follow me round, I'll wear one of those fucking prisoner's tags so you can know where I am twenty-four seven – just please, please, can we try again?'

She could hear the revelling continue in the street outside. Somewhere nearby, drunk and happy people were doing the conga. She sipped her tea. She knew so much depended on what she said next to this man who she had loved for over ten years, who was father to her three children, who knew her better than she knew herself, who really was her best friend and with whom she shared the same sense of humour; the man who could still, *still*, after all that he'd done, after all the pain he'd put her through, make her smile and make her feel safe. Was she being weak? A pathetic, feeble woman who couldn't stand up for herself? She thought of all her girlfriends and what they would say if they were here now – 'Don't give in, Belinda! Don't do it to yourself!' But none of her girlfriends would ever know their relationship like she did. Or know how much more painful it would be to live without him, or how much misery she'd inflict on their kids by making their dad live somewhere else, or how heartbroken Callum was, living away from them all.

No.

Nobody would ever understand that.

She sighed.

'I'm not sleeping in the same bed as you, Callum. Not yet.'

'Of course.' He tried to suppress the joy surging up inside him, terrified she would change her mind if he came on too strong.

'And if it doesn't work, it doesn't work. I can't make any promises.'

'No. But we can try?'

'Yes. We can try.'

And Callum gently took Belinda's hand and she let him kiss it.

'Thank you.' He could barely speak.

And unexpectedly, she found herself smiling at him. 'Happy New Year,' she whispered.

2002

35

Kate looked out at the fields and sheep and trees hurtling past the train window at a hundred miles an hour, and smiled. These were the same dull fields and bored, bleak sheep and lifeless, leaf-shedding trees she'd looked at barely three days earlier, but now the sight of them filled her with joy. How different this journey was from the identical one she'd taken on Thursday. Even the stewed coffee tasted great. This time she was alone in the first-class carriage. No one to see her grinning like a novice drinker who'd just tried sherry for the first time. She stretched out in the capacious leather seat and hugged herself, relishing her delicious secret.

Kate had, until a few days ago, been well practised in managing any thoughts of Callum MacGregor, keeping her promise to herself to shut him away in the cast-iron recess of unwanted memories, to be immediately banished if he should ever dare to wander audaciously into her occasionally unguarded mind. She'd succeeded for the most part because of her uncrackable determination. The same determination that had got her where she was in her career made her strong and defended in other areas of her life, too. But it hadn't always been easy to keep him at bay. The explosion of internet use in recent times had been a particular challenge. She knew it was an option to search for his name online, to sign up to Friends Reunited or some other digital means of communication and track him down. But she also knew that that way madness lay.

It was self-preservation, of course. She'd had to learn to forget him, else she'd never have survived. But now, having seen Callum again just seventy-two hours earlier, it was glaringly obvious to her that this was all she'd been doing for all these years – surviving. Not *living*, just functioning, ticking along on automatic pilot since the night their affair had so brutally and irreversibly ended in 1985. And, to be honest, that strategy had worked perfectly well until now. She'd thrown herself into her career, thriving on the drive to succeed, to become more and more successful with every role she played, ruthless ambition filling the void inside her which she knew subconsciously was there, but which she never wished to acknowledge.

Meeting Matt had been an oasis in the internal desert of her soul – this lovely quiet guy from the art shop, with his dry Yorkshire wit and Scandinavian looks, intelligent, softly spoken, self-assured, and astonishingly sexy – that first time, they'd stayed in bed for thirty-six hours! And yes, he was different from most guys she met; he didn't have the annoying neediness and ego of all the actors she'd been involved with – or the directors, for that matter. And although he enjoyed her work, he wasn't particularly interested in it. He liked Kate the person, not Kate the actress. He was cool, and funny, and gorgeous. And he was the only one – apart from Callum, of course – who'd come close to getting inside, scaling the walls that protected the true and secret Kate, peeping over the edge and momentarily glimpsing who she really was. But then she'd catch him looking in and shoot him back down again before he had the chance to get any closer. Kate loved Matt as best she could, but her best would never be one hundred per cent.

Darling Tallulah was different. Kate *could* be herself with her. This beautiful child had brought such gentle solace to her mother's spiky and broken life, helping to heal it with a daughter's unconditional love.

And yet Kate remembered guiltily how she'd reacted when she'd found out she was expecting – 'I can't possibly go ahead with it, Matt. We've only known each other a few weeks!'

Matt had felt differently, of course, and thank God he had. Thank God he'd fought to change her mind, because now when she thought of Tallulah not being there, never having touched their lives, it was too hard to bear. Matt had done most of the parenting – that's just the way it had to be. Kate's work wouldn't allow her to be a stay-at-home mum, not if she was going to continue on this career trajectory that so far wasn't letting up. But Matt was happy to play along, and Tallulah was happy to be a Daddy's girl. So. Win-win.

And she could probably have carried on like that – with her averagely contented, fine and pleasant life. The black moods she could handle. And the eating disorder, the drinking, the frequent feeling of unmanageability. Sure, they weren't enjoyable aspects of her life, but she knew how to cope with them.

Until three days ago, when she'd unexpectedly stumbled across Callum MacGregor, well and truly upsetting the applecart of her averagely contented, fine and pleasant life.

'Any cakes, pastries, teas, coffees, alcoholic beverages . . . ?' The posh dull monotones of the first-class trolley hostess burst rudely into Kate's daydream.

She smiled back politely. 'No, thanks.'

Suddenly the woman dropped the accent and her bored features transformed as she recognized Kate, launching into a broad Glaswegian exclamation, 'Oh ma Gawd! You're the wee lassie from tha' thing!'

Kate was too happy to be annoyed. 'Yep, that's me!' Though she had no idea which 'thing' the woman was referring to.

'Ah, y'see, ah thunk you're fabulous. Can I git yur autograph just now?' And she thrust a paper napkin and a black biro at Kate.

'Sure. What's your name?'

'Ah, it's not fur me, hen, it's fur ma missus. She's a Kate as well. And she fancies you like mad. Says what she wouldn't do tae ye she got ye on yur own for five minutes down a dark alley!'

'I'm flattered.' Kate's sarcasm was lost on the trolley hostess, who beamed as she watched Kate scrawl her name, before rushing off down the carriage with her trophy.

There were still four more hours to go. When she arrived, she planned to take a taxi to the hotel in Leith, check in, soak in a long leisurely bath – she'd packed some expensive bath oil – then at half six she'd put on the lingerie she'd brought with her, a beautiful lilac silk basque with satin-trimmed demi-cups, matching suspenders and seamed, flesh-coloured stockings. She'd wear the matching lilac silk robe to answer the door to him and her six-inch Louis Vuitton stilettos. Just thinking about it turned her on.

But suddenly, like a slap in the face, she was overcome with doubt. Was she being completely mad? Was this all a really stupid idea?

This journey to Edinburgh was a massive gamble in so many ways – she knew that, of course. She was playing with fire, not just because her lie might be discovered by Matt, but, more importantly, because Callum just may not turn up. What if she'd completely misjudged the situation? Only time would tell. By eight o'clock that evening, she would either be in bed with the man she had never stopped loving, or weeping into a large whisky and contemplating how her life could possibly progress, having rediscovered Callum MacGregor only to lose him a second time. This was a strong possibility. 'Keep it simple, one thing at a time.' That's what her AA friend used to say. Yes. *No point worrying about it till it's happened*, she thought.

She decided to call Matt. Her logic was that if she called him now he would think twice about calling her later, when she'd hopefully be with Callum.

When he answered, he sounded breathless. 'We're in the park. Hetty's pushing Lules on the swings. Tallulah – shout hello to Mummy!'

In the distance Kate heard the thrilled, shrill voice of her excited five-year-old. 'Mummy, I'm going SOOO high!'

'Aw, she'll sleep well tonight!' Kate said.

'That's the idea. How's the journey?'

And because she wasn't lying, she didn't feel guilty when she said, 'It's OK. I've only done one autograph so far! Hey, good night last night, wasn't it?'

And that was true too. The three of them – Kate, Matt and Hetty – had written their names in the Cristal she'd brought home and Matt had quite literally danced on the table. Ironically, Kate hadn't laughed like that with Matt for a long time. Sometimes she envied his close friendship with Hetty, but she suspected now that she might be glad of it in the near future. Because there was a chance Matt might need comforting . . .

36

'Where's Ailsa?'

'Tom's house. I said we'd pick her up later.'

Callum and Belinda were on the sofa, having just finished supper, waiting for the Lottery results. They played the same six numbers every week, and this week's ticket was unfolded and ready in Belinda's hopeful hand.

'You know why she's doing this, don't you? Asking us for lifts all the time?'

Callum smiled. 'Because she's psychologically manipulating us, dear. Thinks she can wear us down with requests to be taken here, there and everywhere, until eventually we'll give in and buy her a moped.'

'Better than a car, I suppose.'

'Ah, see – she's getting to you already. What's wrong with her having driving lessons, like we did in our day, and then borrowing her parents' car – like we did in our day?'

'Because it *isn't* our day any more. It's their day.' Belinda tucked a stray lock of greying hair back behind his ear. 'You feeling old, Callumagico?'

'No,' he lied. And instantly thought about Kate again. Try as he might, he couldn't get her out of his head. Since she'd rung the school on Thursday, he'd hardly been able to think of anything else. Was she really coming up here? He had no way of contacting her, no way of finding out. Other than to go to the hotel itself, and there was no way that could happen. But what if she followed through her threat and turned up on their doorstep? And told Belinda about the other night? He could never lie his way out of that one. What a fucking mess.

He sighed and shut his eyes.

'I know. Two numbers. Rubbish, really.' Belinda screwed up the Lottery ticket and threw it in the wastepaper bin as the TV presenter brought the national draw to a close. 'Still, two more than last week.' She crawled off the sofa and over to the TV. 'So who knows – next time *it could be you*! Now then – Robert De Niro or Jack Nicholson?' She held up two video cases from the local Blockbuster containing *The Score* and *About Schmidt*.

'What? Oh, I don't mind.'

'You're thinking about Beavis, aren' you? Look, you can still go, y'know. I'm not that bothered.'

'It's his third stag night, Bel. The guy's a serial bridegroom. I'll go on his next one, OK?'

She smiled. 'OK, well I'll make an executive decision then. We'll go for the Robert De Niro. Gets me in the mood, does Bob, so you never know – might be your lucky night tonight, MacGregor!'

'Ha! I'll make us a cuppa.' And he headed into the kitchen. The kettle was retro style with whistle, bought for them by the kids for their twenty-sixth wedding anniversary. 'Because you make so much bloody tea!' Ben had told them when they opened it. 'Yeah, and it's retro, like you two!' Cory had chipped in. Callum filled it up and put it on the gas, wondering how he was able to so brilliantly conceal the chaos going on in his head and remain so outwardly calm. He wished there was someone he could tell. Someone who'd advise him what to do.

'You want to see the trailers?' Belinda shouted through from the living room.

'Not bothered. You go ahead.'

As the water heated in the kettle, the sound of its simmering filled the kitchen, piling on the pressure, increasing the tension, getting ever closer to boiling point.

What he did next came from nowhere. He was doing it before he consciously *knew* he was. He didn't know if he was mad, sane, stupid, clever, foolish, wise, or just scared, but his mobile phone was now in his hands and he was dialling their own home number. Two seconds passed. Three, four. His breathing was shallow and loud, drowned out by the water in the kettle, gathering momentum, getting hotter and hotter. And then it rang: the phone in the hallway. Two rings. On the third, he shouted, 'I'll get it!'

Belinda, still on the sofa in the living room, called back: 'It might be Ailsa. Bit early for her, mind.' And she carried on previewing the trailers that came before *The Score*.

Dimly over the video's soundtrack, Belinda could hear Callum taking the call. 'Alright mate, how's it going? . . . Speak up, I can't hear you! . . . No, I can't, pal . . . 'cos I'm havin' a night in with my beloved . . .' At this point, Belinda looked up, curious, grinning. 'No, mate, I can't! . . . Alright, hang on . . .'

He prayed Belinda wouldn't notice his shaking hands as he covered the receiver of the phone that had no one on the other end of it and lowered his voice, saying, 'It's Gary. Says they're all missing me, the bunch of girls' blouses! Said I have to ask you to let me go down there.'

Belinda laughed. 'Go on then.'

'Are you sure? 'Cos I'm not really bothered myself.' Part of him wanted Belinda to say no, to put her foot down and stop him pulling the self-destruct cord.

She whispered, so that 'Gary' wouldn't hear, 'It's up to you, babes. You could just go for one? That'd shut them up.'

Callum turned back to the phone. 'Right, I'm coming for one and that's it, OK? . . . Aye, OK.' And he hung up.

'Don't be surprised, though, if I'm not here when you get back.'

Callum was caught off guard. 'What?'

'I might have left you for Robert De Niro, that's all I'm saying.' And she turned back to the film. In the kitchen, the kettle whistled harsh and loud and shrill.

*

Half an hour later, he stood outside the door of the Lomond Suite at the Barrington Hotel in Leith. She didn't answer straight away, so he knocked again. He'd managed to get past the concierge without being noticed and had scoured three floors in search of the Lomond Suite, praying no CCTV would track him down, his pulse racing with every step. What the fuck was he doing here?

Still no reply after the second knock, so he decided she wasn't there, relief flooding his body with such force he thought he might pass out. She hadn't come. Thank God. He turned to leave, deciding to go straight from there to the club so he could at least cover himself and verify the lie he'd already told about Beavis's stag night. He'd taken three steps away from the door when it opened. He turned. And there she was.

Neither of them spoke. She looked exquisite. The soft glow from the lamp in the room beyond created the perfect back-lighting to the scene and he drank in the whole effect of her, mesmerized by the image: the silk, the face he knew so well, the lips he needed to kiss again, her gorgeous toned thighs accentuated now by the tops of her stockings, and her creamy, flawless skin that he desperately yearned to touch. He was felled. Once more she'd caught him, enraptured him, and made him hers. She held out her hand and he took it. Putting up no fight, he let her draw him inside.

37

'Should we make it a black-tie event?'

'Well if you do, I ain't coming.'

'Oh Matt, you're such a spoilsport!'

They'd been discussing the forthcoming reunion as Hetty painted her nails in readiness for lunch with Adam. The Big Day was nearly upon her and she didn't want to be alone, she was too, too excited! She'd spent the afternoon with Matt and Tallulah and it had seemed pointless going home. So she'd had a bath there, plucked her reprobate eyebrows and 'jimmy-jammed down', borrowing an old T-shirt and joggers of Matt's – 'Because, let's face it, Kate's won't go anywhere near me.'

Matt was flicking through the channels with the TV on mute and tucking into a peppermint tea, having sworn off wine for at least a month after all that champagne the night before. He'd tried Kate's mobile a couple of times, mildly frustrated when it went straight to voicemail. 'And anyway, if you make it black tie, people will expect a three-course meal. And you're only offering them a bowl of cashews.'

'Three choices of canapé to be exact, but yes, you've got a point.'

They sat in silence for a bit. They liked that about each other. Saying nothing for long chunks of time never felt awkward to either of them.

'Why d'you think he's asked me to lunch?'

'Ah, just when I was having a lovely evening . . .' Matt knew Hetty was desperate to talk about Adam. She threw her pen top at him. 'Oh I dunno, because he's probably matured and developed manners over the past fourteen years and thinks he should apologize to you in private rather than wait till the reunion. Personally, I don't think you should go . . .'

'To the reunion?' Hetty was horrified.

'No, you dork, to lunch tomorrow! But then what do I know?'

Matt carried on flicking through the channels. And Hetty thought about the last time she'd seen Adam. She often thought about it, in fact, but more than ever in this past week, since he'd got back in touch.

It was their final term at Warwick. During the previous two and a half years, she'd held on feebly to the notion that she was Adam's girlfriend. Even though she'd never met his parents or even been to his home, and rarely saw him during the holidays. Hetty didn't see this as a bar to their relationship and carried on as if they'd been going steady for years. The feeling clearly wasn't mutual, despite the fact that Adam would occasionally deign to grace Hetty's bed or go with her to see a film or let her buy him a curry. These were the occasions to which Hetty clung as evidence that they were an actual couple.

Adam tried time and time again to push her away, but all to no avail. He would let her down relentlessly, agree to meet then not show up, humiliate her in front of other people, blatantly kissing other girls knowing Hetty was nearby. One time, he met her for a drink in the Union's Mandela Bar, got up to go and make a phone call, and left his drink on the table. Forty minutes later, he still hadn't returned, so she went looking for him. He wasn't at the nearby phone box, or anywhere else in the Students' Union. She went back to the table and sat there alone till last orders. When the Mandela Bar closed and he still hadn't returned, she made her way back to her room.

The next morning, she saw him being dropped off by a first-year student in a yellow 2CV. He was wearing the same clothes as the night before, and was dishevelled, unshaven and laughing. He kissed the girl for an inordinately long time before heading back to his room. En route, he happened to look up at Hetty, sitting forlornly at her window watching him, and shouted, 'What? You're not my fucking girlfriend!' He had so little respect for her that he didn't even feel she warranted being told a lie, let alone an honest explanation. And yet Hetty continued to love him. Her nickname amongst Adam's friends was the Boomerang. No matter how often he threw her away, she kept on coming back.

For a short while, it looked as if there might be a way out of this toxic and dead-end relationship. At the beginning of the second term, Matt had started seeing Lucy, a Chemistry PhD student from Sheffield who was looking for a no-strings relationship, a 'distraction' and nothing more. Which was perfectly fine by Matt. Lucy had a friend called Tim, who she'd met through the rowing club and who both she and Matt thought would make the perfect boyfriend for Hetty. So they set up a double date. To their delight, Hetty got on famously with Tim and agreed to see him again.

But on their fifth date – ten-pin bowling in Leamington – Adam had turned up and nipped the budding romance on the ankles. He told Hetty he needed to talk to her. At first, buoyed up by the enjoyment of her new relationship with Tim, Hetty stood her ground and told Adam he was none of her business any more. Nor was she any of his. But Adam was having none of it. And put on one of his best performances to date, becoming tearful, telling her that he was sorry, he needed her, and he hadn't realized how much she meant to him, that you 'don't know what you've got until it's gone'. And unluckily for Tim, Adam's sorry tale did the trick: Hetty made her apologies and followed Adam out of the bowling alley, never to date Tim again. When they got back to Adam's room he asked Hetty to stay the night and had sex with her. But in the morning he as good as ignored her, telling her his turning up at the bowling alley had been for a dare: to see if he could get her to come back to him even whilst on a date with another guy. And he'd succeeded. And won the bet. 'So thanks for that, but I've got a seminar to get to.'

Hetty was so embarrassed she'd been the subject of a bet that she couldn't bring herself to tell Matt the truth about what had happened. Matt, in turn, had become so frustrated by Hetty's return to Adam that he lost it one night in the communal kitchen and said he had no respect for her as a friend any more. That she could let that moron have such a hold over her and control her life to such a degree – he despaired. And would prefer it if they stayed out of each other's way from now on.

Hetty was heartbroken. She was living a complete lie with a boyfriend who wasn't a boyfriend and who saw her as having nothing more than entertainment value. She had lost the potential of having a *proper* boyfriend in Tim, and, worst of all, she had lost the respect and friendship of her dearest Matty. For the rest of that term she spent every day at the library revising, before going back to her room and crying herself to sleep. Even on exam days, Matt didn't speak to her. Not really. He'd politely ask how she'd found the paper, before excusing himself and disappearing.

Then came results day. They'd been posted on the department board and there was much to celebrate. Both Matt and Hetty had come out with high 2.1s and were delighted. Neither could hide their joy when they bumped into each other at the noticeboard. At first they were shy and clumsy, not having spoken to each other properly for over six weeks.

'Well done, mate,' Matt offered.

'And you, Matty! And you!'

'Did OK, didn't we?'

'We really, really did.'

They both stood there awkwardly for a moment before the tension became too much. Matt was the first to crumble.

'Oh for fuck's sake, come here.'

And he held his arms open for a reconciliatory hug.

Hetty wasted no time in tearfully reciprocating. 'Matty, I am *so* sorry.'

'What've you got to be sorry for? I'm the one who's been a knob.'

'But I should've listened to you about Adam, and I didn't.'

'Listen, who you go out with really isn't any of my business, and I mean that. I'm not just bein' arsey. And obviously you really like him, and judging by what he said at the bowling alley, he really likes you in some weird, Adam-ish way.'

'The thing is, Matt . . .' And she thought about telling him what had really gone on. About the bet. About everything. But then she thought, *Why spoil this perfectly lovely moment?* 'Shall we go to the Union and get completely smashed?'

'Abso-fucking-lutely!'

And they headed off together.

Later that night, after a lot of beer had been drunk and a lot of laughing and farewells and promises to stay in touch amongst the graduands, Matt and Hetty, arm in arm, wended their way out of the Union, stopping occasionally for yet another drunken hug and yet another oath sworn that they would be friends for ever and that no one would EVER get in the way of that. Not even Adam Latimer. At the mention of his name, Hetty, who was the drunkest she'd ever been, decided to go and find him. 'Because let's be realistical, Matthew, tonight is probably the last time I'll ever see him and, well . . . I'm only human, and a last chance is a last chance!'

She headed in the direction of Redelm Hall and Adam's room, with Matt mock-saluting her and shouting, 'You do what ya gotta do, sista!' He laughed at himself for sounding such a jerk before stumbling off drunkenly to his bed.

Hetty knew it was a long shot, expecting Adam to be in his room. He'd probably be in bed with some poor unsuspecting first-year student, or getting stoned at a house party in Kenilworth. She knocked twice on his door – no answer. So she fished in her bag for a pen and a bit of paper – the back of an old envelope would have to do. She scrawled, *I called. I'm drunk. Come and see me, Adam. Please? H xx*

The effects of the booze protected her from feeling undignified as she stuffed the envelope under Adam's door. But somewhere in the back of her mind she knew she'd regret writing the note in the morning. She clambered to her feet and decided to go and find Matt again. Because he always made her feel better. And hopefully he'd have some KitKats.

Matt's corridor was deserted – surprising, considering so many people had had their results that day. Hetty thought there'd be a party on every floor! She knocked gently. 'Matt?' She thought she heard movement inside, so she waited. 'Matt – it's me.' Silence. Hetty squashed her face up against the door and tried talking through the Yale lock. 'I went to his room. He wasn't there. Obviously!' Her voice was sad and resigned. And slurring. 'Are you there?' No answer. 'I wish I'd never met him, Matt. I could've had a much nicer time these past three years if I'd never met him.' She put her ear to the door to listen for more signs of life. There were none, but she carried on regardless. 'Y'know, I was thinking, it's a shame you an' me don't like each other in that way. We'd have made a lovely couple, don't you think? But the problem is I just don' fancy you. So sorry.' Realizing it was pointless to stay any longer, she bid Matt's door goodnight and whispered, 'Nighty-night, Matty. I love you *sooooo* much!' And headed off towards the staircase, bumping into the walls of the corridor as she staggered away.

The next day, she didn't wake up until midday and even after so much sleep she still had a raging headache. She could hear people in the rooms neighbouring hers, packing up, hysterical in their hangovers, shouting affectionate abuse and manic goodbyes. She'd have to start packing soon too, ready to leave that evening. She was feeling very sorry for herself and thinking what a sad and disappointing end this was to her three years at Warwick. She remembered the note she'd left for Adam and she cringed. He'd probably laughed when he saw it. Or chucked it away without even reading it. Had he already left for London, she wondered? And why was she such a complete and utter fool? She considered going back to bed, unable to face the day ahead. Where was Matt? She should get dressed, really, go and see if he was OK. He was certainly out for the count the night before.

But just as she was contemplating all this, a face appeared at her window and she screamed in shock – before realizing it was Adam.

'Come on, open up! I've got a train to catch!'

Thrilled to see him and swept along by his audacity, she pulled back the sliding window and let him climb in, knocking things off her desk as he did so.

'Just wanted to say goodbye,' he said, cupping her face in his hands and planting a big smacker on her lips. It wasn't romantic, or even particularly affectionate, more like stag-night banter, one guy to another – but Hetty would take anything he offered.

'Did you get my note then?' she said.

'What note?'

'I put it under your door.'

'Haven't been to sleep yet, bud. Just thought I'd call in before I skedaddled.'

Hetty didn't want to know who he'd been with the night before; she didn't want to ruin this rare and beautiful moment, instigated by Adam himself.

'So take care, Sweaty Betty.'

She hated the pet name he'd coined for her, but now was not the time to complain. 'You too, Adam.'

And he clambered back onto her desk and out through the window. 'I'll call you, yeah?'

'Yeah.'

She watched him run off in the direction of Redelm, pleased that he'd at least made some sort of effort to say goodbye, but knowing in her heart that she'd never, ever, hear from him again.

'Earth to Hetty? Hello? Come in?'

She'd been completely lost in thought and Matt was staring at her, bemused.

'Sorry, what?'

'I can't get hold of Kate. She's not answering her phone.'

'Well, she'll be at the casino, won't she?'

'What hotel did she say she was staying at, d'you remember?'

'No – but what's the big deal, Matt?'

'Oh, I dunno. She left in such a rush this morning and I didn't really ask her any details.'

'Take the money and run, I would. Ten grand! Her job's bonkers, isn't it? That's a full year's salary to some people!'

Matt ignored her. 'I'll call Cynthia, I think. She'll know.'

Hetty had met Kate's agent on two occasions and thought she was terrifying both times. 'Is that wise? Calling her out of hours like that?'

But Matt had already got through.

'Hi Cynthia, it's Matt Fenton. Sorry to call you on a Saturday night like this, but Kate forgot to tell me the name of the hotel she's staying in . . .'

Hetty watched as the smile fell from Matt's face.

38

'If I go now, I'll just about get away with it.'

'You don't have to get away with it.'

Callum ignored her. He didn't want to start another discussion about where they would go from here. They were lying on the king-sized bed, his head on her shoulder, and she was stroking his arm.

'I've put my number into your phone.'

'When d'you do that?' He sat up, shocked.

'When you were in the shower . . . It'll be easier to stay in touch via mobiles. No more embarrassing phone calls to the school – sorry about that. Just for God's sake make sure you delete any messages from me as soon as you've read them. When do you think you could next get away? I'm filming until—'

He cut her off. 'Hang on, are you insane?'

She looked surprised more than hurt. 'What?'

'I don't know what you think is going on here, but I can't see you again, Kate.' He paused, noticing the pain registering on her face and softening a little. 'It's impossible!'

'It's not.'

Sensing this was heading somewhere very dangerous, Callum got off the bed and started getting dressed, clocking his Dennis the Menace socks lying on the floor and remembering Belinda had given them to him as a stocking filler last Christmas. 'I've got to go.'

She lay there, silently watching him dress. His body had aged well in seventeen years, and he'd lost none of the stamina he'd had at thirty-nine. She wondered if it was down to fitness, and having played rugby for all those years. Or, God forbid, whether he and Belinda still had such an active sex life that he was living proof of the saying 'use it or lose it'. Kate remained remarkably calm as Callum put on his coat and picked up his car keys.

He'd expected a fight, or protests at least, but she said nothing, just smiled.

'Right, well . . .' he said.

'Thanks for the shag?' She teasingly finished his sentence.

'Look, if things had been different, y'know . . .'

This time she watched as he squirmed, awkward, not knowing where to put himself. 'Take care, yeah?' And he headed for the door.

Kate didn't move.

'I'm under K for Kettley's Garage in your contacts list. It *does* exist. In Portobello. In case Belinda should check your phone.'

'I'm not gonna call you, Kate.'

'Fair enough. Just delete my number then.'

He sighed and opened the door to leave.

Just as it closed behind him, she shouted, 'I've still got yours though.'

And she pulled the duvet over her, beaming.

It was gone midnight when Callum let himself into the house. As he approached the front door, he saw through the window the chop-change blue and amber TV rays as they bounced against the living-room walls. Callum steeled himself. Belinda was obviously still awake.

He had his story ready – he'd been to the club but then went for a drink with Gary, who was having women troubles. Gary could always be depended on to lie for him. Not that he'd needed him to in the last seventeen years because, true to his word, Callum hadn't so much as smiled at another woman since being given his second chance by Belinda.

His footsteps were weighty and reluctant as he walked to his fate like a condemned man. He barely made a sound as he closed the door behind him and stood in the hallway.

'Belinda?'

No answer. He took a deep breath, put on a smile and opened the living-room door, probably a bit too keenly, launching straight in with his excuses before he could be attacked. 'I know, I said one drink and now— *Jesus!*' He'd only taken two steps into the room before he backed straight out again.

'*Dad!*'

Ailsa, possibly naked, was clearly in a very private clinch with her boyfriend, Tom, also possibly naked – but Callum didn't hang around long enough to find out. He really didn't want that image in his head. His daughter, for God's sake!

'Jesus, get dressed, will you? And Tom, it's time you went home.'

'Sorry, Mr MacGregor.'

Like many of Ailsa's friends, Tom had been taught by Callum when he was in Year Six at St Mary's and still thought of his girl-friend's father as 'Mr MacGregor'.

Upstairs, Belinda had been woken by the kerfuffle and came out onto the landing in her pyjamas. 'Callum, what's going on?'

He made his way to the bedroom, temporarily forgetting his guilt about where he'd really been that night. His priority right now was the honour and protection of his seventeen-year-old daughter. 'They were . . . y'know, having sex!' he whispered, barely able to say the words.

Belinda looked at him and laughed. 'Callum, she's seventeen, love. They've been going out for over a year!'

'So?!'

'And she's on the Pill!'

'How do *you* know?!'

Belinda was getting hysterical, both entertained and surprised by Callum's reaction to discovering that his only daughter had now grown up. She pulled him into the bedroom. 'Hush! You've embar-rassed them enough already, come to bed.'

Belinda shut the door behind them and watched Callum as he sat down and sighed. 'Aw, love, it's not the end of the world. They're very in love, y'know.'

'Ach, don't tell me any details. It's bad enough I saw them . . .'

'Well, serves you right for coming home late. If you'd only stayed out for one like you *said* you would, then you'd never have walked into the lion's den!'

'Yeah, very funny.'

'What happened to you, anyway?' Belinda got back into bed, switching off her bedside light and settling under the covers as Callum reeled off his well-practised answer.

'. . . Anyway he told me to say sorry. I said, tell her yourself when you see her!'

'Mm-hmm.' Belinda yawned, her eyes shut now, and Callum realized she wasn't remotely interested in where he'd been tonight. He watched her for a minute drifting back to sleep, whilst downstairs the front door shut and Ailsa ran up the stairs. As she passed Callum and Belinda's bedroom she made her annoyance quite clear: 'That was SO humiliating!'

Callum smiled and called out quietly, 'Night, Ails!'

As he started undressing, the insanity of his evening began to sink in. The second unbelievably erotic experience he'd shared with Kate in three days. What the fuck was he doing? His mobile buzzed in his pocket. He took it out as the screen lit up, announcing a text message from 'Kettley's Garage'. He glanced over at Belinda, snuffling and dreaming contentedly. He opened the text:

> *Filming in Newcastle next week.*
> *Only 90 min on train from Edinburgh.*
> *Come and see me.*

Callum sighed and deleted the text.

39

Not wanting to push her luck, Kate made sure she was on the first train back to London on Sunday morning. She knew that she was taking a massive risk telling Matt such a huge lie about the casino – that if he really wanted to he could look into it further and catch her out. But this only made the whole thing more thrilling, and although she knew it was wrong, she couldn't help but feel turned on by it. She was a lost and shameful cause. She knew that now. But what was done was done, and the truth was, all she wanted was to see Callum again. And she didn't care who got hurt in the process. Even poor, lovely Matt.

In the early days, Kate had made a big show about the importance of being honest with each other about their pasts, especially if they were to get married. It was Kate who'd harped on about how vital it was that neither of them had any skeletons in the cupboard to be brought out and dusted down at some later date, causing mayhem and upset and hurt. As a result, there was nothing she didn't know about Matt's history with women. And when he confessed all, in truth she was delighted that there'd been so many – joking that it made her feel less of a slapper.

In return, Kate had told him everything too – from Scott Duncan, who she'd shown her trainer-bra'd pubescent boobs to in top juniors, to James Randell, the twice-married producer of *Lost in May*, the

TV series she was filming when she met Matt in his gallery that day nearly seven years ago.

Yes, Matt knew about every one of the men in Kate's past.

Every single one, except Callum.

She sighed and banished the guilt, plunging herself back into denial.

The train pulled into Euston at midday and by one o'clock Kate was in Mario's on King Street, buying delicious fresh salads and pizza to take home for lunch. She'd spoken briefly to Matt when the train was just outside Peterborough and told him her plans, mustering excitement and enthusiasm for their family Sunday ahead and apologizing again for eating into their weekend. She thought Matt seemed a little distant on the phone, but put it down to her paranoid imagination and headed briskly back to the house. Despite the bite in the air, the sun was shining weakly and the day was actually quite pleasant for November.

Breezing into the kitchen, Kate saw Matt outside in the back garden with Tallulah, who was bouncing up and down with Panda on her much-loved trampoline. She put the pizza in the oven to keep warm, went to the fridge and poured two large glasses of Sauvignon Blanc, convincing herself it was because Sundays were meant for relaxing but knowing deep down that she needed Dutch courage to get her through.

Holding a glass in each hand, she elbowed open the French doors that led into the garden. She hadn't noticed it when she'd first arrived, but now she could see that Matt was smoking. Nothing wrong with that per se, except that he'd given up three years ago.

'Shouldn't you be doing that behind a bike shed?' she shouted.

He turned, surprised to see her. 'Oh. Hello.'

She thought his face looked pale and sad, but wondered if she was looking for trouble when it wasn't really there.

'Yeah, just fancied one.' He let her kiss his cheek as she handed him the wine. 'Thanks.'

'Mummy, Mummy, look at us!' Tallulah was in her element.

'Hey, darling! Did you miss me?'

'Yes!' And she carried on bouncing up and down.

Kate took a big slug of wine. 'God, that's nice.'

They stood there for a moment watching Tallulah, listening to her delighted giggles and shouts of 'WEEEEEEEEEEE!'

Aware that Matt was behaving oddly but choosing to ignore it, Kate lit up a cigarette herself and started wittering nervously. 'I was thinking we should maybe go to Vegas, y'know. Seeing all the blackjack tables last night and roulette – it's given me a taste for it. I think you'd like it. Have you ever been to—'

'What's going on, Kate?' He couldn't bring himself to look at her and she inhaled deeply on her cigarette.

'Sorry?'

'I called Cynthia. She told me she didn't know anything about a job at a casino.'

Kate felt sick. Her mind raced, desperately trying to find a way out of the trap into which she was falling.

'You weren't answering your phone and I didn't know which hotel you were staying in – you didn't tell me – so—'

'Matt, you idiot!'

The only way she was going to pull this off was to launch in with one hundred per cent conviction. 'Of course Cynthia didn't know about it. I was doing it on the side! I don't see why she should get commission on *everything* I do.'

'I didn't know!'

'Well done, you've dropped me right in it now.' And she walked off, a mixture of heady relief, adrenalin and guilt saturating her system. She knew if she didn't sit down quickly she would most likely pass out from the pounding in her head.

Matt watched her go.

Tallulah had stopped bouncing, her little face pressed up against the safety net surrounding her trampoline, and she wondered what was wrong with her mummy and daddy.

40

Hetty had been waiting on Marylebone High Street for twenty minutes and was beginning to think Adam had forgotten about their date. Of course, it wouldn't be surprising – true to form, she thought. Maybe Matt was wrong. Maybe Adam hadn't grown up at all in the last fourteen years. Maybe this was another cruel bet. She wished now that she'd never agreed to meet him.

The Sunday shoppers walked past her, unaware of Hetty's concerns. To them, she was just a woman in a bright turquoise coat and a silly knitted hat that sported a crocheted flower on the side. She'd made an effort today. For a start, she was wearing make-up. Most days she didn't wear any – didn't see the point; taking it all off again was only another job to be done before bed. But today she'd made the effort.

Thankfully, and because she'd planned ahead for the Big Day, she'd had time to realize that the make-up in her trusty old wash-bag had seen better days and that it was high time she bought new. Stuck at the bottom of the bag, and covered in blusher dust leaked from the crack in her old No. 7 rouge, was a green eyeliner that she'd had since Warwick days, as well as a Maybelline lipstick called 'Bilberry Ice'. That was even older, surely 1982. And when she twisted it out of its casing, it simply gave up the ghost in her hand, disintegrating into purple chunks. So she'd gone on a mission in her lunch hour last Friday, braving the make-up counter at Boots.

The friendly but slightly over-enthusiastic assistant – who wore far too much make-up herself – had persuaded Hetty to have a mini demo of products that would suit her 'age and skin type'. Half an hour later, she left the store clutching a bag of brand-new items, her face transformed by colour, shading and bronzers.

When she'd returned to the office, Ivor did a double-take but said nothing. Whereas Glen told her she looked like a drag queen on speed and should take all that muck off before the meeting with their sponsors from the Health Well company that afternoon. She tried to 'take the edge off' at her desk by rubbing her eyeshadow with a tissue. Ivor brought her a cup of tea and told her to ignore Glen. 'You know what he's like about anything fake. Him and his wife split up after she had extensions put in her hair, so it's no surprise.'

'How on earth do you know that about Glen?' Hetty laughed.

'Still rivers run deep, y'know.' And he'd smiled his shy smile.

'Do I *really* look awful, Ive?'

'No.' He decided to be straight with her. 'I just don't think you need it, that's all.'

In his head, he added . . . *because you are naturally, exquisitely beautiful and I love you with all my heart. You could wear a traffic cone on your head and I would still think you were the most attractive woman ever to have graced this planet, but you'll never know that because I'll never have the courage to tell you.*

Hetty continued with her make-up removal and Ivor stared at her for a beat too long, interrupted by Glen, who told them to 'Chop chop,' and said didn't they have work to be getting on with? Ivor went back to his desk, his heart aching, whilst Hetty remained innocently unaware of the torch her workmate carried for her wherever he went.

Suddenly, soft and cologne-scented hands covered her eyes. 'Your money or your life!' It was Adam. She pulled away, giggling too loudly and hoping he hadn't smudged her mascara. 'Wow! You look . . .' he searched for the right word, 'different!'

'Fourteen years, Adam.' She scrutinized his face for a grain of emotion or poignancy, but there was none forthcoming.

'I know! And we've all aged. Myself included.' Before the back-handed compliment had time to sink in, Adam was steering them inside the restaurant. 'Right, come on you. I'm starving. And I'm afraid I've only got an hour.'

Her heart sank and she wondered why. Was he married? Did he have a wife to go back to? Kids? A girlfriend? A job? As they were shown to their table, she hoped the next hour would enlighten her.

41

Kate had locked the door to the gym and put her music on LOUD. Matt knew better than to try and disturb her when she was like this; he wouldn't get anywhere – over the years he'd found this out to his cost. Kate had an incredible propensity for stubbornness. His mother, in her less charitable moments, had said she could be 'a right mardy madam', and Matt was inclined to agree. When she was in one of these moods she was able to carry on as if Matt wasn't even in the room, ignoring his very existence. Yes, she had a great propensity for stubbornness. But she had an even greater propensity for winning the argument – even when she was in the wrong.

He resented it, of course. I mean, Christ, it wasn't *his* fault she'd not told him about Cynthia – she'd never done it before, how was *he* supposed to know? Kate always put *all* her work through her agent – why start moonlighting at this point in her career? And yet here he was, taking the blame again, and apologizing.

Again.

Even though any level-headed observer would say, 'Hey, come on, this is just a little misunderstanding,' he now found himself feeling wracked with guilt for damaging one of Kate's professional relationships. As she was so fond of pointing out, it was her professional success that had provided them with their home and all its accompanying luxuries. He hated it when she said this – partly because it was true, but partly because he found himself want-ing to counteract her claim with an even harsher one – *Yes, but your professional success has cost you your relationship with your daughter, and thank God I'm here for her, 'cos if it was left up to you, Tallulah would probably be in care.* Childish of him. And he'd never say it. Even when Kate behaved as appallingly as she was doing today.

Instead, he scribbled a note and pushed it under the locked door of the gym: *I'm sorry, I really am. I've taken Tallulah to see Cinderella again at the Odeon. See you tonight. I love you, M xx*

Half an hour later, cocooned in the comforting dusty darkness of the cinema, Matt sipped his oversized Slush Puppie, held Tallulah's hand and wondered what to do next. Three years ago, Kate had seen a therapist over several months and it'd really seemed to help. He'd seen the façade drop, the defences come down, and she'd become softer, more open and, dare he say it, more loveable. Then out of the blue she'd announced one day that she wasn't going any more. 'I'm OK, babe. I'm better now – seriously!' And she'd kissed him and the matter was closed. Just like that.

But deep down Matt guessed what must have happened. The therapist must have asked about Luca.

He knew so little about him. He had no idea who his father was or the circumstances Kate was in at the time. And he'd only found out himself by accident.

She'd been eight weeks pregnant with Tallulah and they were sitting in a Harley Street consulting room, facing Mr Chalfont, the benign obstetrician whose smile alone cost £120 an hour. When Mr Chalfont asked Kate if she'd been pregnant before, Matt assumed he knew the answer.

'Yes. When I was twenty-two, I had a baby boy.'

Kate continued looking straight ahead, aware that Matt had turned to stare at her in disbelief whilst the doctor made notes.

'What?' Matt whispered, unable to hide his incredulity as the doctor looked up, sensing that a marital row might be brewing.

And calmly and collectedly, Kate said, 'I had him adopted.'

He surprised himself with his own reaction. Instead of being angry or dumbfounded, when they got outside he simply engulfed her in a huge, loving hug. 'You poor sweetheart! Why didn't you tell me? That must have been . . . well, hell. To give a baby up like that – was there anyone to support you?'

He could tell she was thrown by his reaction – that he didn't ask her about the baby's father. And before long she was sitting on a bench in Soho Square, pouring her heart out to her ever-loving husband. 'I wanted to keep him, Matt.'

'Hey, ssshh . . . it's OK,' he continued to comfort her.

'I did try, I really did . . . but I just couldn't cope. I got into trouble. I was pathetic . . .' Suddenly her tone turned sour and vicious, full of self-loathing. 'Stupid fucking useless bitch that I was!'

'Kate, don't . . .' He was disturbed by this, scared even.

'I was drinking, and depressed, and . . . well, I just couldn't give him what he needed. He was only four months old. I called him Luca.'

'Did your mother know? Your dad?'

'Yes. They wanted to bring him up themselves, but I said no. It wasn't fair on them. Or him.'

'Oh Kate, you should've told me sooner, y'know. Living with this all on your own . . .'

She let him comfort her, her head on his shoulder, wrapped up in his arms till she'd cried it all out. And then, in classic Kate style, pulled herself together, wiped away the tears with her sleeves and announced she was OK now. 'Thanks, Matt,' she said, and he kissed the top of her head.

'Hey, you can talk about this any time you want, y'know.'

'No. Please don't mention it again.' And she'd smiled sadly. 'We've got *our* baby to think about now.'

Matt often wondered about this exchange. He'd kept his word, and they'd never spoken about it since. But he knew that something so monumental couldn't be just swept away and forgotten. If Kate had never allowed herself to grieve for Luca, then the pain would have to come out some time. And maybe that time was now, manifesting itself in her unpredictable and inexplicable, even dangerous, behaviour. Matt shivered at the thought.

42

'Sue text me – they've booked the court for an extra half-hour on Sunday.' Belinda, already dressed for work, vigorously opened the blinds, and let in the reluctant sepia-tinted daylight of a Scottish Tuesday morning.

'OK.'

'And I've done some porridge if you fancy, but you better get a move on. It's five past.'

'OK.'

She sat on the bed and put her hand on his forehead. 'I hope you're not goin' down with this bug that everyone's gettin'.'

'Time was when you'd kiss me first thing, not check my temperature!' he joked, trying to avoid the recurring conversation about how he'd not been himself these past couple of days. 'Yeah, maybe. I'll take a couple of Lemsips to school wi' me.'

Belinda leant over and gave him a perfunctory peck on the lips. 'There we are, see!' She laughed. 'Who says the romance goes after twenty-six years of marriage?'

With that she leapt up and headed for the door. 'I'll be back about seven, after yoga. Put that casserole in when you get home, will you? Gas mark five. For an hour.'

And she was gone, content in the innocent daily minutiae of married life and happily oblivious to the fact that her husband had been unfaithful to her twice in the preceding week.

Callum hauled himself out of bed and headed to the bathroom. 'Good timing!' he said to Ailsa as she emerged, wrapped in a towel, fresh, clean and moisturized, and still unable to meet his gaze after the embarrassing confrontation a few days earlier.

'We're running out of toothpaste,' was all she could muster as she sloped off to her room to get ready for school.

In the shower, Callum thought about Kate and the fact he'd not heard from her since Saturday. The right-minded part of him was hugely relieved. He could put his two meetings with her down to an insane and extraordinary interlude in his otherwise happy and ordinary life. But then there was that little nagging voice inside him – what was it, his ego? – that was really disappointed she'd not been in touch. Disappointment gave way to indignation – who did Kate think she was, marching back into his life like that, stealing him away and showing him what he'd been missing all these years? He found himself calling her a 'prick-tease', a word he never used, and was instantly dismayed at what he was turning into. He held his face under the refreshing, cleansing blast of the power shower, letting it wash away his uncharitable thoughts. Kate's own right-mindedness had most probably kicked in, and they could both brush what had happened under the carpet and get back to reality. And, let's face it, reality was good.

Five minutes later, he was getting dressed when he caught sight of the framed photo on the windowsill, taken in 1982 down on the beach at Portobello. Belinda was pregnant with Cory, and Ben had just built a sandcastle. He smiled, picked up his mobile and composed a text to send to Belinda. It was something he'd never done before – still adjusting to the whole concept of a mobile phone – but guilt and gratitude spurred him on. *I love you Belinda MacGregor x*, he typed, pressed send and smiled. The instant it was sent, the phone beeped abruptly with an incoming text.

It was from Kettley's Garage.

Mr MacGregor your car is due for a service. Please call us at your earliest convenience.

He stared at his phone.

Disbelieving.
Fearful.
Thrilled.

'Dad! I need a lift. I'm too late for the bus.' Ailsa was calling from the landing. 'But you're not allowed to talk to me about Tom, OK?'

He continued to stare at the phone.

'Dad?'

'OK. Coming.' He pressed delete and put his phone in his pocket.

43

This was the second day in a row that Hetty had been out running before work. There were just six weeks left till the reunion and she'd resolved to lose a stone by then. Admittedly she'd been spurred on by the lovely, warm, fuzzy feeling inside her since seeing Adam. And admittedly she wanted to look good at the reunion – not to prove to a host of other Warwickonians that she had aged well, but to impress the man she was still in love with after all this time.

She was on her third circuit of the grubby patch of park that optimistically described itself as a 'public garden'. A few office workers had braved the bleak and overcast morning to drink their pre-work cappuccinos on the park's sparse benches. The combination of exercise and cold November air surprised Hetty's lungs into a light asthmatic wheeze, and she reached for her Ventolin inhaler. Despite the sweat running down the back of her ears, the redness in her cheeks and the discomfort inflicted on her aching chest by her ill-fitting sports bra – she was determined to continue.

Hetty had come away from the lunch with Adam buzzing, and riding a huge wave of delight, despite things getting off to a rocky start. There was no vegetarian option on the menu and Adam couldn't understand why she didn't just eat fish. Worried that he'd get annoyed with her, she found herself challenging her beliefs for the first time in twenty years of commitment to vegetarianism, wondering for a split second whether now might be the time to return to eating meat. Thankfully, the kind waiter nipped this mad thought in the bud and offered her a mushroom omelette instead. And after that, things definitely improved. The wine helped, of course, but it was more than that: Adam was *kinder*. He was *interested* in her. He wanted to know *everything*. In fact, he talked far more about Hetty than he did about himself, and she found this most endearing.

'I often wondered whether I'd see your name up in lights or spot you in some big Hollywood movie!' she ventured.

'Ha! No, my acting days ended with the last Drama Society play at Warwick, I'm afraid.'

'*Blithe Spirit*.' She blushed, feeling like a superfan.

'Well remembered!' And he clinked his glass with Hetty's. 'Though working for Benson Mayfield does require something of an ability to perform.'

She'd never heard of Benson Mayfield, but it seemed they were one of the world's leading companies in scientific research. Adam had apparently scaled the ranks of this vast global organization since he began working for them in the mid nineties, regularly travelling internationally to visit drug manufacturers and develop trade links.

'So exciting!' Hetty was wide-eyed after he told her he was off to Dubai and Bahrain for a month.

'It can be. It's great seeing all the different cultures, of course, and meeting new people, but travel can be exhausting.' And then he looked at her. 'And a bit lonely, if I'm honest.'

She was touched that he'd chosen to open up to her like this. *That was definitely 'a moment'*, she thought. He'd already explained that he, like Hetty, had not yet done the grown-up thing and 'settled down', and that not having someone to share his life with did have its downside. She'd tried to find out if he had a girlfriend right now, but he was vague and dismissive – to the point where Hetty wondered if he was a bit embarrassed to be single. So she didn't pursue it. *Plenty of time to get to know him better*, she thought.

'Have you ever been back?' she asked, when the subject turned to Memory Lane and recollections of Warwick.

'Bizarrely, once. For a stag night. Three years ago. Remember Dom?'

'English and Drama?'

'That's the one. Well, he married none other than Moj – stage manager? Dungarees and a baseball hat?'

'No! But I thought she was gay.'

'Apparently not! Anyway, he chose to have his stag night at the Union. It's changed so much, y'know. The Mandela's gone. And the Elephant's Nest.'

A flash of hurt poked Hetty in the chest as she remembered the humiliation of Adam abandoning her at the Mandela Bar that time. But she brushed it under the carpet of denial and raised her glass instead. 'To Warwick days!'

And Adam raised a glass too. 'And to Dom and Moj. They've got two kids now!'

At the end of the lunch, Adam held Hetty's coat out for her to put on – a proper gentleman, her grandmother would call him – though she slightly ruined the moment with her clumsy inability to find the second armhole.

Outside, he hugged her and kissed the top of her head. She'd savoured all six seconds of the exchange, inhaling his expensive cologne and yielding to the once-familiar feel of his arms encircling her shoulders. She could've stayed like that for ever.

'I'm sorry we lost touch, Het.'

'Me too.'

'But we can put that right now, can't we?'

Hetty inwardly purred. 'I'd like that. It's been so good seeing you again, Adam.'

'You too.' Was he welling up? She was *sure* they were tears . . .

'Look, I'll be away until the day before the reunion, but you've got my email. It'd be nice to hear from you when I'm in foreign climes. Stop me feeling homesick.'

Her heart was positively cartwheeling, bursting with joy that he was being so *lovely*! 'Of course! I'd love to, Adam! Safe journey now.'

'Yes. Bye Hetty.'

And then the final juicy cherry on the softest icing on the fluffiest, best-baked cake in the world was that he blew her a kiss. *A kiss!* She blew one back and, smiling, they went their separate ways.

But she'd only taken two or three steps when she heard, 'Oh, and Hetty?'

She turned around. 'Yes?'

'I completely forgot to ask. How's that friend of yours – Matthew something?'

'Matt Fenton.'

'That's him. You still in touch?'

'Gosh, yes, we see each other all the time. I'm godmother to his little girl.'

'How lovely!' Adam looked impressed. 'I heard somewhere that he married an actress?'

'Yes. Kate Andrews. She's ever so nice.'

Adam smiled and nodded before enquiring, 'And will Matt be coming to the reunion, d'you think?'

'Abso-blooming-lutely!'

'Oh, that's good. Well, do send him my regards. And tell him I can't wait to see him again!'

And with that he turned, leaving Hetty bowled over by this transformation in Adam, who'd become so considerate and thoughtful and had truly mellowed with age. He'd even remembered Matt, for God's sake!

She approached the exit to the gardens and slowed down her pace as she noticed the Romany lady she'd seen there the week before. The recognition wasn't mutual and once again the woman tried to sell Hetty a tatty bit of tin-foiled heather, to 'bring you good luck, luvvy!'

'Oh, I don't need any, thank you!' Hetty yelled, warm thoughts of Adam, her lucky talisman, buoying her up. She was wheezing, sweating and blistered, but inside she positively brimmed with confidence.

44

Kate loved where they were filming. Ten days in Kielder Forest – not Newcastle, after all, but Newcastle*ton*. At least, that was the village where the crew were staying; the cast had all opted for forest lodges, delighted that they came with outdoor hot tubs.

Kate couldn't believe she'd got the location so wrong. 'Babe, I didn't realize till we'd been in the car for hours and not a Starbucks in sight!' She'd laughed about her ignorance on the phone to Matt yesterday lunchtime.

'So you're basically in Scotland again?'

Kate adopted her native accent, Scottifying it for effect. 'Aye, weel it's nae Scotland, pal, but the Borrrrrdurrs if ye want tae be exact!'

'Too far for us to visit, though.'

Kate knew such a journey was out of the question during term time. 'Yeah, but I'd hardly see you even if you did come up. I'm in virtually every scene,' she lied, knowing that on Friday she'd be done by mid morning. 'Still, maybe we could come up here for a holiday at Easter?'

'You'll be doing the film then though, won't you?'

Matt sometimes knew Kate's work schedule better than she did.

'Oh yeah. Duh!' She tried to keep things light. They were only just back on good terms after the Cynthia fiasco and she didn't want the stress of another argument. 'I tell you what, though, I'm going to book myself out for the whole of Lula's summer holiday. We'll go to France for some of it, then somewhere more child-friendly, like Florida. Hey! Disney World!'

At which Matt groaned, as did Kate – neither of them relishing the prospect, though they knew Tallulah would be beside herself.

There was a knock on the trailer door. 'I better go, they need me back in make-up. I'll call you tonight, yeah? From the hot tub!'

'I love you.'

'Love you too.'

And she hung up. Conscious of the glaring difference – in *her* book anyway – between a heartfelt 'I love you' and a common-or-garden 'love you'. The 'I' was the all-important missing ingredient. Hopefully Matt hadn't noticed.

She'd thought about calling Callum yesterday morning on her journey up north. But she had no idea of his schedule or when would be a good time. Was he *ever* alone on a school day? She composed several texts to send – varying from long explanations about how she felt, through to simple two-word messages such as *CALL ME* or *YOU OK?*, through to a solitary exclamation mark. But none of them felt right. And by the time she'd come to the end of the day's filming, she didn't dare risk contacting him.

He could've contacted *her* though, couldn't he? Especially as she'd told him she was filming in Newcastle all week. But she'd not heard a thing and was getting on her own nerves, checking her phone countless times for a text or a missed call. Even Benno had noticed her mobile obsession. 'No phones on set please, Ms Andrews!' he'd joked, but she knew deep down he meant it. Her concentration was rubbish that day. She just couldn't stop thinking about Callum.

Was she kidding herself?

Had she forced him into seeing her?

Well, yes, of course she had. But he could've said no, couldn't he? He didn't *have* to turn up at the hotel on Saturday night. And so she went on like that, berating herself all day. And despite seeking help from a bottle of red and a couple of trusty bedtime Valium, Kate still managed to stay awake till gone two, cursing herself for going to Edinburgh last week, cursing Callum for not getting in touch, cursing Belinda for ever discovering their affair, cursing Matt for loving her when she was such an irretrievably lost soul and so fucking horrible to him, cursing life for being so complicated, cursing, cursing, cursing, until finally sleep came and swallowed her up, before spitting her out again just four and a half hours later.

By eight fifteen she'd got into costume, been through make-up, eaten her paltry breakfast of yoghurt and black coffee, and was sitting on her trailer steps, phone in hand, smoking.

'Five minutes before we go to set, Kate.'

Kate smiled back at Becky, took a deep draw on her fag and dived right in. Surely now he'd be on his way to school, if not *in* school? Surely now it was safe to send a text? And it would come up on his phone as 'Kettley's Garage', so what was the problem?

Before she had time to weigh up the pros and cons – and feeling light-headed from the lack of proper sleep – she composed the message. *Mr MacGregor your car is due for a service. Please call us at your earliest convenience.* She pressed send, deciding to leave her phone in her trailer till they broke at one o'clock so she could concentrate on work and let fate hand out the consequences.

45

The gallery was busy that morning. Matt put it down to Christmas shopping – even though there were still a good six weeks to go. A painting wasn't an obvious choice for a Christmas gift, he'd be the first to admit – the love of a painting was so subjective, for one thing. But many customers had come in and declared, 'Oh, John would *love* that!' or 'Now *that* is so Milly. She'll adore it.' Matt and Pete smiled politely as they carefully wrapped each painting, ensuring the customer knew that the gallery didn't operate any kind of refund policy.

'We're not Debenhams, Madam,' he'd heard Pete say a couple of times.

One woman had asked if they did family portraits. Pete had scoffed at the notion, but Matt thought it wasn't a bad idea and maybe something they should explore.

'And who, pray tell, would be the artist to paint said portraits? Might you volunteer, Matthew?' Pete could be ultra-pompous at times, and it always made Matt smile.

As if on cue, Chloe, the artist from upstairs, popped her head round the door to tell Matt the heating wasn't working in the studio again.

'Ah, Chloe! Come in, come in,' Pete beckoned. 'And tell us, where do you stand on portraiture? Matthew is looking for an artist to do family paintings. Two for the price of one.' Matt rolled his eyes and smiled. 'You could have them in your studio for hours and hours, recreating their dazzling smiles on canvas, and little Jimmy's screeching face. Oh, what fun!'

Chloe, despite her bright-pink hair, was a very serious soul who tended to take things quite literally. She'd once shared with Matt that she was on the Asperger's spectrum.

'I'm rubbish at faces, me. Tried painting my sister once. She looked like a sad goat.'

Matt laughed. 'I'm sure there's a market for that kind of thing somewhere.'

But Chloe didn't smile and Matt changed the subject. 'The radiators just need bleeding. I'll look for the little key.'

There was something so satisfying about bleeding a radiator, Matt thought, as he turned the key anticlockwise and listened to the trapped air slowly escaping, the water rushing in to take its place.

'I could've done it, y'know,' Chloe said, watching him. 'If I had one of them thingies.'

'All part of the service!' Matt joked, but Chloe looked stern.

'I just don't want you thinkin' I'm some kind of useless girlie who has to play dumb to get men to do things for her.'

'What a revolting thought,' Matt said. And Chloe finally smiled. 'There we are, all done.' He put his hand at the top of the radiator to feel its spreading warmth.

'Cheers.'

'How's the riverboat coming along?' Matt knew Chloe had started a new commission recently for a millionaire businessman.

'I hate it. But it's what the guy wants.'

'Take the money and run, I would.'

'Yeah, that's what George says.' George was Chloe's boyfriend, who Matt had met a couple of times. A more unlikely couple he'd never encountered. He was a twice-divorced barrister, who represented big companies in negligence claims. They'd met at one of Chloe's exhibitions and, at forty-nine, George was a good twenty years older than her.

221

Matt headed to the door. 'Everything else OK?' he asked, out of politeness more than anything.

'Yeah, I'm fine. But you're not.' Chloe's directness caught Matt off guard, even though he should have been used to it by now.

'What makes you say that?' He smiled.

'You're not as shiny as usual.' And suddenly she stepped forward and hugged him.

He was totally thrown, partly because he felt a rush of emotion tightening his throat and partly because Chloe had never hugged him before and it felt somehow . . . inappropriate. He was technically her landlord, after all. He wondered what his life was coming to, if virtual strangers like Chloe were feeling sorry for him.

Chloe didn't speak, and finally let him go before turning back to her riverboat canvas. She seemed to instantly forget Matt was there, so he crept out quietly, leaving her to her angry statement-making pastels.

He didn't go straight back to the gallery. The unpleasant mis-understanding with Kate on Sunday had started him back on the fags. And although he'd thought at the time it was just a one-off, he now found himself reaching into his jacket for the third packet he'd bought since the weekend. He was back on twenty a day. It was as if he'd never stopped.

Even within two days, he'd already established himself a quiet little smoking spot behind the shop. The noise from the street was muffled there and he could look up at the backs of all the houses, wondering if any of the dozens of people living in them were in the same mess as him, wondering if any other husbands were question-ing their wife's behaviour, wondering if they really knew the person they were married to at all.

Kate had been so convincing about the casino that he felt stupid ever doubting her, especially when she'd proved she was in Edinburgh by hysterically rifling through her purse, pulling out a used train ticket – London to Edinburgh return – that bore Saturday's date, and yelling, 'There! Believe me now?'

He told her he did.

But he didn't. And he didn't know why.

So when Kate had left for work early yesterday, Matt had got up with Tallulah and made her breakfast as usual, taken her to school as usual, then rung Pete to tell him he'd be a little late to the gallery. He'd then gone back home and switched on the computer. He knew it was a mistake to do it. *Ignorance is bliss, What the eye doesn't see* and a whole plethora of apt sayings had flashed through his mind and warned him against opening this Pandora's box, warned him against googling new casinos in Edinburgh, specifically those opened in the last week, specifically those opened in the last week by TV star Kate Andrews.

And, as if that wasn't enough to confirm his fears, he then called up the tourist board in Edinburgh and spoke to a very enthusiastic woman with a brusque Scottish accent. She'd listed all the casinos in the vicinity and informed him that the most recent establishment had been built three years ago and there were no plans for any more in the foreseeable. Would he like a brochure about the Military Tattoo? He'd stopped listening after 'three years ago' and hung up.

And now he couldn't avoid the stark truth.

Kate had lied about where she was on Saturday night.

Yes, she was in Edinburgh.

But no, she wasn't opening a casino.

So what was she doing there?

46

'That's lunch, everyone!' Benno shouted at the end of the morning's filming, initiating a mass exodus towards the trailers and film-unit base and a three-course meal.

As usual, Kate wasn't interested in the food. And despite leaving her phone behind that morning so she wouldn't get distracted on set, the plan hadn't worked very well. She'd found it so hard to focus, desperate to get through the scenes and not giving it her best. Even the producer had to ask her, 'Where's your head at the moment, Kate?'

'Sorry, sorry. Didn't sleep very well last night.' Which was true. But not the reason she couldn't concentrate.

Mack the facilities guy, who looked after all the trailers, unlocked her door, keen to impress by asking if she needed anything and eager to point out she had *real* coffee in there, 'none of your instant nonsense'.

'Oh, thanks darling. You're a star.' She smiled at him sweetly, silently willing him to leave so she could get on and check for messages.

Once inside the trailer, she slammed the door and leapt at her phone. There were a dozen or so texts – she frantically scrolled through them, searching for his name, which she'd disguised in her contacts list as 'MacGregor's Restaurant'.

Nothing.

Nothing!

She could feel rage rising up in her like boiling oil. What?? He'd had five hours! How the fucking hell *dare* he not answer? She saw there were answerphone messages too and she lit a cigarette, her hand shaking. OK, maybe he'd phoned instead. *Calm down, Kate. And retrieve your sodding voicemails.*

The recorded voice thanked her for calling and told her she had, pause, *six* new messages. She skipped through them, listening only to the first two or three words of each one before disregarding it and moving onto the next: there was only one voice she wanted to hear.

First, it was Matt: *Hi babe, it's me* . . . skip.

Then her agent: *Kate, it's Cynthia* . . . skip.

Then the accountant from the production office: *Hi Kate, it's Jane Dobbs from Accounts* . . . skip.

Matt again: *Oh, and Kate. . .* skip.

Then her dentist: *Hello Mrs Fenton, it's the Park Dental Practice* . . . skip!!

And finally, the sixth message.

Please God, let it be him.

It was her mother: *So you were in Edinburgh last week and didn't come and see us* . . .

She threw the phone across the trailer, where it landed forlornly on the purple sofa.

A knock at the door.

'Go away!'

It was Mack. 'Sorry, sweetheart, I just wondered if you needed any toilet rolls?'

'Mack, if I need anything I promise I will let you know. Now can I have my lunch break, please?'

She heard him scuttling away and shouted after him, 'Sorry, sorry!' kicking herself for being so rude. She wanted to cry, and stood there glued to the spot, humiliated by Callum's rejection, aggressively inhaling on her cigarette, desperately trying to quell the panic that was rising inside.

And then the phone rang.

It would be Matt.

She couldn't speak to him right now, she'd let it ring off.

But even from across the trailer she could see that the name flashing on the screen wasn't Matt's. She walked over to the sofa and looked at it.

MacGregor's Restaurant.

It was him.

The phone nearly slipped out of her hand, she was shaking so much from nerves and sleeplessness and an overdose of nicotine. She shut her eyes as she pressed answer, trying to sound calm, trying to sound unbothered by the fact that he was calling . . .

'Hello you,' she said.

'Hi.' And even this single syllable, uttered in his beautiful, rich, fifty-six-year-old Scottish voice, made her melt.

'I thought you'd forgotten me.'

47

Becky was knocking on the door. 'Five minutes, Kate.'

'OK, sweetheart, no worries.'

Becky walked away from the trailer, confused. *Sweetheart?* Blimey.

Kate was lying on the purple sofa, where she'd been for the past half-hour, talking to Callum and beaming. After the initial awkwardness, their conversation had thawed, warmed up and at one point become positively hot. It felt between them like it had done seventeen years before: easy, unpretentious, familiar.

They'd arranged to talk again that evening between five and seven, when Belinda would be at yoga.

Before she hung up, Kate tried once more: '. . . and I'll be finished by lunchtime on Friday, so if there's *any* chance you can get away . . .'

'There's no way, Kate. I'm sorry.'

'What if I came to you? That hotel again?'

'It's too risky. I can't have two nights out with Gary in the space of a week.'

She knew he was right. But it was so frustrating. 'I'll just have to make do with your voice then, won't I? And you know what that does to me.'

Callum smiled, lapping up the flattery before a tiny voice in his head wondered if he was making a fool of himself . . . but he soon ignored it and chose instead to enjoy the moment.

'Call me anytime,' she said. And when she ended the call, she closed her eyes and took a deep breath. God, he made her feel good.

Callum had only had phone sex once before. It was long before he'd met Kate, when he'd been on a rugby tour to Dublin. He was in his early thirties then. He'd been away from Belinda for three days, and one night he'd abandoned his team mates at the bar and gone to his room to phone home.

They'd talked for over an hour – he remembered the bill had been astronomical. Mostly they'd chatted about the tour and the games and life and how Ben had been that day, and then out of nowhere he'd said to her, 'What are you wearing right now?' It was her black silky robe – the one he'd used to joke wouldn't keep a fly warm, it was so thin. But she'd always said she liked the feel of the silk on her skin.

'Untie it.' There'd been a pause then. And it could've gone horribly wrong. She could've taken the mick, laughed at him with a 'What the heck has got into you, my boy?'

But instead she went along with it.

'OK.' He'd heard her breathing get faster on the end of the line and then she'd said, 'It's untied. Tell me what you want me to do next.'

And he did. And likewise she in turn made her own demands, culminating in one glorious telephonic orgasm that surprised and delighted them both in equal measure.

For years afterwards, Callum often wondered whether the staff on reception in that Dublin hotel had listened in on the call, catching Belinda say, 'I'm coming, Jesus, Callum, ohhhhh . . .'

And him in turn whisper, 'That's it, baby, come on . . .'

The auburn-haired receptionist had certainly looked at him differently the next morning when he went down for breakfast. He shuddered to think. Because it wasn't really in his nature to be so . . . well, *disinhibited*. And yet that evening, there he was, lying on his marital bed in the dark, talking to Kate in her Winnebago, in ecstasy as she told him in detail what she would do to him next time they were together.

When Belinda came back from yoga, Callum was in the kitchen in a pinny, singing along to the radio, laying the table and warming the plates.

'Someone's feeling better then!' she said, surprised but happy to see a much enlivened husband.

'I've done carrots and broccoli. Be about five minutes.' And he kissed her and carried on.

'Old people shouldn't sing!' Ailsa said, coming in with an empty cereal bowl and a book about metaphysical poetry under her arm. But she was smiling, because secretly she loved it when her dad was in one of his silly moods.

After dinner, Belinda cleared up, whilst Ailsa made them a cup of tea.

'So, I'm glad you're in a good mood,' Belinda said.

'Uh-oh. Look out, Dad. I can hear a special request coming.' Ailsa laughed.

'Oh, shush! It's for you as well, this.'

'Go on.' Callum suspected the subject of Ailsa's moped was about to rear its head again.

'My day off on Friday, as you know . . . and Ailsa's got an inset day.'

'How do you *always* know my timetable better than me?' Ailsa complained jokingly.

'So I was wondering . . .'

Here it comes, Callum thought. *I was wondering if me and Ails could go and look at mopeds for her Christmas present.*

'I was wondering if you'd like to pay for me and Ails to go to this new spa over in Glasgow. They've got a special offer, two for the price of one. Elaine was telling me about it at yoga.'

'Seriously? Ah, wicked!' Ailsa was clearly excited.

Callum was, too, but for a different reason. He tried not to show it, playing the part. 'How much is it gonna set me back?' he grumbled.

229

'Hundred and fifty quid. But that's for one night's accommodation . . .'

'Will we share a room?'

'Yes.'

'Cool!'

'And it includes two treatments. Each. It's a bargain, Cal!'

He looked at her. His mind was racing with all the possibilities this would give him. He could see Kate! He could spend the night with Kate!

He sighed as if he'd just been persuaded, calling her bluff.

'Oh I see, so I don't even get a look-in then?'

'Get over yourself, Callum, you'd hate it! Sitting in a jacuzzi, having your nails done! Gossiping!'

He laughed. 'Alright, then. Early Christmas present, OK?'

Belinda came over with soapy hands and gave him a big hug, kissing him all over, saying, 'Thank you, thank you!'

'Yeah, cheers Dad. I might just forgive you now for embarrassing me and Tom.'

Callum shook his head, affecting an outer dismay that belied his inner smile. He was going to see Kate! He knew it was wrong. But he was going to do it anyway. There was no stopping this now.

48

Doug dropped Kate off at three o'clock at the Lodge. She knew Callum was getting in his car as soon as school finished and driving straight there. Plenty of time for her to have a bath, moisturize her skin, do her make-up and get the kit on – some gorgeous French knickers in deep-green satin, matching camisole and push-up bra. Oh, and stockings. All of which she'd hastily bought from a local department store on her way back from filming.

In all that time she hadn't given Matt a second thought. So when her phone rang she was actually surprised to see his name on the screen.

'Hi,' he said.

'Anything wrong?'

'No, I was just thinking about you, that's all. Aren't you on set? I was expecting the voicemail.'

She remembered just in time that Matt would think she was working all day. 'No, there's a problem with the lights or something so I've just come back to the trailer for a bit. You OK? You sound a bit . . . I dunno.'

'I'm fine.'

There was an uncomfortable silence.

'Kate,' he ventured nervously. 'We're OK, aren't we?'

'Of course we are! What's got into you?'

'About Edinburgh . . .'

231

'Matt!'

'I know you lied about the casino.'

Fuck.

Buy some time.

'Alright, thanks Becky!' she shouted in response to a non-existent knock on a non-existent trailer door. 'They want me back on, babe. Look, I'll explain to you properly when I see you, but . . . I had to visit someone. And I promised them I wouldn't tell anyone I was coming. You're gonna have to trust me on this, Matt. I'll call you later, OK?'

'OK.'

And she hung up.

Bollocks.

Callum had been there for three hours. And almost every minute of it had been spent indulging in fabulously filthy, energetic and frenetic sex. It was better than any drug ever invented, and far more addictive. They had devoured each other over and over again, as if there was a finite amount of gratification to be had, desperate to exhaust the supply whilst simultaneously never wanting it to end. They were both privately conscious that their bodies were seventeen years older than they had been, and both privately delighted that age had not suppressed their indefatigability. Callum, in particular, had been impressed – and relieved for the sake of his self-esteem – that his stamina hadn't diminished. *Thank God for rugby*, he thought.

Kate's alarm went off at eight p.m., reminding her to phone Matt. Callum, likewise, needed to phone Belinda. He went outside and told her that he'd gone for a curry with the boys. He was relieved she didn't want to talk much, preoccupied with enjoying her girlie time at the spa. The place was amazing, she said. And actually, maybe Callum *would* like it here, after all.

Kate meanwhile had stayed in the bathroom, talking to Matt. She'd bought enough time with their phone call that afternoon to think up an elaborate but credible story that would justify her trip to Edinburgh and the casino lie. She blamed it all on her school friend Jinny, saying Jinny had been having an affair for eighteen months, which Kate had known about but been sworn to secrecy, promising not to breathe a word. And now Jinny's world was falling apart.

'You could've told me all that though, Kate. Why invent all that crap about a casino?'

'I thought if I told you I had to go to see Jinny for the night you'd have been pissed off. Understandably. Especially after I missed our meal out the night before.'

'Christ, so did you lie about *that* as well? About meeting Paula whatever her name was.'

Kate was trapped. She had to decide in that nanosecond which response would cause the least damage. 'No! Of course I didn't lie – what d'you think I am?'

'I'm not entirely sure, to be honest.'

She'd walked right into that one. There were a couple of seconds of silence before Kate tried again, more gently. 'Look, sweetheart, I couldn't tell you *why* it was so important I went because Jinny made me swear not to tell. So my only option was to make up something to do with work. I handled it all wrong, and I'm so sorry.'

Matt seemed to be absorbing what she said as Kate bit her lip on the other end of the line, hoping to God he'd believe her. She shut her eyes with relief when he said, 'It's OK. I just, well, y'know, I thought the worst, that's all.'

Callum had come back inside, aware that Kate was still on the phone and trying to stay quiet.

'I'll be home soon, sweetheart, and we can spend some proper time together, yeah?'

Her voice was tender, gentle, loving, and hearing Kate talk like that made Callum shiver. He was hijacked by the strangest of feelings – was he jealous? Maybe. But it was more than that – he was thrown by how convincing she sounded. How in love she appeared to be with her husband. If the situation had been reversed and Kate had heard him talking to *Belinda*, what would she have thought?

That he sounded tense and uncomfortable, desperate to get off the phone, ending the call with, 'Right. Better go – my lamb pasanda's calling me.' Not exactly love's young dream. But perhaps more genuine. If he'd really thought about it, what he found disturbing was the ease with which Kate could turn on the charm. Is that what she did with him? Did she never stop being an actress?

Later that night, when they lay on the bed, looking out at the full moon, listening to hooting owls and the absence of traffic, he asked her about Matt. She didn't recoil as he thought she would, or become defensive. She just answered him straight. 'There was only ever you, Callum. I love Matt dearly. But there was only ever you.'

And she turned to him and kissed him so softly, her closed eyes moistening with tears, and he thought: *This can't possibly be an act.*

And it wasn't.

49

Three weeks later, Kate had returned home and was back filming at the studios. It meant a much easier day for her – getting home in time to read Tallulah a bedtime story and share a glass of wine with Matt. Well, a few glasses of wine actually, and a few cigarettes. He joined her now outside the French doors, puffing away in the cold.

'You gonna give up for New Year?' she teased.

'Are you?'

Kate had learnt to handle Matt's tetchiness over the past month or so. He was definitely different, but she couldn't work out why. Of course, it went through her head that he somehow knew about Callum. There'd been all that stuff about the casino, but surely that was behind them now? She put it down to his getting fed up with her work. It was a long job, this: nine months in total, with frequent chunks of time spent away from home. Whenever the moment felt right, she would press Matt to find out what was going on in his head, but each time she'd receive the same answer: 'I'm fine, Kate, don't fuss.'

So she'd just kiss him and say, 'I love you. You know that, don't you?'

And he'd smile a tight smile and say, 'Love you too.'

The missing 'I' was the all-important ingredient, she realized ironically. But she daren't pursue it further, for fear of rocking the boat. And Kate's boat was most definitely sailing on calm and happy seas at the moment.

'I've been thinking about Christmas,' she said, interrupting the silence that had engulfed them as they stood smoking on the patio. 'How about we go to my parents?'

'In Edinburgh?'

She ignored the irritation in his voice. 'Yeah, why not? It'll make a nice change and Mum will be delighted. And when was the last time you celebrated a proper Scottish Hogmanay?'

Matt knew the decision had already been made; it wasn't really up for discussion. 'Yeah, sure. Whatever you want.'

And he stubbed out his cigarette in the garden ashtray and went back indoors. Celebrating Christmas was the last thing on his mind right now.

50

Considering how on eggshells he'd been when he first renewed contact with Kate, Callum was surprised how easily he'd fallen into this happy groove of deceit. There was almost a routine to their long-distance affair, which involved a lot of phone sex and moments filled with the fleeting hope of a potential meeting.

Every morning when Kate was safe to talk she would send the usual text from Kettley's Garage, informing Mr MacGregor that his car was due for a service.

Callum, in turn, would respond when it was safe for *him* and tell her what time that day he could talk. She'd send a swift response back to confirm and all texts would be immediately deleted.

They hadn't seen each other for three weeks now and it was starting to take its toll. Kate frequently showed her frustration by texting him photos of her bare breasts, her breasts in a beautiful bra, her daring buttocks in a thong, or her whole body naked in the bath, her right hand placed tantalizingly beneath the bubbles. There'd even been a close-up of her lips, slightly parted, her tongue peeping out between them, beckoning him in. She knew it was risky, but she couldn't bear not seeing him and this at least alleviated the overwhelming need for fulfilment.

'Can't you come to London?'

'And do what?'

'I can put you up in a hotel . . .'

'. . . make me sound like an escort or a . . .'

'Personal sex slave? What a gorgeous thought.'

They laughed it off, but not seeing each other was no joke.

'I know this is a long way off, but in half-term . . .'

'February? Fuck off, Callum, I can't wait until February!'

'Hey, I'm doin' my best, OK?'

'Sorry. Go on.'

He waited, slightly thrown by her petulance. 'OK, well in half-term, Belinda wants us to go skiing in France with Ailsa. Our friends have got a chalet.'

She interrupted him like a sulky teenager. 'I can't bear thinking of you on holiday with your family.'

Callum ignored this and carried on, 'Anyway, there's also a teachers' conference in Brighton the same week. I'm thinking I could go to that instead – though not be there all the time, of course . . .'

Kate's mood instantly brightened. 'Yes. Do it. It's something, at least. But I mean it, Callum, I've got to see you before then. Whatever it takes.'

They'd finished the call, Callum feeling annoyed that his suggestion – which was a big sacrifice for him – had been met with such an underwhelming response from Kate.

He'd called her from outside the rugby club, where he was meeting Gary for a drink. He'd hoped he could get away without telling anyone about him and Kate, but things were getting tricky and he needed someone he could trust, to fall back on if things got dangerous. He'd already risked using Gary as an excuse a couple of times now and he felt he ought to put him in the picture.

'You're an absolute twat, Cal.' This wasn't the reaction Callum had hoped for, but Gary wasn't one to mince words. 'All that shit that happened before! You're off yer 'ead, pal!'

'Yeah, alright, keep your voice down.' The club wasn't busy – midweek training was still going on – but there were a couple of oldies like them in the bar, and Callum was conscious of eavesdroppers.

'Look, mate, of course I got your back if you need me. But Belinda's unique. I wish I'd met someone like her.'

Callum thought about Gary and his three failed marriages.

'Can't you just get it out of your system and move on?'

'I wish,' Callum said. And he meant it.

'She won't forgive you a second time. You do realize that, don't you?' Gary was uncharacteristically soft. 'And there'll be a whole queue of men knocking on Belinda's door the second she's available.'

'She's fucking amazing though, Gary!'

'Your wife or your bit on the side?'

Callum looked at him. He'd asked for that.

'I know who I'd choose,' Gary said.

'So you could say no to *this*, could you?' Callum got out his phone and brought up the photo Kate had sent him that morning, which he couldn't yet bring himself to delete. She was in the lilac basque again, her hair dishevelled, pouting like some 1950s silver-screen siren.

Gary took the phone and stared at the image. Callum, watching his expression, was bizarrely proud of the effect it was having. Even from Gary's lofty position on the moral high ground, he had to admit Kate was stunning. He whistled long and hard as he took in the glory of the be-lingeried Kate, and Callum couldn't help smiling, smug, peacock-like and preening.

Then Gary shattered the moment. 'Every old man's fantasy, eh Cal?' He handed the phone back. 'You wanna delete that, mate. Before your luck runs out.'

Callum left the club that night irritable and disconsolate. He was pissed off with Gary, but only because, deep down, he knew that what his friend was saying was true. He was fifty-six years of age, for God's sake. Who was he trying to kid?

He got in the car and adjusted his rear-view mirror, examining his reflection, cast in shadow by the lights from the club, which emphasized his tiredness and his lines. He looked exhausted and out of his depth. Because he was.

His phone beeped.

Kettley's Garage reminding him that his car needed a service.

He paused before responding, more reluctantly than usual: *OK* – giving Kate the green light to get in touch. He waited. A few seconds later, her reply came through:

> *Exciting news.*
> *Edinburgh for Xmas!*
> *Santa's coming . . .*
> *. . . And so am I Ho ho ho! xx*

It didn't take much to restore his enthusiasm, and as he readjusted the mirror ready to drive off, he noticed he actually looked a lot younger when he smiled.

51

'What was I thinking, organizing a bloody reunion five days before Christmas!'

Hetty had just finished taking a call on her mobile. 'That's Betsy Barrack cancelling now!'

Matt felt so sorry for her. She'd made such an effort for this party but people were dropping like flies. He watched his friend open a box of yearbooks she'd had specially printed for the evening. She was awkward in her new and very un-Hetty-like dress, which looked like it belonged on someone else's body, with overdone hair and unusually vampish make-up she'd paid a professional to do. He searched desperately for words of comfort.

'Hey, come on! There'll still be loads of people here, you watch! And like you said, even if it's just you and me, that's still technically a reunion!'

Hetty had already put out the name badges on a table. A big home-made banner behind it read WELCOME WARWICKONIANS! CLASS OF '88, an attempt at jollity in this otherwise lifeless function room of the Marmant Hotel. The DJ in the corner was setting up his gear, sound-testing snatches of eighties songs that stopped as quickly as they began, whilst the sombre barman poured complimentary wine into rows of glasses on four large trays.

'We could always drink all of the free booze between us if no one comes.' He was running out of cheery things to say.

'Oh stop it, Matty. I know you don't even want to be here, so let's stop pretending, shall we?'

It was true. Matt was only there to support Hetty.

He'd always made it quite clear he couldn't understand the point of reunions of any kind. 'If we were meant to stay in touch with people,' he'd told her, 'then we *would* have done! There's a reason why Bromsgrove Tom and German Mike aren't a part of our lives any more, and vice versa. You're just a lovely romantic with an idealized view of the world who sees the best in everyone!'

'Including Adam Latimer,' she'd ventured. And Matt had sighed. He wasn't looking forward to that encounter one bit – another reason he didn't really want to be there.

'Be nice to him, Matty, that's all I'm asking.'

Matt nodded and made a mental note to get as drunk as possible. They were travelling to Edinburgh the next day for Christmas, but sod it. If he was hung-over, he could sleep it off on the plane. In fact, he hoped he could sleep for the whole of the holiday.

Things between him and Kate had reached a kind of stalemate. They'd see each other briefly in the mornings before she was picked up for work, then briefly again in the evenings, when they'd rarely eat together, but frequently smoke and definitely drink together, before she'd turn in at ten, needing her beauty sleep.

Sex, unsurprisingly, was non-existent. He'd never known her to be like this before. He'd been used to her manic phases and her periods of self-loathing, and her anger – even rage – which had been known on occasion to turn violent. And, of course, her depressive phases, when she couldn't even get out of bed, lying there, mute, for days on end.

But despite how upsetting those different sides of Kate could be, he now longed to have them back, because he knew how to handle the mania and the self-hatred, the rage and the black, black moods. This new Kate, though, was like nothing he'd ever known before. There was a brightness in her eyes, she was sprightly but calm, friendly yet very, very distant. It was like living with an amenable work colleague rather than the mother of his child and his wife of six years.

It had crossed his mind that she might be having some sort of 'thing' with someone on the TV job – it wouldn't be a total shock. There'd been flirtations before, it sort of came with the territory – much as he hated it, this was a fact. But he'd met the cast of *Shot in the Dark* on several occasions, and the crew. And there was nobody there who set his alarm bells ringing, no one he felt uncomfortable with or sensed anything untoward about. And Kate seemed desperate to finish the job, so that didn't stack up. Almost every day she'd tell him how much she was looking forward to the end of the shoot.

Today was the last day of filming – and Kate would be getting ready right now for the wrap party, less than a mile from Hetty's reunion.

Maybe he just needed to be patient.

Kate would have a few weeks off in January before she started her next job, and maybe a week with her parents in Edinburgh was just what they needed. But he was reluctant to go there now that he associated the city with Kate's weird behaviour, rushing up to see her friend Jinny a few weeks back and the whole strange story about Jinny's affair.

He'd met Jinny several times.

And her husband, Bill.

And a more happy, grounded couple he'd never before encountered, so content in each other's company. He knew it was always the ones you least expected, but still – *Jinny*?

He'd asked Kate if they might see Jinny during their visit and she'd looked at him with disdain, as if he could possibly think that might be a good idea given the circumstances. 'Come on, Matt, get with the programme!' she'd said. And he'd felt about two inches tall for asking.

He ordered a double G&T from the barman, who was confused that Matt didn't want the free wine. But if he was going to have a hangover tomorrow, he may as well make it a good-quality one, not an acidic, cheap-wine-fuelled one. As he took his first mouthful, he made a silent toast to himself: that he would get through Christmas, make a fresh start in 2003 and hopefully get his wife back.

A squeal of delight behind him signalled the first arrival. It was Sarah the Goth! Who, bizarrely, was still a Goth. He watched Hetty transform into the perfect hostess, handing Sarah her name badge and directing her towards the free wine.

In for a penny, he thought and ordered another G&T before heading over to see Sarah himself, to find out if she remembered him. Sarah he could just about deal with – it was Adam he dreaded seeing. And he hoped, despite the hurt it would cause Hetty, that Adam Latimer would live up to his reputation tonight and fail to appear.

52

Kate had always loved wrap parties. Admittedly she'd loved them more in her younger, wilder days – taking coke in the ladies' loos with costume assistants who until then hadn't said boo to a goose, or doing shots with the mild-mannered trainee from the art department; even, once, snogging the face off a nervous young actor who'd had two lines in a scene with her – his first TV job and he got ravaged by the leading lady because the gaffer had dared her to do it. Those days were long gone now, of course. She'd calmed down a lot since meeting Matt and becoming a mother. Yes, she still flirted occasionally – no harm in a bit of that. Usually with the electricians or burly carpenters. She was drawn to their roughness, their witty cynicism, the pinches of salt with which they took everything, and the fact that their skills weren't limited solely to the TV industry, having been sparks or chippies in a previous life. They seemed more real somehow. Yes, she sometimes flirted, but generally, as befitted her age, she had no desire to misbehave these days.

Despite this, a wrap party still felt like the end of term in school. The same mood of recklessness and misrule pervaded. Job done. No more twelve-hour days and six-day weeks – responsibility relinquished and pages and pages of script transformed into hours of screen images, handed over now to the editors and sound engineers, to make of them what they would. There was something liberating about finally letting it go, a year or more before seeing the fruits of their labour advertised in magazines or on the TV channel to which it belonged. *Coming soon, new drama starring Kate Andrews.*

The party was being held in a Spanish restaurant, ironically on Greek Street. With it being five days before Christmas, everyone was doubly keen to celebrate. There was free tapas on tap and mojitos, courtesy of the production company. Clara the camera trainee was already pissed and they'd only been going an hour.

Kate had arrived early, specifically so she didn't have to stay long. They were leaving for Edinburgh at eight thirty the next morning and she wanted to feel good when she travelled. She'd told Callum he could call or text her any time until ten p.m., when she planned to leave the party. 'And if you get my voicemail, leave me a filthy horny message!' she'd whispered to him.

Callum himself was at the staff Christmas bash, school having broken up for the holidays two days earlier. He always felt good at the end of term, but the prospect of seeing Kate was making him even more festive than usual.

It had all been meticulously arranged. She'd booked a room at McKinley's Hotel for the twenty-second, in Callum's name. He would tell Belinda he was going into Edinburgh to do some Christmas shopping – *Alone! I hate shopping at the best of times, you know that – I'll get it done far quicker on my own* – and Kate would tell Matt the same thing.

It would give them three hours together in the afternoon. Then, in the evening, Callum would tell Belinda he was meeting Gary for a drink, and Kate would tell Matt she had to see Jinny again – *She's a mess, Matt, I can't believe it.* This would buy them another three hours, from half eight to midnight. It wasn't ideal, but it was something.

And it was still two days away. For now, Callum had to endure socializing with the staff from North Park Primary, listening to Brian Boyd droning on and on about yearly figures, expanding class sizes, and the cruise he'd booked for himself and his wife next summer. Callum sat politely, smiling and watching Brian's mouth move, not processing the words that came out of it, and all the time hiding his delicious little secret: in two days' time he'd be with Kate again.

Four hundred miles south in London's Greek Street, Kate was doing exactly the same thing – not really listening as Benno talked at her, a dusting of white powder stuck stubbornly to his left nostril. He'd been taking coke and was talking crap at a rate of knots, but she didn't give a fuck. Because in two days' time she'd be with Callum again.

'Oh it's been the most amazing shoot,' she lied, her eyes filling up on cue. 'I'm really going to miss everyone.'

And she thought to herself, *Christ, I'm a good actress.*

53

'Didn't recognize you without your shopping trolley!' An over-weight woman with a faint downy moustache and a sheen of sweat on her forehead had cornered Matt at the bar.

'Sorry?' He didn't recognize her.

'Last time I saw you,' she persisted, enthusiasm bursting out of her as keenly as the upper-arm flesh that refused to be restricted by her overtight sleeves, 'it was graduation night and Martin Bowler was wheeling you past Senate House in a shopping trolley! Weren't we all just *so mad* back then?!'

Matt inwardly sighed. He still didn't remember her, but discreetly clocked her name badge and, urged on by too much gin, faked it to make it.

'Anthea!' He hadn't managed to catch the surname but he knew it began with a 'W'. 'Anthea Williams?'

'Weldon. BA. QTS.'

From the depths of his memory he instantly remembered that QTS stood for Qualified Teaching Status.

'I don't teach, though,' she said enigmatically. 'Never did.'

And she just stared at him, inviting him to ask her why, but he didn't take the bait and just stared back, mystified.

Mercifully the awkwardness was interrupted by two guys, fresh off the dance floor, approaching Anthea, one of whom put his hands over her eyes and said in a cod Birmingham accent, 'I don't care if it's a sit-in, where's me bloody cushion!'

Anthea screamed with delight. 'Phillip Beddon, as I live and breathe!'

Hugs all round. Matt, once again completely at a loss as to who the two men were, looked round for a sneaking-off opportunity. Too late.

'Matt! You're not wearing your name badge!' Hetty was at his side, jokingly admonishing him.

Before he could make his excuses, the voice he'd dreaded hearing all night boomed, 'Doesn't need one! How could we forget the infamous Matty Fenton!'

It was Adam, of course.

Matt realized in that instant that the thing he'd most been fearing was finding Adam *attractive* when he saw him. Since their liaison at Warwick, there'd been no other encounters with men, putting paid to any possible doubts Matt might have had about his sexuality.

He was still slightly curious though, waiting for an unexpected rush and the return of those alien but uncontrollable sensations Adam had once engendered. None came. No feelings at all. Not even repulsion. Just confusion that he'd ever felt that way about him. He looked older, Matt thought, a bit fatter, and very . . . ordinary.

'Matt? You remember Adam?' Hetty prompted.

'Yeah. Yes, of course. How you doing, alright?' And he shook his hand, looking him straight in the eye, refusing to be remotely intimidated.

'All the better for seeing you again. Hetty's been filling me in on all your news, she—'

It didn't take long for Matt to find Adam irritating, interrupting him by offering to get the drinks in and leaving Adam high and dry, mid sentence. Matt headed to the bar with no intention of going back. He ordered himself a large Scotch and downed it in one.

Hetty approached him, scowling. 'Honestly, Matt, could you have been more rude?'

'I can't pretend to like him, Het. The guy's an arse.'

'Just for tonight you *could*'ve pretended. For my sake.'

'I'm gonna make a move.'

'Because of Adam?'

'No! It's just . . . there's only so many times you can say "remember when . . . remember when". It's boring, to be honest.'

'Thanks a lot!'

A cheer of recognition went up and nipped their argument in the bud, as the opening bars of 'It's Raining Men' prompted a surge of thirty-somethings onto the dance floor.

Within seconds Adam had grabbed Hetty, thrown her over his shoulder fireman's-lift style and was carting her right into the centre of the dance floor.

'Come on, Hetty, let's show them what we're made of!'

She screamed with delight, hoping beyond hope that her keep-it-all-in knickers weren't being exposed to the entire room.

Matt was surprised by an overwhelming sense of jealousy as he watched his best mate being carried away.

The double gins were starting to take effect now, and Matt was beginning to feel rebellious. He was annoyed that Hetty couldn't see Adam for what he was, sensing that she would choose him over Matt if she was forced to, and resenting this Johnny-come-lately, no-good ex-boyfriend for potentially ruining their friendship. He was also aware that any frustration or annoyance he might be feeling tonight was in reality down to Kate and her behaviour, and nothing to do with innocent bystanders like Hetty.

Suddenly Anthea Weldon, BA QTS was grabbing Matt's arm and leading him away from the bar, forcing him to dance with her. His first thought was to refuse. But he'd had just about enough to drink to make him surrender.

Feeling overtly competitive with Adam, and trying to drunkenly out-dance him, Matt was soon displaying a vast array of flamboyant moves that would have put John Travolta to shame.

Anthea was delighted as Matt pulled her this way and that, swinging her around with such ferocity and passion that she began sweatily hoping this might be her lucky night.

Adam knew the gauntlet had been thrown and he, in turn, put on a spectacular show of choreography, lifting Hetty, twirling her, dropping her dangerously low to the floor, then swiftly picking her up again.

When the song ended, everyone cheered, breathless and energized, and most people went back to their drinks, laughing. But then the DJ came up with another corker: 'Time Of My Life'. And the competition continued.

This time, though, Matt went straight over to Hetty and pulled her away from Adam, announcing, 'My turn!'

Hetty laughed hysterically as Matt gave her the Anthea treatment.

Anthea turned to Adam, hoping to complete the swap, but Adam was having none of it and marched straight over to Matt and Hetty.

'Sorry, mate, but this one's spoken for!' And he grabbed Hetty back to his side, a little *too* aggressively.

What followed was an undignified tug-of-war, with Hetty becoming an involuntary pulling rope between the two men. At first, she continued to laugh, but then it got out of hand and, after one particularly big pull, Adam lost his grip and Hetty went flying, ending up slumped and ungainly halfway across the floor. Her dress got torn in the process and one of her false eyelashes indecorously dislodged.

'Right, stop it, that's enough!' she shouted over the blaring music. People around them hadn't really noticed and were still dancing.

'You idiot!' Matt shouted at Adam. 'You OK, Het?' He helped her up, feeling partly responsible but glad he could level the blame at Adam.

'Out of the way!' said Adam. 'Here, Hetty, come and sit down.'

'Fuck off, Adam, you're not needed.' And Matt pushed Adam away by the shoulder, making him lose his footing slightly.

Now people *were* watching.

The song continued to blast from the speakers as Adam regained his composure and went for the jugular.

'What's the matter, Matt – can't handle the competition? You feeling left out, honeybun? Bit jealous, are we?'

'Don't be ridiculous, Adam,' Hetty yelled over the music. 'Matt and I are just friends, why on earth would he be jealous of you?' She dusted herself down and examined the rip in her dress.

'Oh, he's not jealous of me, babe. He's jealous of *you*. Isn't that right, Matt?'

And for one moment, his head swirling from the gin and the dancing, and surrounded by a crowd of vague staring faces from a time he'd long since forgotten, Matt thought he was in some alternative, parallel existence.

Hetty looked confused. Adam smirked and Matt shook his head . . . before launching forth and punching Adam squarely in the face. He went flying and screams abounded.

Anthea Weldon felt a stirring primal response to this display of machismo by Matt, who looked at Hetty before walking away.

Matt sat outside the hotel smoking and trying to sober up.

He didn't really want to go home – Kate would probably still be at the wrap party – although at least that would mean he could go straight to bed and avoid yet another fake conversation with her.

And he couldn't stay here. Not after this. Deep down he suspected that his life might be unravelling.

He was on his seventh cigarette by the time Hetty came out. She was carrying one of her shoes. The heel had snapped off during the chaos.

At first, they didn't speak. She sat next to him, clearly still shaken, looking like she'd been pulled apart at her seams.

'Adam says I have to ask you what it all meant. So here I am. Asking you.'

He didn't really know how to explain. It all seemed so tawdry and base. And it was also such a long time ago. He thought a while before answering, his voice sad and dull and monotone, 'It doesn't really matter, Het. Not in the grand scheme of things.'

'I'd still like to know. You've just spoilt the entire evening for me. At least do me the courtesy of telling me what's going on.'

She was right. There was no avoiding it. And actually, the way he was feeling right now, there was nothing much left to lose.

'The night we got our results. You went to find Adam and he wasn't there.' He couldn't bring himself to look at her, to see the trust and naivety drain from her face. 'And then you came looking for me. You knocked on my door, and you sat outside it for a while and you talked about him and how you wished you and I could be a couple instead, because we'd get on so well.'

'That was a joke!' Hetty mumbled, and Matt carried on.

'But you didn't think I was there, did you? And eventually you stumbled back downstairs to your room.'

'I don't really see where you're going with this . . .'

He sighed. 'Well, I *was* there, Het. I *was* in my room. I heard you knock. I heard everything you said.' He took a long drag on his cigarette, filling the air between them with sour smoke as he exhaled. 'And so did Adam. Because he was in the room too.'

Hetty still didn't get it. 'You were hiding from me?'

And he finally looked at her, and saw the penny painfully dropping.

'Was that the only time?' she asked.

'No. No, it wasn't. Look, I can't explain it, and—'

Hetty interrupted him. 'So you're gay?'

'It was a handful of times and it was only ever with him – that doesn't make me gay.'

'No,' she said thoughtfully. As if she was solving a puzzle. 'But it *does* make you unfaithful.'

'Unfaithful?'

'To me.'

And she picked up her broken shoe and hobbled back inside.

54

Kate's mother Yvonne was beside herself with excitement that her daughter and family were coming for Christmas. This was only the second time they had come up to Scotland for the holiday, usually opting to spend Christmas somewhere hot and exotic like Thailand, which Yvonne found bizarre.

'Why would anyone want to eat a turkey dinner in the scorching heat?' she'd said to Gordon.

'I don't think they eat turkey on Christmas Day,' he'd replied. 'That's the whole point. Kate's trying to do something different, and good on her!'

Sometimes Gordon wondered about the gaping holes in his wife's common sense.

Kate and Matt had also spent December in India before – 'Do they even *celebrate* Christmas in India?' Yvonne had asked Gordon incredulously when she heard, to which he'd sarcastically said, 'No.' Which was a mistake. Because that sent Yvonne into a complete spin about Kate and Matt destroying Tallulah's childhood with all this foreign-holiday nonsense. 'That child needs cold weather and Quality Street and Father Christmas coming down a chimney. What they're doing is tantamount to deprivation!'

Gordon ignored her histrionics. He'd found it was the best way.

But when he heard of Kate and Matt's plans to visit, he too was delighted. Apart from the fact that he'd get to see his only daughter and granddaughter, which in itself was a rarity, it also meant he wouldn't have to listen to Yvonne complaining about Kate's weird ideas.

Yvonne had pulled out all the stops, decorating their home to within an inch of its life, putting up *two* real trees: one in the garden that lit up at night, and the other in their spacious living room.

She and Gordon had moved in 1987, a couple of years after Kate had left home and the revelation of her 'troubles'. They never mentioned Luca, or his subsequent adoption – it was all too painful for words. Yvonne had become 'horribly sad', eaten up with sorrow and loss, and Gordon thought moving house would give them all a fresh start. They called it downsizing, and, yes, it was essentially a flat. But Yvonne preferred to call it a ground-floor luxury apartment, it being blessed with three bedrooms, two bathrooms and a study – aka Gordon's little sanctuary. It also boasted a beautiful large lounge with a magnificent fireplace, in front of which Tallulah could put a carrot, whisky and a mince pie for Santa.

They arrived mid afternoon on the twenty-first, just as it was turning dark and Christmas lights were coming on for the night.

Tallulah was sleepy but excited to see her Nannie and Grandy, whom she saw so rarely but completely adored. Especially Grandy, with his funny beard and silly voice.

'Oh come here, wee one, let me get in first with a cuddle!' Yvonne cried as they stepped through the door, scooping Tallulah up in her arms and smothering her with kisses.

'I bet that taxi from the airport set you back a pretty penny, eh Matt?' said Gordon, who always overcame his shyness at initial meetings by asking practical questions.

'Well, it was worth every penny!' Kate answered on his behalf, as she often did. 'Now Dad, how's about you pour us a nice couple of brandies to warm us up whilst I indulge in my horrible nicotine habit. I've gone three hours without one!' she announced, and walked straight through the kitchen to the back garden. Yvonne followed, Tallulah still in her arms, fiddling with Nannie's pearls.

'Don't go scattering your dirty stubs willy-nilly on my patio now, Kate. I've put a special ashtray out there for you.'

'Happy Christmas, Mum!' Kate shouted, realizing the price she was paying to see Callum for a few blessed hours was going to be very high, given that her mother was *already* getting on her nerves.

Gordon looked at Matt and smiled, a silent understanding passing between the two men that they would both require a good deal of patience to endure the next few days and their respective wives' sometimes overbearing personalities.

'Here, give me those cases,' Gordon said, always preferring to *do* rather than *discuss*. 'And I'll make yours a triple.'

Matt smiled. He'd always been very fond of Gordon.

Two hours later, Yvonne was clearing the dishes and Gordon was playing *Guess Who?* with Tallulah, who found it hysterical that Grandy actually looked like one of the characters. Matt could tell that Tallulah's giggling was on the verge of turning to tears, and that it might be an idea to think about bedtime.

'It's OK, I'll give her a bath tonight,' Kate said, and affecting an air of nonchalance she continued, 'And then we need to talk about plans for tomorrow. Because I've still got a bit of shopping to do.' She threw it in casually, almost hoping no one would notice.

'But all the presents have arrived!' Yvonne whispered, careful not to spoil anything for her granddaughter, who was still engrossed in the game. 'I've even wrapped everything for you!'

'That's great, Mum, and thank you! But there's still a couple of things I need to get for a certain someone,' she said, winking overtly at Matt.

He found this out-of-character display of affection a little disturbing, to say the least.

'Right, well, what about the ice-skating, and the Christmas show at the theatre? I've got it all planned,' said Yvonne, unable to curb her enthusiasm.

'Oh, I'm definitely coming ice-skating!' Kate said. 'But then why don't you go to the show, and I'll disappear for a couple of hours and do my thing. Give my ticket to Aunty Norma, if you like.'

'Huh. You won't catch Norma inside a theatre, pet,' Gordon intervened. 'She's terrified the roof will fall in on her.'

'Aye, she has some strange ideas, that one!' said Yvonne.

Kate smiled at Matt and he politely reciprocated as his mother-in-law carried on, 'And will you be seeing Jinny and Bill while you're up? I saw her mother a few weeks back – they'd love to see you, I'm sure.'

Kate's smile dropped and she caught Matt's eye, awkwardly. 'Yes, maybe. We'll see.'

'Aw, you've not fallen out with her again, have ye? Honestly, Matt, those two, they behave sometimes like they're still at school!'

'Don't be silly, Mum. Now, Lules, it's time for your bath, and then bedtime!'

Tallulah complained that the game wasn't finished, but Grandy promised to keep everything exactly how it was so they could finish it in the morning before they went ice-skating. Tallulah seemed satisfied and tootled off to the bathroom with her mum.

Matt excused himself to indulge in *his* recently reacquired nicotine habit, and Yvonne was left with Gordon.

She turned to him and whispered, 'I don't think things are right between those two, Gee. Matthew hardly said anything at dinner.'

'Ach, hush your nonsense, the man couldn't get a word in edgeways,' he said. But secretly he agreed with his wife, and he wondered what was really going on.

Outside, Matt lit up his second cigarette, listening to the faint hum of party music in a house nearby, mixed with cheery pub revelry, even some carol-singing – all drifting in the Scottish night breeze. He wondered if it would snow.

He checked that he wasn't about to be disturbed by Yvonne offering him another mince pie and then took out his phone. He went into his contacts list and scrolled down the 'H's till he found 'Hetty'.

He pressed call, and his stomach flipped nervously; not wanting to have this conversation, but unable to bear not being friends any more. It rang. And rang. Matt knew that on the other end, Hetty would be staring at the screen and choosing once again not to speak to him.

The voicemail kicked in. *Hi, this is Hetty Strong – please leave me a message!*

Matt cleared his throat and began pretty much the same message that he'd left last time:

'Hi Het, it's me. Again. Am in Edinburgh now. Look, I hate us not being friends like this. Adam is . . . well, he's nothing, *was* nothing. And you and me, we're worth far more than all that, aren't we?' He paused. 'Call me, mate. Please. This is really weird.'

He ended the call and sighed.

There was a bit of a fuck-it element in the air tonight, and he knew he had another call to make. He went back into his contacts and found the number he needed. His finger hovered over the call button. He'd been wanting to call for days – no, weeks. But every time, he backed down, overwhelmed by what the conversation might uncover. Maybe it was the wine at dinner or the whisky after it that made him press call. And once again, his stomach flipped.

'Hello?'

'Hello, you. It's Matt, Kate's husband. How the devil are you?'

In the bathroom, Kate sat on the toilet seat watching Tallulah in the bath, lost in her own world of Disney and bubbles and a conversation with a Christmas elf.

Kate had locked the door. If anyone challenged her, she'd say it was force of habit. She knew Matt was outside, smoking, and her parents were still in the living room, discussing the fact that four vegetables on Christmas Day was ample – anything more was simply showing off.

Kate got her phone out. She knew she was taking a risk, but part of the excitement lay in the risk. She wanted to break the rules they'd set for themselves, to go so near to the brink of mayhem that maybe they'd have to jump off. Her breathing speeded up with anticipation. She called his number. If he couldn't answer, he wouldn't. Fuck it.

55

Three miles away, Callum and Belinda's fondue night was well into its second hour.

Fondue night at the MacGregors' had become a bit of a Christmas tradition amongst Callum and Belinda's friends. Always held on the twenty-first, in recent years they'd added a melted-chocolate option to the traditional melted cheese.

Callum was topping up Sue's glass. It was the one time of the year when she was slightly softer towards him, but without fail after her third drink she'd find the opportunity to take him to one side and say, 'I may have forgiven you, Callum MacGregor, for what you did to my friend . . .' At which point Callum would finish off the sentence for her, 'but you'll never forget. Yep. I know, Sue. You don't need to remind me every year!' And he'd move onto another guest before she could start raking over old coals.

Belinda knew she did it too. She'd had words with her several times about it, but to no avail. 'Honestly, Sue! Let it go, babes. I love the fact you're so loyal to me, but the poor man has served his time.'

'Not in my book, he hasn't,' Sue would say, and Belinda would shake her head. Strange that she now felt sorry for Callum getting a hard time from her best friend – his misdemeanour happened seventeen years ago, after all. Belinda decided the only way to deal with it was to laugh it off.

She looked over at Callum now, chatting genially with their next-door neighbour and his mate Gary, and she felt an unexpected surge of love for him. He was looking good, fair play. Actually, he *always* looked good to her, but recently he was looking even better. He'd lost a few pounds in the past few weeks and bought himself some new clothes. Very unlike him to go clothes shopping, but Belinda wasn't complaining! And there was something a bit more sprightly about him; he had his old cheekiness back. She sidled past him heading for the kitchen, sneakily squeezing his bum en route. He looked pleasantly surprised and she winked at him.

In the kitchen she checked on the cheese fondue. A ridiculous idea really – no one except Gary ever really dived in with the cheese – but a few years back, when Belinda had suggested swapping the fondue for canapés, there was uproar amongst their friends. And so it had stayed.

As she gathered together all the accoutrements to take through, her mobile started ringing.

Her hands were full.

Might be one of the kids.

Not Ben of course, who was spending his first Christmas away from home, backpacking his way around the world. No doubt the other two would follow suit when their turn came.

Ailsa was at Tom's tonight and Cory, home for two weeks now since uni broke up, had a bar job in his Uncle Fergus's pub. She'd barely seen him since he'd been back but at least he was earning a few quid.

She just hoped whoever was calling wasn't expecting a lift – Belinda had warned them there'd be none available, not on fondue night. They'd have to sort their own transport. And she hoped they'd remembered, because by now both she and Callum were way over the limit.

But it wasn't *her* phone that was ringing.

It was Callum's.

He'd left it by the sink.

Ailsa had set them both the same ring tone when they'd first got their mobiles, the theme from *Rocky* – it was absolutely ridiculous, but had since become such a family joke that neither of them had had the heart to change it.

Belinda put down the fondue tray and reached for the phone, thinking how silly Callum was to leave it so close to the washing-up bowl.

'Kettley's Garage'.

Strange.

'Callum?' she called out half-heartedly, knowing he was unlikely to hear. And did it really matter? She thought about ignoring it, but then changed her mind, curious as to why a garage should be ringing her husband at seven p.m. four nights before Christmas.

She pressed answer. 'Hello?'

Nothing.

'Hello – Belinda MacGregor speaking?'

Still nothing.

So Belinda hung up, collected the fondue and wandered through to the front room, yelling over the party noise, 'Right, who's ready for a taste of the seventies!'

And the guests all cheered.

56

That night, Kate and Matt lay turned away from each other in Yvonne's rarely used spare bed, neither letting on to the other that they were still awake.

Both were thinking about the phone calls they'd made earlier and the consequences of doing so.

Kate was still in shock after hearing Belinda's voice. She replayed the five-word phone call over and over in her head, recalling the friendly Welsh lilt as Belinda helpfully tried to make contact with whoever was on the end of the line.

Kate hated her for being so friendly. Hated her Welsh accent. Hated that she would be lying in bed with Callum right now.

She wondered what Belinda looked like these days. Seventeen years older. Menopausal by now, no doubt, grey-haired, with a tired old body that surely Callum could no longer find attractive? And at this thought, Kate couldn't help but feel smug. Because whatever Belinda had on Kate – three children and twenty-six years of shared life – Kate would always be the younger woman. The sexier, more attractive, more appealing younger woman.

But hard on the heels of her smugness came heart-wrenching jealousy. And the thought of them in bed together right now, merely three miles away, was enough to keep Kate awake, churning the image over and over in her head.

She was going to look dreadful tomorrow if she didn't sleep. All the effort she'd gone to arranging their getting together would be a complete and utter waste of time if she didn't look her best. She had *always* to look her best. She had *always* to be the better option. She sighed and tried to calm herself down with the thought that at two o'clock the following afternoon, she'd be with him. In that faceless, anonymous, city-centre hotel room.

God, she loved that man.

That man was almost asleep now, the boozy evening having taken its happy toll. He lay basking in the afterglow of another successful annual MacGregor bash.

He could hear Belinda in the bathroom, cleaning her teeth, make-up removed, comfy Scooby Doo nightshirt pulled over her head.

'Ailsa's staying at Tom's. She just text me,' she shouted, her tooth-pastey mouth spitting out the words, barely decipherable.

Callum didn't answer, he was too sleepy with drink to speak now, and he just wanted to lie there and think of Kate and how much he needed to see her tomorrow. He felt himself harden at the thought of being inside her again. Christ, those breasts . . . and her skin . . .

He'd almost dropped off when Belinda got into bed quietly beside him, spooning him and nuzzling his neck.

'Aw, it was a good night, wasn't it?' she whispered.

'Hmm,' he mumbled, losing to sleep his power to speak.

'And you looked so sexy tonight, Callum.' Belinda had been feeling horny most of the evening. She ran her hand slowly along the familiar length of his thigh, higher, then higher, and was delighted to discover that the feeling was mutual.

Callum's eyes opened sharply, the shock of the unexpected sensation of Belinda's hand caressing him. He found himself suddenly very, very awake, and very, very hard. He let her continue. He couldn't stop her, for Christ's sake – she'd be mortified. But the truth was, he didn't want to stop her.

There was no logic to what he was thinking. It defied explanation. But he felt as if . . . as if he was being unfaithful to Kate.

Unfaithful to his lover with his wife! What a head fuck. He couldn't process what was going on.

All he knew was that Belinda, silent and smiling, was urging him now to turn onto his back. She climbed on top of him, guiding him inside her with the deftness that marital familiarity had brought to their lovemaking over years and years spent together in bed.

They hadn't had sex for a couple of weeks, and the last time was such a quickie it hardly constituted sex at all.

'What's got into you, good boy? You getting old?' she'd teased at the time.

'That's better,' she whispered now, holding his gaze as she rocked her hips down and back, down and back and into him, taking him all in.

Callum couldn't look at her. Not because she wasn't still beautiful in her Scooby Doo nightshirt, hoisted up around her thighs for better access and clinging to the curves he knew so well. No, it wasn't that he didn't find her beautiful, it was just that he couldn't bear the guilt. The guilt of what he was about to do tomorrow, and the guilt that if Kate knew what he was doing right now she'd be devastated. So he shut his eyes.

And imagined it was Kate.

And when they'd finished and Belinda lay exhausted on his chest, he looked up at the ceiling, stroking her back, Christmas lights from their front garden flashing festively in celebration, and he thought, *I am a despicable human being.*

They lay like that for a few minutes before Belinda sleepily rolled over to her side of the bed. As she was turning away, settling herself in for the night, she mumbled, 'Kettley's Garage rang, by the way.'

What the fuck?

He feigned sleepiness, despite being as alert as a deer in hunting season.

'But the line went dead,' she yawned. 'I thought we always used Reilly's?'

He didn't know what to say.

His mind raced. He was about to launch into some long-winded

264

explanation about a mate recommending this new place when he heard the gentle, satisfied snuffle of Belinda's snoring.

She'd fallen asleep.

Callum was safe. For now.

57

The waitress put the drinks on the table.

'I'm sorry I've got so little time – I'll have to go after this. The in-laws are arriving at one!' Jinny said, taking a big slurp of her cappuccino and momentarily sporting a chocolate-powder moustache.

Matt liked Jinny. He wished Kate saw more of her, she was such a calm person to be around. 'Thanks for not telling Kate about this . . . about, y'know, us meeting.'

'Well, it feels a bit weird, I've got to be honest, but all for a good cause!'

When he'd rung her the night before, she'd been completely thrown that Matt and Kate were in Edinburgh for Christmas. Kate hadn't mentioned a thing!

Matt tried to play it down, saying it'd been a last-minute decision – that Kate was filming until the day before they arrived and the poor thing was knackered. He was positive Kate would call Jinny in the next couple of days to arrange to meet up. He'd gone on to say he needed her advice – it sounded lame when he said it, but Jinny didn't seem to think so – and she'd agreed to meet him.

He said for Kate's Christmas present he wanted to book a retreat for her *and* Jinny, and needed dates when Jinny could go. But also could she give him advice on what type of retreat he should go for. Yoga? Meditation? Silent?

Jinny, who was a nurse with two small children and little money, was delighted at the prospect. Not just overwhelmed by Matt's generosity that he should be including Jinny in the treat, but thrilled that she was going to spend three whole days with Kate. That hadn't happened since they were in their twenties.

Matt felt a twinge of remorse that his planned trip for them was just a ruse, but needs must. 'The most important thing is that you don't breathe a word to Kate. 'Cos she's bound to call you today, or tomorrow, to catch up, so just keep schtum.'

Jinny mimed zipping her lips.

'And for God's sake, sound surprised when she calls!' he laughed.

They chatted easily, enjoying the festive atmosphere of the busy Haymarket coffee shop, holiday excitement heightened by the backdrop of Christmas pop songs and fake snow.

Matt knew what he was building up to and he sensed he was running out of time. He listened as Jinny talked with love about her kids, and Bill, and found his heart sinking as she did so. Because either she was a brilliant liar and covering up the heartache of her supposed affair, or Kate hadn't told him the truth. And he suspected it was the latter.

Jinny checked her watch. 'I'm gonna have to go, sweetheart. The house looks like a bin. It's been so good to see you!'

It was now or never.

'Hey Jin, listen, I'm glad everything's good with the kids.' He paused. 'And with Bill.'

Jinny started wrapping her scarf around her neck. 'Yeah, well, they do my head in sometimes, but I wouldn't be without them.'

Say it. Say it!

'And I know you asked Kate not to say anything. But she was worried about you . . .'

Jinny smiled distractedly as she searched for the armholes in her coat. 'Sorry?'

'She told me about your affair.'

He watched for a reaction. There was none, so he continued, 'How are things now, because you seem—'

Jinny interrupted him, still smiling. 'What you talking about, Matt?'

Even though he wanted to be sick, even though there was a sudden hissing in his ears and the overwhelming urge to shout out 'FOR FUCK'S SAKE!', Matt knew he had to carry on.

'Kate told me you'd been having an affair for eighteen months. That you were an absolute mess. That you weren't sure how you and Bill were going to move forward.'

'Matt! I don't know what to say . . . Hang on,' – and confusion gave way to a smile – 'is this a wind-up? Are you winding me up?' She started laughing.

'No.' Jinny's smile faded. 'And I can understand you not wanting me to know, and fair enough if you don't want to talk about it – I probably shouldn't have mentioned it. Kate's gonna kill me.'

Jinny took his hand. 'Sweetheart, look at me.'

And he did. Fighting the urge to cry as he saw the kindness in her eyes.

'I promise you, Matt, me and Bill have never been happier. I adore the big lummox.' She shook her head. 'I wouldn't have the first clue how to have an affair – the whole idea is ludicrous.'

'Well, yeah, I must admit, that's what I thought when she told me.'

Most people would have been angry at the insinuation, but Jinny seemed more worried for Kate. 'I just don't understand why she would say something like that though, Matt. It's really bizarre.'

He sighed, longing for a cigarette to calm his troubled soul. And now he knew the truth, he didn't want to stay there any longer, certainly didn't want to tell Jinny about Kate's recent jaunts to Edinburgh to apparently console her friend. He started putting on his coat too.

'Yeah, yeah it is. When did you last speak to her?'

'We've texted a couple of times the past month, but I've not actually talked to her since October. Look, why don't I call her? See if I can get to the bottom of this.'

'No.' He sounded like he was admonishing her. 'Sorry. It's just,

I need to sort this. I think it's best if I do.' He got up now, his hand shaking as he took some coins from his pocket and left them on the table for the coffees. 'She's been under a lot of pressure with work – spending time together this Christmas will give us the chance to talk properly. Please, Jinny, let me do this.'

'Of course!' And she hugged him. 'Matt, I know she can be . . . complicated sometimes. I've been her friend for ever, remember.'

There was an unspoken understanding between them, neither wanting to broach the subject of Kate's instability.

'I'll call you, OK?' And he left.

Outside on the street, three drunken Santas were singing '*I wish it could be Christmas every day*'. He lit a cigarette and started walking towards the ice rink.

58

Callum had been waiting for twenty minutes. He daren't touch any-thing – he felt like an imposter, an intruder, that he shouldn't really be there. Outside in the corridor, he could hear the housekeeping staff going about their duties.

At one point, there was a knock on the door and he opened it, expecting Kate. Instead, a smiley-looking manager asked him if he was OK for water, and did he need anything else? He politely declined and returned to his seat by the window, too nervous even to make himself a cup of tea and trying to come to terms with where he was, what he was doing. He knew Kate found the whole thing exhilarating, that she thrived on the danger of it all. But *he* just felt out of his depth. That this life he was now living belonged to someone else.

That morning, Belinda had been in the best of moods, follow-ing last night's party and the after-party party in bed. She didn't even question Callum's desire to go shopping – if anything, she was touched he wanted to buy her something special. He hadn't said as much, but she knew Callum. That's what he was up to, and given the surge of love she was experiencing for him right now, she wasn't about to stand in his way.

He'd left the house at midday and got a bus into the city centre, heading straight to John Lewis to pick up Belinda's present – a port-able DVD player that she could watch in bed, a pair of black suede boots and a bottle of Chanel. They weren't spontaneous purchases – Kate had helped him choose in advance. Not out of any thoughtfulness for Belinda, of course, but because she knew it would save time if Callum knew exactly what to buy. Go to the shop. Buy it. Head to the hotel.

He'd finished by one fifteen and decided to walk the short distance.

The weather always affected people's moods, he thought. Today, Edinburgh treated its smiling shoppers to frosty sunshine. How different the city centre would feel were it rain-soaked or smothered in Scottish fog. He walked alongside the ice rink, remembering when his kids were little, how they'd loved to skate, round and round in endless circles, no sense of flow, terrified of falling but not wanting it to end.

He saw a little girl stumble and fall on the ice, sliding a few yards on her bum, her face set in a frown, too shocked to cry. She wore earmuffs that matched her little red dress and was carrying a panda. Callum thought how resilient kids could be, smiling at the fact that she'd managed to hold onto her panda despite going flying across the ice. Her dad was there in an instant to comfort her and pick her up, making her laugh, distracting her from feeling embarrassed.

That could be him, Callum thought. Him and Ailsa. And he thought how quickly his own little girl had grown up. Didn't want to think about Tom, though. *No, don't want to go there.* God forbid! Belinda was much more OK about all that than him.

The little girl on the ice was holding her daddy's hand as he led her to the side to join her mum.

It didn't register at first.

Then he recognized the way she flicked her hair over her shoulder. It was Kate.

He was jammed to the spot, unable to move as he stood peering inside his lover's life without permission. The traffic of people passed him in both directions, on a retail mission – things to buy, people to see – but he remained static.

Had she sensed him standing there? She couldn't possibly have seen him, and yet, suddenly and slowly, her husband and daughter unaware, she turned right around and looked him in the eye. And smiled.

It was the tiniest of moments, but it felt like it lasted an hour.

A woman with an inordinate number of shopping bags pushed past him. 'Sorry, pal!' she mumbled, her voice pulling him out of the spell like a drowning man from a lake. He moved away as quickly as his leaden legs would let him. *Just keep walking.*

Suddenly – 'Excuse me?' – a voice came from behind. It was Kate! Kate was calling him! Was this some kind of fucking dream?

She was holding out a camera, whilst Tallulah and Matt smiled at him.

'Would you mind taking a photo?' she said. 'Of the three of us?'

He stared at her and still she smiled. Well used to the incredulity on people's faces when they recognized Kate's famous face, Matt stepped in as he often did and said kindly, 'Don't worry, mate, you're not going mad, it *is* her.'

'I fell over!' Tallulah shouted.

'Yes you did, didn't you, sweetheart?' Kate said, smoothing Tallulah's hair, still holding out the camera. She thrust it towards Callum again. 'It's ever so easy – just press the button on the right.'

From somewhere inside himself, some deep well of self-preservation, Callum found the ability to speak. 'Right. Sure, OK.'

As he took the camera from Kate, their fingers touched – his were shaking. The three happy faces looked straight at him and Matt cued them up to say what they always said in family photos: 'Chugga chugga chocolate cheeeeeese!' The camera clicked several times in succession.

'That's great. Thanks a lot,' Kate said, and took the camera back without so much as a second glance.

She turned back to Matt and Tallulah and the three of them skated off, attempting another circuit of the rink. She didn't look back, and Callum watched her go, his thoughts interrupted by an elderly man who'd been watching. 'That's that Kate Andrews, ye ken!'

'Yeah,' Callum answered, before finally finding the ability to leave.

A knock on the door. He took a deep breath and went to answer it, checking through the spyhole that it was her.

She didn't speak when she came in. Pushed him against the wall, held his face in both hands and kissed the life out of him. Breathless and excited, she looked him straight in the eye. 'Hello. Again.' And she took her coat off, desperate to be naked.

'Kate, what were you thinking? Jesus!'

'Oh shut up, you loved it,' she teased as she undid her jeans.

'I did *not* fucking love it. It was sick!'

Kate was down to her bra and pants already. Callum remained dressed.

'I mean, what did Matt say? And your little girl? I was stood there gawpin' like an idiot – they must've noticed!'

'We've got three hours. We doing this or what?'

And Callum's indignation began to dissolve, once again floored by the force of Kate's intoxicating confidence.

He pulled off his shirt.

'That's better,' she said.

59

The skating had been such good fun. The most fun they'd had, Matt thought, in months.

He tried to remember the last time they were all together like that. It must've been late September – when Kate had had a week off from filming and they'd gone to Center Parcs in Sherwood Forest. They were a proper little family then – and that's what it had felt like today, blending in with all the other proper little families, circling on the ice at a snail's pace, pretending they were in some Scandinavian fantasia. He'd really made Kate laugh when he nearly fell over, doing some elaborate footwork on his skates to regain his balance just in time. It made him want to cry when he saw her light up like that. Made him want to whisper, *Come back to me!* But he feared it was already too late for that.

They'd posed for a family photo, asked some stranger to take it, and Matt had felt protective of Kate's anonymity when the guy clearly recognized her, staring at her like a loon. He knew how to protect her from over-zealous fans. He just wished he could protect her from whatever it was she was living through in that head of hers. But she was unreachable. Her No Entry signs stood bold and forbidding.

At one thirty they met with Yvonne as planned, who was treating them to *Santa's Dilemma* at the theatre, a Christmas show for the under-sevens.

Kate kissed Tallulah on her earmuffed head. 'Be a good girl for Daddy and Nannie, and Mummy will see you later for your tea!'

Then she turned to Matt – 'Right, I'm off to buy *you* something exciting!'– gave him a perfunctory kiss on the cheek, and left.

He watched her go, weaving her way through the crowds, a woman on a mission.

Yvonne was doing up Tallulah's coat, telling her all about the characters she was about to see in *Santa's Dilemma*. She mumbled to Matt that her friend Maureen Maclean had taken her grandson to see it and said it was very good, but the main girl in it wasn't a patch on Kate.

Yvonne liked to think her daughter was the best actress ever to walk the earth. She wittered on, but Matt wasn't listening. Gripped by a notion so strong he felt instantly possessed, he found himself saying, 'Yvonne, you take Lules and I'll see you there.'

And with that he headed off at a pace, his mother-in-law calling despairingly behind him, 'What? Hang on – what about the . . . You can't just . . . WELL I'LL LEAVE YOUR TICKET AT THE BOX OFFICE!' he heard her shout. But he didn't look back, keeping his focus on the moving target ahead of him.

It didn't take long for Matt to gain ground and soon he was only a dozen or so paces behind her, blending into the crowd but never losing sight of Kate's designer jacket. He already knew that if she happened to turn around and see him, he'd say, 'Surprise! I thought I'd join you!' But Kate was walking with such determination now he doubted anything could distract her enough to look back. Heading along George IV Bridge, she niftily dodged any passers-by who got in her way, one or two turning with a look of *Was that . . . y'know . . . whatshername?* but mostly she kept her head down and ploughed on. This was a woman with a destination firmly in mind. And he didn't think it was Marks and Spencer.

She turned so quickly onto the steps that led down to Grassmarket that he almost missed seeing where she went, temporarily losing her. But then she was there again, almost running now, heading straight for the McKinley Hotel.

What the fuck was she doing there? Meeting Jinny? Had Jinny been lying to him, after all?

Who was he trying to kid?

He followed her through the double doors, adrenalin racing through his system, his mouth dry with dread but his need for clarification growing with every step.

The lobby was packed with revellers; a large Christmas tree bedecked in silver held court in the centre, whilst all around it drinks were drunk, jokes were shared, and from the wall-speakers twee and senseless lyrics blared out, reassuring listeners that all was well with the world.

No, it wasn't.

Kate headed for the lift and Matt panicked. He couldn't get in with her, of course he couldn't. But he would lose her if he didn't. Fuck. *Make my dreams come true, All I want for Christmas is you!* He watched helplessly as the doors opened and Kate got in. He walked towards her – was it time to give in? To ask her outright what she was doing here and listen whilst she invented yet another lie? He was within three yards of the lift. Two other women were already in there. Kate held her head down, avoiding recognition. He was about to call out to her, to throw in the towel, when one of the women asked her which floor she wanted. 'Three,' she said. And the doors closed.

Matt had already spied the staircase doors opposite the lift. He barged through them and started running, three steps at a time, up and up, floor one, floor two . . . almost knocking over an elderly couple making their way slowly down the stairs.

'Sorry. Emergency!' he hissed.

Floor three. He stood outside the fire door, panting, waiting for the sound of the lift to come to a halt. *Ping.* He'd just made it.

He allowed a couple of seconds before peering timidly through the door onto the third-floor corridor. There was no one there. He was too late.

But then, from the other direction, he heard a knock a few rooms down the corridor. He watched, trying not to breathe, terrified the slightest sound would give him away.

He could see Kate standing outside room 308, tousling her hair in preparation and smoothing down her jumper. It was clearly important that she looked good for whoever it was she was meeting.

The door opened.

Kate smiled.

At whom, Matt couldn't see.

And then she went inside, the door slamming cruelly behind her.

He stayed in the same position for what felt like minutes, but was only seconds in reality. If someone had seen him, they'd have thought he looked ridiculous – every muscle tensed, one foot held off the ground behind him.

The alcove opposite the lift boasted a large potted plant, as well as two rarely used armchairs for any passers-by needing a rest. Or any husbands following their unfaithful wives who needed somewhere to sit and gather their thoughts. He walked across and slumped into the nearest one, the tensed muscles in his body slowly unfurling, his breathing gradually returning to a normal pace.

He didn't know what to do.

He just didn't know what to do.

60

Hetty glanced down at her mobile, silently flashing Matt's name on the screen. She let it ring off, unanswered. Again. She couldn't face talking to him. And anyway, she was at her Christmas bash with the people from work. It'd be rude to take a phone call right now. They were at a new vegetarian restaurant in Covent Garden and had just done their Secret Santa. Hetty had been given a 'pebble chest' – a beautifully hand-carved, lidded box, the size of a Rubik's Cube, containing a dozen tiny pebbles, each polished and bearing a word – such as 'self-love', 'faith', 'spontaneity'. The idea was to choose one every morning and to carry the pebble – and the senti-ment – throughout the day. Hetty thought it was delightful. She couldn't be sure, but she suspected Lisa had bought her this and felt guilty and a little unimaginative, because all she'd bought Lisa was a paraben-free moisturizer and some screen wipes.

She should've made more of an effort, she knew that. But she just wasn't feeling herself. Not since the reunion two nights pre-viously.

After talking to Matt outside, she'd gone back into the party, marched straight up to Adam and informed him that Matt had told her everything. Adam showed not one jot of remorse. In fact, he found the whole thing amusing and went on to rub more rocks of salt in the pitiful wounds of her deluded soul by telling her the only reason he'd come tonight was to see Matt again. And what a bloody shame it was the guy had gone home – he'd been hoping they could catch up on old times. Properly.

Hetty's dignity in tatters, she grabbed her coat and left, pausing by the doorway to see Adam one last time at the bar, laughing and drinking with two women (both of whom had done American Literature, she seemed to remember). And as he stood there, centre of attention, lapping up the limelight like an egocentric cat, she finally saw him for what he was: a cruel, rather sad and lonely man, who didn't know who he was or what he wanted, and had no heart or conscience.

He caught Hetty looking over and put on a show of smiling and shrugging, before turning back to the two adoring women.

Hetty had been in love with the *idea* of Adam all these years, but the *reality* of Adam was something quite different.

She'd arrived home at her tiny Hammersmith flat, barefoot and broken-hearted. Not because of Adam – in fact, she was glad now she could close the book on this chapter of her life and put him out of her mind for good – no, it was Matthew who had disturbed her the most. His revelation about Adam at Warwick was so completely out of the blue that it made her question everything – how could she think she knew Matt when all these years he'd been carrying this huge secret? Did he and Adam use to laugh at her behind her back?

She felt her world had been dislodged, uprooted, rotated round and round like a spinning top with no care as to where it landed. For seventeen years, Matt had been her best friend, but now with this *thing*, this lie between them, she felt she didn't know him at all.

'I'll walk with you to Leicester Square if you like,' Ivor said, disturbing her sad reverie. The meal was over and everyone was wishing each other a Happy Christmas, but not Happy New Year because they were all due back in the office on the twenty-eighth, Glen having repeatedly pointed out 'the magazine won't print itself just because we're on holiday!' Hetty rolled her eyes at Ivor and put on her coat.

On their way to the Tube, Ivor said, 'You've been very quiet the past couple of days. How did the reunion go? Only you didn't really mention it.'

She thought about how to answer, not wishing to make an idiot of herself after all her fussing during the build-up to the damn thing. 'Let's just say, it wasn't what I was expecting.'

'Ah.'

And suddenly she was opening up to him. 'You see, Ivy, I've spent a huge chunk of my life – well, almost half of it, if I'm honest – thinking that this guy – Adam his name is – was meant for me. He was my first love, y'see. Well, my only love, actually. But he wasn't what I thought he was at all. In fact, he was a jerk. So I've wasted all that time, all that life, and . . .' Her throat tightened and she panicked that she was going to cry. Ivor was just a work colleague, for God's sake! It would be so humiliating to start weeping in front of him! She shouldn't have had that second glass of wine, because now the tears were coming fast and strong with no sign of any let-up.

Ivor stopped in his tracks, looking round to check nobody was watching.

Oh God, she was embarrassing him! 'You must think I'm such an idiot . . .' she sobbed.

'No, not at all, take your time,' he said patiently. He seemed to be waiting for her to pull herself together. After a minute or so, he said, 'We're an ungrateful bunch really, aren't we? Us humans, I mean.'

'Sorry?' she sniffled, fishing a tissue from her pocket.

'I dunno . . . we spend most of our lives wishing we were some-where else or someone else, or looking forward or harping back. Always thinking the grass is greener on the other side. But it never is. It's still grass. Just a different patch of it, that's all.'

Hetty joked through her tears, 'Yes, well mine's in need of a good watering at the moment!'

He smiled, and for the first time, Hetty noticed the kindness in Ivor's hazel eyes. You never really see someone properly, she thought, until you look at their eyes – well, look *into* their eyes, and really *see* them.

He didn't notice she was staring. He was too busy trying to remember something.

'You a fan of Larkin?' he asked.

'I did a bit for English A-level.'

'Me too.' And he looked into the middle distance, seeking out the lines in his head before turning back to her and slowly, elegantly quoting:

> 'Truly, though our element is time,
> We are not suited to the long perspectives
> Open at each instant of our lives.
> They link us to our losses: worse,
> They show us what we have as it once was,
> Blindingly undiminished, just as though
> By acting differently, we could have kept it so.'

Painfully self-conscious, he looked down at the ground and gently kicked a lump of dirt into the pavement crack beneath him like a gangly, awkward teenager trying to impress a girl at school.

Hetty continued staring at him, in the middle of this Covent Garden Christmas, sniffing, not quite believing this revelation taking place before her.

'Gosh,' she whispered. 'Ivor!'

He looked up, and she thought he seemed a tiny bit irritated when he said, 'Hetty, you have no idea what an exceptional person you really are.'

A nervous giggle escaped her. And with that he patted her on the arm like a family dog and mumbled, 'I think I'm gonna walk home, actually. Could do with the fresh air. Have a happy Christmas, won't you?'

'Oh,' she said, a bit thrown. 'Bye, Ivy! Happy Christmas!'

But he was already marching off in the opposite direction.

A little clatter as something fell to the ground. She looked down.

One of the tiny pebbles had escaped from its box. Hetty picked it up – it said 'perseverance'. She watched Ivor disappear into the throng of festive shoppers, feeling a strange sensation in her stomach and wondering if the nut roast was giving her indigestion.

61

Inside room 308 of the McKinley Hotel, Callum was fucking Kate against the wall. Her legs wrapped around his waist, she held onto the bulk of him, thrilled by every depth he reached.

He couldn't stop, she didn't want him to.

This sex was angry and unhinged and their heads were full of mayhem and guilt and lust and love thrown together in unfathomable chaos.

'I need you to keep fucking me, Callum,' she whispered. 'I always need you to keep fucking me.'

'Jesus.'

They came together, intense and quiet, static against the wall, no words, just their breathing and the bang, bang, bang of their hearts affirming they were very much still alive.

Then the knock on the door.

'And two glasses,' Matt said, having to shout over the traffic of the busy hotel bar.

A woman thrust some plastic mistletoe at him. 'Give us a kiss, gorgeous!' she teased, clearly the worse for wear.

'Ah no, you're alright, I've got cold sores.'

She contemplated this for a moment, debating whether it was such a bad thing, then decided it was and scuttled off.

'Oh, and d'you have a pen?' he asked the barman, who was now filling a bucket with ice and water, ready for the champagne.

Matt had grabbed a compliments postcard from the reception desk and was now scrawling, 'To Susie, Happy Christmas!' across it. He paid with cash and the barman handed over the celebratory-looking tray, adding a sprig of holly for an extra festive touch.

At first they were going to ignore it, their bodies still jammed against the wall.

'It'll just be housekeeping, or turn-down or whatever they call it,' Kate said. She'd had more experience of hotels than Callum and knew all the routines.

'Go and look through the spyhole,' she whispered, still dizzy from the sex.

He slowly disentangled himself, noting his knees weren't what they used to be, and Kate moved away from the wall.

She laughed, grabbing a bottle of water from the bedside table and drinking it down in one, whilst Callum pulled on a hotel bathrobe and shuffled to the door to look out.

'There's no one there,' he muttered, still looking. 'Oh, hang on . . .' And he opened the door.

'Hey, where you going?' asked Kate.

But Callum had already gone out and was stooping over the champagne and card left in the middle of the corridor. 'Not for us – it's for someone called Susie.'

'Nick it anyway.'

'You're outrageous!'

'No one'll know!'

'Susie will.'

'Whoever she is!'

They were both in a playful mood now – the angst from earlier had dissipated after their behemoth session.

'Well, if you won't take it, I will!' And with that she skipped out into the corridor, only a tiny towel covering her up, grabbed the champagne and ran back inside, Callum swiftly following.

The door shut again and Kate's squeals of delight as Callum

chased her onto the bed could be heard down the corridor.

By Matt.

Who'd watched as the stranger from the ice rink had come out of room 308 to pick up the champagne, followed by Kate.

He leant into the vast white plant pot sporting a tired-looking aspidistra. And was violently sick.

62

When Matt arrived back at Yvonne's it was half past six and every-one was having supper.

Gordon answered the door to him with a mock fearful look. 'Uh-oh, someone's in the dog house.'

'Sorry, Gordon, I got a bit carried away.'

'It's not me you need to be apologizing to. Good luck!'

Matt ventured into the dining room, where Yvonne had served up honey-roast ham, salad and new potatoes – *Because we don't want to be overdoing it before the Christmas turkey*. She'd set a place for Matt.

'Help yourself,' she muttered briskly. 'The potatoes are cold now, of course.'

Kate tried to catch his eye, smiling naughtily like a schoolgirl silently supporting her scolded classmate.

'Yvonne, I am *so* sorry,' Matt said, and went to kiss her. She begrudgingly let him. 'I'd had this idea for a present for Kate and it sent me on a wild goose chase, and I had no way of contacting you because—'

Gordon interrupted, 'Because she refuses to get a mobile phone. There you are, see, woman! That's another example of how it would have come in handy.'

Yvonne was on the defensive. 'We've managed perfectly well for centuries without them, I don't see why I should be like a sheep and follow the rest of the herd. Mark my words, they'll be out of fashion this time next year!'

It was Yvonne's most repeated belief. She abhorred mobile phones – 'They're not natural.'

Kate was laughing and Matt managed a dry smile in her direction, but it took an enormous amount of effort.

'Anyway, how was the show, Lules?' Matt asked, picking up his little girl and squeezing her slightly too hard.

'There was a dinosaur!' she exclaimed.

'Really? In *Santa's Dilemma*? So what *was* Santa's dilemma, then?'

'He wanted to *moderrrize* everything . . .'

'It's "modernize", dear,' Yvonne interjected, but Tallulah carried on.

'. . . and change his clothes and his reindeers and his elfses. And nobody would let him.'

'I expect Santa wanted a mobile phone as well, didn't he?' Gordon added, and Yvonne frowned at him.

'Anyway, Matthew, you missed a marvellous show – well, both of you did, in fact.'

'Sorry, Mum. I bet Lules enjoyed having you all to herself, though,' Kate said, and Matt marvelled at what an arch manipulator she was, able to compliment whoever she set her sights on, to get what she needed. He felt an unexpected flash of hatred towards her, and downed a glug of wine to suppress this unwelcome sensation.

'Daddy, I want *you* to read me a story tonight,' Tallulah announced, getting down from the table.

'Your wish is my command, Princess!' Matt replied. 'What shall we read?'

'*Misty and Jake.*'

'Alright. Well, bath-time first, OK?' and Tallulah ran off excitedly whilst Matt took a few mouthfuls of his dinner, eating it to be polite, his appetite diminished since the afternoon's events.

'So did you get what you wanted in the end?' Kate asked Matt, resting her hand gently on his shoulder and stroking his hair.

He fought with all his might not to flick her hand away and say, *Don't fucking touch me!* but instead said, 'Not really. What about you?' and held her gaze. The flinch in her eyes was almost imperceptible.

But because Kate knew that Matt couldn't possibly be aware of where she'd been that afternoon, she simply broke into a smile and said, 'I *might* have done – you'll have to wait and see, won't you?'

He looked away, focusing on the piece of ham on his plate, whilst Yvonne wittered in the background and Kate started clearing things away.

He went back over the events of earlier, how he'd sat waiting in the alcove for two hours, wondering if they were ever going to leave.

Time and again, he'd thought about knocking on the door. At one point, he actually got up and headed for the room. Too afraid to go through with it, he listened at the door – the muffled sound of the creaking bedhead and the stifled moans of pleasure could mean only one thing. He felt he was in a different plane of reality, watching himself standing at the door. This wasn't the life he was meant to live. Surely.

He thought about calling Kate's mobile. But his masochism was already at an all-time high – why do it to himself? Why wait for the call to be either ignored or answered with a lie – *Darling, can I call you back? I'm just in the middle of something* . . . So he headed back to his lookout station, sitting out of sight of room 308, waiting for the door to finally open.

She came out first. He heard their whispered goodbyes. The man had looked cautiously from the doorway before calling quietly, 'See you tonight!'

She'd replied, 'You certainly will!' and laughed, turning and padding towards the lift, head down, the door closing behind her.

She pressed the lift button and waited, smiling to herself. And all the time, Matt watched. The lift eventually arrived and she got in. He heard the recorded voice say, 'Going down,' and thought ironically of the truth in those words.

It was a good ten minutes before the man came out of the room. Matt wanted to properly look at him, take in the whole image of this man who'd just had sex with his wife, figure out what the fuck Kate saw in him and why she was doing this. But he had no time to waste.

As soon as Callum's back was turned, waiting for the lift, Matt sneaked up behind him and slipped through the staircase doors. He raced down the stairs, nearly breaking his ankle in the process as he leapt down, sometimes five steps at a go.

When he reached the bottom, he crashed into the still-packed lobby and waited a few seconds for Callum to emerge from the lift. When he did, adrenalin flooded Matt's body. And he knew he had to keep him in his sights, whatever it took. He had no plan other than that.

His mind was jumbled. Nothing added up. The only real explanation was that Kate had had some kind of spontaneous liaison with this complete stranger – a passer-by who'd happened to take their photo that afternoon at the ice rink, then gone on his merry way. But how did Kate connect with him unless it was pre-arranged? And if he was a stranger, which he surely *must* be, how was it all planned? It just didn't stack up! So could she actually *know* this man – was he in fact no stranger at all? So many questions were flying around his head, he thought it would explode.

They reached a bus stop on the Lothian Road. Matt kept his distance as the man stood in the queue. His mobile phone rang and Matt drew closer, wanting to hear him talk, desperate for his own breathing to shut the fuck up, so loud it was, and the pounding of his heart in his ears.

'Callum MacGregor speaking . . . Oh hello, John . . . Yes, Merry Christmas to you! How can I help?'

Callum MacGregor.

Callum MacFucking MacGregor.

Callum MacGregor has been fucking my wife and is going to fuck her again. Tonight. That was all he could think.

Eventually, a bus destined for Portobello arrived and Callum got on, still talking into his phone. He interrupted the conversation and said, 'Single to Sutherland Avenue' to the bus driver, paid his fare and found a seat.

There were two passengers in front of Matt in the queue. When it was his turn to pay, he copied Callum exactly, then headed for the back of the bus. He sat two seats behind him for the whole journey and didn't take his eyes off the back of his head.

He's almost totally grey. Matt thought this would make him feel better. But it didn't.

The journey lasted about twenty minutes. When Callum got off, Matt was relieved that three other people got off too, helping to camouflage him. He waited at the bus stop and watched Callum walk down the road for a few paces before setting off in pursuit.

Matt followed for another five minutes or so, till Callum reached Number 24 and headed up the small driveway. He fumbled for his keys and let himself in.

It was dark now, of course, so Matt could stand across the road and watch Callum MacGregor walk into his front room and kiss what must be Callum MacGregor's wife.

'Darling,' – Kate was talking to him, she seemed a little distressed – 'I've just had a text from Jinny. I'm afraid I've got to go and see her.'

Lying bitch.

'Oh dear, what's happened?' he said, perversely eager to hear the story Kate would concoct.

'She's had the most awful row with Bill. She's walked out of the house, she's distraught.'

'Poor Jinny!'

'I know. Look, I'll try not to be too long, but don't wait up for me. I'll keep you posted, yeah?'

'Sure. I really hope she's OK. Send her my love. If it's appropriate.'

'It's probably not, to be honest.'

'No,' Matt smiled. 'It's probably not.'

63

Belinda was in the spare bedroom, wrapping presents. Three more to go – some novelty socks for Callum, this year's had Christmas puddings on them, then only two Terry's Chocolate Oranges – another sad reminder that Ben wasn't home this year. It'd become something of a tradition that the kids each got a Terry's Chocolate Orange every Christmas, but there was no point sending one to Ben in Australia. It'd never make it through customs, and if it did it'd most likely melt or get crushed in the process. She couldn't wait for him to come home. Her eldest baby. Not long now – middle of March, he'd said. And then, no doubt, Cory would be off on *his* travels.

Belinda wondered how she'd manage once Ailsa left home and she and Callum would be left suffering the frequently discussed empty-nest syndrome. Would they downsize? Wasn't that what was expected on reaching a certain milestone in life? But as Belinda quite rightly pointed out every time it came up in conversation, who's to say the kids wouldn't want to come home to live again? And even if they did get their own place, where would the grandchildren sleep when *they* came to visit?

Belinda had a habit of projecting into the future, of filling her head with what-ifs. And Callum would calm her down and say, 'Bel, we none of us even knows what's around the corner, let alone what'll happen in five years. So just stop worrying and enjoy today.'

None of us even knows what's around the corner.

The doorbell rang. She'd have to go: Callum was out with Gary – again! – and Ailsa was at Tom's – again! She smiled to herself and headed downstairs.

'Mrs MacGregor?' the man on the doorstep asked her. There was a black cab a few yards away, the engine still running.

'Yes?'

The guy looked at her for a moment. He was well dressed, mid thirties, maybe – handsome! – and wrapped up against the cold. She noticed what strikingly blond hair he had.

'Are you going to sing me a carol?' she joked. But he didn't smile back. And he looked too anxious to sing.

'You don't know me, but my name is Matthew Fenton.'

'Right . . . ?' Belinda folded her arms, suspecting there was some door-to-door sales pitch coming or, even worse, a Jehovah's Witness sermon.

'My wife is called Kate and I have reason to believe she is currently with your husband Callum in room 308 of the McKinley Hotel.'

They looked at each other in silence. The tinny music from the black cab's radio filtered through the still air and the Christmas lights from the garden flashed in time to Paul McCartney as he sang, *We're simply having a wonderful Christmas time . . .*

64

'I've got you a present,' she said. And she handed him a gift bag.

'Kate!'

'It's not a big deal. And you can say you bought it yourself.'

He looked in the bag; the present wasn't wrapped, so he saw it straight away: a TAG watch.

'You serious?' He was incredulous, though conscious he didn't want to hurt her feelings. 'How am I meant to explain this to Belinda? That I forked out hundreds of quid on a posh watch for myself?'

'Aw, you'll think of something,' she said, and snuggled up to him. They'd just had a bath together and were having some quiet time, conscious the clock was ticking on this special day.

'Well, thank you.' He kissed the top of her head. 'I haven't got you anything.'

'Oh, you gave me my present this afternoon,' she teased, running her fingers along his arm. 'D'you think we could see each other again, before Christmas?' she whispered, and he could hear that her voice was a little choked.

'Sweetheart, it's so difficult.'

'I know.' She waited. 'I love you, Callum.'

And it was the easiest thing in the world to say back, so he did. 'I love you too.'

They lay there in the safety of the silent night, gently dozing.

The knock on the door was so timid, he thought at first he'd imagined it.

'Kate?' he mumbled, sleepiness stopping his mouth from working properly.

'Hmm?'

And then it came again, more confident this time.

'There's someone at the door.'

'What time is it?'

'Half nine.'

'Just ignore it. It'll be the cleaner. We've still got ages.'

But whoever was outside the room wasn't giving up. They knocked again.

Callum sighed, got up and put on his bathrobe, making his way slowly to the door. He looked through the spy hole but could see no one there.

He was about to go back to the bed when the knock came once more. This time he didn't look to see who it might be, just opened the door.

There was no time to register what happened next.

Belinda barged past him and into the room, followed by Matt, less ferocious but still determined.

Callum had no words.

And Kate screamed, before angrily shouting, '*What the fuck?!*'

This was the strangest of gatherings – three people whose lives had been entwined since 1985, now joined by a fourth in Matt.

He hadn't planned for her to come with him. He'd imagined he'd be confronting them on his own. But within minutes of his arrival on the doorstep, Belinda had grabbed her coat and her keys and was climbing into the taxi with him.

Hell hath no fury.

The journey was tense and unreal. At first they hadn't spoken, both looking out of their respective windows, lost in their own unfathomably sad thoughts.

And then Belinda had started speaking, explaining the whole sorry mess that had started seventeen years ago when Kate began working at the Lamb and Flag with Callum. The sorry mess she'd presumed, she'd hoped – she'd fucking *believed*! – had been left behind in 1985.

They talked dates, Belinda's voice shaking as she confirmed that on the night of Kate's school visit Callum said he'd been with an old college friend, Paul McGee.

They actually both laughed when Matt explained that Kate's excuse for staying late in Edinburgh that night had been that *she*'d bumped into *her* old friend – Paula McGee.

'How pathetic.' Belinda shook her head, but no amount of mockery or bitter scorn could alleviate the pain of this deception.

Matt told Belinda that Kate's story about her friend Jinny hadn't added up, so he'd checked it out with Jinny himself, realizing that Kate had been lying all along.

'That's who she's meant to be with tonight,' he said quietly. And then they'd fallen back into silent contemplation.

In the hotel room, Kate, still naked in the bed, had covered herself with the sheet, her knees pulled up in self-protection.

Belinda just stood there, speechless, breathless, hyperventilating with anger.

Nobody knew what to say. It was all too awful.

Eventually Belinda said, 'Well, happy fucking Christmas, Callum!'

'I'm sorry,' was all he could manage.

'Sorry for being caught, or sorry for fucking my wife?' Matt jumped in.

'Neither,' said Kate. And she stood up, wrapping the sheet around her slim body, which Belinda hated herself for noticing and envying.

Kate calmly walked over to Callum and stood next to him, taking his hand.

He let her.

'We're sorry you both had to find out like this, of course we are. But at least now we all know the truth. Seventeen years ago he chose you, Belinda. That was a mistake.'

'Ha!'

'And so now he's choosing me. Aren't you, Callum?'

2003

65

It was Matt's mother who'd raised the alarm. A call came through to the office on Hetty's first day back, three days after Christmas, during that weird No Man's Land of a week.

'Someone called Sylvia Fenton?' Lisa said, and Hetty assumed Sylvia must be ringing to try and play mediator between her and Matt.

'Oh Hetty, thank goodness I've got you – I didn't have your mobile.'

'What's happened?' Hetty asked, thrown by Sylvia's urgent tone.

'It's Matt.'

Was she surprised? Not really. She liked Kate a lot, but if she was being honest, she'd never completely trusted her. Of course, she'd never told Matt that, but there was something 'off kilter' about Kate that had always made Hetty a little uneasy. So hearing that she'd rekindled an affair with an older man who she'd first met seventeen years ago didn't really shock her at all, though it made her heart break for Matt. And Tallulah.

She had a spare set of keys to their house, which had been very useful over the years when it came to babysitting or watering plants. She hadn't, however, ever expected to use them to let herself in to check that Matt was still alive. Sylvia couldn't face finding out, and she begged Hetty to venture over there and see if she could raise him. If, indeed, he was even there.

Nobody had heard from Matt or spoken to him since a couple of days before Christmas. Kate had revealed all this when she'd rung Sylvia, looking for him, explaining in a cold, formal tone that she and Matt were separating because she was in love with a man called Callum MacGregor, also married, also separating from his wife. Kate had apologized for the timing, saying that she'd have liked for things to happen more slowly, but this was the situation and they were all going to have to get used to it. She'd not heard from Matt since he'd found out and she wanted to know he was OK.

Kate, it seemed, was still at her parents' house. They were looking after Tallulah most of the time, whilst Kate went back and forth to the hotel where this Callum chap was staying. Sylvia had gleaned this from Kate's mother Yvonne, who was as distressed as she was about the devastating news.

'Matt?' Hetty called out timidly, edging into the dark hallway. The alarm wasn't on, so she assumed he must be at home. A strong smell of bins wafted out to meet her as she headed into the kitchen – unsurprising given the amount of half-eaten takeaways, cigarette ends and beer cans that were scattered on every available work surface. A defrosted chicken lay in the sink, abandoned in its juices. This made her gag, and she headed hastily into the living room.

The tinny sound of a low-volume radio show was ploughing on oblivious in the background. There was no light – even the Christmas tree was sad and dark. No surprise there. Over on the capacious leather sofa, under a pile of coats and a rug, Hetty could just about make out the silhouette of her friend. Fast asleep. But breathing.

'Thank God,' she whispered to herself, wondering how best to wake him without giving him a cardiac arrest.

On the floor next to the sofa was a near-empty bottle of Jack Daniel's and an overflowing ashtray. She stepped back into the hallway and turned on the table lamp, gently illuminating the living room through the doorway.

Still no movement. Just tiny breaths.

She went over and sat on the sofa, reaching out for his hand, clammy and scared, and holding it tight.

'Kate?' he mumbled.

'No, sweetheart, it's me. It's Hetty.'

He turned and she took in the full picture of this broken man, silently cursing Kate Andrews for ever coming into his life.

'Alright, mate! How you doing?' he croaked, his voice ravaged by copious cigarettes.

He clearly hadn't shaved for days, his lips stained with stale red wine and whisky, saliva collecting at the edges of his mouth. He was in a T-shirt sporting remnants of his last takeaway, and his hair was greasy and lank.

She'd never seen him look so dreadful. 'I'm gonna run you a bath, petal.'

That had been over six weeks ago now and she'd seen him every day since, their friendship once again made rock solid by what had happened. Understandably, the events of the reunion night had paled into insignificance.

But one evening in January, Matt brought the subject up. Hetty was dropping him off after a session with Dervla, his therapist.

'I won't come in,' she said. 'But please take these bananas.' Food was Hetty's solution to most of life's problems.

He was still fragile, still finding it hard to talk much. 'Dervla was asking me about sex tonight,' he said.

'Oh, heck!' Hetty tried to make a joke to hide her discomfort. This wasn't something she and Matt ever really discussed.

'I used to have great sex with Kate . . . before it all, y'know, died away.' He'd got a bit choked then, reliving his frustration and incomprehension at what had happened to him.

Hetty stayed silent. She'd read in a Sunday magazine that depression could make people disinhibited. *Just let him talk*, she thought, cringing.

'Dervla asked me about sex with other people. I think she was reminding me Kate wasn't the only person in the world I could sleep with.'

Hetty smiled.

'I told her about Adam.'

'Oh.'

They both stared out of the car window, too embarrassed to make eye contact.

'It was such a long time ago, Het. And it was all so weird. But I really liked it at the time. I'm sorry, but I must've done to keep going back.'

They sat there in silence for a while longer, then Hetty said, 'Yes, I really liked sex with Adam too.'

They both contemplated this, and then she remembered something.

'Except . . .'

'What?'

She was clearly embarrassed to ask and kept looking straight ahead. 'Well y'know, when he . . . y'know.' He looked at her and she shut her eyes, mouthing the word *came*.

'This conversation's not remotely awkward, is it?' he joked.

'Did he make a funny noise?'

'Sorry?'

'Like a sort of . . . lowing . . . y'know, like a cow . . . like . . .' And with that, she went on to do the most extraordinarily accurate impression of Adam having an orgasm.

'Gnnnnnnneeeeeeooooowwwwwwwwwwwrrrrrrrrrrrrrraaaahhnn-nnnnnnnnnnnng!'

It seemed to last an age. And Matt just watched her the entire time, utterly mesmerized by her commitment to the performance. When she'd finished, there was a pause, and then he laughed so long it became infectious. Soon Hetty was joining in, until they both howled with such joy that their laughter tripped over the cliff edge of hysteria and transformed into sobs.

Eventually, Matt caught his breath. 'Oh Het,' he said. 'You are such a fucking tonic, you really are.'

He thanked her for the lift and got out of the car. That night was the first proper night's sleep he'd had in weeks.

66

Please mind the gap.

The Tube was at Victoria – only a couple more stops to go. Kate had wanted him to get a cab there and back – 'It'll only take ten minutes!' – but Callum already felt out of his depth with the cost of living in London. The last thing he wanted to do was waste money when he didn't have to.

Kate found his thriftiness endearing and frequently told him so. He said she was patronizing him just because he was almost a pensioner and she'd laughed. 'You're not ready for the scrapheap yet, MacGregor. We'll get another eleven years out of you yet!' And she'd cracked an imaginary whip.

He'd been that day to meet the Head at a primary school in West Kensington. Christ, what a difference. In so many ways. He loved her open-mindedness, the diversity of the pupils and the resources available to them. He'd agreed to two weeks' supply, though there was the possibility of the contract being extended. 'Let's just see how we get on,' the Head said, her attitude and flexibility a million miles away from that of Brian Boyd at North Park Primary.

They'd been in London for a month now, and although he wouldn't say he was enjoying it, there were things about it he definitely liked. Travelling on the Tube was one of them.

Kate thought this was insane – she never travelled on the Tube, citing claustrophobia, commuter body odour and recognition by fans as her three main reasons.

But Callum loved its anonymity and the fact that nobody ever made eye contact. He subtly looked around him now, whilst pretending to read the *Evening Standard*. Several passengers were unashamedly carrying flowers that ranged from ostentatious bouquets to a single red rose in a box.

Valentine's Day.

He and Belinda had always taken the mickey out of it. Occasionally she'd buy him some little chocolate hearts when she remembered, and he'd sometimes buy her a bunch of mass-produced roses. But both were dismayed by the money-spinning con it had turned into over the years. And now he couldn't remember when they'd last sent each other anything to honour the patron saint of Love.

Thinking of Belinda inevitably made him sad. They'd not spoken for weeks, apart from a brief conversation when he told her he was moving to London. She'd written down the address of the luxury apartment Kate's director friend Milosz was lending them – 'I don't need to know any of that, Callum, just give me the address. Ailsa will want it.' After taking down the details, she'd told him Ailsa wanted a word, and before she handed the phone over she said, 'I feel so sorry for you, Callum.' He knew it would be unwise to respond.

When Ailsa came on the phone, she was sweet as ever – the only one in the family who could bear to speak to him – telling him she missed him and asking when he was next going to see her.

This was his life now. Flipped upside down and smack on its face. A series of never-ending arrangements and rearrangements, of travel and logistics, of catch-up phone calls with Ailsa, of pretending that everything was fine and never discussing the undercurrent of sorrow they both felt and which threatened to pull them under at any given moment. Cory refused to speak to him at all, and Ben was still on his travels.

And here he was, a former deputy head in Portobello, now grateful for any supply work that came his way. Kate would ask him daily if she was worth it. And daily he'd say that she was. Of course.

When it first happened, the one saving grace was the Christmas holidays – at least he didn't have to contend with going back to work for ten days, on top of everything else. At least they had space to organize and to think.

Kate extended the booking at the hotel, and that became his home for the next three weeks. He'd stayed there that first night with Kate, both of them lying silent, holding onto each other after Belinda and Matt had long left, both in shock, both wondering what they were going to do.

He'd waited twenty-four hours before calling Belinda. She sounded predictably terrible.

'I need to get some things,' he'd said, as gently as he could.

'You can come over tomorrow morning at ten. I'll go out for an hour.'

'Thanks.'

'And Callum?'

'Yeah?'

'I do *not* want you here when I get back. I never want to see you again. D'you understand?' Her voice broke on the last word, revealing the pain in which she was subsumed.

'Of course.'

Ailsa was there when he arrived. He could tell she'd been crying but was trying to keep up appearances – she gave him the biggest hug and told him she was missing him already and surely all that needed to happen was for him and Mum to sit down together and talk things through.

'Joely Parks in my year, her parents got divorced, went to Relate and now they're getting remarried!' Ailsa's sweetness made him want to cry and he didn't dare speak.

'Do you love her, Dad? – this Kate woman?' She was brimming with hope that the answer would be 'no' and they could all get back to normality again.

'Ails, it's all so complicated,' he'd said, avoiding the question.

'And we all just need time to work out what to do.' He sounded like a politician, practised in vagueness and dodging the point.

He'd packed two bags – mainly clothes for school, and his training kit, shaving things, and a family photo in a frame, taken three Christmases ago. Ailsa had seen him pick it up and her heart gladdened – making her feel that a part of him wasn't quite leaving them all behind.

As promised he was gone within the hour, feeling nauseous when he left.

When he'd started back at school for the Spring term, everyone had heard the news. Gossip travelled fast, especially when it came to other people's personal tragedies, and Callum had found himself the focus of staffroom speculation.

Brian Boyd asked to see him in his office during break time on the first day back.

'Bit of a mess this, Callum, wouldn't you say?' He'd frowned at him over his half-moon specs.

'Yeah. Look, it'll all settle down. I know it will.'

Brian sighed. He knew this didn't bode well. He was also secretly smug that he'd seen the whole thing coming. He'd said to his wife when he heard, 'I *knew* it! I knew there was something going on between them!' But he showed none of his inner self-congratulation and remained stern with Callum.

'The way I see it, you're a good teacher and we don't want to lose you. The parents love you and so do the kids. But something like this . . . She's in the public eye, for Pete's sake. If there's any hassle from the press you'll have to go. I'm sorry, but you'd leave me no choice.'

Kate had talked of the press too, but Callum thought she was being melodramatic.

'It won't come to that, Brian,' he said and got up to leave.

When he was at the door, the Head added, 'Oh, and Callum . . . for the record, I think you're a damn fool. Belinda's a good woman. A bloody good woman.'

Callum nodded and said, 'Yeah well, as you said, I'm a good teacher, Brian, and I do a good job. Your opinion of my wife is irrelevant, and my marriage is none of your bloody business.'

And he left Brian Boyd silently fuming.

'This is Embankment. Please change here for District, Northern and Bakerloo lines.'

Callum stepped onto the platform and headed with the crowds towards the exit. The escalator ascended slowly, passing people coming down on the other side, all with their own agendas, he thought, each one with their own story to tell, their own secrets to keep, their own heartaches to hide.

The night air outside was crisp with cold, exhaust-fume heavy and noisy with the London rush hour. He hesitated by a flower stall, tempted to buy Kate some token to mark Valentine's Day, like so many other commuters. But then it struck him. He had no idea what she thought about Valentine's Day. No idea whether she thought it a load of nonsense like Belinda did or whether she was a big romantic at heart, who'd be disappointed if he didn't come home with at least a tatty-looking rose.

In fact, it struck him there were so *many* things he didn't really know about Kate.

67

Their paths hadn't crossed that morning because she'd been picked up for filming long before Callum had surfaced.

Kate had started work that week on *Hunted*, her new feature film. She was surprised by how remarkably calm she was, handling work on top of her domestic upheaval, but she'd told Callum that she was one hundred per cent committed to being with him, and that whatever life threw at her, she would rise to the challenge and never complain.

Admittedly, she was glad things had turned out the way they had and that they were now living in London. She'd have made Edinburgh work if she'd had to, but London was going to be so much simpler all round. She even thought that in some weird way she was doing Belinda a favour. At least now there was no risk of her bumping into Callum by chance.

The gossip at North Park Primary *did* die down within a couple of days and at first it looked as if things might return to normal – at least as far as work was concerned. Living in a hotel was a strange existence though – and at the end of their first week, Callum broached the subject of getting a flat.

In Edinburgh.

She hadn't been totally against the idea – there were plenty of pluses, after all: she'd have her parents there for childcare and there were daily flights to London; even the train only took four and a half hours. So she began looking into local schools for Tallulah, darkly joking with Callum that maybe they should send her to North Park Primary.

Callum didn't find this amusing in the least. He already felt guilty enough about the disruption he was causing his own family, let alone this innocent five-year-old girl, whose teachers in Chiswick would soon be missing her when term began.

Tallulah was getting used to living with Nannie and Grandy. Despite Yvonne's horror at her daughter's affair, she had only her granddaughter's interests at heart and was happy for Tallulah to continue staying with them for the foreseeable. Whatever gave her the most stability.

And Kate had been grateful for this. She knew she'd need to be back down in London soon for work and to fetch more stuff – after all, they'd only packed enough for a week over Christmas. She also knew it wasn't fair on Matt for him to be living four hundred miles away from his daughter.

But she also wanted to keep Callum happy, and for Callum to be able to keep working at North Park. So there was a dilemma. And she needed a solution. In the end, the matter was taken out of her hands.

Since the evening of the revelation, Kate and Callum had spent their nights together at the hotel, with Kate returning to her parents' home in the morning to be with Tallulah, trying to retain as much normality as possible.

Christmas Day had been horrendous. Tallulah spent most of it crying, saying she wanted her daddy and refusing to open any presents, and try as they might to comfort her, she was utterly inconsolable.

Kate left several messages on Matt's voicemail. 'I know you hate me and I know you're beyond angry, but don't do this to Tallulah. She needs to speak to her daddy on Christmas Day, for God's sake!'

But despite becoming more and more desperate with every plea, she still heard nothing back from Matt.

Two days later, Kate realized she was going to have to enlist help from elsewhere. There was no answer from Hetty's mobile, so she assumed Matt had told her what had happened and Hetty wanted nothing to do with her.

The only other option was to call Sylvia, Matt's mother. Once she'd got past the recriminations and disbelief, Sylvia agreed to go to the house and find out if Matt was there.

It was New Year's Eve before Kate finally spoke to Matt, encouraged by Hetty, who was by his side the whole time.

Kate put Tallulah on the phone and Matt managed to keep it together long enough to tell his little girl that Daddy was fine and he'd had to go to the shop to sell some paintings.

'But did you see Father Christmas?' she sniffled, and Matt had to fight hard to keep his voice from breaking.

'Yes I did, sweetheart, and he told me he'd got you some lovely presents!'

'I miss you, Daddy.'

'And I miss you too, poppet.'

When they'd finished talking and Kate came back on the phone, she suggested that it might be easier to communicate via email from now on. And warned him she was looking into sending Tallulah to school up in Edinburgh.

Matt was too knocked by this shocking announcement to carry on talking and handed the phone to Hetty.

'Kate, I think you must be having some kind of breakdown,' she said. 'To destroy all this . . . to just wreck people's lives like this . . . it's so brutal. And so sudden.'

Kate sighed, strong in her conviction, utterly without self-reproach or remorse for what she'd done. 'Hetty, I wouldn't expect you to understand because you've never really had a relationship, have you, but Callum and I were always meant to be together, it's just other things got in the way. So now we're picking up where we left off. That's all.'

Hetty looked at Matt as he lit a cigarette, his head down, his hands shaking, and said, 'Is that what Matt and Tallulah are to you now? Things that got in the way?'

Kate sighed, losing her patience. 'If you could just tell Matt I'll email him.'

'Yes, I will,' Hetty replied. And then in a calm and level voice, added, 'Oh, and Kate?'

'What?'

'I think you're a fucking bitch.'

The following week, Callum kissed Kate goodbye in the hotel car park, before getting in his car and setting off for school.

Fifty metres away, the rapid click of a long-lens camera captured the moment, before the photographer got in a car driven by his colleague and followed Callum all the way to North Park Primary.

Fifteen minutes later, the driver, Melanie Stokes, a freelance tabloid journalist, had parked up and was on the phone to her editor.

'He's a teacher, by the looks of things.'

'Or a very well-turned-out school caretaker,' the photographer added, and she hit him playfully on the arm before continuing the call.

'And they've been staying at the McKinley Hotel . . . Yes, very posh . . . OK, I'll see what we can get you.'

She ended the call and turned to her colleague. 'Right. You up for this?'

After pressing the intercom buzzer at the school reception, Melanie heard the officious voice of the school secretary, Mrs Crocombe, come booming out: 'Can I help you?'

'Hi, yeah, we need to contact the owner of a green Ford Mondeo, registration M235 KSO.'

'Are you the police?'

Melanie looked at the photographer, shrugged and crossed her fingers. In for a penny!

'That's right.'

And Mrs Crocombe buzzed them in, the photographer hiding his camera under a jacket thrown over his arm.

They waited a few seconds in the foyer till Mrs Crocombe came bustling out. 'That's Callum's car you're talking about.'

'Callum . . . ?'

'MacGregor. He's on his way.'

'Thanks.'

'He's not in trouble, is he?'

But before Melanie could answer, sixty schoolkids aged five to seven burst through the doors on their way to assembly, Brian Boyd not far behind, and two other teachers shepherding them into the hall. The noise was deafening and Melanie had to raise her voice to be heard.

'Callum MacGregor?'

'Yes?'

And with lightning speed the photographer whipped out his camera and started snapping away.

Callum was confused and the flash from the camera caught the children's attention, shutting them up in an instant. Melanie thrust her Dictaphone at Callum and launched in with a barrage of questions.

'What's it like living with a TV star, Callum?'

'What? Sorry, who *are* you . . . ?'

'We know all about you and Kate Andrews, Callum, so you may as well give your side of the story. Don't you feel guilty breaking up her marriage like that? She's got a little girl, after all . . .'

'It's none of your bloody business!'

Brian Boyd had put two and two together, realizing that his fear of press intrusion had been well founded. He stepped forward to intervene.

'I'm Brian Boyd, Headmaster. You have no permission to be on school premises and are therefore committing an offence. Please leave immediately, or I shall call the police.'

Mrs Crocombe was mortified. 'I thought they *were* the police!'

Melanie ploughed on, ignoring Brian's warning. 'Are you in it for the fame, Callum? Looking for a little mid-life adventure?'

'Don't be ridiculous!'

'Actually, Carol, call the police,' Brian said, frustrated.

But Mrs Crocombe was rooted to the spot. 'In fact, I think they *told* me they were the police!'

'GET ON THE BLOODY PHONE, WOMAN!'

At which point, the gobsmacked pupils, thinking this was some kind of game, started egging each other on.

'Sir said "bloody"!' began to spread, gaining momentum and turning into a playground chant: *'Sir said "bloody"! Sir said "bloody"!'*

Alarmed by the mounting chaos, Brian Boyd summoned up his leadership skills from deep within, yelling firmly and concisely at the children to 'BE QUIET!', which instantly shut them up. Then he turned to the photographer, took him by the arm and manhandled him out of the main door. The photographer continued to snap away through the window.

Next Brian went for Melanie, who wouldn't go down without a fight and as she was bundled out shouted, 'Are you married yourself, Callum? Have you got any kids? Should think yours are pretty much grown up by now, aren't they? Wonder what the governors and parents will think about your lack of morals, Callum?'

Brian turned around and gathered himself, addressing the children in the calmest voice he could muster.

'Right, show's over, everyone. Into the hall, please. Recorder group on the stage – Ellie Fairfax and James McBride give out the song sheets.'

Then he turned to Callum. 'Mr MacGregor, can I see you in my office, please?'

Callum decided to jump before he was pushed and handed in his resignation on the spot. He told Kate it was a relief, and that he couldn't have carried on working there anyway, having everyone knowing his business, making comments on the way he lived his life.

Kate struck the hot iron and suggested that it may be a blessing in disguise, that a clean break might be the answer – would he consider moving to London? She'd caught him when his defences were down, and he agreed.

Within a week she'd found them somewhere to live – a riverside apartment in Lambeth, with spectacular views of the Thames, three bedrooms and a parking space. It would do them for now, until the divorce settlements were sorted.

She'd been optimistic Callum would get supply work within days, and that living in London would be the best option all round. It had cost them their privacy, of course – a double-page spread in the *News of the World* exposing their affair and displaying some fairly uncomplimentary photos of Callum at the school. He was mortified, but Kate said it sadly went with the territory and the best thing was to dust themselves down, pick themselves up and get on with the rest of their lives. Together. At last.

68

Valentine's Day was unavoidable from the moment Matt woke up. On Capital Radio, listeners were phoning in and dedicating songs to loved ones; even when he switched to Radio 4 there was a discussion underway about the *real* St Valentine. Who, it turned out, was an advocate for monogamy and a big believer in marriage. How ironic.

He couldn't help but think about Kate waking up that morning, Callum spoiling her with breakfast in bed and a dozen white roses. Callum would, of course, know by now how much she loved Valentine's Day – more than any other day of the year, in fact – and that she loathed red roses but adored cream and white.

'Right. That's your lot!' he said to himself, which he did most mornings after indulging in his daily ration of self-pity and series of 'what-if's about Kate. He leapt out of bed, pulled on his tracksuit and trainers and headed downstairs to fill his water bottle. Matt was going for a run.

He was into his fourth week. Dervla the therapist had suggested it. Apart from the endorphins physiologically fighting the depression, it also gave him some routine to his day. The first time he did it was horrendous, his lungs giving up on him within five minutes of starting, and his legs only managing a couple of circuits of the block. After staggering home, wheezing and purple-faced, he decided there and then to ditch the cigarettes.

And gradually the daily slog became a gentle jog until two weeks later he was running 4 or 5K every morning, followed by some weight training in Kate's abandoned gym.

Only now, nearly two months after the break-up, did he feel he might be capable of mending. He no longer felt tempted to stay in bed all day after downing a bottle of Jack Daniel's, or that life was utterly meaningless and bleak. It had taken eight sessions with Dervla – still ongoing – and a lot of tough love from his mother and Hetty to pull him out of the hellish pit into which he'd so heavily fallen.

He'd been shocked by his own reaction to what had happened. Having always prided himself on being a pragmatist, with a hardy Yorkshire spirit, he'd imagined he might handle it so much better, especially as he'd known for some time that things weren't right between him and Kate.

But Kate's affair had floored him. He was overwhelmed by the magnitude of her love for Callum MacGregor – and the fact that he'd been part of Kate's life long before Matt had even met her. He felt that Callum, weirdly, had some sort of claim over Kate that superseded his own, even though he was married to her! And on top of everything, his ego had taken a bashing – because Callum, at fifty-six, was an astonishing twenty years older than him. What the fuck, Kate? What the fucking fuck?

And then the thought struck him.

Like a punch to the stomach.

Of course! He should've realized: Kate's baby – little Luca, born, she'd said, in 1986 . . .

Callum must have been his father.

He stopped running and caught his breath, pausing to take in the enormity of it all. He wondered if Kate had ever even told Callum of Luca's existence. Kate's mind and the madness of her world made him shudder, and he thought with crippling sadness how little he had ever really known his own wife. It hadn't stopped him loving her though, and he couldn't envisage a time when it ever would. He continued with his run, comforted by the steady thud of his feet upon the ground and the regularity of his pace, telling himself over and over that everything was going to be alright.

Having Tallulah back – albeit part-time – had made a massive difference to his recovery. It had taken a good three weeks before he felt able to see his little girl again, and when he finally did it filled his heart with joy.

By now, Kate and Tallulah had moved down to London with Callum, where they were living in some riverside apartment. Tallulah told him she could 'look out of the window and see the big clock! And the giant wheel!'

If Matt had felt strong enough he would have put up a fight, insisted that Tallulah would not live in the same place as a man he'd only met once, in very sordid circumstances. But Kate was too powerful a match for him, and when he'd voiced the weakest of objections, she'd told him he was being ridiculous, that Callum was her partner now, that she'd known him over seventeen years, and this was not up for discussion. She was happy for Tallulah to spend half the week with Matt – they just needed to arrange collection and drop-off. Like Tallulah was a parcel at a post office.

Although Matt was getting stronger by the day, he still didn't want to see Kate in person when it came to picking up Tallulah. So he'd enlisted the help of his mother Sylvia, who in turn enlisted the help of her best friend Peter, who in turn *wanted* to enlist the help of his partner Julius, but Sylvia put her foot down, saying she didn't want them turning up to collect her granddaughter mob-handed. Julius was the most disappointed by this as he'd secretly planned to give Kate Andrews a piece of his mind – the disloyal, hedonistic, self-centred, callous, marriage-wrecking, hard-hearted harlot, who, whilst he was at it, was highly overrated as an actress. Especially in that thing she did on ITV set in Gloucester.

When Sylvia and Peter had arrived at the apartment building for the first time, it took them a while to locate the correct door-way and intercom. Which made them slightly late. Which added to Sylvia's stress. Kate buzzed them up, her voice bright and breezy as if they'd arrived for afternoon tea.

'Hi Sylv! Hi Pete! Come on up!'

Kate opened the door eleven floors later, and Sylvia was shocked to see Callum there too. Peter squeezed her arm for support, knowing it would knock her for six seeing her daughter-in-law's lover standing there bold as brass as if butter wouldn't melt. ('And what she sees in him I will *never* know! The man's the same age as me if he's a day!' she'd whispered to Peter later when they were getting in the car. Peter thought Sylvia was pushing her luck with that one, but he didn't feel it appropriate to point this out, given his friend's distress.)

'Sylvia, this is Callum,' Kate said firmly.

Callum held out his hand, but Sylvia refused to take it.

'Let's not make this difficult, shall we?' Kate warned. 'For Tallulah's sake.'

'Didn't think about Tallulah when you were jumping into bed with a man old enough to be your father, did you?' Sylvia hissed, and Peter rapidly changed the subject as he spied Tallulah peeping round the corner, her faithful Panda in tow.

'Is that Princess Tallulah-bella Mozzarella Fenton I see?' he exclaimed like a character out of a pantomime.

This made Tallulah giggle. It was a game she and Peter always played and he was grateful now for the ice-breaker. She came running out to see them, shouting, 'My name's NOT Tallulah-bella Mozzarella!'

'Erm, I think you'll find it *is*!' he teased.

Kate picked up Lula's overnight bag and handed it to Sylvia. 'There are a few things in here, but all her stuff is at the house, of course.'

'Well, of course it is, that's her home.'

'Sylvia, we can't have this sniping every time, OK? We'll see you back here on Wednesday night.'

Sylvia bit her lip. It was challenge enough for her not to unleash all that was in her head, and she managed to remain silent, turning her attention to Tallulah instead.

'Come on then, sweetheart, shall we go and see Daddy?'

'YEY!' she squealed and Peter picked her up, teasing her all the while to make the transition as smooth as possible as he carried her through Kate's front door.

'Bye, darling!' Kate kissed her on her head. 'Say bye-bye to Callum!'

'No!'

'Tallulah, don't be silly now!' Kate said with a mixture of annoyance and embarrassment, sensing Sylvia's smugness.

'NO!' she shouted even louder, not because she was upset, but because she was playful, and Peter was her best friend right then, not Callum.

'Tallulah! Don't be so rude!' Kate was feeling really stupid now.

'Leave it, Kate,' Callum said quietly. And Kate looked suitably admonished.

'I'll say that for him, Matt, he's not afraid to stand up to her!' Sylvia had told her son when she'd brought Tallulah over that first night.

And he'd turned to his mother, tired from all the sadness, and said, 'You don't need to tell me anything about Callum, Mum. Or Kate. All I care about is my little girl.' And that's what was keeping him going right now. Patching himself together until he couldn't see the joins, getting fit and looking to the future. A future without Kate, but a future that would always have Tallulah in it. He didn't need to think about anything else. Not for a while, anyway.

69

Glenda McCloud had an irritating habit of taking sharp intakes of breath as she read, as if being intermittently electrocuted. She was looking through Belinda's case notes whilst Belinda sat opposite her, patiently waiting for Glenda to speak.

Sue's sister-in-law Josie had recommended Glenda as 'the best divorce lawyer in Scotland', which Belinda found annoying for two reasons: firstly, how could Josie possibly know that? and secondly, she didn't *need* the best divorce lawyer in Scotland. She just needed someone to fill out the forms, send them to the court and get the whole thing done and dusted as quickly as possible.

The decree nisi had come through yesterday. Now it was just a case of sorting the settlement whilst awaiting the decree absolute in a few more weeks.

'So. He's happy for you to stay on in the house till Ailsa is eighteen, but then you'll have to sell and divvy up the profit.'

Belinda could feel the blood draining from her face. 'You're not serious?'

'Afraid so. I have to say, this lawyer of his . . .' – she looked at the name at the bottom of the page – 'Emmerson Shaw – nasty piece of work. Has Callum used him before?'

'Of course not. It'll be *her* solicitor, won't it? *He* wouldn't have a clue. But I know one thing, Callum wouldn't want me to sell the house.'

Glenda looked at Belinda long and hard, biting the inside of her lip as her mind raced ahead of itself.

'He's got every right to make the request, I'm afraid. Of course, if you spoke to him, you could maybe get to the bottom of—'

'No way,' Belinda interrupted before Glenda reached the end of her sentence. She hadn't spoken to Callum since the day he'd told her he was moving to London.

Since then, they'd communicated either via Ailsa or their solicitors. And that's the way she wanted it. She knew Callum was desperate to see her, to try and make things a bit easier between them. But Belinda was rock solid in her determination never to contact him ever again. She simply didn't trust herself: because she would either scream her head off at him for ruining her life, or she'd crumble and beg him to come back to her. Neither was an option, so she wouldn't take the risk.

'OK, that's your prerogative. And, of course, Ailsa's not eighteen for another six months, so you've got a bit of time. But unless you can come to some mutual agreement, he's every right to insist on the sale of the property.'

It was Belinda's third visit to Glenda McCloud. Each time she'd left there feeling low in confidence and high in stress.

She headed to the patisserie nearby, where she ordered a massive choux bun and the biggest coffee they made, sat in the window and caught her breath.

She knew she was going to have to contact Callum. She didn't have a choice. Apart from anything else, she wanted him to know what antics his solicitor was up to on his behalf. There was no way the man she'd married would want to sell that house, the place his three children had been raised, the home that had witnessed so much love and laughter, that had been at the heart of their long and lovely journey as a family – well, long and lovely until last December.

She knew from his letters and his emails – to which she'd never replied – that the guilt he felt was already crippling him, and she knew he'd find it impossible to increase that burden by forcing her to sell their home. Unless he'd changed, of course. Maybe he'd been with 'Hated Kate', as the kids called her, for long enough now to be influenced by her ruthless mind. Maybe she'd persuaded him that *You paid most of the mortgage on that house, Callum, and the kids are practically all grown up now, don't be a wimp, fight for what's rightly yours.* She wouldn't be surprised.

Bitch.

Belinda caught her reflection in the mirrored wall of the patisserie. She didn't mind looking old. She was fifty-five now, after all, and she'd never been one of those women who worried about age. 'Comes to us all,' she used to say, 'if we're lucky!' She'd put on weight since he'd left – mainly due to seeking solace in choux buns and no longer playing tennis. Ha! The irony of that – she'd lost not only a husband but a tennis partner to boot.

No, it wasn't the lines around her eyes that bothered her, or the extra pounds or the greying hair. It was that she'd lost her spirit. She'd lost her Belinda-ness. Because she'd lost her faith. In love.

It was eighteen years now since his first affair with Kate. Back then Belinda had thought she would dissolve into nothingness. The pain was suffocating, debilitating. And she'd have put money on their marriage not surviving the onslaught. Because once it'd been invaded by that army of doubt and distrust, how could she ever forgive him, or like him, or love him, or even be in the same room as him again?

But she'd dug hard, scrabbling around for the tiniest remnant of love and hope, till she'd scraped together enough to get them going again and move on; slowly at first, timidly and without much confidence of success. Until eventually they made it back to the old Callum and Belinda, Cal and Lind, Callumagico and Bel. And Kate Andrews became just a shadow in their past, a spectre exorcized and gone. They'd watched the kids grow up, reached so many milestones together: the GCSEs, the driving tests, the graduations, the first loves, the first fights, the first drinks, and all the other ups and downs of life – Callum's mother going into care, Belinda's father dying, Callum's promotion to deputy head, and even the good old menopause . . . all the grime and glory that comprised a strong, enduring marriage. They were watertight. Safe. Protected. Until the intruder had returned and stolen Callum from them, smashing up their happy little home for good.

A big juicy tear rolled down Belinda's cheek and splashed into her cappuccino. *All loss is sad*, she thought. *But the loss of faith in Love is catastrophic.*

She decided she would email Callum that evening.

70

'You look brand new,' Chloe, his 'artist in residence', said as she stared sternly at Matt.

'Shouldn't I be saying that about you?' He laughed. 'You're the one who's been doing all that yoga and stuff!'

Chloe had just returned from a month in India, partly taking photos and partly experiencing life on an ashram.

'I don't feel any different,' she explained. 'But you! You look shiny again. Bye.'

And, abrupt as ever, off she skipped to her studio, ready to lose herself in her art again.

Matt certainly did feel better. The exercise regime was paying dividends and he'd even joined a running club.

'It's good for you to make new friends,' Hetty had said, admiring his six-pack like a new hat.

'Stop trying to find me a girlfriend!' he'd laughed. 'I'm still technically married, y'know!'

'Not for much longer. Hey! We could have a decree absolute party!'

'What is your obsession with parties? You'd celebrate the opening of an envelope if you could!'

She'd hit him playfully on the arm, thrilled that the old Matt was returning to life. Tallulah had played a big part in this, of course.

She was with him every Sunday to Wednesday, and he'd also started doing more during the rest of the week – not dating, he wouldn't be ready for that for a while, but as well as the running club he'd started hot yoga on a Thursday and Italian on a Monday. He wasn't sure about Italian at first, it being a Tallulah night, but Hetty had dived in and offered to babysit, solving the problem in a heartbeat.

And then, of course, there was the Friday-evening quiz. He'd gone along initially as a one-off replacement on Hetty's team. She'd been going to the Dog and Duck in Shepherd's Bush for the past eighteen months with her workmates Lisa, Robbie and Ivor, and it'd become ultra-competitive for them. But when Robbie had had to pull out for family reasons Hetty had begged Matt to stand in, otherwise their chances of winning the league would be ruined.

'I bloody hate pub quizzes!' he moaned when she called into the gallery with Ivor one lunchtime.

'That's what Ivor said first of all, didn't you, Ivy? But now he comes every week and he loves it.' Ivor smiled unconvincingly. 'Oh *please*, Matt!'

As usual, he couldn't say no to Hetty, and so he turned up at the Dog and Duck that evening and was welcomed into the inner sanctum of Team Vegelicious. And despite his protestations and low expectations, he'd really enjoyed himself. *And* they'd come third. So it didn't take much to persuade him to come back the following week.

The fifth time he went, he found himself buying drinks with Ivor during the break. He liked Ivor. He'd thought he was shy and silent at first, even a bit miserable, but as he got to know him, he grew to enjoy his dark sense of humour, his intelligent take on world politics and his sardonic wit.

'I can see why you changed your mind, Ivor! It's pretty addictive, isn't it, this quiz malarkey!'

'Not really,' Ivor replied. 'I still loathe it.'

Matt was confused. 'So why do you come?'

Ivor took his change from the barman, along with a deep breath, and said, 'Because I'm in love with Hetty. And I'm addicted to her company. Even though it makes me miserable knowing that she's not remotely interested in me.'

Matt decided not to mention it – it really wasn't up to him, was it? But then what if Hetty was missing out on her perfect man? What if Matt was standing in the way of true love just because he was too cowardly to speak out?

He looked for clues as to how Hetty felt about Ivor, watching the body language between them during the rest of the night. They certainly got on; he made her laugh – a lot. And vice versa. And yes, there was something sweet and tender between them. But what if she only felt friendship towards him, and if Matt said anything their friendship would be spoilt?

The decision, thankfully, would be taken out of his hands.

71

In the end, it'd taken Belinda a whole week and over twenty attempts before she'd composed an email she was happy to send. It simply said:

Callum
Your solicitor informed my solicitor you want me to sell the
house.
Not gonna happen.
Belinda

All the other drafts had been much longer, of course. In some of them, after 'Your solicitor informed my solicitor you want me to sell the house' she'd written:

and deprive our three children of the home they grew up in,
which would break their hearts, but then what the fuck do you
care about hurting our children when you've already smashed
their lives into smithereens, you selfish, arrogant, heartless
cunt.

It'd felt good calling him that. Even for the few seconds it stayed on the screen before she deleted it. She'd also written a postscript in one version:

*PS: Kate seems quite thick to me, so I don't expect she's good
enough at maths to work out that in four years' time she'll still
be in her mid forties, whereas you'll be eligible for a bus pass.
Maybe you should point this out. Perhaps she should think about
getting a carer in to help when you're incapacitated and can't
wipe your own arse any more . . .*

Sue had told her to write it all down.

'Get it all down, sweetheart, say everything you want to say,
then RIP IT UP! Cos you must never, EVER show him how hurt
you are.'

When she finally sent the email that Wednesday evening at
eight p.m., she'd worked out it was 112 days since she'd last seen
him. She switched off her computer till the Friday morning, when
she noticed there were three replies. The first was sent within half
an hour of receiving hers.

*Bel
So good to hear from you.
Can we talk about this?
Callum*

Then on the Thursday morning he'd sent another one:

*If you'd rather stick to emails, that's also fine.
Callum*

And finally on the Thursday evening, email number three:

*Or homing pigeon?
C.*

A tiny smile flickered across her face when she read that, disappearing the instant she became aware of it.

72

Ivor ended up walking Hetty home after the quiz. Nothing new in that, Hetty's flat being only ten minutes from where he lived in Turnham Green. Once they'd reached her front door, though, Ivor told her he had something to say.

'I'm leaving *Vegetarian Living*, Het. I've been offered a job in Belgium.'

'Why?' It seemed like a stupid question.

'Well, because I applied for it.'

'But why?'

'Because I'm finding it impossible to live in London.'

'I know what you mean. It's so bloody expensive. The other day I worked out—'

'Hetty, shut up a minute,' he said gently. 'I'm finding it impossible because I've fallen in love with someone . . .'

'Oh Ivy, how wonderful!'

He ignored her and carried on, 'I've fallen in love with someone, but I don't think it's reciprocated – in fact, I don't think they're even aware I exist half the time, and seeing them every day is killing me. So I need to remove myself from the source of pain.'

Hetty had looked at him, putting on her serious listening face. 'Darling, have you told her how you feel? I'm presuming it's a she?'

This had irritated Ivor. Great, so she wasn't even sure if he was straight!

'Yes, of course it's a she!!'

They stood there for a moment, traffic zooming rudely past.

'I gave you the Secret Santa. The thing with the little pebbles,' he said.

'What?'

'And I sent you the Valentine card.'

'That was you!'

She had indeed received the most beautiful home-made Valentine in the post at work and had no idea who could've sent it. *Be My Valentine*, the card had commanded in an elegant font on a lilac background, with a simple silver heart beneath. Inside, the hand-written message declared: *You are still exceptional.*

'Gosh Ivy! That was you!' she repeated. 'No one's ever sent me a Valentine before,' she said, realizing how self-pitying that sounded. 'Except my dad when I was seven.' She knew she was wittering but couldn't help herself, trying to buy time whilst she absorbed the news that *Ivor had sent her a Valentine card!* 'He did it to be sweet really, but I didn't see it like that, of course, and I got ever so cross with him because I—'

'Oh fuck it!' Ivor interrupted. At which point Hetty *knew* something was amiss because she couldn't remember ever hearing him swear before. And before she could say another word, he cupped her face in both his hands, closed his eyes and kissed her for twenty-seven seconds.

And during the first three of those twenty-seven seconds, Hetty realized that she'd got Ivor completely wrong all the time she'd known him, and that she didn't in fact know him at all.

'Like when someone surprises you,' she told Matt a few days later, 'by being a really good cook or an accomplished dancer or a brilliant linguist, and yet you'd never have thought they had it in them. Well, when Ivor kissed me, it was the most amazing and tender and well-constructed kiss I've ever had in my entire life – not that I've got a huge amount to compare it with, but still . . .'

*

The following Monday, Hetty called Matt half an hour before she was due at his house to babysit. 'Matt, it's me. Hetty.'

'Yes I know. Your name comes up on the— Oh, never mind.' What was the point, he smiled to himself.

'Anyway, I've got something to tell you.'

'You're cancelling on me?'

'No, I'm ten minutes away. But I thought I'd better warn you,' she whispered hard into the phone, 'I won't be alone!'

'Right . . .' Matt was intrigued.

'Just don't say anything when we arrive!'

'OK, but—'

Too late. Hetty had hung up.

So when Matt opened the door ten minutes later to Hetty – and *Ivor*! – he did what he was told and didn't bat an eyelid, inviting them in, offering them both a cup of tea.

Tallulah, however, was not so discreet. 'Are you Hetty's boyfriend?' she asked Ivor as she sat next to him on the sofa, drawing whiskers on his face with a purple eyeliner.

'Yes he is, Lules,' said Hetty. 'Now, hot chocolate before bedtime?'

It wasn't till Matt got home from his Italian class three hours later that he managed to corner Hetty in the kitchen under the ruse of making tea and made her spill the beans, while Ivor watched TV in the living room. She spoke in short, sharp, whispered sentences, laced with hysteria and delight.

'So I invited him up to my flat . . .'

'Right . . .' said Matt, checking over his shoulder.

'. . . and bonked his brains out!'

'*Bonked!?* Hetty, that is so not a you word!'

'Sssssshh! OK, shagged! Fucked! Screwed! Jumped! Baked some mamajolambas! Whatever you want to call it, we did it. All night. And all weekend. And we haven't looked back since.' The tears were streaming now and she was laughing. 'Matty, I love the very cuticles of that man!'

73

She was in two minds. The coffee-coloured silk was so classy and looked gorgeous next to her skin, but the black chiffon was much sexier. Should she go for class or sex?

Standing in the changing room of an obscenely expensive boutique on Bond Street, Kate was choosing a designer dress to wear to the BAFTAs. She'd been nominated for best actress for her role in *Second Sight*, a TV drama she'd filmed the year before.

Callum teased her the day she'd found out, as she leapt about the apartment, screaming for joy. 'I thought you said awards didn't mean anything?'

'They don't!' she yelled excitedly. 'Until you're nominated for one!'

She'd laughed it off, but deep down had been slightly annoyed that he hadn't made more fuss about the nomination. *It's a BAFTA!* she'd thought. But then quickly reminded herself that Callum wasn't au fait with her professional world – why should he be? – and that was one of the reasons she loved him. He was down-to-earth. He had a *proper* job.

The ceremony was only a week away and she'd left it till the last minute to choose her dress so she'd be as thin as she could possibly be. She'd booked the make-up artist and the stylist to come to the apartment beforehand at two, then she and Callum would leave together at six in the pre-ordered limousine, which would take them to the theatre in Drury Lane.

It would be a red-carpet affair, of course. Kate was used to them, knew how to stand, how to smile, what to say to the TV crews and journalists who'd be lining the barriers on the way in. She'd tried speaking to Callum about it a few times, but he always brushed it off.

'You don't need to worry about me saying the wrong thing, 'cos I'm not gonna utter a word!'

And she'd smiled, and kissed him, and made him promise never to change.

'No danger of that,' he'd said.

Since moving to London, he'd been going regularly to his new rugby club in Richmond. She was glad he'd joined – it made her feel like he was putting down roots, though he said it irked him as a Scot to join an English club.

'Well, swings and roundabouts,' she'd said. 'At least you're too old to actually play for them, so you're not being that disloyal.'

He hadn't laughed as much as she thought he would. She was always asking him if he was happy, if he felt he'd made the right decision. And always, always, he would say yes.

They'd got into a routine now, which seemed to be working well – Tallulah was with them Wednesday night through to Sunday, and as Kate was filming again, she'd employed a part-time nanny, Celine, to look after her when she couldn't be at home because of work. Matt had offered, through Sylvia, to extend Tallulah's time with him instead. 'It just makes sense, dear,' Sylvia had said to Kate patronizingly, 'for Tallulah to be with her father when you're not available, rather than some poor young girl who can barely speak English!'

But Kate was insistent. They were going to stick to their routine if it killed her. And if Matt, or Sylvia, put up a fight, they could go to the courts and have an official custody battle. 'And let's face it, we know they'll only side with me, so why waste our time?' she'd replied through a fixed smile.

Kate was thrilled that Tallulah had so readily accepted Callum as 'Mummy's new boyfriend'. At first she was shy of him, hiding behind Kate's legs and timidly peeping out, refusing to speak. But because he was such a natural father, he became a lovely stepfather too. And soon Tallulah felt happy and comfortable in his company. Kate knew he missed his own kids, of course – it was three months now since the split and still only Ailsa would speak to him. She'd been to London twice to visit, though she'd refused to stay at the flat so Callum had put her up in a cheap hotel, which was all he could afford. Kate had offered to book her in somewhere more upmarket, but Callum said he couldn't possibly let Kate pay – it would be morally wrong somehow.

Ailsa seemed to enjoy the adventure of it all, with Callum meeting her at St Pancras on the Friday night, then spending the entire weekend with her. They'd gone on a river cruise and the London Eye, and he'd taken her to eat at Ed's Diner. Kate had put on a brave face, insisting she was just happy that Callum was spending time with his daughter. But inside she was desperately hurt that Ailsa would have nothing to do with her. *Give it time*, she told herself. *You've come this far.*

Callum had also been back to see Ailsa in Edinburgh three times since Christmas. Kate had gone with him, of course, and they'd stayed at Kate's parents'. Yvonne was just about speaking to her now, but it had taken weeks for her to forgive the 'appalling way' Kate had behaved.

Yvonne tolerated Callum with good manners that veiled her contempt. Gordon, on the other hand, rather liked the guy. In fact, he felt a bit sorry for him, having gotten into such a mess. Yvonne claimed Gordon only liked Callum because they were of a similar age. 'Don't be ridiculous, woman,' he'd said, though secretly he thought she wasn't far wrong.

Whenever Kate asked Callum about Belinda, he'd clam up. He said what was done was done and there was no point dredging things up and dissecting them – best for everyone to just get on with their lives. She wanted to ask him if he missed her, if deep down he thought he'd made the most terrible mistake. But all the signals warned her off mentioning Belinda's name. Whenever she felt insecure, she turned to what she knew best – keeping their sex life well and truly vibrant. She was always coming up with new and exciting scenarios, procuring little tablets that would keep them both going all night, dressing up, dressing down, inviting him to share his most private fantasies with her. But he'd just say, 'It's you, Kate. You're my fantasy.' And a tiny part of her felt patronized.

She looked at herself now in the changing-room mirror – her body adorned with the coffee silk she'd finally chosen to wear. It had more edge, she thought. Though it wasn't just the press she wanted to look good for – she was fighting a constant battle to look good for Callum. Never quite believing she'd made the mark, no matter how many times he reassured her. And it wasn't just her appearance she worried about – she was continually trying to find out if he was happy. In London. With her.

A few weeks back, they'd gone to a rugby match together. Kate had procured, via her agent, two international tickets for Twickenham. They were to be guests in a hospitality box sponsored by a big chemical-engineering firm. There was to be free booze and posh food all day, and they'd get to watch Scotland play England. She was so excited when she presented him with the tickets.

'A hospitality box!' he'd exclaimed. 'Me and Belinda always got the cheap seats and a curry on the way home.'

He rarely mentioned Belinda, so her name was left hanging awkwardly in the air, neither of them commenting on it, Kate feeling sick with jealousy. But, ever the actress, she didn't show it and ploughed on.

'Well, it's a first for me. You'll have to guide me as I lose my international rugby virginity!'

The price to pay for free tickets was that she had to be on celebrity duty all day. It was a bit tiresome being hounded by fans when all she wanted was to have a special time with Callum, to give him something she thought he'd enjoy, to share in his love for rugby. But, as ever, her fame got in the way of it all.

Callum had got on very well with the host and MD of the

company, an affable Liverpudlian called Stuart. During half-time he stood with Callum at the bar, both enjoying their pints. They watched Kate in action as she chatted with the other guests, working the room, having her photo taken, always glancing back at Callum for some kind of approval.

'Landed on your feet there, mate, didn't you?' Stuart had said. And Callum had just smiled, giving nothing away. He'd be lying if he said he hated it when men his own age envied not only that he was with a beautiful woman seventeen years his junior, but also that she was rich and famous.

They'd ended up having a great day – getting hopelessly drunk, of course. During the game, Kate whispered to Callum to meet her in the disabled toilet for a quickie, but he was having none of it. She actually thought he seemed a bit disgusted at the prospect and she teased him, 'Not turning into a prude already, are you, Callum?'

'No, it's just . . . well, it's a rugby game, isn't it? Time and place an' all that . . .'

She'd smiled and turned back to cheering on her national team.

Scotland won, which was the icing on the cake, and Kate announced to him that night in bed that she was a definite convert to the world of rugby. She'd never felt so patriotic, belting out 'Flower of Scotland' before the game and cheering on the boys in blue. When could they do it again? Should she get them tickets for the France game?

'Maybe,' Callum said, and turned over and went to sleep.

Kate tried to ignore the doubt that was gnawing away at her confidence.

'How you doing in there?' came the voice of the sales assistant, interrupting her thoughts.

'I'll take both!' she said, putting on the charm. 'And I'll let my boyfriend decide!'

74

That afternoon, Kate felt secure in the warm glow of domestic life.

After buying her dress, she met Callum, who had taken Tallulah for a milkshake nearby. She loved seeing them together, especially when Callum carried her daughter on his shoulders and made her laugh. Then they went back to the apartment and had a lazy afternoon, Tallulah watching Kate paint her nails, Callum reading the Saturday papers and flicking through the sports channels. This was what she'd longed for. This was how it was meant to be.

The knock at the door was a surprise because visitors always used the intercom buzzer. Kate and Callum looked at each other, presuming it must be one of the neighbours – though sometimes, if the security door was left open by accident, guests just made their way up to the apartment.

'I'll go,' Kate said, shaking dry her freshly painted nails. Tallulah, now bored of playing make-up, turned to Callum to 'play sharks', which involved him sliding around on the carpet trying to grab her by the ankle. She so delighted in being scared.

Kate opened the door. Standing there was a young man, tanned, handsome, nervous. 'Does Callum MacGregor live here?' he asked. She detected his Scottish lilt straight away.

'Who wants to know?' Kate replied.

Thirty seconds later, she was showing him into the living room, where Callum was singing the theme tune from *Jaws* and Tallulah was squealing with delight as he chased her slowly around the floor.

'Awww – what a pretty picture,' the young man said.

Callum stopped and looked up. 'Ben! My God!'

He clambered to his feet, but Tallulah wanted to carry on playing. 'Again! Do it again!'

'Was he being a shark?' said Ben, his sarcasm lost on Tallulah. 'He's good at that. Aren't you, Dad?'

Kate took Tallulah's hand and led her out of the room.

'Come on, come and help Mummy in the bathroom.'

'But I want to play with Callum,' she cried as they left. Kate shut the door behind them.

The two men stared at each other.

'I like your new family, Dad.' Ben's voice cracked a little. 'Very sweet.'

'Look . . . just sit down a minute,' Callum said, offering him the sofa, 'I haven't seen you in over a year. Tell me about your trip!'

'What? Think this is a social call, do you? Think I just happen to be in London, so hey – I know – I'll take my holiday snaps over to Dad's and meet my new stepmother and her little brat?' Ben was seething now, months of frustration boiling up inside him, months of wanting to tell his father what he thought of what he'd done but knowing he could only do it face to face.

'Come on – she's five, she's innocent in all of this.'

'Innocent? What about my mother? And my little sister? And my brother? Eh? Aren't we all innocent too? Jesus!' Ben hated himself for starting to cry. He walked over to the window to calm himself down, looking out at the view of the Thames, a view that in any other circumstance he'd have admired.

'What d'you get off on, Dad?' he said, quietly. 'Is it the fame and the money? Or are you just a sad old man who fancied his chances with some slapper twenty years younger than him?'

Callum knew this was not the time to admonish his son for being rude about Kate. 'It's not like that. We knew each other . . . before . . .'

Ben scoffed at this. 'Yeah, I heard about your little secret. Think

338

that makes it better, do you? The fact she's not some one-night stand? That you knew her back then, back in the fucking eighties, when . . .' he faltered, 'when *I* was five for Christ's sake?'

'Ben . . .'

'You were lying to us all even then – you bastard!' His anger got the better of him again and he lunged forward with a punch aimed squarely at his father's jaw. Callum ducked out of the way just in time.

'Whoah! Please, Ben. I know you're angry – of course you are. But this isn't the answer . . .'

Wiping the tears away as fast as he could, Ben turned on Callum, his voice choked with pain. 'I used to be so proud that you were my dad. When we were in school an' that – all my mates thought you were brilliant, 'cos of your rugby and 'cos you never talked to them like a teacher. I really loved the fact that I was your son.'

'I'm so sorry.'

'But now I'm just ashamed. I *hate* you!' he wept.

And he launched forward again. Callum thought he was going to throw another punch. But instead he grabbed his father hard, pulling him into a desperate hug, sobbing his heart out like a little boy. 'Please come home, Dad,' he begged.

Feeling totally helpless, Callum wrapped his arms around his eldest boy and kissed the top of his head, comforting him like he'd done when he was younger. He looked up and saw that Kate had come into the room without Tallulah.

She smiled sadly at Callum and said gently, 'The best way forward for all of us is to accept that this is how things are now.'

She hadn't banked on the aggression in Ben as he pulled out of the hug with Callum and hissed at her, 'Who asked for your opinion, you fucking whore?'

'Oh, how predictable!' she laughed.

'Hey Ben, come on!'

But Kate was made of stronger stuff and she held Ben's gaze as she said calmly and levelly, 'Listen, sunshine. I'm sorry that this is so painful for you, I really am. But I love your father and we're together now, and the sooner you acknowledge that, the sooner we can all start getting on with our lives as a family. And that can include you too, Ben, and Cory and Ailsa.'

'No chance. You're off your 'ead, woman.'

She ignored this and carried on, 'And, of course, you are more than welcome to come here whenever you like. As long as you respect me and my home and my daughter.' And with that, she took hold of his arm – he was too shocked to shake it off. 'But if you *ever* come here again and start mouthing off like this when there's a five-year-old child in the other room, you will have me to answer to, and believe you me, I don't take any prisoners. Got it?'

Stunned by the outburst, Ben turned to his father for support and said, 'Well?'

But Callum couldn't look at him and said nothing.

Ben headed for the door and, turning before he left, he whispered, 'You fucking coward.'

75

Callum
Thanks for your email and for speaking to your solicitor about
the house. My solicitor has now confirmed you will not be
seeking sale of Sutherland Avenue.
Ben said he saw you.
He was very upset.

She *had* wanted to write, *Ben said he saw you and your marriage-wrecking slag of a girlfriend – I hope you're proud of yourselves and the hurt you've caused this family, you selfish, inconsiderate, arrogant wanker.* But she didn't. And she forced herself to end on a positive note, writing:

Ailsa loves her new moped. Thank you for buying it.
B.

76

Callum had been emailing Belinda for four weeks now. His heart soared every time he saw her name in his inbox, which wasn't very often – even though he checked it, hoping, every day. Her messages were always curt. But at least she was communicating with him. And he always replied straight away.

Bel
So glad Ailsa liked the moped.

He'd taken a loan out to buy it, but he wasn't about to tell Belinda that. Or Kate.

Please make sure – I know you will – that she wears the helmet at all times, and never ever, ever has a drink before getting on it.
Yes, Ben came and yes he was upset. I'm sorry, obviously.
Old Watsonians played well against Saracens last month, didn't they? Though I think they need to rethink the back row.
Bye for now
Callum

He'd wanted to write, *PS: I miss you every fucking day.*
He'd also wanted to add an *x*.
But he did neither.

Nor did he tell Kate that he'd had any correspondence with Belinda whatsoever.

77

Matt loved days like this. The week before Easter: fresh, clean sunshine with a hint of cool in the breeze; daffodils, optimism and Lindt chocolate bunnies. He'd always preferred Easter to Christmas, but given the events of the past five months, he felt it even more so now.

The gallery had been quiet that morning. He didn't mind – he was quite enjoying the peace. He'd left the door wide open to welcome in any passing trade, but secretly hoping no one would bother. He was reading a good book that he rather wanted to finish.

Peter was away for the week. Copenhagen with Julius. 'No better place on earth!' he'd said. Matt had made a half-hearted attempt to find cover for him by asking Chloe if she'd like to do a couple of shifts and earn some cash, which he knew she must need.

'No.'

'Oh. OK.'

He was used to her brusqueness most of the time, but sometimes it caught him off guard.

'I don't like shops.'

'Well, it's not a shop as such, Chlo.'

'You sell things, people buy things.'

'Yes, but it's Art!'

This clearly didn't matter to Chloe. And she'd headed upstairs to the studio, Matt shaking his head with a smile. She was getting very close to finishing her latest piece, a spectacular riverscape, on the biggest canvas he'd ever seen her use. He'd sit up there sometimes, watching her paint. She didn't seem to mind, as long as he didn't speak.

That had suited him fine in the early days after Kate left. Each time he'd tried to get back to work and failed miserably, Peter would send him upstairs just to sit quietly with Chloe. Sometimes he would sit there for three hours at a time, in complete and utter silence, apart from the dull scraping of pastels on canvas as Chloe set about her creation.

At lunchtime, he decided to shut up shop and go for a little wander. He walked out to the back steps and shouted up to the studio, 'Chloe? I'm getting a sandwich, d'you want anything?'

'A packet of ham!' she shouted back. 'And a peach.'

Fair enough, thought Matt. Nobody could accuse Chloe of ever being vague.

Out on the high street, the approaching Easter weekend made the air buzz with delight. Everyone was in a good mood, light on their feet, exchanging unsolicited smiles.

He always crossed over the road to avoid Porto's. He'd not been in there since he and Kate had split up; certain places, certain people he just couldn't face. He had a checklist in his head, to mark off and monitor his progress. Seeing the solicitor had been a big one, but with Hetty's help he'd got through that, and in two weeks' time he and Kate would finally be divorced. He would soon be able to refer to her as 'my ex-wife'. And he was alright with that now. Though it had taken a while to get there.

Contacting Kate for the first time had been another major hurdle – he couldn't remember speaking to her on those two occasions early on. But Hetty had told him that Kate wanted to communicate via emails. And that suited him. After a few weeks, they had progressed to texts – simple messages such as *Tallulah left her horse book at yours* or *Mum will come at six tomorrow to collect T.* It'd taken a little longer to actually speak to her again on the phone. Though the anticipation had been far worse than the actual event and he knew, when he'd done it once, that he could do it again.

She'd sounded so friendly – so kind, in fact – asking him how he was, telling him that she hoped they could get through this and ultimately be friends again, because 'I'll always love you, Matt.' He thought when she said this that it would wrench his heart apart, but whether it was a self-defence mechanism or whether he just didn't believe her, hearing her say it had no effect whatsoever.

He talked to Dervla the therapist about it and she suggested he just went with the flow. That there was no right way or wrong way to get over the break-up of a marriage. And no timetable for the change in his feelings, from excruciating pain to indifference and nonchalance.

He called into the little delicatessen on the corner, owned since 1975 by Alessandra, an octogenarian Greek-Cypriot, and her Turkish husband, Osman. The smell of fresh herbs and brown paper bags made him smile every time he went in there. He picked up some Greek sesame-seeded bread, halloumi and hummus – home-made by Alessandra's daughter – two juicy beef tomatoes, and an avocado. He bought Chloe's ham and even found her a peach ripe enough to eat.

'Hey, Matteus!' For some reason, Alessandra was always delighted to see him. 'My beautiful boy, you look the better every times!'

Whether it was her age or her Mediterranean disposition, Alessandra was always emotional, whether discussing the political state of Cyprus or the fact that she'd run out of goat's milk that day. She wrapped up his goods and put them in a pink and white stripy carrier bag as thin as cobwebs.

'You are getting it back, huh? Matteus is coming back now!' And she winked at him.

He didn't quite understand her but said thank you anyway, assuming whatever she meant was a good thing.

He headed off to the gallery and let himself in through the back, shouting up to Chloe again, 'Got your stuff!'

She didn't answer at first.

'Chlo?'

Sometimes she didn't hear him, so lost she was in the world of her painting. And sometimes she didn't answer him because she simply didn't want to. He presumed it was the latter and made his way upstairs.

'It's done!' she said, sensing he had come in but without actually looking round. She was standing with her back to him, facing the canvas, and wiping her hands pointlessly on a cloth saturated in pastels.

'Wow. Chloe.'

It really was magnificent. He'd seen it at different stages, of course, but these past couple of weeks he'd not ventured up here to look. Big sweeping lines, boisterous and joyous, captured the river's vitality and flow in a vivacious explosion of colour.

The French doors onto the little balcony were open, letting in the celebratory daylight of this glorious spring afternoon. The sounds from the high street, softened by distance as they wafted upwards, created a holiday atmos akin to lying on a busy beach. He put down the food on the little paint table and went and stood next to her.

'That is truly mind-blowing.'

'I know,' she said.

He turned to her and smiled, finding her self-belief so refreshing and honest.

'Saying "Well done" doesn't really seem adequate!' he said, and was taken by surprise as he noticed for the first time that her pink hair was really quite exotic. As were her vibrant green eyes.

She didn't smile back. Just started undressing, never dropping her gaze from his, and announcing, 'I want some sex with you.'

Unquestioning, Matt started taking his clothes off too and simply said, 'Yes, that seems like a good idea.'

He didn't open the shop again that afternoon.

78

Dear Bel
Do you think next time I come to Edinburgh to see Ailsa, that you
and I could meet up?
Callum x

79

Dear Callum
No.
Belinda

80

Dervla had assured Matt life would only throw at him challenges which he could handle. And so whether it was the astonishingly life-affirming afternoon of sex with Chloe that did it, or whether he was just ready to jump the next hurdle in what Dervla called 'the healing process', he woke up that Sunday morning and decided that today was the day he was going to face Kate.

Sylvia usually collected Tallulah from Kate's apartment at ten a.m. every Sunday morning and brought her back to Chiswick. Matt looked at his phone – it was half eight. He called his mother and told her of the change of plan. She instantly went into meltdown. 'You can't, love, it's too soon.'

'No it's not. It's fine.'

'Then let me come with you, at least,' she begged.

'Mum, you've been really kind and I honestly don't know how I'd have got through these past months without you, but today I'm collecting Tallulah myself and it's going to be absolutely fine.'

He got in the shower, holding his face under the cleansing hot water, thought about Chloe and laughed out loud. It had been so deliciously messy, so unexpectedly erotic and fuckably delightful – paint getting everywhere, pots knocked over, palettes dropped, easels toppled; all positions covered – standing up, sitting down, on top, under up, sideways, longways, which ways, any ways . . . months and months without sex getting their comeuppance – for

Matt, quite literally. And when they'd both finally exhausted themselves three hours later, they simply got dressed, sat on the floor and
ate the lunch he'd bought earlier.

'Thank you very much,' Chloe said formally.

'For the peach or the sex?' he laughed.

'For the peach and the sex and the ham,' she said, not laughing
back.

He hesitated, knowing he needed to nip this in the bud before it
did any real harm.

'Just so you know, Chloe,' he said tentatively, 'I really loved all
that just now, but I don't want to have any sort of relationship yet.
I'm not, y'know, boyfriend material or anything.'

She looked at him, peach juice running down her chin. 'I've got
a boyfriend,' she stated, without a trace of defensiveness. 'I don't
need another one.'

'Ah. OK!' Matt replied, slightly thrown, and sank his teeth into a
chunk of Greek bread smothered in hummus. He sat there smiling,
and contemplated the fact that he was finally emerging from one
of the most traumatic phases of his life, marked by the most lovely
and uncomplicated afternoon of sex, which would never again be
repeated.

He pressed the buzzer for Apartment 29, his heart racing, sweat
popping out on his forehead. *You can do this.*

Suddenly, the beautiful voice of Tallulah came bursting out of the
intercom. 'Hello Nana, come on up!'

Matt had no time to explain that it was Daddy, not Nana, the
loud buzz of the door urging him to open it. In the lift, he focused
on Tallulah – on staying calm for her, on being polite to Kate – he
wouldn't have to stay long, just collect his little girl and go. But as
the lift slowed down he wanted to go back – he'd changed his mind,
this was a stupid idea. Then the lift door opened and all his fears
evaporated the second he saw her – in all her five-year-old glory, his
gorgeous Tallulah, waiting to meet and greet.

She was so delighted to see Daddy not Nana that she screamed,

'DADDY! DADDY! DADDY!' and leapt into his arms, clinging onto him like a baby koala. 'Come and see my bedroom!'

The door to the apartment was only a couple of metres away, and had been left ajar. Holding his precious cargo for luck, he felt braver now as he ventured inside, ready to face Kate for the first time in nearly four months.

Except she wasn't there.

Instead, looking equally surprised to see Matt, was Callum.

'Oh,' Matt said.

'Hi,' said Callum.

Thank God for Tallulah. 'Can we go to the cinema today, Daddy? Panda wants to go.'

'Yes darling, maybe. D'you want to go and get your stuff?'

And she wriggled out of his arms, dropped to the floor and ran off to her bedroom, leaving the two men in awkward silence for what felt like an age.

'Kate's not back yet. She's had to get a new bag or something,' – Callum paused – 'for tonight.'

Matt nodded. Time was when *he*'d be in Callum's place right now, getting ready to support Kate at an awards ceremony, congratulating her when she won, comforting her when she lost. He felt a twinge of jealousy and said, 'Funny old things, award ceremonies.'

'I wouldn't really know.'

'No.'

More awkwardness. Both men desperately hunting for something to say, desperately wanting to be somewhere else. Matt had never seen Callum so close up before – that time in the hotel room he'd barely been able to look at him. But now he noticed the lines around his eyes, the greying temples, the slight middle-age spread, and he genuinely wondered what Kate saw in him. He seemed quiet and kind, he supposed. But then wasn't Matt both those things?

'CALL-UM?' Tallulah yelled from the bedroom. 'WHERE ARE MY SHOES?'

Callum looked at Matt – the usurping father, usurping fatherly duties, knowing something about Matt's daughter that Matt didn't know himself: the whereabouts of her little shoes. Callum had no choice but to answer. 'Have a look under the bed, sweetheart.'

A punch to the stomach for Matt. *Sweetheart? Take my wife, and now my daughter.*

'Excuse me a minute,' Callum said, glad to have a reason to leave Matt, who stood there, megalith still, hardly daring to look around the plushly carpeted home of his soon-to-be ex-wife and her lover. He noticed there was already a framed photo of the three of them – Kate, Callum and Tallulah – taken surely just a few weeks ago. Kate's new family.

He could hear them talking in the bedroom, Callum and Tallulah, checking her bag, making sure she hadn't forgotten anything, and Matt felt like he was standing outside of himself, watching his life trickle by.

Suddenly the front door opened and in she blustered.

Kate.

She didn't see him straight away. 'Sorry I was so long, babe, they had to call a different branch and I— Oh!'

'Hello, Kate.'

It had been such a shock for Matt to see Callum that seeing Kate now felt like a walk in the park. What he hadn't bargained for was the hug she launched into.

'MATT! Oh my God, Matt!!'

He barely reciprocated the embrace, just about managing a gentle tap on her back. It felt so weird to be this close to her after not even seeing her for such a long time. She smelt different. A new perfume, perhaps? Or shampoo?

She looked at him. 'Why didn't you say you were coming? Oh, this is so lovely! I thought it'd be Sylvia!' She was getting tearful. 'Come and sit down, let me get you a drink.'

'No, we can't stop. Tallulah's just getting her things.' He called out, 'Lules? How you doing?'

'COM-ING!'

Kate was staring at him, full of admiration. 'You are looking *so* good! Have you been training?'

'Yeah. Joined a running club.'

'Well, it's really paid off. You look amazing.'

He knew it was shallow and superficial, but fuck it – he couldn't help but internally high-five himself right now. *You think I look better than him, don't you?* All those weeks of training were worth it just for that single moment of glory.

Tallulah came running in with her little pink rucksack on her back, shoes on, coat done up, Panda firmly cuddled.

'Right. Let's go disco!' Matt said.

It was just a subtle thing and she didn't need to do it. But when Callum followed Tallulah into the hallway, Kate linked arms with him, as if to say defensively, *I don't care how good you look, this is my man now, I made the right choice.* Matt forced himself not to let his eyes flicker down to their interlocked arms; he knew Callum felt awkward that she'd done it.

'Good luck tonight, Kate.'

'Will you watch it on telly?'

'Maybe – might be a bit late for this little one,' he said, smoothing Tallulah's hair.

'Oh, she can stay up for once. It's a special occasion, after all.'

'We'll see.' Matt smiled. He wasn't about to have a row over parenting in front of Tallulah's new stepfather figure.

And then from somewhere, a good place within him, Matt found the courage to hold out his hand to the man who'd stolen his wife. 'All the best, Callum.'

Callum shook his hand back, and fleetingly there was a moment between them, an acknowledgement of something that couldn't be articulated. All Matt knew when he closed the door behind him was that he was filled with an overwhelming sense of relief.

Not because this first dreaded encounter with Kate was now over.

But because Kate was no longer his responsibility.

81

'Do I look any different, d'you think?' Hetty was eating cheese and onion crisps and staring at her reflection, sat in front of her tiny dressing table, still in pyjamas despite it being almost midday. She ran her forefinger inquisitively along her cheeks and jawline, exploring their shape. 'My face is wider, I know.'

Ivor had been watching Hetty from the toastiness of their tangled bed, taking in the sight of this glorious being with whom he'd fallen even deeper in love. He clambered out from under the sheets and stood unselfconsciously naked behind her, his hands resting on her shoulders as he, too, looked at her reflection. She had no idea how beautiful she was. And this he adored.

'I could eat you,' he whispered as he kissed her neck, simultaneously nibbling and inhaling the warmth of her skin. He moved his hands confidently down inside her T-shirt, cupping her gorgeous morning breasts, unencumbered now by underwear, and felt himself harden as her nipples pinged to attention at the touch of his thumbs. 'Your tits are fucking fantastic.'

Hetty sighed with bliss and shut her eyes. She loved it when he talked dirty. It thrilled her that the private Ivor was so different from the public one, that this mild-mannered, unassuming work colleague who behaved like a lamb in the office was like a lion in bed.

She absolutely loved having sex with him. She was making up for her time in the wilderness, as she'd come to think of it – the barren, fallow land in the otherwise fertile continent of her life. How on earth had she survived for so long without it? More than that – because the sex was just a lovely bonus – how had she survived for so long without *love*? Without the reassurance of Ivor's toned and silky-skinned arms wrapped adoringly around her, or the way he kissed the top of her head or held her hand when they went off on their weekend hikes, helping her up over tricky terrain, tucking her straying rain-soaked hair back behind her ears, laughing at the muddy state in which they often found themselves.

She'd just put up with it, that's why. Conditioned herself, like an animal in captivity, acclimatizing to this absence, these self-imposed restrictions. And yes, they *were* self-imposed. Because it had been her choice to delude herself into thinking that Adam was the only man for her, and that if she couldn't have him then no one else would do. What an idiot. And what a waste of time – all those years she and Ivor could've spent together, merrily fucking away the day, enjoying mornings like this, luxuriating in post-sex sleepiness, deeply content and at ease in each other's company.

They'd become so familiar with one another's bodies now, having had weeks of practice in getting to know every inch of delicious skin, every delightful bump and crevice and each adorable idiosyncrasy. Hetty had come alive since they'd met – of that there was no doubt. And so had Ivor. Two lost souls, previously flailing around in the darkness of their lonely lives, had finally found each other, touched and connected. They'd also laughed. A lot. And discovered they had more in common with each other than they could ever have imagined, discovering coincidence after coincidence, each one met with the joyful exclamation *Me too!* Neither needed anyone else any more; both had landed and settled.

'We're like a pair of Canada geese,' Hetty declared. Not the most romantic of comparisons, Ivor thought, smiling. But actually, uncannily apt.

It was only when Hetty thought about Matt that she was slightly wrong-footed by guilt. Even though she knew he was over the moon that she'd found Ivor and was now stuck to him like pins on a magnet, she still felt she'd abandoned Matt for this beautiful new man in her life. And she no longer turned to Matt in the way that she'd once done – he'd been usurped, replaced. Because Ivor wasn't just her lover, he was also her new best friend. It was how it was meant to be – she'd accepted that. And in all honesty, she'd realized there were things she could talk to Ivor about that she'd never dream of saying to Matt. But still she felt like she'd had to let him go.

'Don't be silly, Het,' Ivor had comforted her. 'He's always going to be your friend.'

She smiled, nodding. 'I'm going to see him tonight. I need to tell him.'

'Best do it on your own, d'you think?'

'Yeah,' she said, turning round and pulling off her T-shirt. 'Now how about a quickie before the farmers' market?'

82

'Beans or peas, Cory?'

'Beans. Oh Mum, tell her!' He was play-fighting with his sister in the living room.

Belinda was in the kitchen making Sunday supper, which was always fish fingers and mash with peas or beans. Funny, the little customs they'd developed as a family over the years. Hearing Cory and Ailsa messing around was strangely comforting. But she feared the time when they'd no longer be there for Sunday fish fingers and she'd be on her own. Not as she'd ever imagined, but still. Onwards. She had to look to the future now. The decree absolute had come through a week ago. She'd not told the kids yet – wanted to get used to the idea first.

The day it happened, Callum had emailed her, of course.

Dear Bel
So it's official then.
No longer married.
I feel so fucking sad.
Callum x

She'd cried when she read it. She hated herself for crying, but then she thought, *Nobody need ever know that I did*. She didn't reply. Not for five days. And when she did she simply said:

Callum
Why sad?
Life moves on.
Good luck.
B.

She'd wanted to write:

Why sad? You're living in a luxury penthouse apartment in London with a rich, famous, beautiful younger woman who loves you so much she's prepared to do anything to get you – including destroying the lives of at least six other people! You should be celebrating!

But she'd suddenly felt very tired of being angry. And she knew that if she was to even begin getting over the loss of the only man she had ever truly loved, then she would have to begin to forgive him. And wish him well. For her own sake, she would have to do this.

She served out the food and shouted, 'Come and get it!'

Cory and Ailsa bounded in, and Ben came down from upstairs. Ailsa loved having both her brothers home – Cory was back supposedly to revise, his finals looming, and Ben had been home over a month now. He claimed he was looking for a job, but Belinda sensed he was there to protect her, that somehow without his dad there any more she'd become some fragile, vulnerable woman in his eyes.

'It's very sweet of you, love, but I really can cope, you know. And I don't want you turning into one of them stay-at-home kids, still livin' here when you're forty!'

He said he'd wait till the summer, then think about moving on. Belinda felt so blessed to have such loving children. She knew it would be breaking Callum's heart that his boys wanted nothing to do with him. In time, she'd talk to them about trying to mend that broken bridge. But she wasn't quite strong enough yet. And at least Ailsa was still in touch with him. Belinda never wanted to ask too many questions when Ailsa had seen her dad. She tried to do it subtly. It wasn't so much out of envy or jealousy, her wanting to know how he lived his new life. She just wanted to know he was well. That 'Hated Kate', as the kids still called her, was taking proper care of him.

'I'm going to Tom's after this,' Ailsa said.

'Drop me off at Lenny's?' Cory asked her through a mouthful of beans.

'OK.'

'Make sure he wears a helmet!' Belinda said.

'Yeah, and don't make her go fast, Cory,' Ben added.

In all fairness, Ailsa had been so good with that moped, respecting the speed limit and taking her time. She knew her mother worried about her every time she went on it, and whenever she saw her dad he would grill her on her safety routines.

'Are you staying over?' Belinda asked. The answer would most certainly be yes.

Cory, as usual, ribbed her for having a boyfriend, Ben as usual told Cory to shut up and flicked a pea at him, Belinda laughed and told them off for food fighting, and all the time in the background, unnoticed by any of them, the TV showed coverage of the BAFTA red-carpet arrivals.

83

He couldn't stop fiddling with his hair. Kate had insisted the make-up artist put some gel in it – 'Just to neaten things up a bit' – and now, like a dog with a new collar, he couldn't leave it alone. He looked great. As Kate hadn't tired of telling him.

'So easy for men with these things. Tux and dicky bow, job done.' And she straightened his tie for the umpteenth time. 'You're sure this looks alright?' she asked him, also for the umpteenth time, about her dress.

'Kate, you look absolutely stunning, and when we get home tonight I'm gonna shag you senseless, OK?'

He knew that's what she wanted to hear and he was right. She beamed. She loved it when he paid her compliments. It didn't happen very often – not because he didn't fancy her, she knew that, but just because he was a man and flattery was not the default of most men, let alone a shy fifty-six-year-old schoolteacher from Edinburgh.

The limousine turned the corner and Callum found the sight before them overwhelming. 'Jesus, they're like a bucket-load of ants!' A hundred metres of red carpet lined the centre of the closed-off road that led to the grand entrance of the Drury Lane Theatre. Barriers on either side held back fans and the banks of journalists, paparazzi and news crews from all over the world. On the red carpet itself were scores of famous actors and actresses, stopping for photos and interviews, as well as headset-wearing security guards and event producers busy checking that everything was running smoothly.

The limousine drew slowly to a halt and Kate turned to him. 'Right. Ready?'

'No,' he replied, seriously regretting having agreed to this.

She touched his face and softly said, 'Don't panic. Just smile and stay close to me. And don't utter a word.'

'No danger of that.'

'You get out first, then come round to my side and open the door for me.'

He was a bit thrown by this. 'What, like I'm your bloody manservant?'

'Callum, just do it.' She sighed with a hint of irritation.

He did as he was told. And as soon as Kate stepped out, there was a barrage of camera flashes and shouts from the crowd as well as the photographers.

'Kate! Kate! Miss Andrews! Over here! Nice to see you out with your new man. Callum, over here, over here!' They sounded like a barn full of geese at feeding time.

'I hate that they know my name,' he whispered to her.

'They know everything,' she whispered back through her fixed and well-practised smile. She grabbed his arm firmly, whilst trying to look as feminine as possible, and led him up the red carpet, stopping every few steps to have her photo taken or to sign an autograph for a fan. Eventually they made it to the entrance and she stopped, and through her still fixed smile quietly instructed him further: 'OK, now turn around and kiss me. And then wave.'

'Jesus, I'm like a performing fucking seal!'

He tried to do what she'd asked, but in the awkwardness and anxiety of the moment, their noses banged and they looked a bit ridiculous. Ever the professional, Kate laughed it off, though inside she was mortified. She'd wanted to look so good for the cameras.

A short way off, one of the paparazzi turned to his mate and said, 'Hasn't trained him very well yet, has she?' and they laughed, both chuffed that they'd captured the nose bump. It'd make a great pic.

Inside the foyer, Kate was greeted by Nikki, one of the event organizers. 'Kate! You look fantastic!'

'Thank you. This is my partner, Callum MacGregor.'

Callum smiled, but didn't say a word. As instructed.

Embarrassed, Kate made a joke, covering up for him. 'He's a bit shy tonight, I'm afraid. Right, what's the plan?'

'OK.' Nikki was looking at her clipboard. 'As you're a nominee, we have you sitting fairly near the front – I'll take you there now – but first of all, Sky News would like to do a quick interview?'

'Sure. Lead the way.' As they walked, Kate could tell people were staring at her – 'Kate Andrews, look!' – and she knew she looked out of this world.

The Sky News journalist couldn't hide her admiration, mouthing 'Love the dress!' before launching into the interview proper.

'So, Kate Andrews! You're up for best actress tonight – how do you think you'll do?'

Kate had perfected the art of sounding demure and modest, avoiding arrogance and always acknowledging the people with whom she'd worked. This was like water off a duck's back and she answered elegantly, aware of the camera lens, never looking at it and always, always smiling.

Callum, on the other hand, couldn't help but look down the barrel the entire time Kate was talking.

'Well, who knows what the night will bring? I'm just really honoured to have been nominated and to share that honour with actresses such as Gabriela Heinmann and Holly Grove. It's all really exciting.'

An hour later, Kate was holding Callum's hand tightly as the MC introduced veteran Hollywood star Nicholas Reynolds to the stage to present the award for best actress. A cameraman was poised two feet away from Kate, with another near Holly Grove and another near Gabriela Heinmann. Kate had already drilled it into Callum not to look at the camera and he tried hard not to, but didn't always succeed. It was like a magnet for the eyes; he didn't know how Kate managed it.

'And the BAFTA goes to . . .'

Callum could feel the sweat seeping out of Kate's palms. She was shaking, and he, too, felt full of nerves, dreading her not winning and how she would react.

'KATE ANDREWS!'

Thank God, he thought.

Kate leapt into action, looking first shocked, then humbled, then tearful. She immediately turned to Callum and kissed him long and hard, whispering, 'I love you.'

It was all too public for him and he felt he was on display. So all he could manage was an underwhelming 'Well done!' as he watched her get up and head to the stage to collect her award.

84

Hetty had surprised them both. They'd been down to the river and Gunnersbury Park that afternoon, and now Tallulah was exhausted, curled up on the sofa, nestled into Matt as he read her the story of the Grumpy Gorilla. He'd said they could have pizza as a treat, so when the doorbell went he presumed it'd be the chirpy delivery chap from Pete's Pizza Parlour.

But it was Hetty.

'Surprise!' she shouted. 'Is it a bad time?'

'It's a perfect time.' And he gave her a hug. 'I've missed you, mate! I'll have to have a word with that Ivor, stealing my best friend off me,' he joked.

Hetty giggled and squealed when she saw Tallulah, and all three of them flopped down onto the sofa in one big cuddle.

'Where is he then? Please don't tell me you've split up?'

'No. Quite the opposite.' She'd been bursting to tell him for over a week now. 'Oh Matty. We're gonna have a baby!'

It was true, he'd really missed her. Since Ivor and Hetty had got together, they'd rarely spent a night apart, and although the baby-sitting had continued so that Matt could carry on with his Italian and his running club, Hetty and Ivor were now firmly a duo, and Matt couldn't remember the last time he'd spent an hour in Hetty's company alone. He didn't mind. Not really. After all, she'd had years of 'Matt and Kate' – it was just his turn to play gooseberry now. And he couldn't be happier for her. Little Hetty Strong was having a baby! She'd be the best mother in the world.

They caught up on gossip, including, once Tallulah had gone to bed, the only exciting thing to have happened to Matt this year: Chloe.

'*Oh my God!* You did *not*!' Hetty was exhilarated, shocked and delighted all at once.

'Yeah. But it was just a one-off.'

'Really?' Hetty didn't quite believe him and she screwed up her eyes suspiciously.

'Oh God, yes, seriously. It did me the power of good, but that was it.'

'She's got pink hair!' Hetty announced, as if telling Matt something he didn't already know.

'And a boyfriend,' added Matt. 'No, it was nice, Het, but she's not the one for me.'

Hetty took his hand. 'Talking of which, how's Kate?'

'Oh bollocks. I'm meant to record the BAFTAs!'

He reached for the remote control and flicked through the channels till he arrived at the right one. Miraculously, the Best Actress category was about to be announced. Hetty and Matt stared at the TV screen.

'KATE ANDREWS!'

And weirdly, despite all the pain she'd caused, all the upheaval and heartache, Matt and Hetty were happy for her and jumped up and down on the spot to show their appreciation.

'Aw, well done, Kate!' said Matt.

They watched as she kissed Callum in a close-up shot and Matt sighed, but it didn't tear him apart – nowhere near, in fact. And they watched as Nicholas Reynolds handed her the BAFTA and hugged her like he'd known her for years.

'She's never met him before in her life, y'know!' Matt laughed – he was well out of all that fakery now and the world of fraudulent showbiz friendships.

Kate took the microphone, centring herself, catching her breath, before winning the audience over with an opening jest, pretending to drop it: 'Christ, this is heavy!' Then she gathered her thoughts and began to talk, low level but loud enough to be heard. 'This . . . is amazing,' she began, admiring the heft of the big brass mask that bore her name at the bottom. 'I cannot begin to tell you how humbled I am to have been nominated alongside such great actresses as Gabi Heinmann and Holly Grove,' – at which point she nodded in both their directions and shook her head admiringly. 'They continue to inspire us all with their outstanding work, and for that, we are all grateful.' A ripple of appreciation from the audience.

'I'd like to thank the cast and crew of *Second Sight* – what an incredible show that was to work on. And especially the director and genius that is Denholm Merrigan.' Again, more applause.

'I'd also like to thank my darling daughter, Tallulah.' Her voice breaking with well-timed emotion. 'She is my angel and my shiny bright star and she makes me smile every time she walks in the room. She's stayed up late tonight, especially to watch,' – at which point, Kate looked directly at the camera and said, 'I love you, Lules!'

Back in Chiswick, Matt turned to Hetty and feigned fear.

'I won't tell if you won't,' Hetty whispered quickly without taking her eyes off the screen. 'You've recorded it, she can watch it in the morning!'

'And finally, to my partner, Callum MacGregor.' The cameras swooped straight into a close-up of Callum, who looked for all the world like he wanted his brushed-velvet theatre seat to swallow him up for its tea. 'Callum, you've been my rock these past few months, and I wouldn't be here without you.'

'Well, that's not even technically true,' Hetty said.

'Babe, you complete me,' Kate said in Callum's direction, as if it was just the two of them in the theatre, finishing her speech by blowing him a kiss and shouting, 'Thank you, BAFTA!' over the applause as she left the stage.

'Oh my God, that was so cringe,' Hetty said, and she grabbed a piece of cold pizza from the box. '*You complete me*? Dear Lord! And did you see Callum's face? Talk about fish out of water – he stared right at the camera like a trout!'

'I know.' But Matt wasn't laughing. 'Oh poor Kate, I hope she's not . . . y'know, going off the rails a bit.'

Hetty looked at him, disbelieving. 'You are incredible, Matty. How can you feel sorry for her?'

'I dunno. I've just got a bad feeling, that's all.'

85

The party was in full swing, the air electric with congratulation and flattery. Waiting staff were passing round cute cordon bleu nibbles like mini fish and chips and mini mash and banger. Callum took a couple whenever they went by, failing to see the attraction of these minuscule portions. He'd spent most of the post-awards bash on his own, realizing that if you weren't 'somebody', the chances were you'd get ignored. He didn't mind. He was quite happy to people-watch and wait for Kate, who was currently talking to some big-shot producer from the States. Occasionally she'd look over to him and mouth a concerned 'You OK?' to which he'd nod back enthusiastically, and she'd return to the conversation in hand. Her BAFTA never left her grasp. And he noticed she hadn't eaten a thing all night.

A lot of people were very pissed by now or high on coke. Earlier he'd had to disengage himself from a very boring conversation with an actor called Lloyd something or other, who was gurning at a hundred miles an hour and claiming he'd once worked with Kate.

'So where d'you hail from then . . . erm . . .'

'Callum. Yeah, like I just said, Edinburgh.'

'Och aye the noo!'

Jesus save me, thought Callum.

'I did a play up there once.'

'Yeah, you said.'

Kate was standing next to them at the time, embroiled in conversation with a tough-talking director who *everybody* wanted to work with, apparently.

'But she's just fantastic, isn't she? . . . Kate is. Isn't she?'

'Yep.' Callum wished he was drunk.

'I mean a real . . . y'know, lady. Everyone loves her.'

'Right.'

'And just so . . .' At which point, Lloyd lost his train of thought, gurning manically as he tried to find it. 'So, where do you hail from then, Callum?'

'Istanbul.' Callum pulled away. 'I think I'll get a bit of air.'

And he headed towards the veranda.

Outside, people were smoking and chatting in twos and threes. Callum made his way to the balcony and looked out over the city skyline. Behind him the party continued, this alien party in this alien world, and he suddenly felt very lonely. He took out his mobile and went into his contacts, flicking through his numbers till he found Belinda's. His thumb hovered over her name. He so wanted to talk to her.

'Bit mental in there, isn't it?' A grey-haired man in a designer suit had joined him.

'You could say that, yeah.'

'You're Kate's partner, aren't you?'

'Er . . . yes.'

'You don't sound too sure!'

'Sorry . . . it's just taking a bit of getting used to, that's all. Callum MacGregor.' And he held out his hand.

'Tony Matthews – producer of the *Maggie Lane Show* – I'm a good mate of Kate's. Honest!' And Callum laughed. 'You know we'd love to have you both on as guests tomorrow.'

'Don't be daft!'

'No, seriously. I mean, having BAFTA-award-winner Kate Andrews on the show is one thing and that's brilliant. But having her new partner on *with* her. That'd be a proper coup.'

Callum was about to protest further when Kate came out and joined them, linking arms with him and snuggling up. 'Has Tony persuaded you yet?'

The producer smiled. 'I'm trying my best, aren't I, Callum?'

'Come on, babe. The publicity would do us both the world of good – let the people hear our side of the story . . .' And she looked at him with big, needy eyes. 'Please?'

86

The car was picking them up at seven thirty a.m. They were due on air at nine. Callum had hardly slept. He'd tried persuading Kate to let him pull out, but she wouldn't hear of it. She was trying to keep him happy, humouring him, doing whatever she could to keep the mood light, even making them Bucks Fizz and smoked salmon for breakfast.

He came into the kitchen looking for his phone and was thrown by the prettily laid table. 'Bloody hell – bit excessive, isn't it?'

'Darling, I won a BAFTA last night! And we're celebrating our first TV interview together.' She poured him a glass and handed it to him.

'I can't. I don't . . . it's just all too much . . .'

'But you're not working today!'

'I know, but all this excess and booze and partying and . . . I'm a teacher, Kate. Not even a full-time one at the moment.' She looked like a kicked puppy. 'Look, I'll do this chat-show thing today, but no more, OK? It's not me.'

'Oh baby, is that it? You're nervous!'

'Well yeah, I am actually. But why shouldn't I be? I'm not a bloody celebrity, am I? It's ludicrous.'

And suddenly she turned on him. With a sourness and anger he'd not seen before. Actually, no, he *had* seen it before – nearly eighteen years ago, when she'd lost it with him at his house, the night Belinda walked in on them.

'Yeah, well I have to live with it all the FUCKING TIME! YOU HAVE NO IDEA WHAT IT'S LIKE!'

He was confused, more than anything, couldn't understand why she was behaving like this. And then it dawned on him. 'Are you drunk?'

'Don't be stupid.'

But he didn't have the energy for a row. He needed to phone Ailsa – she had her English exam that morning. 'I'm going outside to make a call.'

'Why can't you do it here?'

'Well, because . . .'

'You're phoning Belinda, aren't you? Why can't I hear what you've got to say, Callum? Are you seeing her behind my back?'

Callum was disturbed by the outburst, shocked at this ugly change in her, like Kate had transformed into somebody else. 'Sweetheart, what is wrong with you?' he said gently. 'I just wanna call Ails – to wish her luck, that's all.'

And then she dropped the bombshell. 'I know you've been email-ing Belinda.'

He stared at her. Not knowing how to react. If he denied it, he'd be lying. But then the indignation he felt at being spied on rose up in him. He was incredulous. 'What? Jesus, have you been reading my emails?'

'Yes.' She was unashamed.

'You're unbelievable,' he said, and he went outside to make the call.

As he closed the door behind him, Kate threw her Bucks Fizz at the wall, glass shattering everywhere, champagne dripping onto the cream carpet. And she fought back the tears.

Half an hour later, they were sitting in the back of the car, silent, each looking out of their own window.

Callum thought about Ailsa. He'd left a message on her mobile but hadn't managed to speak to her. It was always so hit and miss communicating with her, and because Ailsa was the only one who *would* talk to him, it always hit him hard when he couldn't get through.

He hated feeling so cut off from his family like this. Who was he trying to kid, living so far away? Cory hadn't spoken to him since he'd left, and Ben still refused to take his calls ever since the visit to London. The whole thing was a mess.

He looked over at Kate, lost in her own world, hurting, no doubt, from this morning's row. She'd looked so shaken up when he'd gone back inside and hadn't spoken a word to him since. He'd messed her life up too, really. He should have walked away all those years ago, not given in to his bloody ego. Kate could've been quite happy now, he thought, with Matt, and little Tallulah. Not sat in the back of a car on her way to do a TV interview with a man she didn't really know, just thought she knew, just thought she loved. He felt such compassion for her in that moment that he reached out and took her hand.

At first, she wouldn't look at him, wiping away her angry tears.

'Come on, sweetheart, this is mad,' he said quietly, conscious the driver could hear every word. 'We can't go on live television not speaking to each other!'

She sniffed sadly. 'I'm scared, Callum.'

'Of what?' He genuinely didn't know.

'Scared that you're gonna go back to her.'

The chances of that were non-existent. He knew that, but for some reason he didn't dispute it, gave her no words of reassurance, so Kate carried on. 'You still love her, don't you?'

He paused. 'It doesn't . . . y'know, just . . . *stop*.'

'Fucking brilliant.' And she snatched her hand away.

'But I chose you, didn't I?' He tried to touch her again, but she hissed at him, not caring whether the driver heard them or not. 'DON'T!'

'Jesus, Kate, you're doing my head in.'

They'd arrived at the London Studios now, and the driver, eager to be rid of them and their embarrassing argument, interrupted them chirpily. 'Here you go! You need to walk down to that security door at the end.'

'Thanks,' Kate snapped, and jumped out of the car.

She was immediately besieged by a group of five autograph hunters. 'Miss Andrews, will you sign? Will you sign?'

And without her usual care for professional decorum, she turned on them and yelled, 'OH FUCK OFF, YOU BUNCH OF WEIRDOS!'

A bored-looking photographer loitering nearby had just had his day made, catching the whole exchange with his camera, but Kate ignored him and carried on towards the gate.

Callum caught up with her. 'Kate!'

'It's been a life sentence,' she hissed. 'I had to stop myself thinking about you every single day, I had to DELETE you from inside my head . . .'

'Keep your voice down, for Christ's sake!'

'And the only thing that distracted me was work. Couldn't stand still for a second. Had to keep it turning over. Had to be successful. Had to earn money, because it stopped me from falling . . .'

'Seriously, you've got to lower the volume.'

They were approaching the security gate when she turned and whispered, 'If you leave me again, I will *die*!'

'Don't be so fucking melodramatic, Kate!' He was getting angry now, anger born out of fear.

Suddenly she stopped, her mind racing, weighing up whether or not to say it. And then she did.

'I didn't go through with it, Callum.'

He stared at her, confused.

'The abortion. I didn't go through with it.'

And she paused to take in his reaction.

'What?'

'I had the baby. All those years ago – our baby.'

He could see desperation seizing her with a feverish grip. 'Kate. Stop this.' He grabbed her firmly by the shoulders. 'Look at me. *You need to calm down.*'

'I had him and I called him Luca and I had him adopted because I couldn't— He was beautiful, Cal.' There was a wildness in her eyes that terrified him, made more disturbing when she suddenly softened, smiling as if expecting him to congratulate her or fill up with tears of joy.

'OK, listen, I don't think you're very well, sweetheart. This is . . . you're delusional, OK? You've been working really hard these past few weeks and—'

'You don't believe me, do you?'

He didn't. But he didn't want to upset her further.

'Kate, I think you just need to rest—'

She gasped. Incredulous. Before slapping him hard across the face.

'Well, fuck you then!' she said, and turned on her heel.

He followed close behind, deeply disturbed by the desperate and psychotic measures she was willing to take.

The security guard pretended he hadn't noticed the row. In all fairness, this wasn't the first domestic between guests he'd witnessed outside the gate. And the paparazzo photographer thirty metres behind them thought all his Christmases had come at once – clickety-clickety-clickety-click.

87

Ailsa had left Tom's house in plenty of time. She wanted to get to school forty-five minutes before the exam started. Just so she could be ultra-ready. She was gonna smash it, she could feel it in her bones.

At the end of Tom's road, she felt her phone vibrate. That'd be Dad again. She'd seen a missed call from him already that morning, but she wanted to keep her head clear. Talking to Dad always made her sad, and she couldn't be sad before this exam.

She'd followed all the correct procedures: checked her mirrors, indicated and slowed down.

But still she didn't see it coming.

It was a clean hit.

Smack.

Thud.

Crunch.

And the wheels of the upturned moped spun slower and slower until they finally gave up the ghost.

Silence.

Then someone started screaming.

88

'Who says New Year's resolutions have to start in the new year?'

Belinda was laughing on the phone to Sue, holding it to her ear as she carried a large plastic crate, covered in dust, through to the living room. She was clearing out the attic, one of the items on her to-do list. She'd promised herself that once the divorce had come through she'd make a start – and she'd taken the day off work to do it.

'Why do we save things like boxes that once contained hair-dryers or radios or Moulinex mixers? Christ, some of this stuff must go back to the late seventies!'

'Don't chuck it out, Lind, it might be worth a fortune!'

'Oh, great help you are.' Suddenly she stopped laughing. 'Bloody hell.' On the TV she'd just seen a trailer for the forthcoming *Maggie Lane Show* on ITV, and a photo of Kate bumping noses with Callum, taken at the BAFTAs the night before. On screen it said, 'Next: Kate Andrews and her new man.'

'Lind? Belinda? You still there?'

'Turn your telly on, Sue. ITV. And stay on the line.'

89

Once Carla the make-up artist had finished brushing his hair, Callum ruffled it up again. Kate, who was sat in the make-up chair next to him having her lips painted, rolled her eyes at him.

Carla smiled, she was used to this. 'I'm just gonna take a bit of shine off, sweetie, OK?' And before Callum could work out what was going on, she dived in with her powder brush, gently dabbing his face.

'What you *doing*?' he shouted.

'Making you less shiny, sweetie!'

'Christ, Callum, let the woman do her job, will you?'

An over-enthusiastic runner came in, headset and clipboard his badges of honour. 'OK, we're ready for you now!' he said, too loudly.

Kate got out of her chair, smiling sweetly at the make-up girls. 'Thanks, ladies!' Then, dropping the smile, she hissed at Callum, 'Let's get this over with.'

90

'This is torture,' Belinda said. 'I should really just switch it off, shouldn't I?'

'Don't you dare!' said Sue, on the other end of the phone.

'It feels a bit . . . voyeuristic.'

'The man's on TV, Belinda! About to make an arse of himself, no doubt. It's not like you're spying on him through a peephole. Oh, here we go, here we go!'

Five miles away, the ambulance had arrived and the paramedics were gently loading Ailsa onto the gurney. A policeman at the scene was going through the contacts on her phone. He found 'home' and pressed call.

The line was engaged.

91

The brightly lit studio looked much bigger on TV than it did in actuality and Callum felt too tall and cumbersome, nearly tripping over some of the camera cables as he was shown to his seat. The studio manager, Harry, smiled at him whilst simultaneously motioning to him to stay quiet. The commercial break was just coming to an end, and the up-tempo sting that started every segment of the show blared out of the studio speaker as Harry counted in the host, Maggie Lane.

'Back in five, four, three,' he shouted, then mimed, 'two, one,' followed by a huge hand signal to Maggie.

'Welcome back!' she said in bright notes that blended in with the fake jollity of the show. 'Now my next guest won a BAFTA last night for best actress and the tabloids have been singing her praises. But they've not always been so kind, and she's been the subject of some intense media controversy lately with the press dining out on her highly publicized affair. Here to put the record straight is actress Kate Andrews and her partner, schoolteacher Callum MacGregor. Hey, congratulations on the BAFTA! Did you bring it with you?'

Kate laughed. 'Er, no, it's that heavy you'd need a crane to lift it out of the house!'

Maggie smiled manically, simultaneously listening to her producer in her earpiece saying, 'Get to the affair, ask about the affair.'

'So you've been in the headlines a fair bit recently – your private life, as in your affair, became very much public property. How on earth have you coped?'

Kate, despite her hangover and earlier upset, was expecting the question and knew how to handle it with professional expertise. 'The thing is, Maggie, affairs are tricky things – even though lots of people have them! And I think you have to know one hundred per cent that you've made the right decision. And when you have that confidence in your decision, you can take whatever blows life deals you.'

The camera focused on Callum, who sat there frozen like the proverbial headlight-blinded rabbit. Kate carried on, ignoring the fact that he was making them both look really stupid. 'I never had any doubts that Callum was the One,' she said in all seriousness. 'I still don't have any doubts.'

92

Belinda was sitting on the edge of the sofa, glued to the TV set, Sue still on the phone. Both in complete disbelief at what they were seeing.

'He looks absolutely terrified, Lind! I mean, if I wasn't so angry with the guy, I'd actually feel sorry for him!'

'I know. What was he thinking, agreeing to do this? Oh my God!'

The two women were silent as they watched events unfold in front of them, Belinda accustomizing herself to seeing the husband she'd not laid eyes on for over four months. *He looks tired*, she thought.

Suddenly the theme from *Rocky* could be heard, distant and muted. Callum's mobile phone was ringing. But rather than ignore it, he took it out of his pocket and looked at the screen.

'Hey, who's that? Your ex-wife?' the presenter joked, slightly embarrassed by Callum's lack of awareness when it came to live-television etiquette.

Kate turned to him, still smiling but clearly serious. 'You're not actually going to answer that, are you?'

It said Ailsa was calling. He answered: 'Hi, can I call you back?'

'Callum, you *idiot*!' Belinda shouted at the telly, partly delighted, partly cringing, partly defensive, despising Kate for what she'd turned this once lovely man into.

The TV host was going with the flow, treating it like some kind of comedy act, watching as Callum listened, his face turning ashen. 'Maybe it's someone trying to sell him double glazing!' she joked with Kate, whose inner fury was well disguised by her outward charm.

Suddenly, Callum stood up. He looked dazed, stammering, 'I've got to go.'

'Callum. Sit down!' Kate said quickly.

'It's Ailsa . . .' And with that he just walked off the set; his radio mike lead, refusing to follow, stretching behind him until it snapped.

Quick to cover the embarrassment that sometimes came with the territory where live TV was concerned, Maggie Lane announced it was competition time!

Belinda dropped the receiver. Sue was still on the other end, shouting, 'Lind? What's going on? You OK?'

She reached for her mobile, lying switched off in her handbag, her hands shaking with fear. It took what seemed like an age to come to life. She finally opened her contacts, searched for his name, then pressed 'Callum'.

It rang once.

His voice was small and quiet. 'Ailsa's been in an accident.'

93

It was the same driver who had brought them there that morning. He didn't speak. He didn't dare. He'd seen the other half leave ten minutes before and hail a cab. *God knows what's been kicking off there*, he thought.

Once she was settled in the back, Kate tried calling Callum. It rang, he didn't answer. All she wanted to know was what was going on. She tried again. Nothing.

'Fuck this,' she mumbled to herself, and looked out of the window at London's South Bank coming to life in the mid-morning sunshine. Tourists taking photos, cabbies stopping for fares, street performers putting on a tireless display of tricks. Happy-happy. And inside she just wanted to die.

It was over.

She'd known it for a long time really, but had tried not to admit it to herself. There'd been an air of resignation about Callum pretty much since the night they'd been discovered in the Edinburgh hotel. She wondered whether he'd not so much *chosen* her over Belinda as surrendered to the inevitable: knowing that he had no other option. Because there was no way Belinda would take him back a second time. So where else could he go? She might be wrong, of course – maybe it was just the excruciating guilt that made it impossible for him to let go of his old life and embrace the new. A life that shrouded his days in sorrow. He'd never said so, of course. He'd have known it would be pointless.

She shivered at the thought that her theory might actually be true. And she felt herself sinking into the quicksand of despair, unable to resist being swallowed up by overwhelming humiliation and failure and utter self-loathing.

'Can you pull over to that shop, please? I won't be a minute.'

It was a mini-mart. She went straight to the counter and asked for forty Marlboro Lights and two litre bottles of gin.

94

He'd only had to wait half an hour for the train. Thankfully, it was quiet. He sat himself down in a corner and stared out of the window, willing the four-and-a-half-hour journey to fly.

The phone rang several times: mostly Kate. But he just couldn't face speaking to her right now. Couldn't face thinking about their relationship and the mess of what had happened that morning.

He sent her a text – *Ailsa been in accident. Am on way to Edinburgh. Will call. Sorry Kate.* He didn't put any kisses, no frills or tenderness. He just couldn't think about her at the moment.

All he wanted was to see his little girl and be told that she was alright. He shut his eyes, praying for the journey to be over, making a deal with God – *I'll do anything. Anything. Just please make it be OK.* He remembered once before when he'd made a deal like that. And he'd not kept his side of the bargain. Maybe this was God paying him back.

When he arrived at Edinburgh General, he was sent to the Critical Injuries department, where a very kind receptionist told him there was no news, but if he'd like to take a seat in the family room, someone would be along shortly with more information.

It was only a short walk. He opened the door. Belinda stood with her back to him, staring out of the window. She turned around. They looked at each other. And the most natural thing in the world was to draw close and hug. Which they did, without saying a word. The mother held onto the father, who held onto the mother, of the daughter who was lying ninety feet away, holding onto her life by a thread.

It wasn't until the doctor came in five minutes later that they finally separated.

'Mr and Mrs MacGregor?'

'Yes?' they both answered, and Belinda grabbed Callum's hand, holding it so tight it hurt, waiting to hear the worst.

'I'm Doctor Anderson. Your daughter's not very well at all, I'm afraid.'

'Oh God.'

'But she *is* improving. Slowly. Come with me and we'll go and see her.' He turned and they followed. Belinda realized she was still holding Callum's hand and she pulled it away quickly.

95

It had been a combination of things. Hetty had seen the disastrous interview on *The Maggie Lane Show* and told Matt about it. Matt was already worried about Kate, but when Kate's mother called him, alarm bells started ringing. Yvonne said she'd heard on the local news about Callum MacGregor's daughter being involved in a moped accident. It was touch and go as to whether she'd survive. Callum had been seen at the hospital with his ex-wife, and Yvonne had been trying to get through to Kate for two days now, but no joy. Did Matt think she was alright?

He offered to go round there and check, asking Hetty to look after Tallulah while he did.

There was no answer. But after some persuading, the concierge agreed to use his pass key to let Matt into the apartment, on condition he stood by to check nothing untoward went on. 'She's famous, y'know!' he said to Matt. Matt was tempted to say, *Yes, and I used to be married to her*, but he thought it just sounded mealy-mouthed and petty.

The TV was on and the apartment stank of cigarettes. He'd not noticed it when he'd come around the time before, and Kate always swore she didn't smoke indoors because of Tallulah. With the concierge two feet behind him, he looked first in the bathroom and then in the bedroom, but the bed hadn't been slept in. Then he ventured into the living room.

And that's when he saw her.

Slumped face-down on the sofa. The empty gin bottles lay on their side next to her. 'Jesus!' He ran over to her and turned her round.

'Shall I call an ambulance?' the concierge said, panicked.

Matt ignored him, trying to get a response out of Kate. 'Kate! Kate, can you hear me?'

Slowly she opened her eyes and smiled. 'Hey Matt! Whassup?'

Matt turned to the concierge. 'She's fine. You can go now.'

'I'm not sure, y'know, I shouldn't really—'

'She clearly knows me – she just said my name. Now please.'

Begrudgingly – because he wanted to make the most of the drama – the concierge left, and Matt managed to sit Kate up. 'I'm gonna get you a drink, OK?'

'OK,' she whispered, her head flopped down, arms in front of her.

When he returned a minute later with a jug of water, she was still in the same position. He poured her a glass and she began sipping very slowly.

'That's it.'

And they sat like that for a good twenty minutes, him stroking her back, watching as she took the water down, sip by hungover sip, dry-retching in between. There was no need for words, the two of them unmoving, save for the stroking and the sipping. Eventually, he spoke.

'Hey, y'know what I did the other day?' he ventured softly. 'I started sorting out the attic.' Kate stayed silent, becalmed by the soothing familiarity of Matt's gentle voice, as if he was telling her a bedtime story. 'Very cathartic. Boxes and boxes of . . . just stuff.'

The glass shook uncontrollably in her hands and he took it from her, resting it on the floor. Kate leant her head on his shoulder.

'I found some of your old theatre programmes in there, all the shows you've been in. There were loads.' He paused for a moment. 'You were in *Snow White*, weren't you? At Coventry Belgrade. Nineteen eighty . . .' He struggled to remember the date.

'Nineteen eighty-five,' she mumbled, barely audible. 'My first job.'

'Well, I worked it out. You and me . . . we met before, y'know! We met that day you auditioned – don't know how we didn't realize before!'

She turned to him now, confused, unable to process what he was saying.

'I was getting some props and stuff for this show at uni, and you were waiting to audition. I tested you on your lines. D'you remember?'

Kate shook her head and a big tear, fat with sorrow, rolled down her cheek.

'Such a small world, eh? Our paths crossing like that.' He smiled at the memory. 'I wished you luck.' And he drew her to him and kissed the top of her head. 'I'll always wish you luck, Kate.'

'Me and Callum are finished.'

'Oh sweetheart.'

'I bet you're glad, aren't you?'

He sighed. 'No. No, it's really sad.' And he meant it.

She was finding it difficult to speak, the effects of the gin slowing down her enunciation, her mouth sticky with dehydration. He poured her some more water from the jug. Obediently she drank it.

'Maybe I should come back with you. Come home for a bit,' she said.

Matt thought how strange life was – that had she said those words even two months ago, his heart would have burst with joy.

'Babe, you know that can't happen.'

'Why?' She couldn't focus through both eyes, so she put her hand over one and tried to look at him. 'I know I've been really stupid,' she said. 'I know that. And I know it'll take a while, but I'll get some help. I'll go back to the counsellor – he'll help me.'

'Well, I think that would be a really good idea, mate.'

'Yeah, and we'll get through it like we did before. And I promise you . . . I promise you I won't be such an idiot again.'

Matt looked at the ugly, sorrowful mess his beautiful wife had become and stroked her face. Never had he felt such compassion for her as he did right now.

'Listen to me . . . Kate, listen to me. You're not coming back with me.' Despite his words, there was no malice in what he was saying, no self-righteousness. 'Our marriage is over now. You have to see that.'

'*No!*'

'Yes, it is.' And he pulled her to him even tighter. 'I love you.' It was his turn to cry. 'I'll never stop doing that . . .'

'So take me home!'

'. . . and I will help you as much as I can. But your mother is on her way to London. I'll stay with you until she arrives and then she'll look after you. Till you get yourself straight.'

'But I want *you* to look after me.'

And he kissed her head again, rocking her gently, comforting her child-like sobs. 'It's not my job any more, pet. Sorry.'

2017

'You should've brought the selfie stick, you moron!' Fourteen-year-old Jack was berating his twin sister Dorcas as she tried desperately to squeeze all three of them into the shot.

'Just get my dad to take it, dopey!' Tallulah laughed. She adored the twins, and had always treated them like her kid brother and sister, despite the absence of any blood connection. She'd always considered Hetty to be a close relative, so it made sense that she'd think the same of Hetty's offspring. She'd known them all her life, and, being an only child, enjoyed the power of this pseudo sibling relationship, as well as the authority afforded her by being six years their senior.

'Dad! Take a photo!' She handed her mobile to Matt. He duly obliged, faking ignorance as to which way round the handset should be held.

'Uncle Matt! Stop it!' Dorcas giggled.

Age suited Matt. The laughter lines that had come with the passing of time and a long-found contentment with his second wife Carrie – Tallulah's beloved stepmother – had been more than kind to his already handsome face.

It was a joyous occasion – Tallulah's graduation from UCL and a happy, happy day. Kate had not long left them. She'd stood proudly alongside Matt in the grand hall, cheering on their clever daughter as she lined up with the hundred or so other graduands to accept her degree in Economics.

'God knows where she got it from, eh Matt?' Kate had whispered, tears in their eyes as they applauded their little girl, now nearly twenty-one, and watched as she stepped up to the stage to receive her mock scroll from the university's Chancellor.

It was easy between Kate and Matt now. The hurt long healed, their lives long moved on.

'You sure you won't join us?' Matt said. Hetty and Ivor had booked them a table at Chez Martin as a treat to celebrate Tallulah's special day.

'Ah no. Things to do, places to go, people to see!'

Matt knew better than to try to persuade her. Although Kate had been sober for years, she still found big social occasions a challenge, and preferred to slip away quietly, letting the revelry carry on without her. He also knew that today was a big day for her, too. And not just because of Tallulah's graduation. He engulfed her in a big hug before she left.

'I'm on the end of the phone, remember. So is Carrie.' They'd looked over to where Matt's second wife stood talking to Ivor and Hetty. She had such remarkable poise: poise that at another time in her life Kate would've envied. Now, when she looked at Carrie she felt relieved. And secure. That the father of her little girl had finally found a woman who loved him, a woman who deserved him.

'I'll let you know how it goes, OK?'

Matt smiled at her and winked. 'Good luck!'

Kate blew kisses to the excited party and headed off to the Tube.

Ailsa was still at her mother's house. She'd popped over that morning for a catch-up. The doorbell went and she made her way into the hallway to answer it – it took her a little longer these days, her ever-progressing pregnancy slowing her down.

'Mummy, can I get it?' four-year-old Alfie asked, not waiting for the answer and running ahead to look through the letter box.

'Can you see who it is?' she said.

'It's Grampa!'

Ailsa opened the door to let Callum in. 'Hi Dad.'

'Nice surprise!'

'Yeah, Mum had this one for a couple of hours while I had a kip. I'm absolutely knackered.'

'Not long now, sweetheart. Good curry, that's what you need,' and he kissed his daughter before picking up his grandson. 'Where's your Nana then, son?'

'She's in the bedroom. She said she's putting her face on.'

Callum laughed.

'Hey Alf, don't be giving away a lady's secrets!' Ailsa smiled at her dad. 'So where you taking her today?'

'Thought we'd drive into the centre and walk up Arthur's Seat. Haven't been up there in years and it's on our bloody doorstep!'

'You sure your knees are up to it?'

'I've taken an Ibuprofen.' He winked at her.

She looked at her seventy-one-year-old father and smiled. She had to hand it to him, the man had perseverance oozing from his pores. Once a week, for nearly fourteen years, he'd taken her mother out on a 'date'. Sometimes it was the cinema, sometimes it was a stroll up to the castle; when the Festival was on it might be to see some new comedian or a concert in the Assembly Rooms, and whenever he could get tickets for the internationals at Murrayfield, of course they'd go and watch Scotland play. Whatever it was, he never gave up. Always striving to restore the faith he'd long since extinguished from their marriage.

Belinda had made it clear to Callum that she would never take him back again and they would certainly never remarry, but if he wanted to woo her for the rest of his days, or until he got bored, she'd grant him permission. 'Just don't expect anything more than my scintillating company and unwavering friendship,' she'd said. ''Cos that's all you're ever gonna get.'

Ailsa's accident had made them all rethink. It had taken eighteen months for her to make a full recovery. Then, when Callum had moved back to Portobello – to a one-bedroom flat, not the family home – Belinda had been glad to see the rift mend between him and

397

his three children. She in turn grew to forgive him. But she would never, ever forget. 'Not twice, Callum,' she'd sadly smiled. 'What d'you think I am?'

For the first year he'd begged her and pleaded with her, thinking he'd eventually grind her down and persuade her to give in. But the day came when she had to put him straight, laying the deal down on the table and telling him it was either friendship or nothing at all.

And as time went on, and Ben and Cory and Ailsa started families of their own, Callum and Belinda learnt to be grand-parents with a difference: they probably got on better than many non-divorced couples their age. She knew if she said the word, he would marry her tomorrow. But it just wasn't ever going to happen. And finally he'd accepted it.

Belinda came downstairs now, looking smart. She always made an effort for their weekly dates. At the age of sixty-nine she still looked after herself, just adding a bit of glam with a touch of mas-cara and a smidge of lipstick.

And every week he'd say to her, 'You look lovely, Bel.'

And every week, with a twinkle in her eye, she'd reply, 'Well don't get your hopes up, MacGregor, 'cos you're not gonna shag me, OK?' Only she didn't say it this week because little Alfie was there, and it wouldn't be nice for him to hear his Nana being so rude. She was a respectable old lady now, after all.

'Is it cold out?' she asked him.

'It's Scotland, woman, what d'you expect?' And he held her coat out for her to put on, Ailsa watching them and smiling.

'Right, don't be going into labour till we get back, young lady,' Belinda said as they headed out of the door.

'Oh don't worry, I'm off home now. Tom's doing tortillas.' And she watched her parents wander down the drive towards Callum's car, chattering away like they'd always done, looking for all the world like they had done forty-three years ago on that international day when they'd first met.

*

'I got my special coin last night, look.'

She held it out to Maria, the counsellor, who took it and admired it. 'Fourteen years sober. That's pretty amazing, Kate.'

'I know.'

'You're still getting to meetings regularly then?'

'At least twice a week. I'm being a good girl, don't worry.'

Kate hadn't seen Maria for a while. They caught up with each other once every few months these days, just to 'check in', or whenever Kate needed to see her.

'Well, you're looking good.'

'Don't worry, I know you don't mean fat!' Kate laughed.

They sat in silence for a few minutes. Kate knew this was the way it went. When she'd first started seeing a therapist – a different one way back when – she used to despise the silences and feel obliged to fill them. But she was a different person in those days, less honest, less in touch with what was really going on inside.

She knew the rules now. They could sit in silence till the hour was up if that's what she wanted. But it wasn't. She'd also learnt over the years, through the pain of getting sober and the endless hours she'd sat in AA meetings crying her heart out, or listening to other people crying *their* hearts out, that it was always better out than in.

'Tallulah graduated from uni this morning,' she said, the tears of a proud mum springing to her eyes.

'That's a bit of a milestone,' Maria said. 'How did you feel?'

'Amazing. Obvs.' She laughed. 'A tiny bit of guilt crept in when I saw her on the stage thingy being handed her scroll, but then I thought, fuck it, she's turned out OK, has Lules, despite my early attempts to mess things up for her. I've done my time on the old self-pity, haven't I?'

'I would say so, yes.'

More silence. 'It was nice standing there with Matt and Carrie. Who'd've thought it, eh? Me and them, the best of friends, cheering on our little girl. We're the shining example of what's apparently called a "blended family".'

And again more silence. 'So . . .' Maria gently edged the conversation forward to where she sensed Kate wanted to take it. 'Big day today?'

'Yep.'

'Where are you meeting him?'

'Secret Garden Café in Regent's Park.'

'Nice and neutral.'

'Nice and neutral,' Kate repeated and bit her bottom lip in a vain attempt to stop the tears of fear. But then she knew they'd have to come out at some point, so she may as well open the floodgates now and let them flow.

She arrived an hour early just in case she couldn't find it, and drank three coffees in quick succession. She was shaking. But it wasn't down to the caffeine.

She looked at her watch. Again.

He wasn't late.

Not yet.

She could just walk away, of course. She didn't *have* to put herself through this. But then how would it feel to never know, to never find out?

And then she heard it. His voice.

'Kate?'

She looked up and there he stood. Smiling. Scared.

Thirty-one years of age.

He looked just like his father.

And instantly she loved him.

'Luca.'

'It's really good to meet you, Mum.'

Song credits

Lyrics on p.8 from 'Careless Whisper' written by George Michael and Andrew Ridgeley

Lyrics on pp.31–32 from 'Lord Of The Dance' written by Sydney Carter

Lyrics on p.44 from 'Running Up That Hill (A Deal With God)' written by Kate Bush

Lyrics on p.66 from 'Got To Have Your Love' written by Bryce 'Luvah' Wilson, Kurtis el Khaleel and Johnny D. Rodriguez

Lyrics on p.118 from 'There Must Be An Angel (Playing With My Heart)' written by Annie Lennox and David A. Stewart

Lyrics on p.142 from 'Come On Eileen' written by Kevin Rowland, Jimmy Paterson and Billy Adams

Lyrics on p.162 from 'Your Love Is King' written by Sade Adu and Stuart Matthewman

Lyrics on p.269 from 'I Wish It Could Be Christmas Everyday' written by Roy Wood

Lyrics on p.276 from 'All I Want For Christmas Is You' written by Mariah Carey and Walter Afanasieff

Lyrics on p.292 from 'Wonderful Christmastime' written by Paul McCartney

Acknowledgements

What a lovely journey into the world of novel-writing this has been
... I'd like to thank my fellow travellers at Transworld, especially
Frankie Gray my editor for her astonishing patience, creativity
and optimism, Alison Barrow, Vicky Palmer, Bill Scott-Kerr and
Larry Finlay for their gorgeous support and enthusiasm. And Kate
Samano for putting up with my grammar tantrums!

To the team at Curtis Brown a massive thank-you, but especially
to Jonny Geller, for his invaluable advice from the very start and for
just taking a punt on me as a novelist.

To Les Edwards, my A-level English teacher at Porthcawl
Comprehensive – now departed this world, but who gave me a love
for literature for which I'll always be grateful. I want your family to
know that, Les. You were the coolest teacher.

Thank you to my lovely, lovely friends who have supported me so
loyally on this venture as well as everything else – you know who
you are and I am forever indebted to you all.

To Dawn of Cornwall for convincing me I could do it.

To Mark, Julian and Maria for always supporting their drama
queen of a sister – I love you all so much. (And Maria, I hope your
book club doesn't slate this – 'cos that would be so embarrassing
for you.)

To my beloved Peetlets – Fiona, Louise and Alex – for your continued love and joy-giving.

To my dear, dear mother, Hannah, who has encouraged me to write since I was little. Mum, you are the best (and I'm sorry about the swearing).

To my beautiful father, Richard, no longer with us, and painfully missed every day. I know you are proud, Dad, wherever you are.

And finally to my wonderful husband, David, for always inspiring me and for giving me the confidence to do this. I wouldn't have got here without you, my darling.

Ruth Jones is best known for her outstanding and award-winning television writing – BBC One's *Gavin and Stacey*, in which she also played the incorrigible Nessa, and Sky One's *Stella*, in which she played the titular role. She has won acclaim for her performances in BBC dramas *Tess of the D'Urbervilles*, *Little Dorrit* and *Hattie* as well as comedies *Little Britain*, *Saxondale* and *Nighty Night*.